DRAU BLOOD

thank you!

Book 1
A Cerberus & Cerberex Novel

DRAU: BLOOD
E.S. STEPHENS

First published 2019
Written by Elizabeth Stephens
All rights reserved. Apart from any fair dealing for the purpose of study, research, or review, as permitted under the Copyright Designs and Patents act, 1988.
No part of this publication may be reproduced, stored in a retrieval system, or transmitted in any form or by any means, electronical, chemical, mechanical, optical, photocopying, recording, or otherwise, without prior permission of the author.

May your daggers remain sharp, your arrows strike true, and the Master be forever in your shadow.

THE NORTHERN PLAINS

THE RIVER ANGOSEN

SHEVE

THE BOWL OF ARTUS

IMET

THE WILDLANDS OF KURTH

RIVER ACONITE

AGRELLON

THE FER

THE ARGON OCEAN

THE BAY OF TEARS

THE GORGON'S HORN

N

THE URG

SOUTHERN STRAIGHTS

HOGVOROD

MARIDA

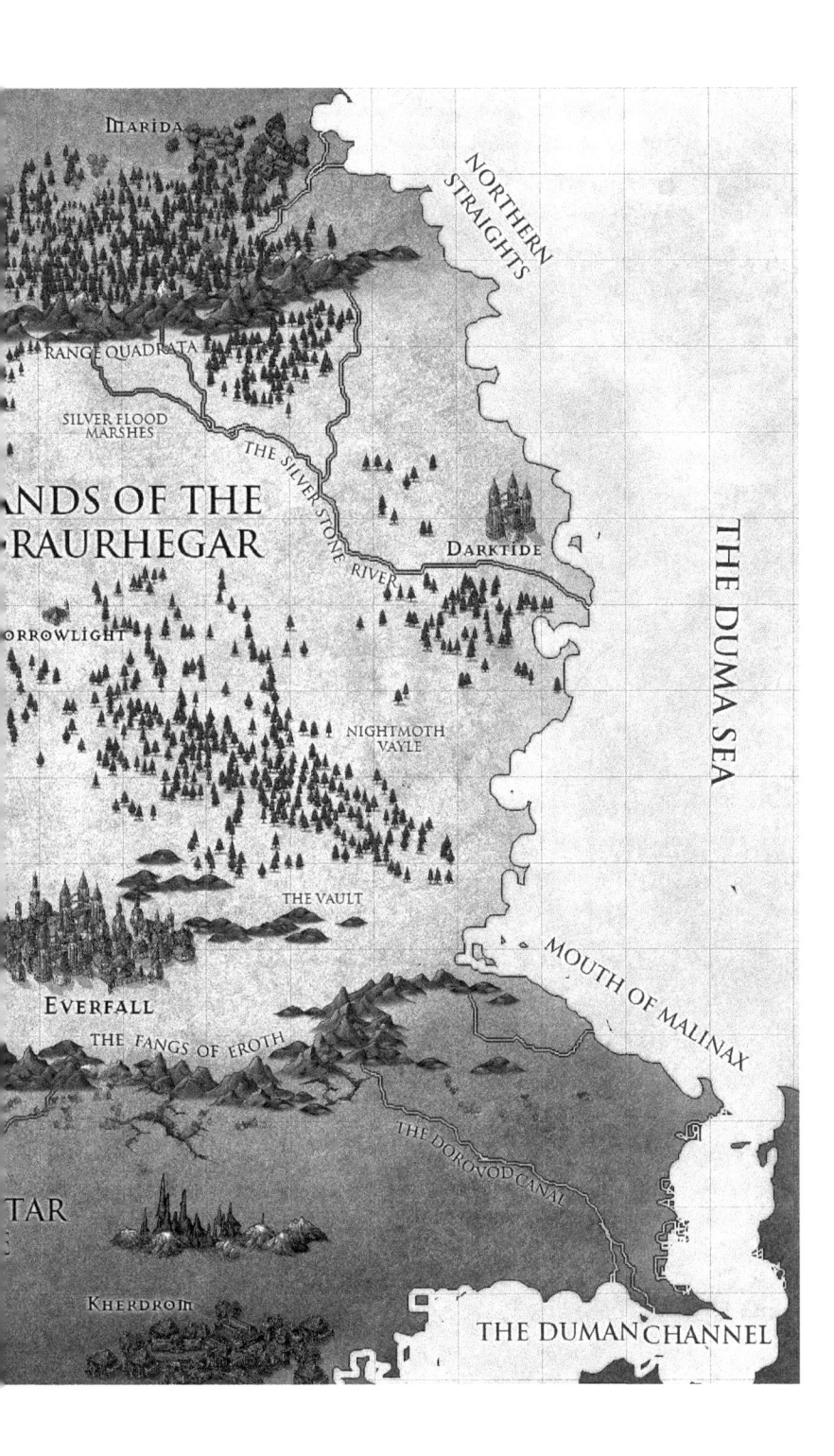

RANGE QUADRATA

SILVER FLOOD MARSHES

THE SILVERSTONE RIVER

NORTHERN STRAIGHTS

NDS OF THE
RAURHEGAR

DARKTIDE

ORROWLIGHT

NIGHTMOTH VAYLE

THE VAULT

THE DUMA SEA

EVERFALL

THE FANGS OF EROTH

MOUTH OF MALINAX

THE DOROVOD CANAL

TAR

KHERDROM

THE DUMAN CHANNEL

Prologue

Selwyn pulled down his scarf and squinted into the rising mist. The air was chill, unfamiliar, and clean. He raked a hand through his ash grey hair tucking a loose strand behind an elongated ear. "I do not like this Dendrion," he muttered. "This mist moves all wrong. It all but blinds the senses."

With barely a whisper a second Drau emerged from the mist behind him his head and scarf pulled back in a similar fashion to reveal dark skin and a stream of dead straight, white hair. "Peace Selwyn, the caravan will arrive soon enough and our contract fulfilled. We need only the patience to see it through." Dendrion's eyes glinted with a ruby sheen as he placed a hand on Selwyn's shoulder whispering, "relax old friend, you'll be back in my sister's arms soon enough."

"If that is so then why task all five of your Chosen to perform a day's wet work?" Selwyn twitched at the muffled sound of a snapping twig. Looking back, a third lithe silhouette stalk through the gloom before disappearing again. "Or is this just another opportunity for you to show off to the young assassin?"

Dendrion's lips curled at the corners. "Well Cerberus has to learn sometime. Better he cock up a caravan grab than something more ... important." Ten feet away a pair of blood red eyes moved forwards now soundlessly. There was a slight limp to the younger Drau's gait.

"You train him too hard Dendrion. Your son is barely one hundred and fifty. Is it really necessary to make him suffer the same way we did? Times change." Selwyn hissed under his breath.

Dendrion frowned. "You may be my First Selwyn, but don't presume to school me on the subject of children. He will need to perfect all these skills if he is to someday take my mantle - when the time comes of course."

"Ever the fatalist." Selwyn gave a smile. "You are of course right ... Master." He crossed his arms across his chest and bowed slightly before stiffening as Dendrion raised a finger.

"They are here," Dendrion muttered peering through the mist. "Time for our work to begin." Selwyn nodded and as one both Drau parted melting into the banks of tall grass and tree growth.

The caravan's wake was heralded by a storm of hooves pounding soft earth and the trundle of wheels. A faded sigil on the leading wagon had been poorly sanded off yet still bore the marks of a pair of crossed staffs once rendered in ivory now scrubbed to a pale echo of their former lustre. The livery of the house-guard surrounding it was a claret red. Rudimentary efforts had been made to disguise it beneath heavy cloaks of black wool, but the bulk of plate and mail would not obscure so easily. Selwyn took a brief head count as they pulled to a slow. A single wagon, covered and so far as could be seen, unarmoured. Four house-guard from House Gal-Serrek by the colouring. An odd twist of fate yet it would not be unusual for a lesser house to adopt the livery of a parent family or indeed for a rival to use the guise of his enemy to escape suspicion. He had done similar himself a handful of times. A further two well dressed individuals headed the group. One male the other female dressed in no particular house colour but richly adorned. Selwyn imagined the necklace of the lady must have cost in excess of three hundred black dinarah given the size of the bloodstone - a princely piece indeed. The male on the other hand exuded grace and standing with poise more than physical baubles. Selwyn had been privileged to visit the royal court more than once to know that the posturing of noble blood ran through that one's veins. So seven or possibly ten at a push. Not an unreasonable number. Yet given the cargo's anticipated value, fewer than he had expected.

"There should be more than this," Selwyn whispered, crawling through the undergrowth toward Dendrion. "It is not like the Gal-Serreks to take such a weak force even if they are looking to avoid attention."

Dendrion inclined his head toward Selwyn's. "Now whose the pessimist?" He glanced over his shoulder and then left into the tree line before nodding. "Sisendra is in position and should anything go sour, well..." he gestured behind him. "There are reinforcements if needed." He checked the miniature bow held beneath his left arm brace and unsheathed his rapier. "If we allow this casual thievery to go unchecked it could destabilize the fragile alliances we fought to make. Better to bring about an end to this now while its still young and make an example. The Gal-Serreks wont tolerate failure in their ranks. They'd sooner declare these fools to be nothing but imposters, but it will have the right effect all the same." Dendrion shifted his weight fractionally in preparation.

"Be careful." Selwyn smiled. "None of us are as young as we were back then."

Dendrion snorted. "Speak for yourself! Are you growing old on me Selwyn?" He leaned forwards. "You are forgetting the first rule." He smirked. "Assassins' don't play fair." With that he sprang towards the caravan keeping as low as he could. Barely a sound to mark his passing.

It was the horses who felt the assassin's approach first. Their nostrils flaring as they paced the ground at the sense of oncoming danger. Herd instinct took hold but it was too late that their riders heeded their warning. Dendrion vaulted atop the first charger severing the jugulars of two house-guard before they were so much as aware of the blade at their throats. Jewels of crimson ran along the rapiers edge dispersing to the ground with a flick. A hail storm of black and silver fletched bolts soared past placing a third out of action and maiming one of the wagon's horses as it pulled the other atop it.

"Dendrion!" A female voice called out from some where ahead. "The wagon."

Dendrion looked up just in time to see Selwyn leap across the body of a fallen horse and send a dagger spinning into the torso of an emerging house-guard from within the wagon's interior. The dagger held true but despite the force of the throw, scored little purchase against the armour. Selwyn bent back as his opponent returned the favour with a backhand swing of a barbed sword. Dendrion locked a bolt into his crossbow and fired watching it sink pleasingly up to the fletching. The house-guard sank to one knee in surprise giving Selwyn the only opportunity he needed to knife the fool from ear to ear and kick him back into the dirt. He had no time to mutter thanks as three more had begun to appear from within. Selwyn shrugged a razor edged, curved sword from the scabbard at his back in preparation.

Dendrion allowed himself a prideful nod. Selwyn was a masterful swordsman he could take care of himself. Reaching into a pouch at his waist he pulled out a black metallic orb and gave it a furious shake. From pin-prick vents on its surface a black smoke began to erupt and the smell of phosphor permeated the iron tang of blood-filled air. Sprinting, he weaved his way towards the wagon. Moments later a high pitched scream brought him to a sudden halt.

A hundred feet away Sisendra sank to her knees as the point of an elaborate blade sank into her side. The bejewelled female gave a sinister smile as she gave it a twist extracting a further scream from her prey and yanked the blade free in a welter of blood. Sisendra dropped her daggers and clasped a hand to her side as runnels of red escaped dripping from her hands. She looked over to Dendrion her already alabaster skin appearing to turn whiter still.

Dendrion hurled the smoking orb at the wagon before twisting under a falling blade, spinning in a bid to reach her. As he turned a lithe form sped past him, its speed rendering it merely a smudge in the gradually receding mist. Cerberus interposed himself between Sisendra and her attacker. The lady stepped back in surprise before inclining with an understated curtsy. She launched at him with a flurry of lightening fast blows. Blades crossed and Cerberus parried ... just. Behind him Sisendra gasped falling backwards as her eyes began to roll.

"Cerberus!" Dendrion reached into his pocket and withdrew a crystalline vial of amber liquid that pulsed with a low glow, flicking it towards the younger Drau. Cerberus twisted away from a slice meant to gut him and rolled, grabbing it an instant before it hit the floor.

From the other side of the battle Selwyn's voice rose above the din.

"We need to finish this. More are coming," Selwyn called as he joined Dendrion from behind. Blood not his own was sprayed across one cheek and several heavy scratches were sliced into the black leather of his armour. He pointed as more forms began to surge out of the mist. "Better to leave and live friend. They knew we were coming. We are betrayed."

Dendrion nodded at the wagon now engulfed in thick choking smoke. "House Dhal-Marrah does not flee when the job is half done. Go greet these new 'friends' I'll see to this." He pulled his scarf up over his nose and headed towards the wagon, his footfalls filled with purpose.

For a moment time slowed as the smoke enveloped him, muffling the sounds of combat. The numb cold and reassuring scrape of a knife from his belt permeating the sudden calm. He spun the blade and wrenched the wagon's coverings. The air blasted before him. Pieces of the wagon hurtled across the battlefield, sending Dendrion flying backwards before landing heavily on his side. From the wreckage, seemingly unscathed, stepped a figure swathed in a cowl of crimson velvet that seemed almost monastic. No weapon rested at his hip or hand, no badge or staff denoted his loyalties, but his hand flickered with a pale green haze of tiny sparks. Without word or issue the figure stepped measuredly towards him. Flexing, Dendrion pushed himself to his feet only to wince at the familiar stab of pain from a cracked rib. "Warlock." He snarled the word like a curse. " I should have known that this confounded mist was magically wrought."

The figure's hood twitched with what may have been a laugh as he stepped ever closer. The air around him hazed in his wake as his fingers flexed, plucking the air like a stringed instrument. Arcane words hissed from within the hood. Yet the heat of the curse barely caressed Dendrion's skin as he dropped to the ground. A blur of movement barrelled into the warlock bringing his aim off by a fraction. With a heavy gash that rendered the left side of his armour useless, Cerberus held out a hand. "Father." Dendrion knocked the boy down to the floor with a hamstringing kick as a flicker or witch-fire seared the air where the boy's head had previously been.

The pounding of feet and hooves signalled the arrival of a fresh column of house-guard. Dendrion looked between them but could see no sign of Selwyn as he and Cerberus found themselves encircled. Unlike the others this new arrival wore their house colours proudly dispensing with any cloak for the preference of javelins. Teal green hide that had been hammered with brass rivets adorned those Dendrion could see and the badge of a coiled serpent around an unsheathed sword was engraved upon the right shoulder.

"Stay close," Dendrion whispered to his son as the circle tightened. Cerberus did not respond but Dendrion could feel the tautness as the boy prepared for the strike. He surveyed the sea green hues and drew himself up. "I am Lord of House Dhal-Marrah under contract to return stolen property of the crown. We have no quarrel with the House of Trileris. Our contract extends only so far as procurement of this caravan. Leave and none of you need feel the kiss of my blades." Dendrion lowered his rapier slightly and waited.

"So this is what passes for the mighty House of Dhal-Marrah." A male voice heavy with aristocratic resonance floated through the air. Several teal dressed bodies parted to allow a young Drau of noble bearing access. "I must say," he continued. "I was expecting something more."

Dendrion lifted his rapier in a salute. "I don't believe I have had the honour. Then again I have no need of sell swords."

The noble smiled. Pinkish eyes glinting as he gave an elaborate bow. "My apologies, where are my manners? Malinar, heir of House Trileris, or at least," He held out a bloodied bloodstone necklace. "I am now."

Dendrion gave a curt nod. "So, Lord Trileris sends his little boy does he." He gave a laugh. "He must really be terribly attached to you."

The indulgent smile on Malinar's face dropped to a scowl. "Your time wanes Dhal-Marrah. Your family may be the power behind royal privilege but times are changing old man. The Gal-Serrek's have promised a considerable reward for you and your brat's head and I fully intend to collect."

The corner of Dendrion's mouth curled. "Old man is it? The Gal-Serreks would do well to remember who brought the body of their lord home rather than let him be feasted by crows. For such a seasoned warrior you talk far too much." He eyed the ring of guard. "You know, there is a saying we call the Third Rule." Malinar's eyes narrowed. "Don't..." Dendrion glanced around. "Get..." He looked back at Cerberus over his shoulder. The boy was grinning. "Close." As the word left his lips he pushed his fingers into his ears watching as Cerberus immediately did the same. The others were less lucky.

A high pitched whine pierced the silence. Malinar looked at the Trileris guard in confusion for a moment before the agony swept him and a number of others up like a ship at sea. Soon he was rolling on the ground grabbing his head while others began to bleed from ears and noses dropping their weapons as they sank to the dirt screaming. A smell of ozone and a heavy popping sensation revealed a female Drau appear within the confines of the ring to a reception of scraping steel. She held up a hand as those still standing reached for their weapons. "I would not recommend it."

Her skin was the colour of pyre smoke and her hair hung in wisps of deep grey the colour of a brewing storm. Dendrion smiled as she passed by, daring a brisk kiss. "Your timing is as always, impeccable my darling."

The lady nodded the black lace of her robe giving the suggestion that she floated. "Getting our son into more trouble I see Dendrion." She tutted quietly under her breath as she worked her way around to Cerberus's side. "At least you appear to have kept him in one piece this time."

Dendrion flashed her a full smile for a moment before the air fizzed with sudden static. Slowly the circle of guards that still stood, backed away as they looked up. Above the sky had turned an unnatural purple punctuated with sudden flashes of energy. A sound breaking thunderclap sent all sprawling as a fork of eldritch lightening scorched the ground a mere hands-width from Dendrion charring the earth black. With surprising strength he turned and pushed Cerberus into the lady's arms.

Dendrion stepped back looking this way and that. "Elryia, take Cerberus and go." Cerberus looked at his father as if stung. "This is no place for an apprentice. Go. See that the others know we are betrayed," he shouted above the storm. From behind him gentle footsteps stalked towards him as a familiar figure in red stood poised, hand outstretched. Dendrion growled. "I know not what fiend you formed your pact with traitor, but when Eroth devours your worthless soul I hope for your sake, it was worth it." Before the last few words had left his lips Dendrion sprinted towards the warlock flicking his blade out in a curve. He did not see Elryia's eyes suddenly go wide as the Warlock's hands moved with strange dexterity weaving a baleful trail of reddish vapour. He did not hear her call as she wove the last elements of her teleportation magic, loosening her grip on Cerberus's shoulder.

Cerberus seized the opportunity his face a mixture of anger and betrayal. With the speed of youth, he sprinted towards the warlock while plucking two throwing knives from his belt. As he passed Dendrion, he narrowly missed his father's grasp. "Cerberus!" He ground to a stop at the paired voices of his mother and father. Twisting on the spot, he brushed two fingers across the ground for balance as he turned to see their look of sudden panic. The air smelled of fire and brimstone almost too hot to breath. As time slowed to a crawl his mother ducked to the dirt, his father still running towards him. Cerberus took a step to aid her and then there was only pain

It was like nothing he had felt before. No poisoned blade or enchanted weapon compared. A burning, soul scouring pain that pulled the life out of him. He felt the heavy weight if his own body strike the ground and tasted the iron and grit of bloodied dirt. Before the blackness pushed the edges of his vision, he saw his father blown off his feet, a mixture look of surprise and agony wrought across his features. He looked at the scorch mark across his chest and slumped forwards. Then there was only darkness.

Heavy hands dragged Cerberus's prone form through the slick grass as the rain lashed his face. He looked up blinking as the daylight stung his eyes as he coughed wads of coagulated blood onto his chin. The hands let go and he gasped in pain as his body hit the ground once more. Selwyn's face swam into view. Remnants of his armour still clung to him and an angry red cut scored down one side of his face. "Eroth's fangs, he alive!" Cerberus heard Selwyn say as his vision blurred in and out. "Elryia! He's alive!"

Hurried footstep thundered towards the two of them. Elryia's hair swept on end as if she had stepped from the winds of a hurricane. Her face coated with tears. "Help me get his armour off Selwyn. I need to see what we are dealing with."

Cerberus felt the buckles of his leather cuirass loosen followed by hot pain and a stickiness as it was removed and he was turned on his side. Cold fingers probed the fist sized wound in his lower back and he let out an involuntary scream before a numbing warmth swept over his body. For a moment his vision cleared but the pain it cost him to breath was almost more than he could bare. Slowly at first the pain began to ebb and the warmth grew till Elryia gave a sudden gasp and the heat abruptly ended.

"He is pact-marked," she panted looking at Selwyn. "I have done what I can to ease the pain but this is beyond my skill to heal."

Cerberus rolled himself onto his back groaning with immediate regret as the damp earth beneath seeped onto the wound. "Uncle?" Selwyn cradled him into a sitting position. Cerberus looked around. "Uncle," he winced. "Uncle, where is..." his voice drifted off as a fallen shape on charred earth struck him as sure as any knife. Tearing himself away despite the pain and the protestations of those around him he limped to the body laid out to the sky. "No," he whispered as he came close. "No."

Dendrion's breaths came in ragged gasps that filled his mouth with blood that slipped from the corner of his lips. There had been intense pain but he had lost all ability to vocalise it. Now there was simply a penetrating, bone chilling cold and unimaginable weariness. He couldn't help but give a slight smile when he saw Cerberus's face suddenly come into view. Part of him had been sure the boy had died out right as the witch-bolt hit. To see him still standing after such a blow that was truly Dhal-Marren. He reached up to his neck piece and pulled at a silver inlaid brooch. Tugging it loose with a jerk and pushing it into Cerberus's hand. The boy took it and looked him in the eye. No tears. "Swear it." The voice that came from his lips sounded haggard and strange. "Will you uphold the honour of this house?" Cerberus nodded. "Will you stand with your brothers and sisters against the darkness?" Again the boy nodded. Familiar footsteps came towards them. He looked at Cerberus, meeting his gaze.

"I will," Cerberus whispered pushing back a choke. As he bowed his head Elryia moved next to him and grabbed his right arm. Cerberus looked up at her the sweat of exhaustion beading on her forehead as she spent the last dregs of magic she had. He gasped as a needle-like pain stabbed at him. When she removed her hand a thin white sub-dermal scar, almost like the imprint of a tattoo, throbbed where her hand had been. Its shape resembled the winged dragon and crossed knives of the Dhal-Marrah sigil.

Dendrion forced a smile. "Welcome assassin." He hacked a cough and shivered as the cold worked its way through his body. He grasped Cerberus's hand tightly. "A war is coming my son. House Dhal-Marrah must answer. You must protect this family." He felt his breath tighten, unable to feel his hands as they slipped to the ground. The last thing Dendrion Dhal-Marrah saw before the embrace of death came was his son, his wife, and his friend. He could not have asked for more.

Cerberus let a tear slip down his cheek as he watched the last dregs of life slip from his father's face. The sudden weight of his departure crushed him as surely as any mace. With trembling hands he pinned the badge to the cloth of his shirt and reached for his final throwing dagger. Closing his eyes he ran his hand along the blade letting the blood run between his fingers before dripping onto the open wound across his fathers chest. "I swear I will not let another Dhal-Marrah fall. I will avenge your passing." He gritted his teeth squeezing his fist tightly. "I will be the last thing they see before their souls are sent to burn." Opening his eyes, for a moment Cerberus was certain that his hand was pulsing with a faint crimson glow. He blinked away the tears pricking his eyes and when he looked again there was nothing but blood.

Chapter 1:
Thieves

The lands of the Draurhegar. All that lay between The Range Quadrata to the north and the Fangs of Eroth to the south. Where once a barren plain long abandoned by the sea had spread, now a new ocean of life ran as far as the eye could see - it's crowning jewel the mighty city of Everfall. In the maze below it's streets hummed with activity. Lords, ladies, merchants, and commoners mixed in a melting pot of life and to the casual onlooker, in comparative peace.

High upon the skyline a Drau threw himself into the five foot leap between two rooftops with vigour. Far below a handful of citizens had the sense to look up as a dark shadow flitted past followed shortly by another a matter of moments later. The street was a good twenty feet below and while coloured awnings of silver and blue or purple and red broke the drop at intervals, a single mis-judged step or ill-calculated jump would result in crippling injury if not outright death. Sky running was not necessarily an illegal nor unusual act in Everfall. The dark grey-blue stone of the buildings were easily scalable to someone with the skill or correct gear. Over time these warehouses, stores, homes, and services had been added to, extended, or modified to create an altogether eclectic skyline unlike any other this side of The Fangs. Every hundred yards or so the spire of a watch tower punctured the flat-lay of buildings like knives that reached for the sky. Each had once denoted the bounds of the kingdom in its day and was proof at just how much the Drau had thrived and expanded. If onc scaled these pinnacles, the view was spectacular. Some had now been left abandoned but others flew bright pennants and banners of coloured silk particular to one of the noble houses that claimed dominion over the labyrinth of streets.

Another jump and the first Drau made a three-point landing before dusting himself off. He was tall and clad in leather panelled trousers and black leather arm bracers with a plain shirt and long coat. His hair was lightening white, mid-length, and partly pulled back from his ashen skinned face and deep red eyes. He looked back grinning to his friend still catching up a little way behind. "Come on old man, keep up!"

The second Drau landed more heavily a few moments later. A purple black hood and scarf of some heavy woven material obscured his face save for a pair of silver flecked eyes. He was dressed head to foot in an intricate leather armour that overlapped while still offering excellent flexibility, tailored made for his physique alone. "It would help if you didn't cheat." He pulled his

his scarf down past his face revealing a cool storm grey coloured face and flashed a smile. "In short. You're an arse Cerberus!" His eyes sparkled in jest.

Cerberus sprinted up the pitch of the roof to the next jump. "Excuses Kane," he yelled over his shoulder.

Kane sighed and stretched a shoulder. He was fractionally bigger built if only by a fraction than the more lithe form of Cerberus, with broader shoulders and thicker wrists. His eyes darted as they followed Cerberus speeding across the next roof, sizing up the potential destinations he could be heading to. A short way ahead the streets and buildings were dominated by House Gal-Serrek. Beyond that the architecturally unique Palace District. Cerulean blue domed roofs and silvered spires gleamed against the Palace proper - a sharp edged building of marble and black obsidian. He sighed. "Looking for trouble then Cerberus." Kane leaped from the roof top taking an alternative route.

Cerberus felt the wind race through his hair and the adrenaline course through his veins - this was to be alive. Using an awning as a springboard, he neared a tower that rose a hundred feet from the ground and hung with runners coloured red and lined with black. The three swords, the sigil of House Gal-Serrek, shone in gold thread and glinted from the rose coloured sunlight. As Cerberus approached the tower's wall, he mixed with the shadows. There was little love between the Gal-Serreks and the Dhal-Marrahs. Those bridges had long since been burned. The King's house were just as likely to kill him on sight as soon as arrest him for trespass. Sizing up the surrounding buildings he could make out at least six guards patrolling the roof tops. He counted under his breath, mentally mapping their patrols, then double checked. His timing would need to be on point. Slowly he crouched like a coiled spring readying himself for the dash. He had no fear of Gal-Serrek paid guard. They had little enough finesse and thought between them to fill an egg cup. Still, a crossbow bolt to the shoulder or worse the leg, would certainly hurt. He pressed half his face against the stone of the tower. Three. He peered around and kept his eye on the nearest guard. Two. He checked the grapple connection to the bolt and loaded it into a miniature crossbow under his right wrist. One. He sprang across the short gap and ran for all his worth.

A shout from the top of the tower alerted the guards to his presence. Then more shouts as they prepared to take aim. Cerberus weaved this way and that seeking to wrong foot them. A red fletched bolt hissed passed his head followed by a second he had to physically twist out of the way to avoid. As he crossed the half way point of the building, two Gal-Serrek guards rushed to meet him with jagged blades in hand designed to cut through flesh like steak knives. Cerberus shifted his weight before bending backwards to duck underneath the swing of the first and rolling as the second sliced down just behind him.

He laughed as they cursed at him. "You're getting better boys. Keep up the practice and one day you might actually hit something." He gave them a mock salute as he spun away to miss another bolt aimed for his left eye. Turning, he fired his grapple through the narrow gap between the surrounding buildings watching it embed itself in the outer wall to the Palace before tying his own end of the metallic cord around a banner pole. Tearing away the banner itself and throwing one end over the cord, Cerberus wrapped both ends around each hand and jumped.

The impromptu zip-line dropped him down ten feet between the buildings scratching the leather of his trousers as he picked up speed. A torrent of bolts from a fast repeating crossbow clattered against the walls around him as he sped on. He could still just about hear the shouts of the guards behind him followed by a ripping sound as a final bolt tore its way through his coat.

He let go of the rapidly fraying banner seconds before the zip-line would have smashed him into the wall. He reached for the ornate stonework ridge that ran along its edge grimacing a little as he took hold and the muscles in his arm pulled slightly. With born practice, his fingers curled over the edge and with a strength that a stranger might have been surprised by, pulled himself up and over on the soft earth. He landed in a well manicured boarder of exotic plants and stood silently. An arm hooked around his neck pulling him further into the foliage. A second later twelve heavily armed palace guard in plate armour thundered by, taking him by surprise.

Cerberus looked back at his restrainer as he was pulled behind a Yunkol tree with waxy leaves the colour of brain matter. Kane, hood pulled up and scarf replaced, held a finger up to where his mouth would have been while holding him securely with the other. Only once the tremor of armoured boots had fully subsided did he let Cerberus go.

Cerberus massaged his throat. "Was that really necessary?"

Kane raised and eyebrow and pulled down his scarf a fraction. "Well I could always call them back if you would prefer." He paused. "Master."

Cerberus folded his arms. "Sarcasm doesn't suit you Kane."

"I wasn't intending it as sarcasm." Kane smirked.

There was a moment of sudden tension before Cerberus couldn't help but grin. "So what took you so long? I thought you'd got lost."

"Lost?" Kane laughed keeping an eye on the area. "I've been sat here waiting for you to show up!" He slunk back quickly as a crystalline laugh pierced the garden's quiet. Three young Drau ladies passed the hiding place exchanging gossip and secrets. They slinked along the path with almost feline grace. Each had a spill of pale hair that tumbled to their waists and their pointed ears sported an array of jewelled earrings linked with fine silver chain.

"Queen's ladies," Kane whispered. "We should probably leave before we become the subject of choice in tittle tattle conversation. Wouldn't want to be found uninvited."

"What could you possible mean Kane? As I understand it you're more than welcome within the Palace," Cerberus teased.

A smile passed Kane's lips. "I didn't say I wasn't welcome."

A few yards away one of the ladies stopped and looked back. Cerberus and Kane froze. Tentatively the lady paused inquisitively for a moment before the summons of her friends demanded her attention.

The pair breathed and Cerberus inclined his head reluctantly towards Kane. "As you say. Wouldn't want to overstay our welcome." He waited patiently for the group of ladies to turn out of sight before hopping up the wall and back over into the street below startling a human street beggar. Kane followed him a second later.

They made their way back through the markets. Exotic goods from across the known lands were arrayed for all to see. The smell of spice and baked goods, the riot of coloured fabrics, and the ebb and swell of the crowds blinded the senses. Kane loosened his armour and pulled off his scarf as they passed among the stalls electing to keep his hood up. Cerberus on the other hand walked with an easy grace that could be construed as casual. He stopped at an extravagantly dressed stall of jewelled items making a passing inspection. Shards of bloodstone a jewel of deep red with black veins, lay cut in various unique designs. His hand lingered on one shaped into a twisting dragon.

"You have superb taste sir, it is one of our best pieces." A Drau merchant stood beside the stand with a welcoming smile. Judging by his girth he'd made a good living and the satin lining to his attire suggested he lived comfortably.

Cerberus nodded. "I dare say it is possibly the best piece here, Gerino," he flattered grinning.

The merchant's brow furrowed for a moment and stepped back as Cerberus looked up at him. "My Lord Dhal-Marrah, I'm... I'm honoured." He took a deep breath and regained his composure. "What can I help you with today. I have some simply superb dragons-eye pendants or perhaps you are looking for something special? I have just acquired some stunning obsidian charms - very rare, only mined in the Dwentar Lowlands."

"Ah Gerino as always you never fail to impress." Cerberus smiled all charm and ease. "Unsurprising when one such as yourself has such a timeless jewel to act as their muse. Tell me how is your wife these days?"

The merchant's smile temporarily faltered. "Quite, my Lord I could not create such beauty without her. Alas she has not joined me on this particular trip."

Cerberus sensed Kane move behind him, "careful Cerberus," he warned.

Cerberus smiled at the merchant. "Of course Gerino I quite understand. A lady like that is a bright spirit and demands every freedom." He performed an over accentuated bow enjoying the merchant's flustered look. "But I am not looking for something so extravagant. This perhaps?" He plucked a silver ring inlaid with a single pearl and sapphire shards from a velvet cloth.

The merchant raised a small quartz glass to his eye. "This my Lord? Surely not. This is slavish, human work."

"Cerberus." Kane whispered.

"Indeed, but it has a simplicity I find quite pleasing," Cerberus replied ignoring Kane for the moment. "And surely it is the right hand that makes the ring?"

"It would my Lord. Well if you insist. This piece is yours for a mere forty skathes." The merchant beamed.

"Ah as ever you run a hard bargain Gerino. It is as you say, human workmanship. Say twenty-five and we have a deal." Cerberus folded his arms without breaking eye contact.

"Twenty-five my lord? Absolutely not! I have a reputation to maintain and a family to feed," the merchant replied with a look of surprise and horror.

"Cerberus?" Kane muttered again.

"You have no children Gerino and your family are as wealthy as any want-to-be lord of this kingdom. Thirty then or I will take my business elsewhere. Perhaps the jewels of Maestro Lorelen have more lustre at a reasonable price." Cerberus's eyes hardened.

The merchant snorted. "Lorelen? He wouldn't know the difference between diamond and a piece of rock." The merchant's shoulder sagged. "Very well my Lord, if you insist, then thirty it is."

"Cerberus!" Kane shouted.

Cerberus stifled a jump and rounded on him. "Eroth's teeth Kane! What is it?"

Kane rolled his eyes and pointed down the row of stalls with a slight smirk. A little way off four children - part Drau and part something else, ran through the crowd. Cerberus' hand moved like lightening to the where his purse should have been in his pocket.

"Ah. Please excuse me Gerino. Thirty it is. Have the piece ready, I will be back to collect momentarily." Cerberus turned and motioned to Kane as he ran after them.

Two boys and two girls split into the crowds as they turned to see Cerberus and Kane heading towards them at speed. Cerberus pointed Kane towards a side ally in the hope of cutting them off. He had to be slightly impressed. Not everyday did someone managed to sneak past him without notice. Were it heritage, they'd have made some promising apprentices. One young thief looked behind and fled into a sprint, pushing his way through and upsetting barrels and baskets as he attempted to put as much distance as possible between them. Cerberus smiled as he caught sight of a familiar velvet purse clasped firmly in his hand. Well if they wanted a chase then he would oblige.

Approaching a vintner muttering under his breath as he attempted to stand the barrels that had been toppled, Cerberus lightly leaped on to one before pulling himself up the wall side. He was met by a handful of curses. Atop a short balcony he watched as the children wove back together like a team before darting left down a crawl space between two warehouses. "Oh you're quite good!" he chuckled to himself.

Moving across the roofs, Cerberus watched from above as the children emerged into the street beyond. First one to check they had not been followed, then the other. They were wise to be careful. The laws of Everfall were not merciful to pick pockets and thieves no matter their age. The older boy was last to emerge keeping as much to the shadows as possible before running across to another access alley the other side. Cerberus followed silently from above keeping just out of their line of sight should any of them decide to look up. Ahead a small ball of Gal-Serrek retainers made their way towards the market areas. The children flattened themselves against the walls as they moved past with a speed that only practice could achieve. Ducking down beside the ruin of an abandoned tower the older boy prised open the purse.

Cerberus leaped down onto them and grabbed the culprit dragging him behind the building. The other three yelled and dispersed like sand into the warren of back routes that spread behind these buildings. For a second he took a quick look around. Kane was no where to be seen. Seeing the attention of his captor momentarily split, the boy made a wriggle for freedom. Cerberus turned in a second. "Oh I don't think so." He grabbed the boy by the throat and held him to the stone wall of the tower.

Cerberus could get a better look at him now. He had soft grey skin but rounder features and dirty brown hair. He wagered that there was something most likely human in his make-up. Clothes that had once been smart were now thread bare and worn and he wore the thin white line of a scar crossed his top lip. He looked up at Cerberus with water blue eyes, the pupils small with terror. Cerberus smiled as he watched the boy desperately try to escape. "Now I believe you have something that doesn't belong to you." He put the boy on his feet maintaining a firm grip.

The boy's eyes flicked briefly to the purse in his hand and then looked back at Cerberus. With some surprise, Cerberus watched as the boy's lips began to curl into a smile and his eyes hardened before he threw the purse a short distance away. As Cerberus looked for the purse's location, the boy wriggled out of his grasp and fled a short way out of reach. Cerberus turned to lunge at him only to feel the prick of cold steel in the small of his back.

Cerberus smiled and made a show of raising his hands. "Well, now you really have my attention." He turned slowly. "Trust me that in your case, it's not a good thing."

A slim figure in deep blue commoners clothes and a hood pulled heavily over the face, held a thin sword against his chest. With a burst of speed Cerberus batted it out of the way with an arm brace and pulled a dagger from his belt. He barely had time. The whistle of the sword cutting air came for his stomach and he parried it away backing into the wall before barraging the assailant with his own attack pushing them back. "You shouldn't be allowed one of those if you don't know how to use it." He sniggered, easily dodging a haphazard slash. "Now I'd love to teach you the basics but I'm afraid I simply don't have the time." A well placed hit with the hilt of the dagger followed by a rough spin and the sword clattered to the floor followed by a grunt of pain as the figure was pushed face first into the wall. Cerberus released the pressure a fraction and pushed his own blade touching the middle of their back. "I really wouldn't move if I were you. You see a single push from me and you'll loose your ability to walk out of this."

"Release me this instant!" The voice was commanding and female.

Cerberus flipped the figure around and pulled back the hood. Pale skin with the merest hint of colour was framed by a waterfall of silver hair that moved gently in the breeze. Her eyes held a diamond sheen and her skin seemed to smell slightly of violets. Cerberus was fairly confident that his face must have been a picture of surprise.

Heavy feet sounded along the street as Cerberus and the female Drau stared each other down for a matter of moments. As a second knot of Gal-Serrek guards moved past, Cerberus pressed against her, giving the impression of two commoners sharing a passionate moment - not totally unknown and certainly not on Gal-Serrek turf. As he drew back a fist smacked him clean in the jaw. He turned away and growled quietly as he pushed the jaw between thumb and forefinger with an audible click and grinned. "Worth it."

Behind him the female Drau held her second punch. "Wait. I know your voice." She lowered her hand and looked sideways at him. "Cerberus Dhal-Marrah?"

Cerberus turned slowly still grinning and inclined his head. "Lida."

Lida took a step back. "You... You've..."

Cerberus laughed. "Not like you to be speechless. If memory serves you had a wicked tongue when we were younger." He bowed his head. "Your Highness."

Lida blushed slightly and looked around. "I wouldn't say that too loudly."

A boyish look of delight spread across Cerberus's face. "Oh, no one knows you're out here do they." He raised an eyebrow. "Well that does explain your dress sense I suppose." He gestured to the cloak and took a step closer. "But then again you did look good in almost anything if I remember," He whispered, watching her squirm. "I imagine that your brother's face would be quite something if he could see you now."

Lida placed her hands on her hips. "Tread carefully my lord, you are addressing a queen whether she be in rags or riches."

"But of course." Cerberus fell into an elaborate bow. His head snapped up full of glee. "However, right now your nothing but a commoner and these," he gestured to the surrounding streets, "are the domain of Gal-Serrek. Take it from me. They don't treat trespassers gently."

"Then you had better make yourself scarce." She smiled and leaned towards him. "I am meeting..." she paused. "A person of interest."

"You think because you've bound yourself to that old bastard, you're immune do you?" Cerberus's eyes narrowed.

"That bastard is a King." Lida huffed. "Try to remember that when you're seeking to bring up ancient history Cerberus."

"Ancient is it?" Cerberus scoffed. "But as you insist, it's no issue with me. Will you at least allow me to escort you back?"

"I'm sure I can manage." Lida looked up seeing Cerberus's face turned to cool anger at the slight. Her face softened. "It's not personal. We live in different times and the kingdom is dancing to a different tune. Your appearance would cause, " she paused, "unwanted attention."

"I see." Cerberus forced a smile to his face and bowed again more formally. "I was unaware that the House of Dhal-Marrah had fallen that far from grace." He rose stiffly and sauntered over to where his purse lay in the dirt, picking it up. "I forget my manners. It must have been the surprise at seeing Your Majesty mingling with the rabble - I imagine the King would find that very unbecoming."

Lida drew up her hood and turned to leave the ally, muttering something under her breath. She gave him a look before her physical form ghosted before him.

He sensed her leave and smiled to himself. "You haven't changed all that much then."

"Did you get it back?" Kane leaped down from the roof above.

Cerberus waved the purse in answer. "I've changed my mind on the bauble." He watched Kane stop in surprise and shrugged. "I have papers that need my attention and preparations to make at the house."

"You hate paperwork and family duties in equal measure. Who's rubbed you up the wrong way?" Kane placed a hand on Cerberus's shoulder holding him still for a moment before it was shrugged of.

"My uncle is visiting nothing more." Cerberus smiled. "Plus Cerberex might have woken up by now and I do so enjoy it when she has company over."

Kane raised an eyebrow. "Company you say?" He rubbed a hand over his eyes. "Oh Cerberus tell me you haven't. Not again!"

There was a chuckle and Cerberus turned to face Kane with a hardly innocent smile. "Well what can I say? She has terrible taste!"

Kane shook his head unable to contain the smile for much longer. "Then you're quite sure you don't want to pick up that ring? You may need it as a bargaining chip."

"Quite sure." Cerberus glanced in the direction he'd last seen Lida. A handful of boot marks in the dirt were the only indication she had been there. He shook off the familiar feeling of regret for things unsaid, before springing off a stack of discarded crates towards the nearest rooftop. "She'd have to catch me first," he added as Kane followed. "Now, do try to keep up this time."

Kane rolled his eyes.

Chapter 2:
Family

The house of Dhal-Marrah rose three stories into the air from grey-black stone hewn into gothic design. Intricate carvings over its lower facing had eroded with time or were partially obscured by crawlers. Turrets flanked both sides, perfect vantage points, and the roof flattened at its peak such that should the house come under attack, archers might fire at any oncoming foe that breached the perimeter wall without fear of repercussion. Yet despite all its imposing nature, Cerberus and Kane both knew the house's greatest treasure lay not within its walls or in its location but beneath its foundations.

A house-guard in black and silver stood to attention as the two passed the iron work mastery of the main gate that was wrought into the dragon and blades of the Dhal-Marrah sigil. Beyond, paved stone lead to the door of the house a good fifty feet away, flanked by borders of sweet scented flowers of deepest mauve and chalk white. An aged Drau in simple grey robes attended them pulling away twisted weeds. Noticing their presence, he gave a simple nod. The gardener's eyes twitched towards the house for a second and returned to the pair. Kane's eyes narrowed, trying to perceive his intention. It didn't take him long. In the silence of the afternoon his sensitive ears could pick up shouting and the unmistakable sound of something large and probably expensive smashing to the ground. From the first floor a window swung wildly open as something hit it.

"Oh she is pissed at you!" Kane laughed.

"It would appear so." Cerberus grinned. "Well, she always did have an evil temper."

Kane looked sideways at him. "Has the Master met his match?" Another window opened and a small metallic item sailed through it bouncing off the ground below and rolling under a large bush. "Isn't that..."

Cerberus's eye's narrowed. "My room? I believe it is."

Kane snorted derisively, turned and patted Cerberus on the shoulder. "I'll take my leave I think." He nodded back towards the house. "Good luck." He strode away across the grounds, circumventing the house via the stables and chuckling to himself.

Cerberus ran to the bush and retrieved the item he had seen hit the ground. A small silver box. The lid had come away from its housing but thankfully appeared to be in a fixable condition. It was only the size of a small plum but the craftsmanship was superlative. Tiny shards of raw diamond gave the appearance of ice caught in the process of thawing. Not something that admittedly happened in the climate of Everfall overly much but Cerberus had seen plenty of ice on his few visits North. Carefully, he put the box into one of his belt pouches and headed up the steps to the double doors of the house.

The entrance hall was eerily quiet as he entered, abnormally so. House Dhal-Marrah owned more than thirty servants, Drau, Human, the occasional Elf. That he was not greeted by any on his arrival was - unnerving. A handful of bookcases and side tables adorned the hall and a large staircase rose to a landing that haloed it from above. Keeping his wits about him, Cerberus made his way towards and up the stairway. He moved cat-like, not a whisper of noise as he approached the door to his room. It lay slightly ajar and the metal catch had been busted by what seemed to be a well placed kick.

Thunk. Cerberus dodged behind the door as an arrow embedded itself in the heavy wood. "Cerberus!" The voice was loud, female, and carried an undertone of intense frustration. He peered out. High on a beam that spanned the width of the hall's roof supporting a large candelabra, a single Drau the paler mirror of himself, crouched wielding a wicked bow and wearing an interwoven leather jacket and matching trousers in deep grey-greens and black-browns. Thunk. Another arrow hit its mark fractionally away from the other. "Afraid brother? You should be."

Cerberus pressed his back against the door and looked around his room. On the desk the other side, precisely where he had left it in the light of a thin shaft of sunlight from the window, a silver rapier lay plain in all regards save of the 'D' Cerberus knew to be engraved on the nub of the pommel. He felt the impact of a third arrow. "All this over a little lordling Cerberex?" He called out. "It's not like you can't get another." In one swift move he rolled across the room and grabbed the rapier before turning and inching the door open slightly, noting that Cerberex had moved from her perch. Stooping into a slight crouch he slithered around the door onto the landing.

The crack of a fist hitting his jaw spun him for a second. "Every time Cerberus. Every time!" Whack. Another fist connected with a rib. "Is no one good enough?" Cerberex asked through gritted teeth.

Cerberus caught the third fist and rose to full height a fraction taller then her, and leaned in. "I'll let you know." He smiled at the scraping sound of a knife and pushed her back as she unsheathed two hunting knives. "Oh, you were rather keen on this one then?" he cocked his head to one side with a malicious smile. "Sorry, not sorry." There was a metallic 'plink' as he parried away a knife meant to cut him from neck to naval.

"At least I have taste. Something you're still working on brother." Cerberex spun her blade right to left forcing her brother back a step. "Tell me how was that red-head human girl. Couldn't find yourself a proper lady?" She hissed her second blade up forcing him back again. "Or maybe it's just that none of the Drau ladies will have you."

Cerberus caught the third strike against the hilt and twisted forcing her arm down. He could feel the bannister behind him. "I believe she was ... exceptionally satisfied with my company." He leaned underneath another strike. "She didn't leave till morning," he whispered leaping backwards and balancing on the bannisters edge. "Which judging by your comments last night, is not something your bed partner quite managed." He grinned at the surprise on her face, using the opportunity to leap down to the floor of the entrance hall with seamless grace.

Cerberex sprung towards the bannister as she watched him leap embedding the blades in the wood and reaching back for her bow. "How dare you listen in to my private conversations!" She notched and fired.

Cerberus laughed as he dodged lightly out of the way. "Listened in? Oh dear sister. I imagine the entire house may have heard your 'private' conversation." Another arrow hissed across and smashed a small but intricately painted vase. Cerberus looked back. "I do believe that was mother's." He wagged a finger.

Cerberex notched another arrow and held it braced to fire. "You would not dare," she hissed through clenched teeth.

Cerberus gave her an evil smile. "Oh my Lord," he cried out adopting a high pitched voice.

"Stop." Cerberex fired and slung the bow across her back. She grabbed her knives, splintering the wood, and leaped down after him.

"Do watch where you put your hands," Cerberus continued placing the small table between them. Another 'plink' and he batted away a knife thrown at his head. "Oh you are a big boy!"

Cerberex choked. "I never said anything like that!" Already she could feel the colour rising in her cheeks.

"No but the colour of your face says it was implied." Cerberus pulled the knife out of the wooden bookcase behind him testing its weight for a second before hurling it back.

The knife snickered past Cerberex's cheek. She lifted her hand in surprise feeling the hot, wet sensation of trickling blood as it continued past, finally hammering into the frame of the front door just as it opened.

Both siblings froze as a dark figure in the doorway stepped to the side as the knife struck. A tense moment passed without word as the figure reached up with one hand and pulled the knife away, studying it before taking a step inside and placing it gently on the shelf of a nearby cabinet. He was dressed in an ankle length coat of deep blue with silver brocade and embroidery. A gaunt face that had paled slightly with age, still held sharp unflinching eyes that now rested on the pair as he moved an errant strand of hair away from his face.

"Uncle." Cerberus dipped his head briefly.

"My Lord Charnite." Cerberex sheathed the other blade in a fluid movement and similarly dipped her head respectfully all the while keeping an eye on Cerberus.

"So I see very little has changed while I've been away." Selwyn's gaze shifted imperiously from Cerberus to Cerberex and back before his face twisted into a slight smile. The sound of rapid feet came from down the left hall. Light footfalls that required no disguise. A sudden flash of energy flickered from the shadows before both Cerberus and Cerberex were flung off their feet.

Cerberus winced as he landed heavier than he expected. When he looked up a lady in deep purple lace and silk, her hair rippling from the colour of midnight to the pearl white of moonshine was clasped to Selwyn her lips pressed firmly against his.

"Still tastes like strawberries!" The smile spread across Selwyn's face as he gently pulled away, looking over the lady. "You haven't aged a day," he whispered stroking her chin. Suddenly with surprising strength he lifted her up into his arms and it seemed a hundred years lifted from his face as he winked at her. "I missed you too Maleficent my dear."

Cerberex rubbed her back from where she'd hit a book case. "Aunt Mal." She gave a cough. The lady looked over at the two of them. She was more petite than Cerberex and had the thin line of a smile. She nodded at Cerberex with eyes that spoke of years of mischief.

Cerberus felt a sudden gut wrenching pull as Aunt Mal looked at them. Though they lived in the same house, Maleficent rarely moved from her basement laboratory but on the rare occasion she did it was like suddenly looking into a time vortex and seeing a familiar yet ultimately more feminine face stare back.

Selwyn kissed Mal's forehead and gave the pair an appraising look. "Cerberus, Cerberex, a pleasure as always. As you were." He proceeded to carry Mal back down the hall she had emerged from. A few moments later the click of a door quietly shutting could be heard.

Cerberus got on to his feet and held out a hand to his sister. She batted it out of the way, pushing herself up, her eyes narrowed at Cerberus and a hand on her knife. He took a step back. "Do you really think that I would intervene if any of them really had a semblance of feeling for you?"

Cerberex moved across the room and retrieved her knife. She turned around giving Cerberus a dead pan look. "I wouldn't know. They never wake up."

"Because each of them would likely murder you while you slept, poison your morning drink, or find other ways to rid themselves of the heiress to House Dhal-Marrah." Cerberus sighed. "If you really wish to continue this may I suggest that we do so in an area where we are less likely to break anything valuable."

"Arannis was interested in me." Cerberex countered.

Cerberus pulled a face and pointed the end of the rapier at the ground leaning on it slightly. "Arannis is it? Tell me sister what did Arannis talk about? Which house did he hail from? What were his interests?" He watched Cerberex's face turn dark. "Arannis was no lord. He was the third son of a minor house who sought fame and fortune and was paid handsomely I might add, in Trileris coin to bed you and bring any information you let slip to the current lord and lady of that house. In short, he's lucky he lived long enough to get as far as he did."

"And the others?" A dangerous note entered Cerberex's voice. Cerberus simply shrugged. "You know brother, I'm not an idiot and no matter how you may feel about it, I am entitled to my little bit of fun. It would however, be nice to just once wake up next to a warm body."

Cerberus smiled. "Of course sister. How could I forget just how much you do for this house already," he continued sarcastically and gave a mock bow before heading down a corridor to the right leading to the dining hall and library. "If you'd only improve your taste I might even give them a head start." His voice echoed back to her.

Cerberex listened to him leave until she was sure that she was alone in the entrance hall. "If you'd only improve your taste..." she mimicked and pulled a face. "They aren't the only ones to gain information via subtle means, or do you assume that knowledge of the other houses was simply delivered by courier."

The wilderness that bordered the mountains had a subtle peace to it that only a Watcher could truly appreciate. Heavy pines grew with a density that seemed to be natures way of keeping out unwanted visitors. A hundred years ago Cerberex had sat in her mother's sitting room staring at that line of brownish-green from the window. Her father had once said that she was as untamed as the wild that hugged the doorstep, before handing her the first bow she'd owned and sending her to Agrellon. When she had retuned she had found him and his support of her life choices snatched away.

These days her spirit was tempered by the needs of the house. The families dealt in a web of subterfuge. While her brother duelled with death on a rooftop or on street corners, she bargained a yearly visit to court and her ability to glean information from those immune to the violence Cerberus dealt in, for her freedom of the wild. It was her undoing in many ways - family always came first.

"Paid handsomely to bed you." Cerberus's words haunted her as she entered the first line of trees. She'd have killed him for that comment alone once, should have killed him. Male Drau were not entitled to the same protections as their female counterparts till they had passed their trials and even then they were considered second only. Why for the love of Eroth, she kept him around still baffled even her. She could hear his laugh in the back of her head. Her fists clenching and unclenching until she stopped and pushed her nails into the bark of a nearby tree to calm herself. She felt a nail snap and the tree bleed sap until with a tearing and cracking, she pulled her hand away and ran into the depths of the woodland.

There was a path through the tangle of briar and pine if you knew what to look for. Cerberex knew it by heart, she had memorized every loose stone, every pitfall, so when the ground instead of arching upwards towards the foothills of the mountains, suddenly and inexplicably dropped away into a deep basin, her speed was not impeded. Despite the speed or her run, as the edge dropped away she threw her hands up grabbing a lonely leafless branch and twisting up onto it till she sat perched atop gently swaying. Below the basin was devoid of all foliage save a handful of dead saplings. A single stone stood at the centre its faces smooth like black glass that shone on the rare occasion some light dared to cut through the canopy. She closed her eyes. No bird song, no crawl from the undergrowth, yet just at the edge of her senses she could hear the faintest whispering that she couldn't quite make out. Whenever her anger was at its peak she would inevitably find her way here.

Cerberex inhaled the smell of mulch, dirt, and sweat. The persistent echo of Cerberus's voice diminished and with it the anger and the need for violence diminished also. What need had she to prove herself equal when she was in every respect superior. A smile touched her lips and she rose on the branch standing perfectly balanced despite the drop and the gentle sway of the thin spike of wood beneath her feet. The back of her mind in an adrenaline fuelled frenzy, urged her to jump and see if she could make it to the bottom in a single leap unharmed. Despite the jagged pieces of broken tree stumps that lined the basin and all physical evidence to the contrary, a small part of her said she could do it. Tentatively she took a step across the branch, feeling it bend with her weight Her heart rate quickened.

Cerberex's eyes flicked open as somewhere in the under growth behind her a scurry of movement and the snapping of branches brought her to attention. Cartwheeling off the branch to the safety of the ground, she crouched in anticipation a hand on the ground feeling for the tremor of footfalls. "So you finally mustered the balls to try me in my domain brother," she whispered to herself. "Oh I'm going to so enjoy making you regret that decision." Sidestepping, she merged with the shadows an uncanny trick she'd always seemed to possess, and began stalking her prey.

A short distance away Cerberex picked up the tracks of her quarry. Here where the undergrowth was spongy with moss, the imprint of a boot was quite firmly visible. Ahead the smallest sound of movement through fern caught her attention. To her knowledge there was a clearing ahead, a favourite haunt for small game, where the bramble's receded and thick ferns and larger rubbery succulents grew. Careful not to disturb the ground too much, Cerberex moved from tree to tree like a ghost. From between two ancient firs a whisper of movement shifted in the shadows. So Cerberus thought he could hide from her did he? Very well, let the game begin. With nothing but the creak of gently swaying branches, Cerberex stepped left to wrong foot her quarry. Pausing she waited for Cerberus to fall into her trap - nothing.

Cerberex's eyes narrowed and hesitantly peered past a giant fern leaf to find again nothing. She listened, this was not her brother's handiwork. She'd intrinsically known her brother's style since the earliest days of her memory. Like a sense, she could almost feel his proximity. This was different. Without thinking her hands reached down to her blades. They unsheathed with a hiss and she pressed herself back against the gnarled bark of a tree. A twig snapped gently maybe twenty feet away the other side. Cerberex held her breath looking up. The fir she lay against was still young, its higher branches were too green to support any real weight but perhaps she could get just high enough to be off the forest floor. Placing a foot against a convenient knot-hole, she used her knives like pitons to bring herself a good ten feet up. Gently she eased herself across a branch, wincing as it creaked.

Below and slightly to the right, the shadows shifted again. Cerberex span the hunting knives in her hands, precariously balanced. Unblinking, she leaped. A ring of metal against metal rang through the clearing like the toll of a bell. For a moment Cerberex's vision spun head over heels as her prey used her momentum to flip her over the top and backwards. She rolled with the movement spinning with both knives outstretched only to meet tempered steel. The figure in front of her was unknown but the grace of their movement and hint of physique spoke a language of their own that Cerberex understood well.

The sword twisted locking her knives in place and for second. Cerberex snatched her chance to look into the face beneath the hood. He was male, paler than her brother, with hardened features. His eyes were a mirror of her surprise. She pressed forwards testing the strength behind the sword he wielded with some degree of expertise, before spinning the knives backwards, unlocking them, and taking a step back. She watched him mimic her as they circled till with a twist of speed she pushed herself up and over using a nearby stump for height - a whirl of blades. This time there was no ring of steel or hiss of a razor edge as her knives met air. The leaves kicked up behind her as she spun to a stop confused.

The hood had fallen back to fully reveal his face. Not that much older than Cerberus. She stood up with her knives still raised. "You trespass on the lands of Dhal-Marrah. You had better have a good reason." For moment Cerberex saw a flicker of surprise as his eyes sized her up, he lowered the sword fractionally.

"I could say the same for you - apprentice? I sense no mark - but you're not bad." His voice was rich and bred - unmistakably Drau with the flair of noble birth.

Cerberex did not drop her knives for a moment and commenced circling again, watching as he maintained mirroring her. "An apprentice of what?" She paused surprised for a second. "I am Cerberex of Dhal-Marrah and unlike you, I have every reason to be here." She watched him stop at her name and raise an eyebrow.

"You're Cerberex?" He rested the flat of his sword on his shoulder. "Well you're not exactly what I was expecting."

"And what was that?" Cerberex spun her blades restlessly, anticipating a trick.

"Let's just say that Cerberus's descriptions are - misleading," he replied with the hint of a smile.

Cerberex edged fractionally closer. "Who are you?"

His smile faltered. "I... I am unimportant my Lady. A friend of Cerberus"

Cerberex almost dropped her knives with surprise. "A friend?" Her knives moved back to their sheaths at her sides. "Cerberus has friends?"

"I am... well suffice to say I keep an eye on things for your brother." His head moved to one side. "Surely you didn't think ... but I assumed..."

"Assumed what?" Cerberex edged closer still.

He waved the matter away. "My apologies. If I had known it was you my Lady, I'd have announced my presence. The fault is entirely mine."

"Wait a moment. You work for my brother?" Cerberex rolled her eyes and folded her arms. "So he's keeping tabs now is he? Of course, can't trust sister dearest can we? Wouldn't want her to ruin all his plans, so now we have to send a tag-along to make sure she doesn't get herself into too much trouble."

"Firstly it's 'with', I work with Cerberus or at least I like to think I do. Secondly, I haven't been 'sent' I was equally surprised that you were here. Thirdly, judging by the way you use those, you hardly need someone to make sure you get out of trouble." His head moved from one side to the other.

"What are you looking at?" She asked feeling a little uncomfortable by his stare.

"I'm not the only one staring." He gave a soft laugh.

Cerberex blinked and looked away for a moment. When she looked back he had vanished.

Kane darted over a stump keeping the noise of his passing to minimum before crouching to a halt behind a patch of briar. He could still just make out Cerberex in the clearing and let go of a breath he didn't know he'd been holding, as he watched her leave in the opposite direction. Thank Eroth for shadow walking! He trailed her with his eyes till the foliage prevented him from doing so. Lifting up the end of the leather shoulder guard he inspected a tiny tear roughly an inch and a half long in the sleeve of the shirt he wore underneath. Beneath it a thin line of blood showed a short yet deep cut. Nothing more than a scratch in comparison to others he'd had and it would heal easily enough, yet it surprised him that it was there at all. Cerberus was the only one these days who could score blood blade on blade even if some of the other assassins had come damn close once or twice. He tried to shrug off the irritation of it and crouched for a few moments more, erring on the side of caution before heading back to the clearing and watching her make her way deftly back through the wild.

Chapter 3:
Uncle Selwyn

Cerberex could still hear the siren call of the stone as the pines thinned to briars and then to ferns before a crumbling wall of stone marked the immediate grounds of the house.

"The hunt still calling Cerberex?"

Cerberex jumped, notching an arrow as she twisted in the direction of the voice. She relaxed her aim as her uncle leaned against the wall gently raising his hands with a slight smile that reminded her in every way of Cerberus. "You are the second person to have jumped me today. The third is likely to get shot," she replied coldly.

Selwyn raised an eyebrow. "Oh?" He lowered his hands to his side. "It's not like you to jump at shadows niece." He walked to her side.

"Only when they walk and talk uncle," she countered. "Seems little brother has been having me tailed." She began to walk across towards the house with Selwyn close behind.

"I doubt that." He smiled warmly at her. "In any case you know the wilds like no other. I'm sure you could disappear if you chose."

Cerberex slowed and took in a long breath, forcing the anger out of her head. She smiled. "So, how was court?"

Selwyn gave a mock shudder. "Terribly boring!"

Cerberex laughed. "Well that explains your sudden return. Aunt Mal will be especially pleased. Will you be here long?"

Selwyn smiled. "That's better. I prefer to hear your laughter. Possibly. I have been away for a while and what better way to take a short break than in the one house where I know I'm bound to find some excitement."

"Pah! Excitement? Truly the house has been dead since you last left." Cerberex stopped by a stone bench. "Which begs the question why you would think things are about to get exciting."

Selwyn pulled an accentuated shocked face. "Really Cerberex. How could you accuse me of that." He smiled and reached into a deep pocket of his coat looking furtively around. "I brought you a little something." He held out a small knife with a beautifully carved bone handle the end of which had been turned into a dragon's head. "It is one of a pair."

Cerberex carefully took the blade and turned it over in her hands. "Do you seek to change the subject uncle? It is very nice, but I have many blades and my memory can't be bought with baubles so easily these days."

"Not like this one you don't. It was given to me by your father but as my weapons are of a verbal variety these days, I felt they should be given to those who might show them a bit of use. Do with it as you will my dear but I know better than to buy you with such things." He laced his hands behind his back. "Of course you always have been incredibly perceptive. I came because there have been stirrings since Dhal-Marrah distanced itself entirely from court."

Cerberex tucked the knife into her belt. "Should we be worried?"

Selwyn gestured to the house. "Yours is an old name Cerberex, even my house cannot openly compete with it. Your lack of presence in the court makes you an easy target."

"If you remember uncle there is a good reason why I don't represent the house. Why not ask Mother?" Cerberex slowly made her way down a manicured path.

"Of course how could I forget. No, I have not come to encourage the family to be more active in state affairs. I simply felt I should update your Lady-mother on the state of the growing discontent." Selwyn approached a pair of ornate glass panelled doors and opened one, allowing Cerberex to pass. "The King grows impatient with the Queen's resistance to provide an heir. There has been some accusation that she regrets her decision to bind to house Gal-Serrek."

The entrance lead into the dining hall and Cerberex stopped placing her weapons on the dark, thorn-wood table that stretched almost to its length. "What has this to do with us?"

"It is the first time in over eight hundred years that the presiding monarch has not ruled with a Dhal-Marrah at their side." Selwyn took a seat and steepled his fingers. "There is some talk that the king would..." he paused searching for the words. "That he would encourage the Queen to have an unfortunate accident and perhaps find a more willing wife."

Cerberex looked up in surprise. "That is treason! Under our most sacred laws the Queen is the hand of Eroth incarnate. To suggest her untimely demise is to court the wrath of a God."

"You are an idealist niece and long may you remain so, but this is politics. The King hails from House Gal-Serrek a family that cares little for religious mediocrity, but as I shall repeat it is over hundred years since Dhal-Marrah has enforced the monarch's will or at least been in the background." Selwyn looked around. The walls of the room were hung with portraits of various house patriarchs and matriarchs descending over the years until his eyes rested on the familiar features and stark white hair. "Your father would have seen that tradition continue but well..." He shook his head. "Fate is a cruel mistress."

Cerberex turned the bone knife over and over in her hands as she sat on the opposite side. "Yet it is the Queen's right to chose the when and how of conception. Surely the King cannot force that issue. Physiologically speaking all female Drau have the ability to choose if they will or will not." She smiled slightly. "A perk of the species in my opinion."

Selwyn laughed under his breath. "Quite niece and yet there are rumours that the King has already given Queen Lida an ultimatum."

Cerberex snorted. "Of what nature. The lout may postulate all he wants but at the end of the day he has little to do with it."

Selwyn looked at her sternly. "If the Queen continues to refuse the King, House Gal-Serrek will walk from the alliance and bring civil war to our streets."

Cerberex's eyes widened. "That is preposterous!"

Selwyn nodded. "Now do you see my concern? I would like to think it is merely idle words and Eroth knows how cruel the King can be, but since this came to my attention I have kept my ear very close to the ground."

"Cruel he certainly is, but you cannot tell me that he actually means to follow through." Cerberex shrugged. "Not that I blame the Queen. I couldn't bare the thought of lying with him." She leaned forward across the table. "Surely if he's so desperate for his due, he could take a lover. After all he wouldn't be the first."

"I would delicately suggest my dear, that he probably does. Not that it will give him what he wants." Selwyn leaned back against the chair. "So I come to your house my dear niece to ask a favour."

"Selwyn Charnite." A female voice resonated down the room making Cerberex look up suddenly and Selwyn's smile faltered.

"My dear sister you are as quiet as ever." Selwyn raised his head and looked at the tall female drifting towards them in a gown of grey silk.

"My husband is long gone Selwyn and we are not brother and sister any more." She came to a halt four chairs down.

"Elryia, I shall always consider you my sister." Selwyn stood and gave an elaborate bow.

"Mother, it would appear that Uncle Selwyn has some..." Cerberex began before being cut off by her mother's raised hand.

"I heard quite clearly." She turned to Selwyn. "House Dhal-Marrah is removed from house politics Lord Charnite as well you know. We no longer involve ourselves."

Selwyn's eyes narrowed. "House Dhal-Marrah has always ensured the safety of the royal family. The oath between your house and Lotheri still stands."

An awkward silence filtered across the table, stretching for what seemed an inordinate amount of time. "Then the Lotheri's had best ensure they look after their own." The words were spoken quietly with a dangerous level of calm.

Selwyn smiled but it did not reach his eyes. "With the greatest of respect, that is Lord Dhal-Marrah's decision."

"Then I will say it again. My husband is dead..."

"Damn it Elryia! I am not to blame for your loss. Do you not think that I would go back in time and exchange places if I could?" Selwyn slammed a fist into the table before taking a breath and calming himself. "Please, I am not here to fight with you. You are of course the Lady of the house. However, you cannot hide away forever. When you bound to Dendrion you knew what it meant. Dhal-Marrah must return to court. House Charnite cannot hold alone. There must be a show of strength to give the Gal-Serrek alliance pause."

Cerberex felt an iron grip rest on her shoulder. "My children are not pawns in your political intrigue Selwyn. We no longer hold the cohorts as we once did."

Selwyn laughed. "Do you not? Clearly your sense has dulled a little. Perhaps you should watch your daughter's reflexes or better yet," he paused as he made his way slowly around the table end. "Why not ask Cerberus?"

Cerberex looked up at the sharp features of her mother. "Please mother," she began with the most diplomatic voice she could muster. "There is no harm in asking. He is after all, family and Aunt Mal is always so much happier when he is around." She watched as the annoyance drifted from her mother's face leaving her with a passive look of acceptance.

"At least you remembered something of diplomacy from all those lessons I taught you Cerberex." Elryia forced a smile not breaking eye contact with Selwyn for an instant. "You are of course welcome in this house Lord Charnite, you are as my daughter quite rightly puts it, family after all." Her eyes softened. "And I do not blame you or wish that fate had chosen differently but I caution you against asking Cerberus..."

"Asking me what?" Cerberus stood at the far end of the room his arms folded as he beheld the scene.

Selwyn clapped his hands and walked briskly to the far end. "Nephew!" He embraced Cerberus as he came closer much to Cerberus's surprise. "We must talk," he whispered into Cerberus's ear. "In the usual place."

Cerberus's face did not change and he patted Selwyn on the back. "It's good to see you back Uncle. Perhaps Aunt Mal will finally stop trying to blow us all up for a bit."

Selwyn pulled back, his face split into a wide grin. "Oh I sincerely hope I'll be able to distract her for at least a few days." He glanced back at Cerberex and her mother. "Now, how about we find a decent bottle of something. After all, its not like the family is all together like this very often." His eye caught Elryia's and the two exchanged a hard look, each expecting the other to blink.

Three empty bottles of good wine twinkled in the diminishing candle light as evening fell. Selwyn flopped back in his chair easing into a contented silence. The rose-light of the sun had drifted down to a deep twilight and of the family group only Cerberus seemed to remain comparatively sober. He edged to a far wall on the left keeping his eye on those in the room. Aunt Mal was sleeping soundly against the shoulder of his Uncle who seemed to be well on the way to a wine induced slumber. Cerberex had been the first to leave followed by his mother, leaving just the three of them. It had taken in his opinion, an impressive amount of time to ply enough alcohol to get the rest of them this drunk. Above a portrait of a black clad ancestor in a deep purple cloak, looked down as he raised his palm of his right hand and placed it firmly against the wall. He winced at the sudden burning sensation then withdrew his hand. Thin lines of red the colour of blood, ran down and along the wall as a series of stone blocks roughly two by six turned dark then disappeared into black entirely revealing the illusion. Cerberus disappeared into the darkness beyond without sound.

Cerberus kept his feet on a practiced path in the light-less passage beyond. To misstep was to be dead. These tunnels were riddled with traps designed to eradicate unwanted guests and only those who had been taught the trick behind the 'bladed path' could get through. At least, that's how his father had put it the first time he had taken Cerberus down to the assassins' route. Most of the route had fallen out of use since those days. Once these tunnels would have been a hive of quiet activity. Now only the bunk room, training pit, and blade room saw day to day use. A familiar tickle told him that there were currently only three of the dozen assassins under his command currently in residence. As he came closer to the core, lamps lit the doors and arches leading off to different rooms. Most were covered in a heavy layer of cobwebs. Cerberus smiled as the ring of metal on metal sang to him from the far end.

"Oh come on you're not even trying to hit me."

"Trust me Meera if I was trying you would be dead."

"Scared of drawing a little blood?"

"Not in the slightest."

"Ah! Now that's more like it."

Cerberus smiled as he appeared in the archway looking into the training pit. Two individuals one male the other female sparred with each other. They were superb - as they should be, he had personally trained them both. Kane was the first to notice him, parrying away a flurry of blows, giving him a quick nod. The female looked up a second later with a broad smile. She had dark grey almost black hair cut boyishly short and was straight and skinny as a pole. In her hands she held two ornately hilted blades roughly a foot long. They reminded Cerberus of his sister's hunting knives yet these were far thinner and almost round like a stiletto. Like her they were unique.

"Cerberus! Darling!"

Cerberus inclined his head. "Meera. Keeping those knives of yours sharp I see."

Meera looked down at them before spinning them a wrist flick. "Naturally." She looked sideways at him. "Oh I know that look."

Cerberus smiled. "I should hope so. As my First you're supposed to be able to anticipate my commands."

Meera gave a cheeky grin. "Commands is it?"

Cerberus gave a quick laugh and looked over at Kane. "Not been pressing you too hard I hope Kane?"

Kane rested the flat of the sword across his bare shoulders. "Not really."

Cerberus raised an eyebrow. "Would appear she's scored a hit." He nodded towards the incision on Kane's shoulder.

Kane opened his mouth but Meera got there first. "Oh that wasn't me." She looked back at Kane gleefully before turning and pouting at Cerberus. "He wont even tell me which one of our motley crew scored that." She tilted her head back revealing her throat. "Will you darling?" Kane remained silent. "See." She grinned a pearl white smile. "Well if there's plan afoot I should dress into something more appropriate." She looked down at the torn shirt she wore revealing thin slices of almost dove white skin. As she brushed past Cerberus she looked back at Kane. "Maybe we can perfect on your technique again a little later darling."

Cerberus waited as her footsteps headed down to the bunk room before walking over to Kane. "Aren't you tempted?"

"By what?" Kane moved towards a table on the far side and slid his sword into its scabbard before attaching it back onto his back.

"Oh come on, she's clearly into you." Cerberus chuckled. "Why not go for it? She's one of my Chosen but if your looking for permission..."

"I'm well aware of what she's after Cerberus." Kane adjusted the straps of the harness. "I'm just not interested."

"Not interested?" Cerberus moved towards him. "Trust me when I tell you that's only going to encourage her."

"So it would seem." Kane flexed his shoulders with an almost imperceptible wince. Cerberus grabbed hold of it with lightening reflex. "Ow!"

"So how did you do that?" Cerberus looked at the small wound with interest.

"Looks like a blade if I'm not mistaken."

Kane shrugged him off. "It's just a scratch. Misjudged a throwing knife in practice and paid the price for it."

"Really?" Cerberus watched as Kane headed to the archway. "It must have been thrown at a strange angle to make a wound like that."

"Rule number one Cerberus." Kane's voice drifted back as he left.

Cerberus smiled. "Rule number one: Assassin's don't play fair." He wandered over to the live weapon rack beside the arch and glanced over the selection of throwing knives. "Apparently not," he muttered under his breath, picking up one of the knives and examining it.

"Aaah, still smells of blood, sweat, and tears."

Cerberus smiled and turned, sitting on the table with his arms folded. "I'd be more worried if it didn't Uncle."

"Still got that Meera girl around then?" Selwyn ran a hand down the stone edge of the arch, every ounce of earlier inebriation gone.

"She's very good at what she does." Cerberus watched and waited.

"Didn't you..." Selwyn began.

"Yes," Cerberus replied before he could finish.

"But you're not..." Selwyn continued.

"No," Cerberus continued anticipating him.

Selwyn nodded. "Ah, I see. To business then."

"Eroth's fangs! The mighty Selwyn Charnite." Meera's voice was tinged with surprise. "What a pleasure to see a former First Assassin amongst us."

Cerberus watched as Meera stalked across towards him now dressed in sleek fitting leather armour. "Now, now Meera be respectful."

Meera stopped turning back to Selwyn with a spin. "But of course." She crossed her arms over her chest and performed a deep bow. "No disrespect was intended my Lord."

Selwyn ignored her. "I came to talk to you Cerberus."

Cerberus shrugged. "Meera is my First. Whatever you need to say to me Uncle, you can say to her."

Selwyn looked at Meera before sighing. "As you wish. I am here to ask a favour."

Cerberus leaned forward resting his arms on his knees. "Of course, the route is indebted to you. Ask away."

"I believe, no, I am convinced that house Gal-Serrek intends to make a move on the crown." Selwyn watched as Cerberus looked up in surprise and held up a hand. "Yes, yes I know your sister gave me the same look."

"That's a very strong claim," Meera replied carefully. "One that I can't say seems likely. For what reason? The King himself is of that house. You can't imply that they would move against one of their own."

Selwyn looked at her darkly. "I've witnessed worse." He returned his gaze to Cerberus. "I'm not asking much. Just a tail on their dealings. Enough to ensure that this is simply word and rumour."

"Uncle, why do I get the impression that this is the short version of events. Meera is right. They wouldn't depose their own so you must therefore mean the Queen." Cerberus regained his composure.

"Queen Lida is many things. Beautiful, talented, diplomatic, but she is not loved by all. The binding of her and the King is one of necessity and politics. There are rumours of an ultimatum against the Queen." He paused considering his next words.

Cerberus narrowed his eyes. "Are you suggesting that Lida, I mean the Queen is being blackmailed?"

"Not at all. For the most part the Queen runs her life from her own chambers and the King from his, and therein lies the root of this. For she does not allow herself near him." Selwyn folded his arms. "Not that I can blame her. To be quite frank he's an alcoholic brute with a nasty temper. That said if its true the King grows tired of waiting. Should she continue to..." He looked at Meera and tactfully chose his next words. "Should she continue to 'avoid' him then House Gal Serrek will respond appropriately."

"Oh say it for what it is." Meera rolled her eyes. "She wont bed him and he's a bit upset!"

Cerberus looked up. "That's not what you mean is it Uncle? You're here to tell me that this is about heirs and future Kings or Queens. Kings or Queens with Gal-Serrek blood." He stood still a little shorter than Selwyn. "This is because she either cannot or will not have a child." Selwyn gave a slight nod. "And the rumours say what? That he will find another should she refuse? Wouldn't be the first time a mistress has walked the palace."

"True nephew, but if your father hadn't dragged Nius Gal-Serrek back dead, there already would be." He lowered his voice. "I believe he means to have her killed." He watched as Cerberus raised his eyebrows. "I know it all sounds a bit much but humour me."

"Meera, kindly make arrangements to get intel on the Gal-Serrek goings on so we know what we're dealing with," Cerberus muttered.

Meera looked up surprised. "You can't honestly believe..."

"I'm not going to repeat myself." Cerberus turned his head and gave her a hard look making her take a step back.

Meera regained her composure and bowed. "As you wish." She took two steps back before turning on her heel and walking briskly out of the room.

Cerberus folded his arms. "She's right you know this isn't our line of work."

"Your father wouldn't of considered it beneath him." Selwyn watched Cerberus's eyes harden. "But your right. I confess that I might be using the history I know you two have to my advantage here." He smiled and caught Cerberus's look. "Oh don't give me that look Cerberus. I merely want to ensure that nothing untoward happens and I wouldn't have asked if I didn't think you would be interested."

"That Uncle, is as it was so delicately put to me recently - ancient history." Cerberus sighed. "But I will ensure that nothing goes awry nonetheless."

Selwyn smiled. "I expected nothing less," he replied as he turned to leave.

"Uncle." Cerberus watched Selwyn stop just before the archway. "Why do I think that you know I've already seen Lida today?"

Selwyn turned his head seeing Cerberus out the corner of his eye. "I am aware the Queen has taken to absconding from the palace to meet with less savoury individuals. Individuals who trade is less than legal items in some cases. She isn't stupid. I dare say she is aware of the rumours surrounding the Gal-Serreks. I might even go so far as to say she also wishes to extract herself. I simply wish to ensure she doesn't do herself any harm."

Cerberus nodded and gave a smile that did not filter to his eyes. "Remember Uncle, I am not an apprentice any more so please do not play me for a fool."

Selwyn inclined his head. "I wouldn't dream of it nephew."

Cerberus stalked across the room. "Then you can be assured that I will see to it personally - I can guarantee that nothing shall befall the Queen on my watch." Selwyn gave a second nod and Cerberus watched him walk away leaving the ghost signature of two people entirely capable of killing each other.

Chapter 4:
Starlit Reconnaissance

Cerberus sat resting on one knee with another arm holding him to the spire tip of tallest tower on the house. The pale sun had sunk into the earth turning the sky a deep, bloody red. Behind him a dozen sparks of star light lay scattered across the sky. From this height only the two mountain ranges blocked his view in any direction. Everfall spread out like a dark stain of old blood illuminated in pale silver light as one by one the lamps lit. Thin wisps of smoke danced from rooftops like air elementals. No longer in casual wear, the form fitting leather armour chaffed ever so slightly around the neck and shoulders. Half a dozen throwing knives were wrapped about his waist alongside the silver rapier. The only other adornment was a brooch of silver, mottled with age. A dragon spreading its wings above two crossed daggers. The eyes were shards of ruby and reflected the last rays of the sun much like his own.

A mournful bell echoed from the Temple of Eroth and the sunlight died. Cerberus smiled. "Nice try Meera but you can't sneak up on me that easily."

Meera effortlessly pulled herself up onto the spire top. "You didn't tell me you were planning on making the trip by yourself."

Cerberus smiled. "You didn't tell me you were bringing company." He turned and watched as Kane pulled himself up only a handful of seconds behind Meera. Both were kitted out much like himself. A smaller, less ornate version of Cerberus's brooch decorated Meera's armour.

Meera grinned. "Well we never fight alone." She leaned against Kane with an arm over his shoulder.

"There will be no fighting tonight," Cerberus murmured firmly. "You will look and listen and report back by dawn. If there is anything untoward at work I trust you can find it."

"Darling, I was made to find trouble." Meera whispered sitting next to him.

Cerberus pulled away. "Then you wont need any help. As you've brought Kane along we can cover more ground." He looked back as Kane gave a polite cough.

"With respect Cerberus. I don't think this is a good idea." Kane looked down as Meera hissed at him quietly under her breath. "The contract in this case is familial. Realistically speaking, I am too close."

"True. Sometimes I forget, it seems like you have always been here for as long as I have." Cerberus flashed him a smile. "Of course Meera here might get lonely with out an escort."

Meera glared at Kane as he smiled back. "Oh I'm sure she'll bare up. Besides, I can keep tabs on things here. Some one's got to keep an eye on your uncle after all; he has a way of getting his fingers into things that one."

"You know we have house guard for that." Cerberus gave him a sideways look.

Kane shrugged. "They're not as good at it though."

Cerberus chuckled. "Don't let the guard captain hear you say that." He stood. "Well if you're sure Kane. You are one of my most veteran assassins these days and there are other's I can send to keep an eye." He placed a hand on his friend's shoulder. "You needn't go near the palace, I can check in on her for you."

Kane shook his head. "It's better if I'm not part of this. I'll only find my way there if I am."

"Well I'm sure I can distract you darling." Meera smiled sweetly.

Kane turned to her with a flicker of annoyance. "It's more I could distract you Meera."

Meera pouted. "I'd have thought you'd jump at the chance to see some real action."

Kane's face remained impassive. "More than you know Meera but let's not present the palace guard with bonus targets shall we?"

Cerberus held up a hand as Meera prepared a retort. "Enough we are wasting starlight. You are free to remain Kane, I'll let you know how things are when I return." He watched as Kane nodded and hopped off the edge grabbing the claw of a stone gargoyle before he could fall and made is way back down.

"You give him too much free reign." Meera took a step towards Cerberus.

"Would you rather take his place instead?" Cerberus asked. Meera stayed silent. "That's what I thought." He wandered to the edge. "He's not interested Meera. No matter how much you try to force the issue." A curl of a smile pulled at his lips. "You're just not his taste."

Meera joined him. "Well you would know. I believe that you required a little work to convince." She leaned in till Cerberus could feel her breath on his neck. "And I don't remember you complaining afterwards."

Cerberus didn't turn he could already feel her smile. "I don't believe I was there the next morning to do so." He forced himself to glance at her. Her face had dropped and he couldn't help but feel the smallest bit smug. "Shall we?"

"As you wish." Meera balanced on the edge perfectly. "You weren't there Cerberus but you came back for more - maybe your jealous." Before Cerberus could reply she leaned forwards and dropped.

The city after dark was a different breed of animal. Beautiful and exotic in the silver-blue lamp lights, and altogether a hundred times more dangerous. Murderers, thieves, muggers, and women of the night hugged alleys and doorways. Those who dared the starlit hours were terrors themselves or prey with only a fine line between the two. Like ghosts on the wind, the two sped across the roofs into the city proper. With a snap of fabric and whisper of air to mark their passage, they brought their shadow-walk to an end and swept down a drainage pipe to the street level below. To the casual onlooker it seemed that two shades had simply materialised on the paving. Each keeping in perfect step with each other as they approached the now deserted market districts.

"So?" Meera's thin cloak moved gently just below her knees as she looked at Cerberus expectantly. "What now? With just the two of us and a city to cover, the hours to dawn grow thin even at this hour."

Cerberus maintained his step. "We needn't cover the city. Selwyn believes that the Gal-Serreks are neck deep in this so we shall focus on their domains."

"The Gal-Serreks are known for the strength of their fighters." Meera mused half to herself and smiled. "A little liquor and their tongues might grow loose and easy." She paused with him as they came to a fork in the market. "And you?"

Cerberus's mouth curled. "Selwyn taught me a long time ago, when in doubt follow the purse. Lord Gal-Serrek is the king-pin in more ways than one, so I shall follow the money." He turned and looked east. The palace rose a little way off, hard to miss with its abundance of window lights glittering like fireflies. He turned feeling a hand on his shoulder.

"To trespass there at this hour is to court decapitation." Meera whispered. Her breath caressed his cheek.

Cerberus brushed her hand away gently. "Oh I know," he replied and flashed a grin. "But what's the game without a little risk?" His eyes glittered.

"Naturally darling and of course, the prize of a gawk at her highness while you're at it." Meera returned the grin. Cerberus met her gaze. "Oh come now, I'm sure its entirely innocent." she leaned in and whispered directly into his ear. "because I'm sure Kane would love to hear about you previous dealings with his sister."

Cerberus stiffened ever so slightly. "The past Meera. That was in the past, this is professional." In a single twist he grabbed her arm pulling it back till she gasped with pain. "And I'm not entirely sure Kane didn't know. So if you really are going to try and blackmail me Meera, do try something more current."

Meera winced a little then laughed. "Oh darling, if I was going to blackmail you there are so many other incidents I could choose from." She took a sudden intake of breath as her arm was tugged further behind her back. "Ah, but your point is made." She smiled as her arm was released.

Cerberus took a step away. "You're my First Meera, not Master."

Meera massaged her arm a little. "Oh perish the thought!"

Cerberus nodded and closed his eyes breathing deeply of the night air. "So many options, so little time." He opened his eyes and looked at the palace lights. "If you should find anything, give what you have to Selwyn. Failing that, I shall find you before dawn." He did not wait for her to acknowledge, sprinting between the empty stalls towards the shimmer of the palace. As they parted ways the shadows above them seemed to shift and a shrouded figure stood watching.

Cerberex watched as her brother and his companion parted. She couldn't make out a face or hear exactly what they spoke to each other in their hushed tones, but what she had heard made her sure that the voice of the other had been female. She'd kept pace with Cerberus till the city had closed about him and it had taken all her considerable skill to track him to the market districts. Vendetta drove her on as she picked up the pace, following him as he weaved a convoluted path eastward till hard stone of the palace's outer wall blocked his path.

Carefully, Cerberex notched an arrow. It was rubber tipped. Designed to leave on hell of a bruise but it wouldn't kill. Normally they were used to scare prey into fleeing in the direction of a prepared trap or to knock out smaller creatures. The weight of the rubber made them cumbersome for long distance shooting. Reaching into the quiver by her side, she counted three others among the usual steel tipped variety, though she doubted that if she missed him with one, she would get the chance to shoot another. She smiled watching him like a cornered rabbit size up the sheer wall that rose a good ten feet and prepared to loose - revenge would be so sweet!

Cerberus carefully eyed the wall up and down, picking out the weathering of the stonework. Running a hand across it, he felt the cracks where over time the stone had begun to move as its resistance was cowed by the elements. He paused momentarily and took three steps back. A split second later he ran towards the wall, leaping up and seeming to almost run perpendicular for a second before catching the top with his hands as his momentum subsided. With cat-like grace he swung the rest of his body up and slid down the other side.

"Shit!" Cerberex whispered to herself, lowering her bow as Cerberus disappeared from view. Throwing it onto her back she returned the arrow to the quiver and darted forwards. A little way ahead a rooftop garden with ornate trellis rose up. A gap of four or five feet lay between it and the wall. Tentatively she considered the jump. Ahead she could barely still make out the gentle pat of Cerberus's footsteps within the grounds beyond. Trespass into the palace was strictly forbidden. The status of House Dhal-Marrah might prevent a public punishment if they were caught, it would not absolve them of punishment completely. She took a deep breath and checked the buckles of her equipment. She willed her legs to speed faster and launched herself forward.

Cerberex narrowly avoided missing the wall completely. Her boots just making it to the edge as she swung her arms wildly in an attempted to rebalance before loosing her footing and sliding down the other side. With a crack of bone she hoped her brother didn't hear and a grunt of pain, Cerberex landed heavily onto finely cut stone paving. Forcing herself up, she pushed back against the wall and blended as best she could with the shadows. All sign of Cerberus had evaporated. Her knee throbbed and she could feel a wet trickle run down her leg. Limping, she rested in a bed of shrubbery and trimmed trees a few feet away.

The palace rose up ahead. Sheer walls of obsidian that glistened like oil on water. Massive windows of coloured glass rose from crystalline edged balconies draped in flowering vines of some exotic crawler. Spires and domes swept up towards the sky and shimmered with starlight, mirrored by transparent crystalline roofs. Lights glistened within, twinkling gold and silver and the smell of cooked delicacies and midnight jasmine perfumed the air.

Heavy feet reverberated across the ground. Cerberex instinctively pushed herself down against the dirt, relying on the dark colour of her clothes to cover her from searching eyes. A trio of guards far more heavily armoured than any house guard moved past. They were clad in silvered plate draped with soft mid-blue cloaks of brushed cotton lined with white fox fur. Their faces were covered by ornate helms and each carried a halberd bearing the pennant colours and twin sceptre sigil of the royal house of Lotheri. They were known to those who frequented the palace, as the Queen's Guard. Cerberex didn't need a demonstration to know that she would be cut down in a heartbeat if she were discovered even if it was said that Queen Lida was more compassionate than her counterpart.

Gently Cerberex flexed her knee. It stung badly. Carefully she pushed herself up to a crouch. "I hope you know what you're doing brother," she muttered to herself. She surveyed her surroundings but saw no sign of Cerberus. With a sigh she prepared her bow, placed a hand on her quiver, and prepared to wait.

  Cerberus pressed himself as close as he dared to the ledge of a darkened window some two stories up as the guards passed by below. For a split second he could have sworn he'd seen movement among the shrubberies but Meera's presence was some way west. He glanced above him. Part of the wall had been carved into an elaborate mural of sinuously serpentine figures their outstretched hands held out in supplication while holding aloft a large balcony. Faint music floated from above and the murmur of hushed voices. Springing up like a lemur his arm wrapped around the arm of a serpentine female and he used the momentum of the swing to hook a leg across the midriff dangling momentarily upside down. Above, slight vibrations in the stone told him the balcony above was occupied by one or more individuals. Silently, he hung counting the rhythm. One, two, three, four, five, pause. He listened to it repeat three or four times as his arms began to burn with the effort. A guard then, likely just the one. Carefully he inched his way along the outstretched figure. As he reached the end he felt the stone figure tips crumble to powder under his grip. Instinctively he locked his knees as his hands raked the air, his scarf muffling his alarm. The sentry paused and broke routine, peering over the balcony. The cracking of stone and patter of falling pebbles alerted him. Resting his halberd against the edge, he scanned the ground below. Cerberus watched the pale yellow eyes beneath the helm and held his breath. From here he was in no position to defend himself or attack. A burst of drunken laughter shattered the tense silence. The guard's head pulled back from the precipice and in that moment Cerberus swung to catch the lower rim of the balcony above.

  Vines covered in sweet smelling black flowers wove their way around the baroque palisade of the balcony's edge like a tangled web erupting from two heavy clay planters. Cerberus wrapped a hand around some to pull himself up and felt them snap under the strain leaving a sticky sap on his hand. Cursing he tried to pull more away and reveal the solid stone beneath. Ahead the bright candle light spilled across the space between the edge and the wall turning the obsidian to liquid gold. Across the balcony on the far wall nearest the opening, a water feature of a beautiful elf-like woman rendered in marble at an incredible ten feet in height, washed her naked form from a copper coated urn. The water splashed against the wall behind making its finish dull and pocked. Wrenching the last few vines free, Cerberus pulled himself onto the balcony's ledge and inched his way softly towards the statue.

  "To the King." The clink of crystal chimed from within. "Long may you reign my Lord." Another clink of crystal.

Cerberus braced himself against the statue feeling the cold water seep into his armour. Steadily he walked up the wall before flipping and balancing on the maiden's urn.

"To the succession!" Cerberus froze to the spot as the last word echoed from within. The voice was reedy. Cerberus pulled a pair of daggers from his belt and wedged them in the crack of the wall the better to climb but his attention was focussed on the flickering shadows from within.

"Tie your tongue Malinar. Succession requires a prodigal child something the bitch denies me yet," a second voice slurred.

"She plays a dangerous game to refuse."

"There is more than one way to hold the throne Malinar." The third voice was flint-like and dangerously sober. "You asked for my council and I have given it. Kill her and be done."

"Damn it cousin! I cannot murder her in cold blood - it needs, no it must look like an accident." The tinkling of liquid paused the voices for a moment. "I'll not turn the last of the Lotheri line into a martyr to piss on my parade."

"Then force the issue."

"Oh don't think I haven't cousin. She can refuse me, she can refuse her oaths of binding, but she's still soft. She wont permit others to suffer in her place." A dull chortle was followed by a contented grunt. "And she has quite a lot of ladies."

A burst of laughter made Cerberus leap up to the wall and climb four or five feet as a smudge of silhouette blocked the light. He breathed hard using his daggers to pick his way up the sheer surface, following the path of the crack. An angry part of his brain shouted that he had dallied to long and to stay was to court death.

"I could wet my dick in a new one each day till season's end and not run dry!"

Another burst of laughter. Cerberus reached up now ten or more feet above the balcony his eyes fixated beneath him. He could feel his hands clenching about the hilts. He hissed as his right-hand dagger reached the end of the crack and careened across the glassy surface with a squeal.

"Did you hear that?" The third voice cut through the jovial undertone like a knife.

"Here what?"

"Ssssh you ignorant oaf." The shadow below stepped out fully onto the balcony.

"Oaf is it? You dare talk to your King in that manner?" A heavy thud

Raised voices and the shattering of glass forced the Cerberus to look down.

"Naturally I jest my Lord. I am merely pre-occupied that we are not overheard." Two Drau argued below him.

A second figure twice the girth of the first stepped onto the balcony. "Are you jumping at bats now? You always were a small, frightened shit." The first figure braced himself against the balcony's edge before he was grabbed by the second and pushed back further. His captor holding him moments from the drop, swayed gently in a wine induced stupor. "Jest is it? Am I funny cousin?" The scream of a night-hawk high above broke the tension. The second figure pulled his prey back and let go. "There's nothing but bugs and birds out here." He sniffed and moved back within the adjoining room. "Get back in here you pitiful wretch and be thankful I'm feeling jovial tonight."

Cerberus forced himself to look away as the frivolities continued, feeling his fingernails tear as he pressed them into the fine fractures and slight imperfections of the stonework and climbed inch by inch up its face. He had trained with the best under the most intense scrutiny but it was all he could do to maintain his hold. His arms and legs protested urgently against the abuse. Meera's warning reverberated around his head. Few had ascended the palace without discovery. He glanced around looking for another balcony or lonely gargoyle to leap for. The wall glistened on either side. Twenty feet above, a half domed roof and pale light shimmered across the blue patina of its surface. Theupper most parts of the palace rose above it cornered by knife-like spires. A sliver of lamp light passed a thinly curtained window a good leap to his left. Briefly he thought he caught sight of an aged bone trellis. As he looked he could feel his hands slipping and he calculated he had moments to make a decision.

Cerberus pulled a hand away and reached behind him, pulling free a miniature crossbow. A single bolt was loaded attached to a metallic cord. Pulling back the safety with his teeth, Cerberus fired as his other hand finally slipped. One second, two, three, he felt himself falling backwards. As he counted the fourth, the cord grew taught, skidding him across the sheer surface face first into a matted mess of dead growth. The grapple moved under his weight. Cerberus rammed a hand into the dried vines his grip uncaring of the noise he might make. His fingers closed around a lattice-like structure beneath just in time as the stone crumbled and the end zipped back within the crossbow's attachment. Cerberus allowed himself a moments breath choosing not to think of how events might have played a moment or two later, before making his way up to the roof.

The roof was indeed domed but flattened at its midway point before joining the next wall. A foot gap above its crest ran a bank of three tall windows cast in a pale light from within, roughly twelve or so feet in height. Cerberus crouched as he approached. There was no avoiding them. Thin agate-blue curtains hung across them blurring what he could make of the interior. On the far side one window hung slightly open allowing its curtain to ghost across his face.

Gently Cerberus pulled the window wider pushing back the curtain with his other hand. No candles lit the room beyond. Instead dozens of moon-globes rendered the interior in a pearl-like light somewhere between white and blue. The room itself was easily as large as the dining hall of home. Plush upholstered chairs and elegant tables decorated one side of the room and a harp, two bookcases, and a large cabinet lay on the other. He numbered pairs of double doors, one directly ahead leading presumably further into the palace, and another to his right towards an adjoining room. A third smaller door was recessed into the left wall. Finally, in the centre of the room a silver fluted bath tub stood surrounded by towels. Cerberus padded towards it keeping his eyes open for any sign of movement and dipped his finger into the water it contained. Warm. He wiped his finger dry on a towel. It had been abandoned only recently.

"If you're here to rob me you're doing a very poor job of it." The voice was musical and familiar. "Trespass on royal ground is punishable by public beating and theft by death." Cerberus felt a cold chill come over him, freezing his muscles in place. "That either makes you incredibly brave or extremely stupid and I'm intrigued to see which you think you are."

Cerberus suppressed a smile sensing the light pat of bare feet behind him. "I think you'll find me a little of both."

Chapter 5:
Trespasser

"Cerberus." The voice was laced with disapproval. "This will be the second time today that you have tried to accost me. A third would be ill-advised."

Cerberus craned his head around. Lida stood still dripping slightly in little more than night-wear and armed with a small dagger. Her eyes glittered in the low light, her other arm slightly outstretched. "You appear to have caught me red handed my Lady." His mouth twitched into a slight smile.

"Don't try the charm with me. It wont work." She stepped around him maintaining a good few feet space.

"And why not?" Cerberus grinned again. He watched her intently as she lowered her hand and placed the dagger on a small table. "Now should I be insulted or not?" He stretched as the numbness of his body receded. "You either think I'm little threat, or..." He eyed the dagger on the table. Rough, utilitarian.

Lida rolled her eyes. "Ugh, get over yourself Cerberus." Her eyes narrowed, cold, hard, analytical. She drew herself up straight. "You're here in an official capacity this time I see."

"What gave it away." Cerberus took a step closer and watched her instinctually take a step back. "I'm not here to harm you."

"And yet here you are in the midst of my personal chambers after dark." Lida cut him off. "Give me a reason why I should not call the guards."

Cerberus glanced around the room briefly checking each door. "Because if you had wanted to you would have done so by now." He took at the bath, towels, and dagger again. "You're alone?"

"Evidently; and that is not an answer." Lida replied.

"Why are you all alone? Where are your ladies?" He walked slowly to the dagger and examined it. "This is shoddy human work." Still holding the dagger he returned to the bath. "And this is a lot of towels." He turned to look at her. "Tell me you were not about to do something incredibly stupid."

"You'd do well to remember you place Cerberus," she replied dangerously inching towards a bell pull a few feet from a small desk.

Cerberus reached behind him resting his hand on a small throwing knife. "I wouldn't recommend it." For a moment their eyes held each others gaze.

"You would dare threaten me." Unblinking her hand closed about the cord.

Cerberus shifted the throwing knife to between his fingers. "I am not here to hurt you," he repeated. "My contract states only to assure you're safety."

Lida's scowl lifted into an ice cold smile. "Contract? I am a contract?"

"If you had heard the things I have tonight, you would consider the concern justified." Cerberus secreted the small knife in his sleeve.

"Concern? Does your concern mean anything Cerberus?" Lida's hands flexed. A dozen tiny sparks jolted from them as she let go and took a step towards him.

Cerberus held his ground. "This isn't a personal contract Lida. I came on behalf of another." He watched as her hands began to shake and shifted his weight. "Yes I have heard enough to trouble me but..."

"Get out." The words were barely above a whisper.

"Lida, at least let me warn you about what I have heard."

"Get out!" The words were now a scream.

Cerberus felt his patience thin. "Fine. Fine. I'll leave. After all, you always were content to let others suffer for you." He backed towards the windows. "I'll inform my client you refused my help."

"Your help?" She followed him step by step. "I waited for you to come when they handed me the circlet. I waited years but you never did. Where was Dhal-Marrah when my enemies closed in about me? Where was Dhal-Marrah when my hands were forced into servitude?"

Cerberus stopped. "Being picked off by your lout of a husband and his kin," he growled. "My family bled in silence to maintain your precious peace. My father died to protect yours. Our lands, Dhal-Marrah lands have been cut off piece by piece. My name lies in the mud to hold yours high and you talk to me of servitude."

The air around Lida crackled. "I had no choice. The houses were baying for blood - you gave me no choice but to ally myself to the only ones who could cow the growing mob. When the going got tough, when I needed you the most, you left; and not content with leaving me for the wolves, you took everything with. You - left - me, with no allies, no friends, and no family. I have every possible reason to hate you and see you suffer."

Her final step brought her toe to toe with Cerberus and he could feel the power radiating from her. "So this is how you see us? You're saying we have earned this?" He shook his head, gritting his teeth. "You're right there is no common ground between us. You are more like the Gal-Serreks than I credited you for. What a shame they clearly don't see it the same way." He stepped backwards onto the window ledge. "The Gal-Serreks hate us for doing them the kindness of bringing their fallen home. Their hate I can understand, but you? You I did nothing but ensure your safety. You abandoned us, not the reverse." Cerberus felt the sting of the slap across his face. He was half surprised that it hadn't been a bolt or blast to send him through the window.

Tentatively, he let go of a long breath and slowly turned his head back. The second hit knocked his hood back and let his white hair loose. His teeth ground together until a moment later he caught the third mid-air with one hand.

"I hate you." She hissed, writhing in his vice-like grip.

Cerberus turned his head back and stared straight at her. The anger in them almost forced him back. Her eyes shimmered.

"I hate you." She repeated pulling her head forward.

Cerberus tore his eyes away and loosened his grip, allowing her to yank her fist free. "A lot of people say that." He paused. "I'm not your enemy Lida but there are those within these walls who will harm you and while you may not like it, I can not willingly let that happen." He stepped out of the open window and onto the roof. "A contract is a contract. I will be discreet." Cerberus walked steadily to the roof edge. He could feel Lida's eyes boring into his back as he affixed a fresh grapple bolt to the miniature crossbow.

Cerberex could feel her leg going numb. She'd lost count of how long she'd lain still as death amongst the bushes and cultivated flowers. The only feeling was a dull throb from the poor landing she'd made. Three times the same guard patrol had brushed past her hiding place, oblivious to her but she was fast approaching the point when she would need to make the decision to leave or pursue Cerberus further into the grounds and solid stone walls and paving did not make for bountiful tracks.

Quietly she shifted her position, stifling a gasp as stabbing pain shot through her knee. Peering through the leaves, she could see a lantern heading towards her along the path and she pressed herself flat to the ground. The footfalls were softer, the sweep of cloth, accompanied by low voices. Two then judging by the difference in pitch, lightly armoured given the weight of their step. She held her breath as they came close.

"My cousin is taking too long." The first voice was stern but soft. "And his excesses increase daily. If he cannot bring the Lotheri Queen into line then it is time we took matters into our own hands."

"The king deals with challenges in his own unique way but say the word and I will make the final push." The second was ingratiatingly sweet.

"Don't be a fool Malinar. This is a matter of delicacy. My cousin may be a idiot at the best of times but he is right about one thing. The Queen must lay her own head on the chopping block." The pair paused mere feet from her hiding place. "Oh don't give me that look. We may not need to wait long. My spies in the palace tell me that the Queen has no love for the King. She seeks to be rid of him as much as he of her and I have actively encouraged her animosity, well, from behind the scenes naturally."

"You would have the King murdered then?"

"Of course not. We still need him and the other houses might become suspicious if both of them were to suddenly befall terrible accidents. No, killing my overbearing cousin will never do." A hand reached down just above Cerberex's face and plucked a small white flower, holding it up for a moment before plucking the petals one by one. "It seems the Queen has taken an interest in chemistry of late. Now I for one can fully endorse any activity that expands the mind. Such studies should be encouraged don't you think Malinar?" Cerberex felt the petals drift slowly onto her face.

"Of course - very healthy."

"Quite. In fact I've rather taken her new hobby heart. You see she has made contact with a rather unique benefactor. One with a sympathetic ear and access to some highly controlled substances. They have been engaging with each other by note now for roughly a month. I think it only a matter of time before she will make an attempt on the King's life with her latest concoction. It would be a shame if she were to be unsuccessful and these notes to cross into the wrong hands."

"Such a disgusting act of betrayal would grant his majesty every right to seek retribution." Malinar replied ingratiatingly.

Cerberex felt her temper rise as the two individuals quietly laughed.

"This is the latest note. It wishes her luck in her endeavour and advises her that there is a small party to celebrate the visit of the King's family."

"I was not aware there was such an event."

"That is because you will organise it Malinar. You will make arrangements for a small soiree and invite prominent members of House Gal Serrek to attend. There will be drink and plenty of it, ample opportunity for the Queen to try her luck."

"And what if she doesn't take the bait."

"I'm confident she will, especially if my cousin is serious about pestering her ladies. She is too soft to see anyone suffer in her stead for too long but let me worry about that. You need only prepare the circumstance. Does the King still wear that amulet I gave you the last time we met?"

"Indeed he does."

"Good, its enchantment will improve his ability to brush off the effects of any poison she might try. The attempt needs to be soon. We are on a tight schedule."

Cerberex waited as their conversation came to a close. Moments passed in silence. Had they moved on? She couldn't hear the rustle of fabric or soft tread. Her knee still burned with pain. She reached down into a pouch at her waist and plucked a small capsule from within. Black Poppy was an addictive but had the unique ability to subdue pain and boost the senses for a short while. She placed the capsule between her teeth and bit down, feeling the liquid within slip down her throat. It had a harsh aniseed-like tang to it. She turned her head spitting the empty capsule onto the ground. A moment later and her vision suddenly swam before returning with crystal clarity. The pain in her leg dulled to an almost imperceivable throb as she rolled out of the flower bed.

"Good evening my dear." Cerberex froze where she stood. The voice was immediately behind her.

"Admiring the palace gardens are we. They are truly magnificent aren't they?" Cerberex turned slowly around. The speaker was tall and thin to the point of frailty. His head was entirely shaved, revealing the number of glittering gems that studded his elongated ears. His hands rested inside the belled sleeves of a blood red and old gold robe of heavy velvet and his eyes held her like a cat sizing up a mouse. "Alas," he continued. "The garden's are off limits to all but the most intimate of visitors." Cerberex glanced behind her and took in the distance between herself and the wall. She looked back and saw his amber eyes narrow as if daring her to take the chance. It took less than a second for her to make up her mind. A moment later she spun and ran for the wall.

"INTRUDER!" The shout came loud and clear. "Secure the royal family and arrest the trespasser." Heavy footfalls echoed from around the grounds as guards thundered from their posts, rallying to the call. Cerberex felt the hiss of a heavy crossbow bolt's fletch brush past her ear and she careened around an intervening tree. The second bolt lodged itself in her shoulder causing her to stumble as her studded leather armour took the brunt of the impact. She reached back and tore it free before leaping up the wall ahead using a small statue as a boost. The smell of ozone, the crack of stone, and a flash of pale green light later, and the statue crumbled beneath her foot.

Cerberex hung by the arms as her feet scrabbled against the smooth surface of the stonework. She gasped in surprise as a firm hand gripped her foot.

"Why are you leaving so soon? The party is just getting started." Glancing down she caught sight of a gloved hand and deep green cuff. Urgently she kicked feeling her foot connect with what was probably a nose judging from the yell that followed shortly after. With every ounce of strength she pulled herself up and over the wall and sliding down the ten foot drop the other side. Though she felt no pain, there was a disturbing crack as her leg met the pavement below. Footsteps hurried towards her from the palace grounds she flattened herself against the stone and hoped that the feat of jumping the wall was more effort than her pursuers were willing to put in.

"Where is she?" Cerberex instantly recognised the voice of the bald lord in red.

"The bitch kicked me in the face." The voice of his friend was muffled.

"You fool! You let her escape. She may have heard every word."

"And what if she did? No one's going to believe the word of one street rat."

Cerberex shifted as she felt a thud vibrate through the wall behind her.

"Idiot! You think a self-serving street rat would waste their pitiful excuse of a life just to hide out in the palace grounds? Use your common sense little that you possess! That was a spy. Someone is on to us."

"I will send my own men to track them down. They wont see another morning." The second voice came in hurried gasps.

"See that they don't Malinar or your head will be the first to roll."

Cerberex breathed a sigh of relief as she heard footsteps recede back towards the palace proper. Sinking down to the floor she gently unlaced her boot and looked down at her leg. Even through the leather and padding she could see the knee was offset, possibly dislocated. Slowly she re-laced her boot and began to make her way back hoping against hope that the Black Poppy didn't wear off before she reached the house.

Cerberus heard the yell as he was carefully abseiled down the outer wall using the regular pattern of gargoyles as stopping points. "Meera." He hissed halting his descent and looking down as lanterns and torches darted from their once stationary posts. "You and I really are going to have a conversation one of these days." From this vantage he had a better view of the layout of the palace, the distance and depth of the walls, and the pattern of the guards. Most of the lights were now in the process of converging towards the outer wall on the eastern side. A brief assessment was all he needed to note the guard post on the southern wall was now devoid of lights. As he adjusted his descent part of him hoped that Meera would be cornered in a strange sense of ironic justice. The sensible part of his brain preyed she didn't or he'd be mounting a rescue come morning.

The second his feet touched the bottom, Cerberus was a blur of sudden motion, effortlessly scaling the guard house and leaping from the adjoining wall the other side. He landed softly upon the canopy of a store front and to the paving below. He had to concede the distraction had made his escape child's play as he quietly filtered into the night life of the market districts. The small stalls were all unanimously vacant at this time, yet it was still the busiest route in the city and Cerberus welcomed the anonymity. A loud grinding sound echoed through the streets behind him and the clatter of metal on stone made all in the vicinity look back. Heavily armed soldiers jogged down the market. Small groups dispersing in different directions in a bid to cover the districts closest to the walls. Cerberus looked around for a place to hide or at least to appear inconspicuous before he felt a hand on his back and was roughly pulled backwards into a small niche between two buildings. Cerberus waited as the rush of citizens and house guards subsided. He had not caught their colours but given that they came from the palace it was most likely red. He reached back and grabbed the wrist of the hand still holding his collar and spun around pressing its owner to the back of the wall, one hand around their throat. "Count yourself lucky that I'm the listening type. What ever your excuse, talk fast."

Meera leaned as much as she could towards him. "My, my, now doesn't this bring back memories." Cerberus scowled and squeezed till she coughed. "All right! My goodness, we are in a foul mood aren't we? Wouldn't have anything to do with that one, no two beautiful bruises coming up on that handsome face of yours would it?"

Cerberus let go and Meera bent over gasping for air. "You had your orders. You were given your task. Yet you dare to put a contract at risk for your own petty self gain?" Meera looked up at him in surprise. "I have tolerated your insubordination, I've even turned a blind eye to your utter lack of respect, but this, this is nothing short of a challenge."

Meera sneered. "Get off your pedestal Cerberus and tell me plainly. What exactly are you accusing me of."

"It is 'Master' Meera, 'Master'." Cerberus took a step forward watching Meera press herself against the wall with satisfaction. "You followed me. You thought yourself my equal to the task and now the whole kennel is awake and on the scent."

A look of surprise flickered across Meera's face. "I what? Cer... Master, I did exactly as instructed. I have checked in to no less than three bars and taverns since we parted ways."

"You're a poor liar Meera." Cerberus growled grabbing her by the scruff of her coat.

"If you don't believe me then check my purse. Drunk men make poor losers but losers nonetheless." She gasped putting a hand to a small pouch of coin at her waist that seemed to be stretched to capacity. Cerberus looked down at it and released her, shoving her roughly. "I assumed something had gone poorly and returned to the market districts in case you called for aid."

Cerberus could barely stifle the laugh. "You came to rescue me?"

Meera shrugged. "Of course, not that you would need it Master. Perhaps it was the shadow that's been tagging us since we got into town." Her eyes glittered with joy as Cerberus stood stone still. "Oh, you didn't notice?"

"Meera, don't toy with me. What shadow?" His voice was low and laced with threat.

Meera grinned. "Male or female I'm not sure, but they've followed us rooftop to rooftop since we left house Dhal-Marrah."

"You're telling me we have been tracked since we got here?" Cerberus whispered through gritted teeth, clenching his hands into fists.

"Oh they weren't as fast as us. Their tracking skills however, are superb." Meera smirked folding her arms. The punch arced lightening fast giving Meera less than a second to dodge out of the way. She ducked as the fist collided with the wall behind her dislodging the crumbling plaster.

Cerberus retracted his hand massaging the split knuckles. "We will return to the house and as you seem to see this as a game Meera, you will report to the bunk room when we get back and prepare yourself for patrol." Meera's eyes narrowed and her mouth opened to protest. Cerberus held up a finger. "You think your role as Chosen and First prohibits me from bouncing you down to guard duty?"

"I would not dream of suggesting such a thing." Meera clenched her jaw and felt her hand close around her dagger. Cerberus watched, daring her to try. Finally, she relaxed her hands. "I will of course do as the Master requests though I may think that he seeks to push his own failings on another."

Cerberus opened his mouth to respond but Meera had already scaled the back wall of the building like a cat and was even now shadow walking back to the Dhal-Marrah estate.

Chapter 6:
Post

Cerberex awoke to the smell of dragon flower and a gentle breeze. Opening one eye she looked around. It was her room. She closed her eye again for a second and recounted the events of the previous night. She clearly recalled following her brother across the city, the jump for the wall, the palace grounds, but she had no recollection of how she had arrived here. She opened her eyes and sat up. Her armour had been removed and now hung on the door of a wardrobe, she had been cleaned and dressed in a thin nightgown, and her leg lay bound in white binds not unlike the thin ones she wore perpetually on her wrists. Blinking, she noticed the small oil burner on the bedside table responsible for the strongly medicinal scent.

"It would appear that your quarry last night was a little beyond your skills." Cerberex turned her head to see her mother sat in the plush armchair beside her desk. "But then your brother is not exactly the average." Cerberex watched her stand and seem to glide towards her before sitting on the bed. "Now normally its your brother I'm called to attend at some ungodly of the night so I'm intrigued to know what your excuse is?" A slight smile played at her lips and Cerberex felt the colour rise slightly in her cheeks. "No? Well I'm sure it will come back to you." Again her mother smiled knowingly and patted her leg gently. Cerberex winced in anticipation of the pain but none came.

"Does Cerberus..." She began gingerly pulling away the bandages.

"Know? I don't think so. He'd be far more upset than he was." She replied checking the level of the oil in the burner.

Cerberex studied her knee. The swelling was going down but aside from that it was as if she'd never had a fall. "Your abilities never cease to amaze me mother."

"Careful Cerberex, flattery wont get you everywhere." She stood and headed for the door. "It's late you should get up and eat something, before you uncle finishes what's left of breakfast without you." The door closed with a gentle click.

Cerberex stood from the bed. Her leg felt numb as she awkwardly wobbled to a dresser, pulling out a casual dress of midnight blue. By time she'd changed and pulled a hairbrush through her thick hair the feeling had returned enough for her gait to at least appear normal. Checking herself in the full length mirror before she left, she made some minor adjustments to the neckline before she left in search of breakfast.

The dining hall smelt strongly of cooked meat and toast as she entered. Several plates littered the table to the far end nearest the window. Cerberex had a fleetingly vague memory of a time when the table would have been filled from one end to the other, but a hundred years later and she could not recall their faces. Uncle Selwyn was affording himself a second portion of bread and some yellow viscous liquid imported from some exotic location. He smiled as she approached and sat opposite, helping herself to the last of the eggs.

"You're looking a little paler than usual niece." Selwyn announced between mouthfuls.

"I didn't sleep well." She countered focusing on adding a slice of cured boar to her plate.

"Well I imagine that is rather hard to do when you're playing keep up with Cerberus and his friends."

The silver fork clattered loudly on the dish as Cerberex looked up. "Eroth save me! Who does not know where I went last night?" She looked up at him placing her fists on the table. Selwyn gave her a knowing smile and she sighed. "Ah, so you have been talking to mother." She picked up the fork and a small knife and began to nibble at the boar.

"What can I say Cerberex? I like to keep an eye on you all." Selwyn replied as a red haired human woman entered with a steaming jug of slightly thick brown liquid and heavy clay mugs. He waited for her to place them before helping himself.

"Actually Uncle I think you and I need to have a chat about my baby brother." She looked up and watched him spoon more of the clear yellow paste onto his bread, mesmerized by its glutinous quality. "I'm..." She began. "Uncle what in Eroth's name is that stuff you are putting on your toast?"

Selwyn's brow furrowed as he looked down caught off guard by the sudden change in conversation. "What? Oh this? Honey my dear. The queen is rather fond of it and I've developed a bit of a passion for it myself. Would you care to try?"

Cerberex tipped her head to one side and studied the movement of it within the fluted glass container. "How is it made?"

"Well obviously its imported but as I understand it the plains dwellers in the North cultivate these tiny insects..."

"It's liquidated insect?" Cerberex felt herself push back fractionally with disgust.

Selwyn paused for a moment before turning and studying the contents for himself. "Do you know I don't know?" His face split into a boyish grin at the look of repulsion on Cerberex's face. "It's quite sweet. Your cousin's enjoy it tremendously."

"I think that says more about my cousins than the condiment." Cerberex replied turning back to her plate.

Selwyn continued to grin and put the container down before pouring himself a mug from the still steaming jug on the table. A creak of a door making him look up. "Good day to you too nephew."

Cerberex looked up suddenly at the announcement of her brother and watched Cerberus make his way towards them taking the seat beside her. "What?" he asked catching her stare. Cerberex shook her head briefly and returned to her plate once again as the door at the far end opened for a second time and a young male servant approached Selwyn with several pieces of folded parchment on a small tray. Selwyn's face dropped. "Ugh, the life of a politician." He ushered the boy to get a move on and took the tray placing it to one side with a sigh and counting the number of pieces. "Eroth's teeth! Does it end?" He muttered to himself. "Oh very well, let's see what we have that's so god damned important." He picked up the top one skimming its contents for the salient points. "Seems there was a break in at the palace last night. Looks like general inter-house intolerances again. No surprises there. Oh but they did catch the individual, well that's unsurprising - she's been caught, judged, and oh dear, executed? Well that seems a little extreme. I suppose trespass is trespass."

Cerberex coughed in surprise and disgust as the word 'executed' lingered on the table making Selwyn and Cerberus both look at her.

"Are you all right?" Cerberus gave her a strange look and gently patted her on the back.

Cerberex nodded still choking. "I'm fine. Swallowed something the wrong way." She managed between coughs.

"Oh my dear, please help yourself to some of this." Selwyn pushed forward the jug to her before standing and peering inside it. "I'm fairly convinced that insects were not involved in its manufacture." He sat down again as she waved him away and picked up the next two pieces of parchment. "Boring, boring, boring, one day they are going to realise that I have absolutely no interest in shipping and stop pestering me with these pointless requests." He picked up the final piece and glanced at the seal. "Palace seal is it?" He placed the parchment on the table sliding the a knife beneath the wax to unfurl it. "What do we have here then? A party? How nice. Well lets see the guest list." He flipped the parchment over. "Ah, I see, so mainly house Gal-Serrek will be in attendance. Well that settles that then." Selwyn leaned back. "Boy!"

The young servant had just reached the dining hall door and immediately hurried back to his side. "Send a messenger to the palace with the word that unfortunately Lord Charnite will be unable to attend due to hmm let's see, family obligations." He smiled and patted the boy on the shoulder sending the servant off at a brisk walk.

Cerberex carefully chewed her mouthful and placed her fork down quietly before moving her chair. "Excuse me."

Selwyn sipped at his mug and looked up in surprise. "Didn't you want to talk to me about something Cerberex?"

Cerberex waved a hand nonchalantly. "It can wait." She pushed the chair back towards the table and headed for the door at the end of the hall with all the speed she could muster without looking too hurried.

Selwyn watched her leave and the door close behind her. "She's behaving rather odd today don't you think?"

Cerberus poured himself a mug and sipped at it pulling a face at the bitter liquid. "It's Cerberex when is she not? How do you drink this stuff it's terrible!"

Selwyn looked at the door thoughtfully. "Hmm? Yes she does seem to take after your mother," he replied ignoring Cerberus's outburst. "It does mean however, that you and I can have a comfortable conversation." He turned to him sitting back in his chair. "So tell me what happened? Because that first missive suggests there was an issue and the bruises on your face suggest that something didn't go to plan." He steepled his fingers in front of himself in anticipation.

"It wasn't us." Cerberus murmured pushing the mug away and reaching for a carafe of watered wine. "Meera and I were being trailed since we left the house but didn't see where they went."

"Meera? I'd have thought Kane was the better choice of partner for this." Selwyn's face remained emotionless.

Cerberus took a swig from his glass. "If he'd come I'd have been happy for him to, but I wont make him return back there if he doesn't want to." Their eyes looked up and met across the table.

"And the contract then? If this trespass was not you, that means there are other interested parties." Selwyn leaned forward slightly. "What did you learn of my concerns?"

"Justified Uncle." Cerberus took another swig. "The King has indeed lost patience. From what I heard, he plans to be rid of her though it seems he is less clear on the details of exactly how. His current plan seems to be to bed each of her ladies in a bid to force the issue."

Selwyn's face wrinkled in disgust. "Barbarian! What else?"

"Not much." Cerberus met his gaze.

"And this?" Selwyn gestured on his own face where Cerberus had two small fresh bruises. "Forgive me nephew but that doesn't look like not much."

Cerberus stroked his face feeling it to be still a little tender. "My visit was not welcomed."

"You were seen?"

Cerberus shook his head. "Only by Lida."

Selwyn relaxed back in his chair. "I see. How did that go?"

Cerberus laughed and poured a second glass. "As poorly as you might expect. She's still furious that we did so little to help her when she needed it."

Selwyn looked down at his mug. "How little the lady knows. Of course you realise that Kane could offset all of this by just visiting once in a while. If you can scale those walls, I feel fairly confident he can."

"Of course he could but I wont make him uncle." Cerberus's eyes narrowed as he stared Selwyn down.

Selwyn looked away and sighed drumming his fingers on the table as his brain got to work. "Cerberus given how you were received last night I feel a little reluctant to ask this." He paused and picked back up the parchment with the palace seal. "This party they are holding. It is to officially welcome the King's cousin back to court. The guest list is almost unanimously Gal-Serrek with a handful of other house dignitaries thrown in for good measure..."

"Yes." Cerberus caught himself by surprise by the speed of his reply.

Selwyn looked up. "You don't know what I'm about to ask."

"I do. You want me to sneak in a check that this isn't a poorly disguised attempt on the Queen's life and the answer is yes I will." Cerberus downed the dregs of his glass and set it on the table.

"Well that was easier than I thought it would be." Selwyn looked at Cerberus with a mixture of surprise and suspicion. "Of course, I will pay whatever the bill is. Can't have your First thinking you've become a charity."

Cerberus waved his hand. "Your family. There is no fee."

Selwyn's suspicion grew. "Cerberus, there isn't something you aren't telling me here is there?"

Cerberus stood from the table and leaned over wresting on his knuckles with a wince. "She called me a thief Uncle. That the my word meant nothing. That we have earned everything that has been thrown at us. If gatecrashing this party proves in anyway that any of those statements are untrue, it will be worth every penny."

"This is not a gatecrash Cerberus. The place will be crawling with the King's closest family. You must not be seen - even by her." Selwyn's face was deadly serious.

Cerberus grinned slightly. "Oh don't you worry uncle, I think you'll find I can be very discreet when I want to be." His eyes moved from left to right as he watched a familiar shape move across the rear of the estate through the garden door windows. "Excuse me uncle, I have a wayward individual who is trying their hardest this morning to avoid me."

"Nephew?" Cerberus looked back. "This thing between you and Lida."

"Ancient history Uncle." Cerberus cut him off before heading through the garden door.

Selwyn nodded and returned to re-reading the parchment.

Cerberus skirted the gardens heading to the wooded edge of the estate, taking a protracted route that brought him right into the path of his quarry. Kane stopped with a start as Cerberus emerged a few feet in front of him.

"Patrolling again Kane?" Cerberus watched as Kane's eyes flitted back to the house and then back to him. "So which of us are you avoiding? Meera or me?"

Kane smiled. "Or a little of both." Quizzically he glanced at Cerberus's face. "Not quite as planned then I take it."

Cerberus rubbed his jaw. "You're sister's work."

"I gathered. You're getting sloppy." Kane's grin spread. "I take it she didn't take too kindly to a home visit?"

Cerberus leant against the base of a tree. "You could say that. Actually she was very... honest about her feelings, something I'd like to bring up with you. In fact all things considered, I was surprised you didn't find me and ask how she was."

Kane's face darkened. "You and I agreed that neither of us would dig this back up." He folded his arms. "I left that place a long time ago and now we are here."

"So it's me you're avoiding." Cerberus smiled and kicked the dirt. "See you and I both know its not that simple. You maybe under the sanctuary of house Dhal-Marrah but she is still blood. So ask me Kane." Kane stared at him and Cerberus sighed. "No? Very well. You're sister is beyond any doubt courting a tragic accident. If not in the immediate future, then very soon."

"Has she asked for aid?" Kane murmured.

"No, but she'll get it regardless. Which brings me to my actual point. Once she is secure you really should visit her." Kane took a step back and Cerberus followed. "No ifs, buts, or maybes Kane. You will stop running away from this. I allowed it before but if it brings what little respect the name of

Dhal-Marrah has into disrepute, I cannot let it continue. You have access to the palace and they cannot turn you away even if they wanted to. You need only see her once and then you can return or stay as you wish, but your sister should at least know you are alive."

Kane scowled. "If I go back there I will not be coming back out again."

"Kane, you are a trained assassin. Possibly one of my finest. I'm sure you would find a way." Cerberus replied. Kane looked back towards the house again. "By the way you can stop running patrol. Meera has volunteered." He was cut off as Kane grabbed his arm and pulled him behind a tree out of sight. Looking back he now noticed the lithe dark figure running towards the woodland's edge. Kane was watching it with his eyes as it came closer, pressing against the tree as it passed the open space they had been standing in previously, but not loosing sight of it.

Cerberex had changed into what Cerberus had always considered to be her favoured attire, a set of studded leather armour. She came to a stop a dozen feet away and checked her surroundings quickly before darting over a tree trunk and into the wilderness beyond. Kane let go of Cerberus's arm still watching her through the trees as he leaned in. "We will talk about this another time." He whispered before stealthily moving away along the woodland's edge in the direction of the house as she moved out of sight.

Cerberus watched him go before curiously turning and looking back in the direction Cerberex had just run. "How interesting." He murmured to himself pressing a finger to his lips. Cerberex was not normally secretive about her movements. That she preferred the wilds, had been trained by the Watchers the highest council of rangers, was almost public knowledge, yet she had clearly not been surprised by the notice of a palace intrusion. The night time stalker had to have been of superlative skill to chase not only his best assassin, but also himself across the city and all the while making as much noise as a leaf on the wind. He raised an eyebrow. "What secrets are you keeping sister?" He asked the silence.

Cerberex sat at the edge of the drop, her legs drawn up to her chin. Below her in the bowl of the earth, the standing stone sang to her. It's black surface seemed to flicker and move like molten glass. There was no shame in her feelings of cowardice it told her - all mortals fear. She clenched her fists as thoughts of the bald male and his accomplice entered her mind. What they planned was in defiance of sacred law, death of a god's chosen representative it reminded her. She rolled her shoulders as if trying to scratch an itch she knew was only in her head. The song continued, shifting key. Rainbow hues glittered along the stone's surface. She longed to touch it and feel the glossy smoothness of its surface. Instead she unconsciously chewed her finger nail. Fear. Fear was natural it told her. Fear kept the prey alive. Fear did not rule the hunter. The hunter was fear itself. Fear was a weapon used on the weak and she was weak. Cerberex shook her head. She was not weak. She was the untamed hunter - a child of the wilds. She looked down at her hand now holding the silvered hunting knife. In her mind she fancied she could hear the stone laughing.

Chapter 7:
A Nest of Vipers

Whenever and wherever the rich and powerful descended in numbers the dregs of society naturally followed in their wake, eager to snap up the scraps. Ever had it been and Cerberus was well aware of it.

Dusk had fallen and Cerberus had spent the better half of the day either sleeping or examining the precious few schematic sketches the house library had in its possession. Now the streets around the palace gate were thick with traffic and bathed in a deep magenta half-light. Cerberus fluttered from one group of people to the next like a ghost, analysing the Great Gate from all angles. Carriages bearing the colours of houses Trileris, Estealia, and of course Gal-Serrek rumbled passed ignoring the mob and rabble. Cerberus watched each pause at the gate offering a parchment to a plate armoured captain before the heavy guard presence before the gate itself moved aside allowing the carriage access. He pulled his hood further over his face as he inched closer.

As the final carriage entered the gates the crowds surged forwards. For the most part the guards simply pushed them back, some more forcefully than others; but there were those who filtered through. Among the rabble Cerberus could make out artists, performers, escorts and more. Peering over the shoulder of a rotund sell-sword wearing no particular colour marking his loyalties, he watched a female Drau in sumptuous purple silks approach with an entourage of four or five ladies all elven from the Northern plains past The Range Quadrata. Cerberus was familiar with her if only briefly. Her name if he recalled correctly, was Belladonna. A half-breed of great repute in the city's night life. Her establishment the Black Orchid, was a hot spot for young lordlings with coin to burn and a taste for the exotic. He noticed that two of the ladies in her group were moon-elves. Their tall frame, pearl white almost translucent skin, and elongated fingers made them impossible to miss. So, someone was paying handsomely for the best entertainment in the city - whoever this cousin of the King's was he had to be a Drau in great favour. Belladonna smiled at the captain while her ladies chatted and laughed coquettishly with the other guards. Cerberus watched a purse exchange between them and smiled.

Suddenly Cerberus's view was blocked. He craned his neck as he felt the heavy tremor of the gate open slightly. Bright streamers, and a cacophony of different musics assaulted his eyes and ears. The procession of ten or so strong, wound its way toward the gates. Each was masked and lead by a male

Drau of aged years in a long coat of cerulean blue and gold that looked too elaborate for even a royal soiree. Cerberus mingled into the middle of the group as they passed, pulling his cloak about him in hope that their showing off might avert the guards eyes as he moved with them. They at least wouldn't notice his presence given the heavy stench of Amber-leaf exuding from them.

Their leader spread his arms wide as if to embrace the captain as he approached. Each finger ringed in gems most of which Cerberus noted were almost certainly fakes. "Good evening most excellent men of the guard." His voice was drawling and ever so slightly slurred.

"If you have no invite, you have no entry here. Move on." The Captain slowly moved his hand, making a point to rest it on the blade at his side.

"Behold the bounty of Khathar and join the revelry. " The leader continued, undaunted by the captain's intimated threat. Cerberus twitched slightly at the mention of Khathar. That at least explained the Amber-leaf. Most considered Khathar a false god, but his edicts of pleasure and celebration had been steadily gaining ground among the youth of the city much to the chagrin of the more orthodox Cult of Eroth. "Every joyous action, every intimate celebration is pleasing to the Master of Pleasures and where his worship is made the Children of Kathar may enter!"

Cerberus hunched as much as he could as the captain looked over the motley crew of performers. "So you are what? Actors and acrobats?"

The leader made an elaborate bow. "We are disciples of the Lord of Games, the Celebrant King, and the Happy Sage. We may dance, we may joke, but we follow the true path of pleasures."

Three other guards their faces covered by tall bridge nosed helms, had stepped forward to join the captain. "Actors then. So tell me fool, what role does that one play?" The captain's head nodded in Cerberus direction and he felt a sudden wave of panic wash over him.

The leader turned to look. A brief glimmer of surprise brushed his painted features before he turned back. "Why he plays the part of sorrow of course. For only with sorrow can we experience true joy." Cerberus did his best to stifle the laugh he felt deep in his gut. Fool he may be but this one had a silver tongue and a sharp mind.

For a long time the captain seemed to appraise the group before turning and motioning to the guards still at the gate. "The King is a great lover of the arts, let's see just how good you are."

The rumble of the gates vibrated through the stone slabs beneath his feet. Cerberus felt the press of the performers around him shift and moved with them. As they passed underneath, the leader hung back before stepping into stride with him and wrapping an arm around his shoulders. Cerberus instinctively dipped his head lower. "Welcome little brother. I must apologise that I did not see you before but fear not, those who wish to be born anew will never be turned away from Kathar's embrace." His arms were incredibly strong for his frame. He leant down and whispered into Cerberus's ear. "Oh I know you wished only to see how the great and powerful take their time, but even this small step to witness joy unbound is a step nonetheless." Cerberus wasn't sure if the old coot was still playing the part or if he actually believed his own act. Whichever it was he had little time to consider it before the group was ushered into the palace itself.

Cerberus was not new to the palace and while the others around him looked aghast at the sudden extravagance, Cerberus could vaguely remember a time when the house of Dhal-Marrah would attend the royal court and Drau courtiers would move from their path at the mere sight of them. In those days the ceilings and walkways were hung with the banners and colours of every house. Now the stairs, landings, and halls were draped in the bold red and black of house Gal-Serrek such that the royal house of Lotheri was but a side note. Dozens of servants in black washed around them. Each busy with the sudden surprise of so many guests. An ancient Drau his back hunched with age greeted the entertainers with a curt nod. Cerberus did not catch the words that were exchanged to those few selected for the evenings entertainment in the clamour of the main hall. After a moment or so the group was on the move again laughing and dancing with each other as they jostled forward. Cerberus was content to let them pass as they were lead through a number of small hallways designed to grant the numberless servants and cohorts of guard access through the palace without disturbing their superiors.Eventually, he found himself brought out to a walled garden of exotic blooming flowers that exuded a powerful bio-luminescence and marble pools of crystal water in which swam tiny jellyfish. Floating lanterns of coloured parchments levitated above, held from floating away entirely through some arcane means. The air was heavy with the scent of lavender and violet.

Cerberus hung back and merged into the sea of grey, browns, and blacks of a battalion of servants en route to see that the needs of guests were being met. He pressed himself against the outside wall of the palace as they dispersed and obscured himself behind a planter. Looking across at the guests, he was suddenly very aware how much his dark clothes would stand out against the silks and velvets of the lords and ladies in attendance. The flicker of a fan and the brush of skin brought him back to the here and now as he felt the presence of another at his side.

"It is quite the party is it not?" The female voice was accented and decadent. Cerberus nodded. "Though I feel it is in rather poor taste. I hear the King's cousin is a scholar of the arcane, so he is unlikely to appreciate the quality of the effort." Cerberus glanced to one side and noted the purple silk, the grey yet tinged with brown skin, the full lips painted a earthy red, and the thin scar that ran from the back of the ear all the way down and around her neck. He gave a slight smile. "Though there are some of us here that can appreciate it at least." She caught his eye. "Some I think, weren't even invited."

Cerberus sighed. "You are as astute as ever Madam."

"Ah and there I was thinking you were ignoring me... my Lord Dhal-Marrah." She whispered the last bit enticingly. "Though I must say I am surprised to see you join the party. Perhaps you have a thing for one of the ladies?"

Cerberus laughed quietly. "Alas, I am not here to cause mischief or mayhem."

Belladonna pouted. "And now I am sad. I rather enjoyed your mischief the last time we met." She flicked her fan, doing a poor job of hiding her grin.

Cerberus tilted his head. "You're all work I see."

"Well a lady must make ends meet." She sniffed. "Besides, I don't hear you complaining."

A blast of silver trumpets disrupted the casual atmosphere. "Their royal highnesses, King Aelnar Gal-Serrek and Queen Lida Lotheri." The guests turned and Cerberus pressed himself against the wall.

"Place you arm around my waist and no one will question you. They will think you simply my bodyguard." Belladonna seized his arm and wrapped it around her before forcing him into a bow as the King and Queen entered the garden followed by a heavily robed individual.

Immediately every individual fell to one knee. King Aelnar couldn't hide his smirk as he strode with every air of confidence, dressed in a deep crimson robe clearly meant for an individual a good deal smaller then he was. He strode ahead his arms outstretched. The Queen by comparison was modestly dressed in lavender. A floor length gown of lace and chiffon without adornment save the silver filigree circlet of office that accentuated her ears. Cerberus felt a stab at his ribs and a strong arm force him down further.

"Friends and honoured guests. Not since the day of my binding have I had occasion to throw such an extravagant soiree but today is one of great celebration. It gives me great joy to finally introduce my own cousin to our esteemed company. Too long has he served in the shadow. It is time that he was recognised."

As the King turned away Cerberus drew out of the bow and glanced at the newcomer.

"Vor'ran." The King clasped both hands heavily on the new individual's shoulders who winced but remained smiling. "I am pleased to finally bestow upon you the honour you have so long been denied. You have served as my loyal aide and friend for too long without recompense." Cerberus watched with narrowed eyes as the King withdrew a long golden chain upon which hung a medallion emblazoned with a large ruby and hung it about the Drau's neck. The King turned to the party. "Behold Vor'ran of House Gal-Serrek. Lord Adjutant of the King."

The Drau adjusted the medallion, pulling his hands out of the sleeves that had hidden them and setting back the hood that covered his face. His long coat was a vibrant arterial red. Arcane glyphs has been picked out in silver thread that seemed to sparkle in the light and all this trimmed in white wolf fur. His skin was a mid-grey neither dark nor light and his extra-ordinarily round head was completely shaved of hair. Cerberus didn't need any of this to know he had met him before. Though time had begun to show the signs of age with a slight wrinkle set perpetually above the eyes, running around to both elongated ears. Here stood the nightmare that had haunted his sleep for a hundred years, made flesh and blood and smiling amiably to any who looked at him. Here stood the bane of Dhal-Marrah. Their fall from grace made possibly only by the hands of this Drau and the blood that lay upon them. Dhal-Marren blood, his father's blood. Cerberus breathed heavily, his body seeming to switch from ice cold to burning hot. The transition made him want to throw back his hood and gasp for air, instead his hand held tight to a the rapier he had hidden beneath his cloak, his thumb stroking the engraved 'D' in the pommel. For a moment he was sure his fingers were glowing red, then his hands, then his eyes began to sting. When he looked up Vor'ran had mingled into the party and though it felt like seconds it seemed minutes had passed.

"Are you listening to me?" Belladonna's face creased with annoyance.

"I'm sorry Madam?" Cerberus blinked away the brightness blinding his eyes.

Belladonna glanced under his hood. "Eroth's teeth have you been touching the Amber-leaf?" She scolded and huffed. "Keep your hood up and your face down then I don't want you embarrassing me." Cerberus lowered his head and nodded.

"Madam 'Donna? I don't remember extending an invitation." A skinny individual in handsome emerald green and a coat with antique gold brocade, inclined his head. Cerberus knew this Drau also. Malinar was his name or more usually Lord Trileris.

Belladonna dipped in her skirts just enough to be deemed acceptable. "My Lord Trileris. I simply assumed that in the heat of all the planning, my invite had simply been forgotten." She gave him and evil smile. "Naturally, I couldn't let you simply be hung out to dry after all the work you'd done and a party isn't a party without some entertainment." She brought her head to his ear. "And I am something of collector of the most exquisite types of entertainment as you have seen for yourself once or twice."

Cerberus watched Malinar's face twitch into a smile. "How very thoughtful." He paused. "You seem to be without refreshment Madam. Let us see if we can't do something about that." He held his arm out to her giving Cerberus a curious look.

Belladonna accepted his arm, wrapping both her hands around the bicep. "Oh don't worry about my man here. Simply a precaution to ensure that my ladies and I came across town... unmolested."

"Indeed, perhaps he would like to remove his hood and cloak. It is a warm enough evening, surely." He inclined gently to peer beneath the hood.

Belladonna grasped his chin between and thumb and forefinger. "I would not recommend it my Lord. The beast was facially scarred by his previous owner and I insist he keeps himself covered for the sake of decency."

Malinar drew back. "Well, we wouldn't want that now." He smiled. All ease and friendliness. "I believe I offered you a drink? Come, let's see what the royal wine cellar has brought for us and you can talk to me about all the city's latest rumours. It's been a while since I could get out and about."

Belladonna smiled graciously. "It would be my honour."

The pair moved across the garden. Weaving between the guests, Cerberus followed them while maintaining what he hoped was a reasonable distance. His eyes twitched left and right for any sign of wolf fur trim or a flash of scarlet but he saw only Lords and Ladies familiar to court exchanging in polite, well groomed conversation. Out of the corner of his vision he caught sight of the King and Queen surrounded by a gaggle of over-absorbent lordlings and ladies out to gain favour and a better seat at court. The King seemed to be well into his cups already. As for the Queen, her face was one of deadpan acceptance. Cerberus gritted his teeth. What did she in him? His focus was so bent on the commotion the royal couple caused, he did not catch himself before walking directly into Malinar and spilling his goblet down the Lord's embroidered doublet.

"What in the..." Malinar looked at him angrily as Cerberus rebounded away. "Madam, if you bodyguard cannot behave properly then maybe you are not welcome at this gathering." He hissed, wiping at the deep red stain.

"A thousand apologies my Lord." Belladonna looked mortified before her face changed to one of anger. "You idiot! Be gone until I call for you."

Cerberus gave a deep bow, allowing his hood to slip lower over his face till he almost couldn't see, and then moved in a roundabout way to the table of refreshments being constantly attended to by a handful of human females. Surreptitiously he took a goblet and knocked back the contents before replacing it. It was an extremely fine vintage. I little earthy for his liking but he could appreciate it nonetheless and the brief hit of alcohol was a pleasant relief. His hand went back to his rapier. Where was Vor'ran? It was like the Drau has suddenly disappeared or had vacated the party in some way but the garden was an internal courtyard , walled on all sides by the palace itself and only a single entrance and exit. He moved quietly from group to group all the time keeping his wits about him.

A loud laugh from the growing circle of flatterers around the King and Queen made Cerberus look up.

"So that's when I told the her - lady all I need from you is a shot of Spider Bite and you on a table with your skirts above your head!" The King belched with laughter echoed a split second later by the rest of the gathering. He turned and pushed an empty goblet into the Queen's hands. "Fetch me another," he ordered before catching himself, "my dear." He turned away from her. "These excellent people seem to be enjoying my little stories immensely."

The Queen stared for a moment at the goblet in her hands. Cerberus edged to a closer group, remaining out of sight. "Tell him to get it himself." He urged her mentally, willing her to turn and throw it in the King's face. He watched as she sighed inwardly and made her way to the table before handing it to an awaiting servant. "How low have you fallen?" He muttered to himself in disgust even as he drew closer, masked by a group entranced by the dancing of a nearby moon elf.

"I see you pay continuous attention to the King's needs." Cerberus ducked as Vor'ran seemed to suddenly appear from out of nowhere. The queen simply looked at him, her face a mask of annoyance at the task she had been caught performing and irritation at the complete lack of formality Vor'ran afforded to her. "It's rare to see a Drau such as yourself, still able to perform such menial tasks without the need for others." He patted her arm. She stared at the irreverence of the gesture in fury. "I think it shows a level of modesty many of us could learn from."

"Cousin!" The shout came from the ever growing gaggle.

Vor'ran smiled and waved before turning back to the queen and handing her his own empty goblet. "Excuse me my Lady, it would appear I have been summoned."

Cerberus watched him meander his way towards the King, before returning his attention back to the Queen. Her head was bent over, hands placed squarely upon the table. Cerberus inched up a fraction, peering over the groups heads. She seemed to be ever so slightly shaking and judging by the look of concern on the servants faces, not for joy. Was she... weeping?

She brushed a hand over her face and took a couple of deep breaths bringing her bearing up straight and looking over the guests. Cerberus ducked. Turning back to the table she pulled forward two goblets downing the first and discarding it before pulling forward a third to replace it. Motioning she held up the empty goblet with a look of dis-taste, attracting the attention of the waiting servants. Cerberus didn't catch the conversation but watched as both humans nodded quickly and immediately left presumably for some beverage that more fitted the Queen's demands. As they left she reached down her slight cleavage and withdrew what initially Cerberus thought to be a sliver of glass. Shifting as close as he dared behind a pair lost in the moment with each other and smelling strongly of wine, he realised as she snapped the top away, it was a tiny vial of black liquid; barely enough to coat a knife edge. Deftly she tipped the contents into one of the goblets seizing it to her chest, looking up and breathing heavily.

Cerberus stared, temporarily forgetting about the immediate threat of Vor'ran and the guests almost all of which could recognise him with but a glance at his face. Surely she did not intend to... He didn't have time to finish the thought, she swilled the goblet, muttering a few words before it began to bubble. She seized the second goblet and with hands shaking began to walk stiffly back to the group where the King was being encouraged to sit to save himself from falling.

"You were an age." He slurred grumpily as she handed him the goblet.

"What can I say. One of the wines was gone. I needed another to be brought up." Lida replied demurely.

Cerberus slinked back to his previous spot behind the group not quite comprehending what he thought he was seeing. Did she intend to drug him? Poison him even? How long had she been doing this? His mind filled with a hundred questions but one screamed at him louder then all the rest - why? Why when she had so clearly lost the will to fight against him, when she had been so earnest in her agreement to his rule; why would she attempt to kill him and not just kill but murder in cold blood? The answer crawled out into his head. "Because she is not content to be used and abused by this creature." It whispered to him. "Because she is a Lotheri and a Queen." It called. "Because she has no love for him or his ilk." It shouted at him clear as day. A burst of sudden unexpected joy erupted in Cerberus's chest.

Lida proffered the goblet delicately between two fingers before it was snatched away.

"See that the imbeciles are dealt with for the waste." The King grunted before returning smiling to his captive audience. "Now where was I?"

Cerberus watched Lida stare at Aelnar's goblet. Her hands were visibly shaking at her sides. "Stay calm." He willed her. "Stop shaking." He was only five feet away now, leaning against a statue covered in creeping vines.

The moment stretched for what seemed like eternity. The goblet rose to the King's lips before he set it down again, engaged in his story. Lida's fingers were laced in front of her now. Tiny sparks flashed from them as her hands twitched in expectation.

"And that good folk, is what my cousin here has been doing. Ensuring that our lands stay safe and the imports keep coming." The King belched loudly as he came to the end of his story and reached back, grasping the goblet of wine as his listeners murmured their appreciation. He tipped his head back and drank deeply. Wine spilled from the corners of his mouth and onto his clothes before he set the empty goblet down, wiping his face with his sleeve.

"Well you're majesty puts far too much importance into what I have been achieving on your behalf." Vor'ran smiled and turned to the group. "But it was nothing. Plain's Dwellers are thick as mud. Their agreement of trade so long as we desist the raids on their provinces are all well and good, but for a race as short-lived by our standards, what exactly its worth is..." The King bent over and coughed. Vor'ran patted him gently on the back. "Yes, what exactly it's worth is when we can and always have simply taken what we need - that remains to be..." The King was now hacking and coughing alarmingly.

Vor'ran paused from his lecture. "Are you well your majesty?" His face wrinkled with concern.

"There you are." Belladonna's hand wrested on his shoulder. "Head back to the Orchid and acquire three more ladies..." She paused as the coughing became louder and concern began to filter from the group beyond.

"What is going on?" Malinar's voice spoke up behind him. Cerberus cursed quietly.

A dull thud and gasp of shock and fear whispered through the guests as black liquid began to ooze from the Kings mouth as he fell to the floor. Cerberus looked for the Queen and saw her a few feet away her mouth open in terror, unable to move or look away.

"Eroth! The King has been poisoned!" Vor'ran motioned to a number of others to help him roll the king over. "A dose of Moth-wing if I am not mistaken." He continued forcing the King's mouth open. "Extremely toxic. It must have been something he drank." Vor'ran made a show of looking over the King's symptoms, all the while the King continued to drown in black sludge.

"Should I call for the palace healers my lord?" A young lordling in a rust coloured jacket enquired eagerly.

"Absolutely not! Waiting for them to appear may well kill him." Vor'ran placed his hands one over the other on the King's chest and closed his eyes murmuring quietly to himself. Cerberus watched as the King's eye's rolled, his gaze switching to Lida whose head lay slightly cocked to one side in an appearance of slight confusion.

Vor'ran's forehead wrinkled in concentration as his muttering became more pronounced. It was not a language that Cerberus recognised and judging from Lida's looks, neither did she. The coughing subsided and silence consumed the garden.

"Is he...?" No one dared finish the lordling's question for him.

Cerberus's heart leaped in his chest. Again he glanced back to Lida whose hands were clutched to her mouth. "Yes," he thought. "She has done it." He knew how she felt. The first kill was always the worst strain on the conscience but now the bastard king was finally...

The King's eyes fluttered and he gasped fresh air into his lungs. Vor'ran stood up with a sigh of relief as those around him patted him on the back or knelt to help the King in hope of some small share of the glory.

"I.. what?" The King slurred as he sat.

"You appear to have been poisoned your majesty." Vor'ran held out the goblet. "If I might ask. Where did you acquire this goblet?"

The King stared at it for a minute in confusion. A second later he was standing. His face was contorted with rage as stood and grabbed the Queen by the throat. Several onlookers took a step back from the King's sudden burst of both speed and anger. "You hell-spawned hag! You would dare to try and poison me? Me, you're husband! Your King!" Lida scratched at the hand tightening around her throat. Sparks burst from her finger tips. "Oh no you don't. I'll not let you utter a single word or incantation simply to try again." He squeezed tighter. Lida's eye's bulged.

Cerberus moved deftly between the onlookers who stared at each other in shock. The rapier slid from it's scabbard with barely a hiss.

"How dare you. All these years you have been plotting and now it has come to it. How does it feel to know you have failed?" The King sneered.

"I... didn't...please..." Lida gasped the tinge of blue beginning to blossom on her lips. "It... It wasn't..."

"You're a poor liar." The King placed a second hand around her throat and froze as cold steel caressed the back of his neck and around to his jugular.

Chapter 8:
The Stroke of Midnight

Time stood still. Petals from the wall flowers fluttered in slowly. The look of shock and surprise writ large upon the faces of all those present. Cerberus's shock white hair moved gently as the hood fell back. When time came rushing back it was with the whisper of knives and blades leaving scabbards and hidden sheaths. "It seems you have a problem with your security detail my Lord." Cerberus did not smile. His eyes bore into the King's skull unblinking. In the back of his head the small voice of reason was screaming the word 'idiot' at him. "Don't take it personally."

King Aelnar turned slowly the blade never leaving his neck yet just light enough not to draw blood. Roughly he shoved the Queen away. She hit a chair and sank like a stone clutching her neck and gasping for air. "Dhal-Marrah." the King sneered, a dangerous smile spreading across his pudgy face.

Behind him Vor'ran subtly moved his hands and muttered. He managed a single syllable before a short dagger embedded itself a hair's breadth from his head into the wood of a small planted tree. A thin line of blood ran along the side of his face but he did not flinch. "Dhal-Marrah," he copied. "Always sticking their noses where they aren't wanted. I would have thought your family had learnt its lesson by now." He fell silent as the King raised his hand.

"There is no need for your tricks cousin. Lord Dhal-Marrah has just made a fatale error of judgement today." The King took a tentative step forward. "Not only does he trespass in my home, he threatens me, his King, in front of the entire front bench of the royal court." He glanced back to Lida. "As for you, you have broken the edict of Eroth, you are no longer bound by her protection and I may deal with you as I see fit."

"Then you would anger a god, it was not her that spiked your drink." Lida glanced up as the lie came unbidden to Cerberus's lips. The flicker of a question in her eyes.

Vor'ran tilted his head. "It was you?"

"He came with this half-breed." Malinar stepped forward clutching Belladonna with a dagger at her throat.

"As I have already stated my Lord, I believed he was my usual bodyguard." Belladonna stumbled in his grip before regaining her composure. "I had no idea that it was an imposter."

The King looked from Malinar to Belladonna to Vor'ran. The chiming of heavy armour on stone crashed into the garden. Loud protests echoed as guests were roughly shoved from the newcomers' path. Cerberus counted the steps.

Eight. Eight heavily armoured guard. He focused on the King. So long as his blade was at his throat they would not touch him. A moment later he felt them behind him and and the slight push of a halberd tip rest in the middle of his back. Quickly he began to analyse his choices.

The King's smile broadened. "For years I have sought to rid myself of your murderous family," he whispered under his breath. "Cousin." He called over his shoulder and Vor'ran looked up. "Be so kind as to confine the Queen." Vor'ran had barely time to move before Cerberus stepped forward and pressed the blade a fraction into the neck fat of the King's throat. A tremor of concern vibrated through the guests. The King's face seemed to split with joy. "So that is your target is it boy?" He glanced down at the Queen. "How typical. You Dhal-Marrah's always setting your sights on another's prize."

Cerberus gritted his teeth. "Don't push your luck."

"I think I already have. You're here for her not me." He pressed against the blade but Cerberus did not push. Behind the King the look of terror in Lida's eyes stung like snake-bite.

"Lords and Ladies. You are all witness to this attack. Cerberus of the house of Dhal-Marrah has on this eve, attempted the murder of your King. A traitorous act punishable in only one way." King Aelnar played his audience like a bard. Cerberus could hear awkward murmurs of assent. "Only by the quick thinking of Lord Vor'ran was your King saved from death." More calls of agreement followed. Cerberus watched as a heavily armoured guard - the King's personal protectors, roughly grab Lida's arm and pull her to her feet. The King lowered his voice, staring directly at Cerberus. "You have two choices. You can surrender here and now, or the next time you see her will be at the gallows by your side." His voice was low and filled with the thrill of excitement. Cerberus looked at Lida. Her face was unreadable, her head held high. "Choose quickly whelp."

Lida's words echoed in his mind as he locked eyes with her. "When I needed the protection of Dhal-Marrah most - you left... I have every reason to hate you." The sound of metal on stone rang out like a bell as the rapier hit the ground and rolled. Cerberus felt heavy hands grab his arms and force them behind his back.

"Prestigious members of the court, I am a compassionate King." The King glanced back at the Queen. "My Queen you are forgiven for this transgression. You have delivered a notorious criminal and I accept that by way of apology. You need education rather than public punishment. For this," he pointed at Cerberus. "There can be no clemency. The method of his sentence will be decided before the court on the morrow." He lowered his voice. "But as I am the judge - we can be sure where that will lead." He looked up addressing the party once more. "Send for House Dhal-Marrah. They are called to defend the actions of their disgraced son." He leaned in. "You see," he whispered. "I really should thank you for attending. You just single handedly insured the claim of my house on the throne Everfall in perpetuity, while at the same time destroying what little is left of your own."

Cerberus tried to lunge at him before coiling in on himself as a mailed fist ploughed into his stomach, removing the air from his lungs. A second followed and his mouth filled with the taste of bile and blood before he was dragged away.

Cerberex woke up covered in cold sweat. Her hair was plastered to her face as she sat bolt upright in the pitch black of her room. Rubbing her eyes, she took a deep breath hoping to calm the feeling of an inescapable dread she couldn't quite put her finger on. Like drifting sand through an hour-glass the feeling began to subside and Cerberex began to hear the commotion that had most likely caused her to wake in the first place.

The hammering on the main door of the house was insistent. As she ventured onto the landing, Cerberex could see her brother's door was ajar - another night time excursion. Her mother dressed in a deep blue night gown, cursed as she made her way across to the door on the floor below before flicking the door open with a motion of her wrist. In the pale moonlight a cloaked Drau bowed formally before presenting a rolled piece of parchment without word. Cerberex looked across as a light footstep caught her attention. Aunt Mal and Uncle Selwyn appeared in the entrance hall as her mother stared the parchment in her hand.

"Elryia darling, I'm not one to judge, but if you're lovers will send you letters could they do so at a more acceptable time of day." Mal yawned.

"Shut up Maleficent!" Cerberex watched her mother hold the parchment in front of her like a hot coal. Quietly she began to inch down the stairs looking back up at Cerberus's room. The sudden dread she'd been awoken by was suffocating her again. As she reached the bottom step her mother brandished the parchment at Selwyn. "What did you do?" Her face was taught with anger. "This is a summons so tell me fast Selwyn Charnite, what did you talk him in to?"

"Uncle?" Cerberex called warily as she alighted from the last step, recoiling as her mother shot her a glare.

"Stay out of this Cerberex." She warned.

"My Lady..." Selwyn began taking a step forward wrapped only from the waist down in a long blanket.

"Don't try that with me." Cerberex watched as her mother pointed at him still brandishing the parchment. "Whenever you come to this house, trouble follows you. So tell me now. If I open this parchment what will I see?"

"Elryia." Selwyn took a step forward. "I am no seer. I cannot tell you what is written on that piece of parchment."

"Then tell me I have nothing to fear. Tell me where my son has gone tonight." Her face was almost white now with a mixture of rage and fear.

Selwyn glanced at Cerberex and then back to Aunt Mal and sighed. "You know I can't do that."

Cerberex's eye's narrowed with irritation. A flicker of her her fingers and she plucked the parchment from her mother's outstretched hand and darted beyond her reach, tearing away the wax seal.

Silence reigned as she read, re-read, and read for a third time as her heart seemed to stop in her chest. Limply she held the parchment at her side and stared at the three pairs of eyes turned in her direction. "He's..." She began unsure of exactly where to start. Her eyes turned to Selwyn's. They were calm and guarded. She tilted her head to one side. "You know."

"For Eroth's sake daughter! What does it say?"

Cerberex turned back to the parchment hoping the wording had changed since she had memorized it. "He... He has been arrested."

Elryia snatched the parchment back reading it for herself. Her hand going to her lips. "No..." She murmured and then laughed madly shaking her head.

Cerberex felt the dread begin to burn away. Anger filled the void where it had been. "Where is he?"

"Choose your word's more carefully niece." Aunt Mal placed a hand on Selwyn's shoulder.

Selwyn gently pushed it off. "He chose to attend the palace invitation in my stead."

"Chose?" Elryia laughed dangerously. "Chose you say? You silver tongued snake! You sent my son into a den of wolves to be torn apart - alone!"

"Calm yourself Elryia, of course he didn't." Mal hissed.

"He would not take anyone else." Selwyn and Elryia's eyes did not blink.

"You - He what?" Mal took a step back as if stung. "You, you sent him - you sent Dendrion's only son ... you sent him alone?"

Elryia scrunched the parchment and threw it to the floor. "Yes he did Maleficent and now my son is in a cell beneath the palace until tomorrow morning when they will assuredly execute him." Tears ran down her face.

"Oh don't be so melodramatic! Court doesn't work like that, they'll have to prove he did anything first." Selwyn bent to pick up up the crushed ball.

"He tried to assassinate a King. There are witnesses from the entire front bench!" Elryia shouted.

Selwyn straightened the document. Somehow his composure didn't shatter once. "I did not send him, nor could I even if I had wanted to." His eyebrows raised as he took in the salient points. "What in the hells did he think he was doing?"

"Elryia try and calm down. We will go to court in the morning and tell them that there has been some kind of mistake. That he was drunk or that he is unwell. He is Lord Dhal-Marrah after all. They can't just execute him." Mal drifted across and placed an arm around Elryia's shoulders.

"Actually Mal my dear, I'm not sure that will work. Elryia is right. There are names of two dozen witnesses all of which are from the front bench." Selwyn murmured.

"Well then you had better come up with something else because I am fast running out of ideas." Mal shot Selwyn a venomous look.

Selwyn turned back and began reading the document properly, running his free hand through his hair. Suddenly his head shot up and he glanced around the entrance hall, then the stair, and finally the landing. "Where is Cerberex?" He asked his eyes wide in sudden concern.

Cerberex pulled her ranger leathers on even as she heard them yelling her name. A veritable armoury lay arranged on the bed. Her bow, a full quiver of arrows, her two silver hunting knives, three tiny throwing knives, and a leather ball filled with chalk that would explode upon impact. Scrawling a quick note and leaving it upon the pillow of her bed, she gathered her equipment and opened the window.

A cold breeze stung her face. For a moment she was sure she had seen movement below but as she blinked what ever it was had vanished into the dark. Cerberex sat, her legs dangling over the ledge. Beyond she could see the twinkling lights of the city and rising up like a host of fireflies, the lights of the palace. As it met her gaze she felt dread wrap its fingers around her heart again. She gritted her teeth against them and dropped, landing on three points. Taking a breath, she stood, glanced at the light above from her bedroom's open window, and began running for the palace. In the East, a thin band of turquoise announced the coming sunrise.

The Midnight Oubliette. It had existed long before the first stones of the palace had been laid above it. Light-less. Suffocating. It was not the fate that Cerberus had dreamed would be his. Only the most dangerous of criminals were committed to the depths. Tales were told of the Midnight Madness that took hold of those who were best left forgotten. Those for whom time could never wash away their sins. Cerberus reasoned that at least his captors paid him the compliment of deeming him a single Drau albeit of noble birth, terrifying enough to warrant abandonment in this place.

His armour and weapons had been confiscated. They had searched his pockets, removed the lacing from his shirt, even taken the silver tie that held his hair back from his face. They had not discovered the copper pin in his left boot, not that he could use it or even get to it from his current position. A heavy iron belt rested around his waist to which the manacles for his hands were attached. A three foot chain meant that it was precisely impossible for him to move anything past a crouch.

The darkness surrounded him like a grave. There were other miserable souls here of that he was certain. Dead or alive? Ah well that was a different question. Once or twice he'd flinched away from a low laugh behind his ear only to turn and feel the cold dampness of stone. Alone, Cerberus could still hear the jailer and his assistant laughing in his head.

"Well this one's a pretty boy. It's been a long time since we've had one of the houses come to stay." The jailer's eyes were wide and quite possibly mad. His hair what little there was, lay lank and matted. "Don't worry little lord they all pull that face when they go in. Few of them look so stern when they come out."

"Yeah most of shit themselves before then." The apprentice might have been a son or nephew. He hung back with caution still chuckling. "I could have a play with this one, looks like he could do with loosing a couple of inches." He clicked a large pair of scissors menacingly.

"Many have tried, many have failed. Do you want to see how far up on the list you can make it?" Cerberus felt the sting of the hit before the last word left his mouth. Instinctually he tried to dodge but the king's guard held his arms firmly to his back

"Hold your tongue or loose it." The jailer hissed angrily.

"This one's not for touching." The guard pushed him roughly in the back urging his forward. "He's got an appointment with Eroth come the morning. The king wants him alive and in one piece. Can't have him damaged for the show."

Cerberus smirked through his split lip at the scowl of the apprentice to this news.

"His name is Cerberus Dhal-Marrah. Now he's your problem." A heavy kick to the back of the leg forced Cerberus to the floor much to the glee of the guards as they left.

Cerberus felt the bony fingers of the jailer pull his head up. "Cerberus you say." His breath stank of bad alcohol and decay. "The hound from hell? Well in the short time we have, I'm going to teach you a whole new kind of meaning to that word." He patted Cerberus cheek.

Cerberus jerked awake though his eyelids may as well have remained closed. He hadn't meant to fall asleep. A terrified scream echoed through the walls, high pitched and pitiful. For a soul sucking moment he had the wrenching belief it was his sister's voice before calming himself. Cerberex was at home and with any luck blissfully unaware of his predicament. A shallow laugh followed as the scream died. Cerberus took in a deep breath and let it go. He would not be broken by this place. He turned his head this way and that as his ears picked up haphazard footfalls and a jingle of keys getting closer. Finally, the door to his cell somewhere ahead in the dark, opened.

"Up little dog." The cudgel nudged him in the face. Cerberus growled. "Up or do I need to stick this up your arse? Move it!" The jailer moved around him removing the chain from the metal waist band and snapped an iron collar about his neck attached to a long pole. Cerberus ground his teeth and slowly stood counting the ways he would make this individual pay as the rod pushed him out into the dimly lit hallway.

Cerberus's blinked against the light. As he blinked he could make out the heavy, riveted doors of other cells. He did his best to ignore the moans of victims shuffling within. Bile rose in his mouth as he shuffled through puddles that felt too viscous to be just water. A cackling laugh came from the door to his left. Part of the door had cracked at the bottom and a hand reached out scraping at the floor as they passed. "Snap! Crack! Your head's in a sack." A voice giggled from the other side impossible to make out age or gender. Momentarily distracted, Cerberus almost tripped as a steep stair case curled upwards ahead of him. He choked as he was roughly pulled to his feet by the collar around his neck. A simpering wail whimpered from above.

The room at the top of the staircase was flooded with light in comparison to the rest of the oubliette. The stone floor was worn of any texture and the air stank of blood old and new. A hand reached out grabbing his ankle from a cage making him stumble. The female within had patchy black hair and was barely dressed. Pressed up against the bars, the left side of her face was a mess of blood and scar tissue. Cerberus pulled away in revulsion even as he was forced down into a chair and chained in place. In the far corner of the room the apprentice hacked at a slab of raw meat on a table in the corner. Blood pooled around his feet. Cerberus forced himself not to vomit as he noticed two humanoid fingers lying not far away. Instead he cracked his neck to one side, doing his best impression of nonchalant disdain.

"You were given some fairly explicit orders gentlemen." His voice still sounded small to his ears.

The apprentice embedded the knife into the wood and Cerberus got a good look at him. He was extremely burly. Cerberus's eyes narrowed as he noted the dark hair and vibrant golden eyes before suddenly realising that what stood in front of him was the result of both Beast and Drau. He cocked his head to look up at the jailer. "Well someone fucked up."

The cudgel came down upon is back with a crack. Cerberus bit down on the yell that tried to force its way from his mouth. "The King said he wanted you walking and walking he shall have. He said nothing about anything else." Cerberus felt the cold of a dull blade tear through the back of his shirt as the apprentice stepped behind him. He gave a small smile at the whistle that issued from the boys lips, envisioning the look the pair must have had as they beheld the lattice work that covered his back and the larger knot of scarring that had never healed from the witch bolt he'd taken all those years ago.

The blade tip ran along the litany of scars. "Looks like you've seen my kind of work before." He felt the jailer's breath against his ear. "But don't worry, I'm sure I can find a new tune for you to sing."

Cerberus wrapped his hands into the chain that ran between his shackles, focused on the floor in front of him and waited.

Chapter 9:
Shadows

Cerberex placed her hand on the wall of the palace panting for breath. She had run almost the entire length of the city across rooftop and street, racing the dawn that was bleaching the horizon. She looked back unable to shake the feeling that she was too late, that she wouldn't make it. Nothing but dead leaves whispered across the alley. Her heart was thundering in her chest but it wasn't fear. Her mind was a steel trap of cold intent. Both her and her brother would be walking from here by the time the city woke and woe betide anyone who got in her way.

She adjusted the bow and walked back a few paces before sprinting at the wall headlong, using a discarded cart to springboard her assent. Lightly she balanced atop it checking the space beneath. She had no clear idea of the layout of the palace, but by her understanding, if you wanted to hold someone you generally headed downwards. Cat-like she lowered herself from the wall into the shadow of what judging by the smell, were refuse barrels. To her left the great gate that lead to the city was closed and to her right the palace rose like shards of glass. A quiet clink made her squat in the mire for a moment in expectation. Seconds passed until the door of the guardhouse by the gate opened, spilling golden light across the paving and a solitary palace guard wandered around the side to take a piss. Seizing her moment she ran towards the palace crossing the bright light reflecting from the partially open doors and flattening herself against a buttress bathed in shadow.

A narrow path meandered between the palace and its outbuildings. Cerberex peered in the darkness looking for signs of light beyond before sinking to her knees. The ground here was heavily trampled, heavy boots had wandered this particular route so many times, they had slowly begun to carve a groove in the earth. She traced the line of the most recent print noting its tip pointed ahead. The path was too narrow for more than two to walk abreast. A small guard detail but frequent. If she remained in the same direction as the print she should be able to avoid them depending on how far ahead or behind her they were. Quietly she jogged the first side of the palace turning the corner and squeezing between the palace wall and the palace itself.

A tinkle of falling glass made her pause for a second. Above her a small window swung wildly on it hinges. The crystal had shattered. She glanced at the ground a piece of black feather fluttered in the breeze. She picked it up analysing it closely. A bird then? She looked around unable to see any dead feathered body. She dropped the feather letting it flutter away and looked at the window and the surrounding area. The wall beneath had not seen anything in the way of maintenance and carved blocks of stone had shifted or otherwise eroded away. Jumping, her fingers found purchase tearing away soft moss from a recess. She grunted as she pulled herself up till she could see into what appeared to be a kitchen store room the other side.

Taking a breath she swung her leg in. Her foot skidded on a short round item on the tiled floor below and a ceramic bowl shattered as she went to catch herself cursing. A shout came from the door beyond and the sound of feet. The catch of the door began to move and Cerberex looked wildly around for a place to hide, choosing a stack of barrels near the door itself just before a sliver of gold light crept from the opening door. From her hiding spot Cerberex watched as a small hairless cat slinked through the opening and sat a foot inside the doorway licking its paw. A second shadow moved past it. A servant in simple black robes stepped into the room. Human. Male. Not yet into adulthood but not far off. He raised a blue glass lamp noticing the open window and shattered bowl on the floor. Cerberex pushed the door shut as he moved towards it unsheathing her knife. She stalked behind him as he gathered the pieces of pottery off the floor and stood to examine the window. As he leant to reach forward Cerberex clamped one hand over his mouth and held the edge of the knife against his throat with the other. The boy's eyes looked back at her with terror and shock.

"I want you to listen very carefully to me." Cerberex's voice was cold and calm as she whispered in his ear. The boy nodded. "Very good. Now, I'm going to move my hand and you are going to answer some questions for me. Lie or try to run and I will paint the floor in your blood is that understood?" Again the boy nodded and true to her word she slowly moved her hand away from his mouth. His breath was in terrified short gasps. "The party." She stated simply.

"It's moved inside the palace since the incident. Someone tried to kill the King and now the palace has been locked down by the Kings personal guard." He whimpered.

"Who attempted to kill the King?"

"What? I, I don't..."

Cerberex pressed the knife against his jugular. "You seem to be a clever boy, so just give me your opinion." She stroked his greasy hair.

"I umm, I heard some of the other servants say that a umm Dr... dr.." He stuttered.

"Drau." Cerberex finished for him impatiently.

He nodded. "That a Drau noble tried to stab him?"

Cerberex look at the boy in surprise. "Stab him? Are you sure it wasn't poison?"

The boy shook his head. "I heard nothing about poison."

"And the Queen?" She whispered in his ear.

He squeaked at the tickle of her breath. "She has taken to her chambers. Someone said she weren't feeling well. She has asked for honey and hot water to be brought."

Cerberex paused. If the Queen was poisoned instead she'd hardly be asking for refreshments. "You are sure this order for honey came from the Queen."

The boy nodded. "Yes. The message is written in her hand."

For the second time Cerberex looked at him in surprise. "You can read?" The question was unbidden and she covered his mouth before he could answer. "Never mind." She added, uncovering his mouth again. "This Drau, what happened to them?"

"I, I..." She could feel him hyperventilate. "I think they took him to the cells down stairs." He whimpered.

"Shh, shhh." She comforted stroking his hair again. "Now I'm going to tell you exactly what you are going to do next. I am going to take away this knife in a moment. You are going to go through that door and tell who ever you report to that a bird flew into the window. You will then return. You will not talk of this conversation, you will not mention my existence. If you do, well, I'm a rather good shot." Slowly she moved the knife and watched him back away to the door almost tripping over the cat in the process. As he left she returned to the window and ran her boot over the floor. Something small rolled towards her. Using her feet as a guide she reached down and picked it up. A crossbow bolt no more than three inches long rolled in her palm. This was no bird. Her fingers wrapped around it, her mind clicking through the possibilities.

The door re-opened and the boy returned, this time without the cat. Slowly and deliberately she sheathed her knife and unslung her bow, notching an arrow. "We are going on a little adventure you and me." She aimed the shot at his head. "Do you know where these cells are?"

The boy stood stock still. "Please." He whispered. "Please I don't go down there. I'm just a kitchen boy."

"But you do know where they are." It was more of a statement now. She smiled as the boy nodded. "Excellent, you're going to take me there nice and quietly. If you keep to your word then you can be assured that I'll keep to mine when I say that you will continue to live." She took a step forward as he took a step back, the terror in his eyes making his legs shake. She looked toward the door and nodded her arrow at it. "Lets go."

Cerberus screamed as the tip of the blade pierced the skin and the poison burned like fire through his back. He wasn't sure how long he'd been here for now. He felt exhausted. He clamped his mouth shut and breathed through the pain as his vision swam. The blade tore away and Cerberus arched pulling at his restraints for all he was worth. He closed his eyes and re-opened them. His skin felt like it was aflame. Looking down his hands were red and burning. He could feel the sweat run down his face. His breathing came in rapid gasps. The jailer's face swam into view.

"Oh bravo little dog, bravo indeed. Your quite something. Most of the guests here would be begging me to stop by now, but you, you're not quite done."

Cerberus forced his head up with a wince and he cracked a smile. "Oh you're going to need to do much better than that. I could keep this up all day."

The jailer sniffed and stood back up. "Stick him again." Cerberus's head slumped down as the knife pressed through his flesh before snapping back up as the poison chewed its way through him. He screamed again.

"Cerberus." A voice whispered. "Cerberus." It came again more insistent.

Cerberus blinked and for a moment he had sudden clarity. He could smell violets not his own blood. The lights in the room dimmed and flickered.

"Cerberus." The voice shouted at him and he felt the sting of a hand across his face.

Darkness, utter emptiness. Was he dead? No. Cerberus blinked as a tiny blue orb the size of an egg floated a little way above him. Soft skin touched his face.

"Snap out of it Cerberus."

He tried to rise but the belt around his waist was held fast. Gradually his eyes accustomed to the gloom. He was in a small cell. His clothes were soaked in sweat. A pale figure loomed over him in a coat a size or so large that it was difficult to determine whether the figure was male or female. That faint smell of violets again.

"Lida?" Cerberus's lips barely moved. He looked the figure up and down. "What are you wearing?"

Her face became clearer. A look of relief. She folded her arms. "Well I was going to open with let's get you out of here but if you'd rather stay..."

Cerberus's eye's slipped closed and opened again as another slap came across his face.

"No you don't. Do not close your eyes do you hear me? Don't you dare close them Cerberus." Lida placed her hands on the manacles. "Hold still, these are about to get very hot." She closed her eyes, clenched her hands around the chain, and very slowly the metal began to heat.

Cerberus bit down as the metal grew warm, then hot. White sparks hissed across the metal and the smell of burning filled the air till with a high pitched whine, the waistband sagged in two. He gasped for air before pulling away as Lida reached for the manacles and reaching into his boot for the pin he had secreted there. A moment or two later his wrists were free.

"Can you walk?" Lida placed a hand on his shoulder in a oddly friendly gesture.

He blinked and shuddered as for a moment Lida was gone and he was back in the chair if only for a second. He blinked and he was back in the dark. Lida pressed her hands against his face and pulled down the lower lids of his eyes, spotting the bloodshot vessels and hissed under her breath. "We need to get you out of here now." Cerberus inched into standing, still sore at the waist. The corridor beyond was darker than he remembered and wider than it had felt. Soft whimpering echoed from any one of the other cells. Lida lead the way stopping every so often and listening. Cerberus welcomed the slow pace as he tried to bring the contents of his head back in order. His thoughts came back with a jolt as the sound of footfalls behind them, followed by a pause and the creak of a door hinge.

"What the?" The apprentice's voice echoed. "Oh shit! Prisoner loose! Prisoner Loose!"

Lida's head snapped around at the noise. "Go, go!" She whispered, ushering Cerberus further forward. "The door at the far end - as fast as you can." She gave him a push. He held firm. "You're in no shape for heroics at the moment. Go!"

"Hey who's down there?" A flash of a tinderbox and a beam of light from a small lamp hurried down the corridor.

Lida coughed and did her best to lower her voice. "I am Lord Lotheris, by royal warrant you are ordered to stand down."

Cerberus skidded and almost fell. The male impression was terrible!

The apprentice held the lamp. "Lotheris is it? Strange, ain't been no princes down here no sir." He took a step forward. "But we was told that a certain lady might pay that one a visit." He grinned.

Cerberus placed one foot on the first step and watched. Lida stood her ground. Her hands twitched with sparks that flickered like fire flies. Though no air moved in the corridor, the coat she wore seemed to move slightly.

"Little tricks don't scare me pretty lady." The apprentice was no more than five feet from her now.

Cerberus looked at the stairs for a second then back.

"You know not to whom you speak." Lida barely whispered.

"Oh he's aware my Lady. Jethro just doesn't care - and our orders come from the King." Cerberus looked up just as a well placed boot sent him sprawling down to the floor and the jailer joined them. Lida glanced back wide eyed. The Jailer smiled, his grin missing more than a few teeth. "Did you think that a few friendly charms would keep me busy love?"

"You will talk to me with respect." Lida replied evenly.

Cerberus felt the pressure of the foot on his arm as he tried to roll away. "Will I?"

"I am your Queen." Lida almost growled at them.

The jailer gave a slight shrug. "Seems to me that position's pretty vacant right now." He glanced down at Cerberus's wriggling fingers. "'Cause the way I see it, I'm just looking at the newest heads on traitor's row."

The apprentice grinned at Lida and lunged grabbing her shoulder and pulling her arm back. Like lightening Lida twisted and slammed an open palm into his face sending coruscating energy searing through his skull. Cerberus seized the distraction and punched with every ounce of strength he had into the side of the Jailer's knee feeling a knuckle crack as it connected. Surprised, the Jailer pulled his leg away releasing Cerberus's hand. He rolled to his feet slamming another knee into the Jailer's groin barely suppressing a smile as the Drau bent double with a wheeze.

The apprentice fell like a brick as Lida removed her hand from his face, his eyes far off and staring as he gave a few involuntary twitches. Roughly, Lida grabbed Cerberus by the collar as she passed, yanking him up the first few stairs while she took them two at a time.

The Jailer groaned as his ability to breath began to return. Cerberus watched him reach into a pocket and bring a small silver whistle to his lips. At first no sound reached his ears, then somewhere above him the toll of a bell struck once, then again, and again, till it was joined by others. Cerberus turned and ran up the stairway.

Cerberex and her impromptu tour guide stopped as somewhere within the palace a bell tolled. The boy's eyes widened. "What is it?" Cerberex hissed at him. They had made it through a maze of corridors with little disturbance but the tone of that bell gave her the idea that their luck might be changing. "What is it?" She repeated.

"It's the oubliette lady." He panted.

"Oubliette?" She spun him with a single hand. "Where?" The boy looked down at his feet. "Beneath us?" The boy nodded. "How do I get in?"

The boy's eyes raised up to hers in surprise. "Wh, why? Why would you..."

Cerberex pulled an arrow back in her bow and aimed at his head. "How do I get in?"

The boy was shaking and turned a corner leading to a staircase that headed down below the ground level of the palace. How he could see anything Cerberex had no idea. Humans' seemed to have appalling vision even in broad day light, but even she struggled to maintain an even footing as the steps grew steeper. A bead sized point of yellow light was the only indication she had that the stairs had an end to them. Below the persistent tolling was louder and she could make out bulky silhouettes move across the opening.

Cerberex returned the arrow and reached out grabbing for the boy's shoulder. "Guards?" She whispered.

"Sort of." She heard him whisper back.

Cerberex stopped. "Sort of? What does that mean?"

The boy turned almost bumping into her. "I don't know lady. I don't go down there."

"Then how do you know you are going the right way." Cerberex hissed.

"Because this is the way the woman came yesterday before she was..." Cerberex didn't need excellent night vision to know that he was pulling a finger across his throat.

As they headed nearer the opening the sound of running grabbed her attention. "Seems their worked up about something."

The boy paused. "It's the bell."

"What about it?" She replied pausing again in frustration.

"Someone's trying to escape the palace lady." The boy paused as a shadow blotted out the light ahead then moved. "Sometimes they ring it when one of the servants tries to make a run for it. They don't get far."

"How do we get passed them?" Cerberex cut him off. She could feel him turn in surprise.

"I... I... We can't! It's impossible!" He stuttered loudly before Cerberex pulled a hand over his mouth cursing.

"Keep your voice down and your legs moving." She hissed into his ear before carefully pulling her hand away.

"Lady I can't. If they catch me here they'll kill me for sure. Please lady, I don't want to be executed." He whimpered.

Cerberex swore. "I'll tell you what. How about I execute you right now and save you worrying about it?" The boy fumbled as he tried to step away. "Move it." She growled. The boy swallowed and nodded turning back and slowly making his way down the stairs, his hands visibly shaking at his sides. Cerberex sighed, they were making painfully slow progress.

As Cerberex approached the final stair she squinted in the sudden light. The boy crouched against the edge of archway, hugging it like an old friend. She dared a glance beyond. Lamps lit the way in both directions every few feet. Several male Drau affixed leather armoured guards to their shoulders and chest. They wore the palace colours but their armour was far and away lighter than palace guard plate. Cerberex pondered how many she could take out before one of them called for back up. Two, three, maybe more if they were slow. They seemed to be some kind of light militia and judging by their agitation, clearly unused to being called to action at this hour.

"I don't know the way past lady, please ... please let me return to the kitchen's now," the boy whispered.

Cerberex peered out again. The militia had suited up and were now jogging down the corridor beyond to the right. It occurred to her suddenly that the bell had stopped ringing. She was sure it had been a sign that her brother had managed somehow to extract himself from his predicament - had he been recaptured so soon? Hauling the boy to his feet and pushing him forward, they entered the corridor beyond. He stank of urine and in the light Cerberex noticed the boy's trousers were wet. She sighed under her breath. How he'd survived being brought here she honestly had no idea. For his sake, she hoped he was new. The City of Everfall was no place for the faint hearted.

Distracted by the scent of her guide's terror, Cerberex heard the returning footfalls too late. Swiftly she turned around looking for a place to hide.

"You!" The voice made her stiffen to a halt. "Turn around. What business do you have here?" The hiss of metal on leather caught her attention. "Servants have no place down here - show me your colours."

The boy whimpered and then suddenly sank to his knees. "Please sir, it's not my fault! The lady..." Cerberex cursed under her breath, turned, and fired the arrow she'd kept slack in her bow through the boy's neck. He gargled as the steel head jutted out below his chin, before his eyes rolled back and he fell forward.

Time stopped. Cerberex felt her hand automatically reach for another arrow, string and aim. As the arrow loosed time came rushing back in sudden fast forward. The Drau turned and the arrow danced across the edge of his paldron with barely a kiss. Angrily, he shouted behind him for aid, simultaneously drawing a short sword. Cerberex flung her bow over her shoulder and drew her hunting knives in one fluid motion. Leaning back she rolled beneath his swing and sprung above him using one of the walls as a launch. A resounding screech of metal echoed around her as he used the edge of his blade to push her attack sideways. She pulled her blades back like a pair scissors and crouched patiently in defence. His blow was heavy. Designed to cleave through her shoulder and shatter her collar bone. Riposting, Cerberex's wrist jarred at the ferocity of the attack. Twisting her second blade around, she pushed her advantage feeling the opposing pressure of his armour and sudden release as the blade sank into stomach. She held it in place as his eyes went wide and his sword slipped form his grip.

"I am looking for my brother." She winced. Her voice seemed hideously loud.

The Drau coughed a laugh. "You're here for the red-eyed traitor?" He shook slightly. "Little shit's got it coming for him tomorrow."

Cerberex felt her blood run murderously hot. She spun the second blade and pressed it home, feeling a lung burst. The Drau yelled, blood bubbling across his lips. Looking down at him as he sagged with pain, she resisted the urge to twist. "Wrong answer. Where is he?" He looked up at her. Blood dripped from his chin onto her hand. "Tell me where, and I will ease your passing."

She leant forward as he drew a ragged breath, spitting a gobbet of viscera and phlegm in her face. "Go to hell."

Cerberex ground her teeth and wiped her cheek on her shoulder. She sneered. "Gladly, but not before you." She twisted the blades within the wounds, mincing what ever organs they had pierced and withdrew them. The Drau sank to his knees as he tried to keep his life-blood within. It poured through his fingers and onto the floor. She patted his head almost caringly and stalked past. A second later he was sprawled, staining the flagstones red. Cerberex's heart thundered in her chest.

Chapter 10:
The Knife Edge

Lida and Cerberus launched themselves sideways through the nearest unlocked door of the corridor above. The sound of a dozen feet as reinforcement pursued them. Cerberus glanced around them as Lida pushed the door closed, whispering to the lock until it replied with a resounding click. Taking a moment to catch his breath, Cerberus reasoned that they had made it at least two floors above where he'd been held. He glanced about the room. A heavy thud shook the rivet studded door, forcing his stomach up into his mouth. The room was plain. For a second Cerberus thought they had merely traded one cell for another till he registered the boxes stacked high with seemingly random assorted items. Necklaces, talismans, gloves, small daggers designed for self-protection, lace scarves, cutlery, small animal skulls, and the list went on. There was no rhyme or reason to the collection. Cerberus held up a necklace of pearls stained yellow with age. He prized open the stained locket at its heart. Within a picture of a young Drau male cut in the colours of a lesser or possibly even extinct house stared back at him through broken glass. A pinch of short, blonde hairs scattered to the ground.

The door shook again louder, the lock protesting loudly. Lida, brushed passed and climbed a stack of boxes to where a high window was lit with the pre-light of dawn. She pushed it expectantly. The window stayed shut. A heavier thud came from the door again and something within the lock squealed in protest.

Cerberus took a step back. "We're going to need that window open." He called to her looking around for some kind of weapon.

"What does it look like I'm doing!" Lida retorted pushing as hard as she could. The rusted hinges of the frame squealed in protest.

The wood by the lock of door splintered. "Well, you might want to do it a little faster." Cerberus pushed his weight against the door, holding two small daggers that were dubiously sharp, designed more for show than anything else.

"Do you want to swap?" Lida hissed, the frustration evident in her voice as she fought to force to window wide.

Cerberus felt his feet slide as someone tried to push the door from the opposite side. He gritted his teeth and forced it shut. "Get a move on!"

Lida looked back at him angrily. "I'm trying!"

The door jolted and Cerberus skidded across the floor as it flew open with a loud bang. The jailer's familiar voice carried over as several lightly armoured prison guard pushed their way in, weapon's drawn. "Cut down the female, but the devil is mine."

Cerberus slashed out with the daggers as they entered, scoring a hit across the face of one and producing little more than a scratch. He swore under his breath and leapt backwards. As he thought, they were little more than letter openers. He pressed the hilts into the palms of his hands and proceeded to use them between his fingers like knuckledusters. If finesse would not suffice then brute strength would have to. Standing in the space between Lida and the guards he slammed his fist in an uppercut designed to punch through the lower jaw of the first. The guard pulled away howling as he caught the blow and the blade pierced through his hand instead. Cerberus tried to pull away, kicking out as he did so. The blade snapped to reveal nothing but cheap tin at its core, leaving the pointed end impaled in the guard's fist. He threw the useless hilt to the side and it skittered across the floor.

The window screamed and finally flew wide, precariously swinging on a single functioning hinge. Lida cried out in surprise and joy then again in fear as a gloved hand grabbed her by the back of her coat and yanked her from her makeshift pedestal. She yelled, landing heavily on her back as a boot pressed against her throat. Desperately she tried to force the words out of her mouth and unleash her arcane might against her attacker but the pressure made it impossible to utter a breath. Uselessly she clawed around her for some form of improvised weapon.

Cerberus's vision swam as the flat of a blade caught the back of his head, momentarily distracted by the screech of the window and Lida's triumphant yell. He turned enough in time to watch her fall from the stack of boxes and blinked stars from his vision as he flung his remaining dagger with all the strength he could muster at the guard leering over her. It sunk hilt deep into the shoulder, taking him off balance enough for Lida to suck in a lungful of air and stretch out her arm, muttering under her breath. As if caught in a gale, the guard slammed into the ceiling until gravity exacted its influence once more and he dropped back to the floor with a sickening crunch of broken bone and a shower of paintwork and plaster.

Cerberus turned, his fists clenched awaiting the next attack. The first connected with his jaw before he could process the number of guards behind him. His head snapped around and a tooth loosened in the back of his mouth. Cerberus wiped a dribble of blood from his nose. His vision blurred as the sweat poured from him. The heat he realised, how could it be so hot. He gasped for breath but it was like breathing flame. Stumbling forward he stretched out his hand, grasping the nearest guard. The guard directly in front of him screamed, desperately trying to tear his arm away from Cerberus's grip. Cerberus looked down and watched the leather arm guards bubble and blister as they curled in on themselves, burning away beneath his touch. The acrid smell of torched flesh crawled into his nose as the Drau's hand blackened and charred. In surprise, Cerberus let go and stumbled back, looking down at his own smoking hand. Two shadows fell over him as he fell back against a stack of boxes. He looked up and prepared to take the hit, inadvertently ducking as suddenly their heads snapped back. Cerberus cocked his head to one side. It took him a second to realise that the tiny silver studs in their clavicle were actually arrowheads. They gasped to breath and sank, slowly drowning in their own blood.

From the doorway, the Jailer knelt on the floor grasping at his throat as a bow string slowly garotted him. Cerberex stood, arrows spent, her hair and face flecked with blood, and her knee placed against the Jailer's spine forcing his throat against the bow. Her lips were split in a slight smile but her eyes were icy cold. Cerberus's mouth opened and then closed as he tried to form some kind of appropriate response.

"You seem to be in an awful lot of trouble brother." Cerberex's voice was chillingly calm.

Lida dusted herself down as she picked herself up and looked with a level of thinly veiled admiration. "Is that...?"

Cerberex's head snapped in her direction. "Well I should have guessed that you were involved," she paused giving a slight incline of the head. "It's been a while."

Lida took a step forward. "What can I say Lady Cerberex? Times change."

Cerberus stood rubbing his jaw and feeling the bruising begin to swell. "Ladies, it's lovely you're catching up but..." The sound of movement in the corridor stopped him mid sentence. For a moment they all looked at each other in silence before climbing over the piles and stacks of personal effects in their race to reach the window.

With the slight adjustment in pressure the Jailer gasped for air and reached behind him, drawing a jagged blade. "Cerberex!" Cerberus called out as he saw the shimmer of metal in the Jailer's hand. Cerberex immediately made to pull the bow string taught but the blade snicked through the cord with surprising ease. Like a cat he pounced forward to Cerberus who recoiled backwards. The blade missed his sternum and careened through the air, tearing a gash into his leg. Cerberus winced as his shin erupted in hot pain and planted his other leg into the Jailer's face, crushing his nose and knocking him unconscious. He looked down at the tear, feeling the wet trickle of his own blood run down into the foot of his boot. For the crudeness of the knife it had cut through leather, cloth, and into the flesh beneath like they had been nothing but butter. He blinked away the pain and pushed into the darkest reaches of his head, giving the Jailer a vengeful kick in the ribs with the other leg and feeling a rib snap as his foot connected.

Cerberex was first through the window, a squeeze even for her thin frame. She had to squirm and writhe to ease her hips over onto the soft earth, terrified of attracting unwanted attention. She twisted and reached back down, offering a hand to Cerberus. She gave him a look of concern as he gasped in pain. "What's wrong?"

"Nothing. I didn't move fast enough." Cerberus waved her away. "I can deal with it." Cerberex narrowed her eyes but turned back to help Lida. As she turned away, Cerberus stumbled slightly. The wound still felt aflame. "So?" He looked at Cerberex expectantly.

Cerberex helped pull Lida the rest of the way through the window and tuned to look at him. "Well don't look at me! I wasn't really convinced we were getting out of this."

Cerberus's head twitched. "But.. well how did you get in?" He asked incredulously.

Cerberex got onto her feet. "I climbed the wall." She looked back at Lida. "You know for a place that has suffered trespass and attack in as many days you really should consider hiring some more guards."

Lida looked up. "We have over a hundred."

Cerberex shrugged. "Well not from what I saw. I climbed the wall, made my way around the side of the palace, and went in through a kitchen window a bird had knocked open. Not a single soul noticed."

"A bird?" Cerberus repeated.

Cerberex grinned. "What can I say brother, luck just seems to smile on me more than you."

Cerberus suddenly looked her square in the eye. "It was you." He watched as she recoiled from the sudden accusation. "You were the trespasser. You followed me into the city that night."

Cerberex's eyes narrowed. "I wasn't the only one snooping in places I shouldn't but if I'd known you were risking our house for a midnight tryst..."She glanced at Lida. "I might not have bothered."

Lida stepped back. "I assure you that there was far from any trysting involved." Cerberex's look was anything but one of belief. Lida rolled her eyes. "Dhal-Marrah's." She whispered to herself as she cautiously made her way along the wall to a stone palisade barrier.

"Where are you going." Cerberus called after her, keeping his voice low.

"Well we can't just sit here." Lida hissed back and turned, looking over her surroundings.

"We?" Cerberex looked at Cerberus with a grin.

"Oh knock it off." Cerberus sighed and limped towards Lida.

Lida shifted as Cerberus approached. "We're in the lower gardens. The walls here are too high to climb and the closest entrances lead only into the palace itself." She pointed towards the palace walls. "Guard towers keep an eye for anything unexpected." She turned and pointed right. "You see where the palace juts out there?" Cerberus nodded. "A little beyond that are the royal stables and a little more are the main gates."

"That's your plan?" Cerberus looked at her with barely masked disappointment. "You're planning on what - asking nicely?"

Lida shot him an angry look. "Do you have a better one?" She looked back. "We have to get to the stables first, which means getting passed them unseen." She gestured to the guard towers.

Cerberus looked up at the sky. Only one or two of the brightest stars still shone and the clouds were flecked with tiny patches of gold. "Then we had better get a move on." He replied looking back to the garden. The lower gardens were a patchwork illusion of grass, cultivated flower beds, and enclosed patios partitioned and separated by low decorative walls and hedgerows and yet despite all its manicured beauty Cerberus noted one important factor - nothing was above two feet tall.

Cerberex watched and waited. Her eyes firmly affixed to the tiny silhouettes of two palace guard patrolling the top tier of the guard tower a little beyond. They had waited under the protective cover of a large crystalline moth house for the dawn. Now a thin mist had risen and the ground up to a foot high, glistened silver. The silhouette shifted and Cerberex ran, sprinting across the divide and skidding gracefully to a crouched stop beneath a line of erotically shaped shrubs. Sunlight shimmered atop the wall and where ever the ground turned from silver to gold, the mist receded to nothing. Cerberex glanced back up at the tower and then waved to the next. Lida shortly followed by Cerberus, quickly followed. She caught sight of the wet blooded patch on his leg slowly growing. Their eyes met.

"Don't." Cerberus whispered dangerously.

"I didn't say anything." Cerberex retorted her eyes turned to watch the movements in the next tower.

"You were thinking it." He hissed.

Cerberex pursed her lips. "You first then." She gestured to the open space leading to a short wall of black stone some twenty or thirty feet beyond. She glanced at the tower again. "Go!" She gave him a pat on the shoulder.

Cerberus grimaced and let out a groan as he stumbled over the hedge row and ran across the intermediary gap keeping low to the ground. Every footstep was murderously painful.

Cerberex's heart thundered in her chest as she watched him go. "He's not in a good way is he?" Lida whispered so close that Cerberex almost jumped out of her skin. Cerberex shook her head. "This is my fault." Lida muttered again.

Cerberex tore her gaze away from Cerberus and looked over to her. "Why do you say that?"

"Anyone who's known your brother a while knows that the easiest way to elicit a response from him is to tell him not to do something." Lida smiled.

Cerberex opened her mouth to ask but caught herself. "He's quite capable of getting into trouble without provocation too." She leapt over the hedge and sped across the gravel and grass beyond. A spear of sunlight pierced the ground a few feet ahead forcing her to suddenly change direction and leap across a flower bed, barely making it to the sanctuary of the wall before the guard atop the nearest tower returned to his post.

Cerberus gave her an encouraging smile as she slammed her back against the stonework and pressed into its shadow. "Not bad."

Cerberex raised an eyebrow. "Not bad for what?" To her irritation, he simply shrugged.

A few painful minutes later the guard shifted his post again and Lida bolted across the rapidly illuminating lawn. She came to a skidding stop the ivory of her coat speckled in green and yellow stains from sap and leaf litter. Looking at her, Cerberus couldn't help but think that she couldn't have looked less like a queen. Deftly, without her noticing, he plucked a small red leaf from her hair.

Cerberex peered above the wall. She could see the stable now. A few solitary individuals seemed to be moving within. She looked back at the pair. "There's movement in the stables."

Lida smiled mysteriously. "Oh don't worry about that."

Cerberex wrinkled her nose in annoyance and looked at the distance. The stretch was at least a hundred feet of open ground. Sunlight had burned away most of the mist and the path was broken with a maze of low flower beds. The scale ensured that the area was overlooked by not one but two of the guard towers. Timing would be vital.

For five long minutes Cerberex did nothing but watch the guards' movements, counting quietly under her breath. Finding the pattern to their routine, she looked down at Lida. "Count slowly to ten when I go, then run yourself." Lida nodded. Cerberex checked her timings and ran. There was no avoiding the sunlight now. Now it was speed that was important. A large statue rose up a few feet before the stables. Cerberex focussed on that and willed herself to speed up. Counting quietly to herself, she dared to glance behind her as she reached nine. A moment later she could see Lida leap the wall and begin to run. She turned back around just in time to force a leap across a wide circular flowerbed recently dug and covered with a fine net to keep out unwanted pests. Her foot came back down barely an inch away from its edge.

Lida caught up with her only a few moments after Cerberex's hand touched the grey stone base of the statue. She didn't look as Lida placed a hand on it breathing heavily, her eyes focussed solely on Cerberus. He was moving with all speed towards them but he was slowing, his limp becoming more pronounced with every step. Cerberex glanced at the nearest tower. Ten seconds. She looked back at Cerberus barely half way as he made his way around a flower bed rather than leap. Eight seconds. She looked back at the tower. Seven. Cerberus stumbled slightly shifting his balance. Six. The top of a halberd came into view it's pennant featureless against the brightening sky. Five. "He's not going to make it." Cerberex whispered more to herself than anyone listening.

"He will. He has to." Lida sounded like she was trying to convince herself.

Three. Cerberus came to the larger flower bed painfully aware of the time it had taken and did his best to forced his legs to jump. It was leap that should have been ridiculous to even consider missing. It was not the leap he should have made. His injured leg met the ground the other side and betrayed him instantly. It crumpled under his weight sprawling him forward and forcing him to bring his other leg down prematurely to try and prevent him falling over. It snagged behind him caught in the netting of the flower bed.

Cerberex saw the jump and winced as Cerberus crumpled like a wilted rose. "Shit!" she swore loudly and made to run out to him. Lida grabbed at her to pull her back but she shook the hand away.

Cerberus pulled, trying to free his good leg all the while grimacing against the searing pain of the other and fighting not to yell out. Cerberex skidded down next to him and severed the net with a single swipe of a hunting knife just as a sharp bleat of a horn followed by a distant yell sounded. Cerberex looked up as the horn blast was taken up by the next watch tower and then the next. She pulled Cerberus's arm over her shoulders and hauled him to his feet. "Stand brother! You must keep moving." She didn't wait for a response and half helped, half dragged him the remaining distance towards the statue and the stables beyond.

Heavy armoured shapes came thundering out of the nearest entrance to the palace and charged across the grass. Cerberus gasped in pain as he pushed Cerberex away. "Go on, leave! It's me they want."

Cerberex grabbed his collar and hauled him forward. "Will you stop trying to be a hero for Eroth's sake!"

Lida took the lead as they bolted to the stable house and breathed a sigh of relief as a young Drau female gowned in grey silk and modestly bejewelled ran to meet them. "Cynthia!" Lida placed her hands around the startled looking lady with relief. "Is it done? Did you manage what I asked?"

Cynthia nodded and curtsied keeping her head low. Her voice when she spoke was soft. "It is as you commanded my lady. The horse is ready and waiting and we have procured this." She held out a soft black bundle that clinked as Lida took it.

"And the other thing?" Lida muttered quietly as a young boy, Drau or at least in part, brought a dappled grey horse from within.

Cynthia looked up at Lida and her eyes were surprisingly full of energy. "The healer has been called and paid and your ladies know what it is they are to say if the truth is discovered." Lida smiled and moved past to the horse but Cynthia grabbed her arm. "Do not be gone too long my Queen. I do not know how long the ruse will keep him at bay."

Lida paused taking her hand. Her eyes narrowed. "What has happened?" Cynthia tried to pull back in alarm but Lida held her firm. "Tell me." She commanded.

Cynthia leant forward. "He took Aeris last night." Her voice barely above a whisper. Lida's face darkened. "She is not in a good way."

Cerberex half carried Cerberus over. "We have company." She looked between the two. "What's wrong." She asked uneasily.

Lida clasped Cynthia's hands in her own. "We will resolve this when I return. Do nothing that would put you or the others in danger. I could not bare to have your blood on may hands." She smiled and turned to Cerberex helping take the weight of Cerberus as Cynthia sped back towards the palace.

"What was that about?" Cerberex asked.

"Nothing. Here." Lida shoved the bundle into her hands.

"What is this?" Cerberex turned it over noticing the embroidery of a tiny silver dragon on a collar and the hilt of silver rapier.

"What your brother brought to the party." Lida motioned for the stable hand to help get Cerberus up as shouts began to echo closer and the clatter of plate armour became more pronounced.

Cerberus rolled doing his best to maintain his balance. A dark cloud was gathering at the edges of his vision. He saw the bright silver and red figures charge towards them."They're here," he croaked.

Cerberex swung herself up behind Cerberus taking the reins in one hand and pulling the horse around. Holding a hand down to Lida. The horse whinnied in protest at the weight as she swung behind and Cerberex urged it forward into a canter up the slight slope towards the front of the palace.

Glancing up, Cerberex caught a glimpse of the Great Gate and accompanying guard house. Palace Guard blocked them and the gate itself was firmly shut.

"Can you shoot them?" Lida called to her shoulder.

"They're wearing plate." Cerberex replied and looked back to see that they were slowly being boxed in. "I can try." She urged the horse forward and released the reigns, then reached back for her bow only to feel the slack bowstring as she brought it forward and the lightness of her quiver, remembering that the string had been cut only a hour or two earlier. Cerberex looked up as a wave of fear passed over her. "I.." A guard went down left centre his hand grasping at his throat. Then another, a black feathered fletched bolt sticking out of his eye. A third collapsed under his own weight as another shattered through the knee cap.

Cerberus panted and lolled against the horses neck. He tried to look up, surprised as the silvery figures toppled as if they were nothing but wooden skittles. He smiled at the skill in the shots.

Lida stretched out her hand and closed her eyes wrapping the other firmly around Cerberex's waist. "You are truly an expert archer Cerberex Dhal-Marrah." She spoke as tendrils of pale blue energy filled her outstretched palm.

Cerberex looked in confusion at her empty quiver. At the periphery of her vision she thought she saw a black shape perched atop the skewed roof of a water storage but when she turned to see what it was, it was gone as if it had been nothing more than smoke.

Lida's eyes flashed open, the silver of her iris now writhing with electric blue as she unleashed the growing energy in her palm almost falling off with the recoil of it. The gates flew wide as if they were made of paper. Guards still patrolling the exterior were flung from their feet into the street and those few merchants looking for an early morning's barter with the low-life suddenly threw themselves into the gutter. Cerberex dug in her heels and urged the horse into a full gallop down the city streets. In her arms, Cerberus's head lolled and his body seemed to slump.

Chapter 11:
Consequences

Rain. Rain drumming, then the sudden vibration of far off thunder. A cold draft that made the skin prickle. Crackling. The soft pop of dry wood on a slow burn. Laughter. Dry laughter. "Not going to break easy are you?" The stink of old blood then the memory of pain - the pressure of the knife, the sting of coursing poison, the tear of skin. Cerberus sat up with a yell, sweat beading off his torso and across his head. He blinked and the darkness receded. Rain. He blinked again. It was running past the window. He rubbed his head and forced the visions away. Slowly the setting became familiar. The deep red curtain drawn partially across the window. The small stone fireplace. The wardrobe with one door that would never fully close. He knew these. They were his. This was his room - this was house Dhal-Marrah. He groaned trying to put the pieces of his memory back in order.

"How much do you remember?"

Cerberus' head snapped up in the direction of the voice. Lida sat in the armchair by the desk on the other side of the room. Her head was tilted watching the rain and her hair fell like a silver waterfall down the side of her neck - starkly bright against the plain black shirt and trousers. He furrowed his brow in concentration. "Are those mine?"

Lida's head turned to him with a smirk. "Well, it's not like I had time to pick out a wardrobe before I left and your sister is well, she has very unique taste."

Cerberus snorted and rubbed his neck. "Oh we can all agree on Cerberex's uniqueness of dress sense." Lida smiled. Cerberus looked down to see the covers of his bed tastefully drawn up over the little enough he was wearing. "Speaking of which, where..."

"You were in need of some patching up. We needed to ascertain what needed fixing." She turned away to watch the rain again.

"There's that 'we' again." Cerberus glanced around the room before noticing a pile of folded clothes at the bottom of the bed.

Lida chuckled. "Oh don't worry Cerberus you're not the first I've seen in the altogether and your mother presumably gave birth to you, so I feel confident she's more than accustomed to your particular shapes."

Cerberus leaned back in the pillows with a slight grin as he folded his arms across his chest. She was trying to mock him. "Oh really? So tell me my Lady, did you like what you saw?"

Lida's eyes shot back and the colour rose in her face a fraction. "I was rather shocked actually."

"Shocked." He repeated. "Well that's definitely a new one. I don't believe it's ever been called shocking." He grinned.

Lida's eyes narrowed. "I was referring to the top half. When I saw it I wondered what had been done to you."

Cerberus looked down at himself, wondering what she was referring to and then realised she was speaking of the lace work of thin scars across his back and front. "Ah."

"You are lucky that you weren't sliced to ribbons because I would not have put it past him." Lida's eyes sparked with concern. She stood and wandered towards him. "The oubliette is a place were the worst of our kind are left to be forgotten. It's charms manifest and shape to break your mind without the need to break your body." She leant against the wardrobe. "But it's not unheard of for my... for the King to return to more barbaric methods from time to time."

"Well, these are..." Cerberus searched for the word and his eyebrow twitched. "An occupational hazard."

The corners of Lida's mouth curled ever so slightly. "Just like you Cerberus to make a joke about anything serious." She sighed. "You didn't answer my question. What do you remember?"

Cerberus shifted with the sheets and reached for the clothes before dressing beneath the covers. "I remember the party, watching you be spoken to as if you were nothing but a beggar and the tears falling from your face. I..."

"Why did you do it?" Lida cut him off abruptly.

Cerberus laughed and laced the front of the trousers. "You are my Queen. It'd be remiss of me if I did not jump to your aid." He looked up to see her stern expression and sighed. "Because I don't like him or what you have been forced to become. So considering your choice of words the last time we spoke, I wanted prove a point." He swung his legs over the side of the bed and winced as he caught the bandage covering the slice he'd received. He looked up at her. "You weren't exactly doing a fantastic job by the way."

Lida blinked in surprise. "Was I not?"

Cerberus stood. "Absolutely not. You were shaking like a leaf. You're not a killer." Gently he crouched down and felt under the bed for a pair of boots.

The door knocked twice and opened. "Cerberus! Eroth's eyes! I thought you'd woken up." Cerberus groaned as a heavy arm grasped his shoulders.

"Good morning Kane, or is it afternoon. I honestly have no idea right now." He carefully pushed Kane's arm away and sat back on the bed pulling on a pair of black leather boots.

Kane whistled. "You had me..." He paused. Cerberus was smiling. Kane's eyes narrowed. "You're not alone." It was a statement rather than a question.

"Nope." Cerberus replied simply.

Kane's eye's closed slightly and he forced a smile. "Who is it this..."

"Kane?"

Kane's eyes went wide and his face drained of colour. Cerberus grinned, raising an eyebrow. Slowly Kane turned. Lida looked at him the shock writ wide across her face. Awkwardly, he performed a modest bow. "Ahem, my Lady." A second later and he was bowled backwards as Lida flung her arms around him. Cerberus looked away unable to shake the grin from his face.

"I have missed you so much." Lida's voice came muffled through Kane's clothes and leather cuirass.

"Umm." Kane turned to Cerberus with terror, dread, and the look of a man with no idea what to do next. Cerberus merely looked back enjoying the discomfort his friend was obviously feeling.

"I should not have done what I did. I'm so sorry Kane." Lida pulled away and wiped the beginning of a tear from her face. "You were so right about the Gal Serreks, the coronation, all of it. I should have listened to you brother."

"I... umm... I'm sorry too Lida." Kane patted her shoulder.

"Right, well." Cerberus stood and shrugged on a shirt. "I'll leave you two to get re-acquainted." He moved behind Kane and into the doorway. "Don't be too long Kane. We are probably going to be quite busy with the ah family business." He paused and caught Lida's eye, inclining his head. "My Queen." and gently closing the door.

Out of habit Cerberus slipped quietly across the house, limping slightly as he crossed the entrance hall.

"Cross the threshold of this house once more Cerberus Dhal-Marrah and you will not be crossing back."

Cerberus froze and looked back. At the top of the stair his mother stood like a black spectre against the light. Her hand rested against the bannister as she observed him. Cerberus stood straighter and brushed a hair behind his ear, mustering a smile. "Wouldn't dream of it mother."

Elryia made her way regally down the stairs towards him. "Do you have any idea of the trouble you've caused this house?"

Cerberus laced his hands behind his back. "I have a general idea. However, it was needed." He felt the sting of the slap across his face before he had a chance to step aside.

"You dare speak to me of needs. These are the needs that killed your father. They are the reason that House Dhal-Marrah lingers on the edge of extinction." Still a little taller than him, she seized his chin and force him to look at her. "It is by my will that your little league of heroes is tolerated beneath this house and what do I have for thanks. You leave at every hour of the night. You return battered, bruised, and in this case near death."

"House Dhal-Marrah is the house of assassins mother. It is the legacy that I have inherited and swore to uphold." Cerberus growled.

"I have lost a husband and lord to it boy - I will not lose a son and to drag your sister into it tells me that for all your playboy bravado, you have no idea what you are doing. You have not only brought the name of your own house into disgrace, you have brought those close to you under scrutiny." Her voice hissed with anger.

Cerberus twisted from her grip. "I did not bring Cerberex along with me. She came by herself. She has been tracking me herself. I have upheld the agreement we made upon my mastership to keep the family business from her but she is still a Dhal-Marrah and if accident of birth is anything to go by, that song is singing in her blood regardless." He turned to leave.

"I mean it Cerberus." She called after him. "Dendrion would never have done something so reckless."

Cerberus turned ready to argue as the front doors opened. Wind and rain swept into the house and a familiar figure stepped in out of the elements.

"Nephew!" Selwyn shrugged his coat and though soaked to the skin, strode across the room and embraced Cerberus with both arms. Elryia recoiled from him as if confronted with a wild animal. "It is so good to see you up and about this quickly. I did say they would not keep you down for long." Selwyn gave a joyful laugh before straightening and nodding to Elryia. "Lady Dhal-Marrah."

Elryia laced her fingers in front of her. "You have something good to tell me I hope."

Selwyn twitched at her abruptness. "Indeed." He glanced a Cerberus. "A fine mess you got yourself into nephew. Luckily, you were not as alone at this fiasco as we thought. A number of House Valouris were in attendance and thanks to a little coin applied to the right people, they now swear blind that the person they saw was not Cerberus Dhal-Marrah. Naturally House Charnite is playing devils advocate on your behalf. I have announced to the court that without a prisoner to be produced it is impossible to say exactly who is responsible. Dopplegangers have been used in the past to confound crimes So I have suggested a thorough search of the palace be made." He smiled. "I may have also dropped in that the group thought to be responsible for his entry, is a cult of notoriety known for its narcotic fuelled visions."

Elryia sniffed. "You told them they were drugged. This only stalls proceedings."

"Oh quite the contrary. The council will need to make a choice. They can let the incident go and sweep it under the proverbial rug my dear, or they can make it public knowledge that the King is a supporter to Cults of Khathar and risk the wrath of the Matrons of Eroth in the process. Something I would not wish in his position if I valued my crown." He leaned in to Cerberus. "Not that I'd mind."

"I'm sure Cerberus is very thankful for your help." Elryia muttered coldly.

"My help?" Selwyn feigned shock. "My good lady, he should thank Eroth that he has an ingenious sister from what I hear." He bowed low, his hair dripping water onto the floor. "We'll talk later." He whispered low enough that only Cerberus could hear him.

The window rattled in its frame against the storm outside. Cerberex frowned at it as she entered the small library and pulled the curtain closed, muffling the sound. The library was little more than six bookcases a handful of document drawers, and a desk at its centre. Her mother could often be found in the chair reading or re-reading some book but what with her brother's latest stunt, the room was empty and for the most part silent. A black bundle rested on the desk next to an open book and a silver rapier leaned to one side. Looking around for any sign that she was not alone, Cerberex moved quietly over to it and ran a hand over the cloak that wrapped it. It was soft velvet, not the heavy stuff. This was light and glided over her fingers. The tiny embroidered dragon with crossed knives beneath shimmered in silver thread, a nice touch if modest. As she unwrapped the cloak things clinked against each other. There was armour within, leather, not unlike her own but firmer. Plates had been inserted to the chest allowing flexibility while still strong enough to give a wayward arrow pause. It was form fitting of that there was no doubt with fur lining for comfort - wolf if she wasn't mistaken. As she turned the cuirass over in her hands two tiny vials clinked and rolled out of some pocket and onto the desk. Catching one she held it up and studied the liquid inside. Thick syrup appeared to crawl in the glass. Cerberex had a collection of interesting poisons and venoms herself that she had extracted in her years of hunting the monsters of the wilderness. This was unlike any natural excretion but more a synthesized reduction judging by its viscosity. Carefully she placed them standing upright.

Three tiny knives were hidden in the chest piece. Cerberex found them by accident as she ran her hands over the smooth leather to find hidden recesses beneath. She held each one up and allowed the lamp light to dance on their edges before replacing them in the order she had pulled them out. A second metallic glint caught her eye and she picked up and arm guard the leather tooled to display the same dragon and knives motif. She turned it over and examined the mechanical component underneath. To her eyes it appeared to be a tiny crossbow. Within the mechanism was a bolt no more than three or so inches long. Cerberex turned her head to one side as she brushed the black feather fletching just visible. "What have you been getting yourself into brother?" She whispered to herself.

"What are you doing Cerberex?"

Cerberex almost dropped the guard in surprise as her uncle entered the library.

Selwyn moved around her glancing at the items on the desk. "Does Cerberus know your looking over his things."

"I was just..." Cerberex began.

"No he doesn't." Cerberex flinched at the sound of her brother's voice.

She held up the arm guard to show off the bolt secured within. "I've seen this before."

"Well it's a bolt I'm sure there are hundreds around." Cerberus replied casually as he approached and re-wrapped the cloak around the items.

"Not like this." Cerberex insisted.

Cerberus shrugged. "I had it custom made. Maybe the weapon-smith liked the design and chose to make more. What can I say? I'm a trend setter!"

"Why haven't I seen others with them then?" Cerberex demanded.

"Well they are small for a reason sister." Cerberus picked the bundle up and cradled it under his arm.

Cerberex looked at him angry with his dismissive attitude. "What about this then?" She pointed at the segmented black leather of the cuirass. "Is this also a new trend? I have seen something at least similar to this too."

Cerberus's eyes narrowed. "What?"

Selwyn took a step forward placing a hand on Cerberus' shoulder. "Leather armour is everywhere Cerberex. Undoubtedly you've seen something like this before."

"Well this set trespassed on Dhal-Marrah land not a full day ago." Cerberex huffed and folded her arms.

"What?" Cerberus repeated, his eyebrow raising.

"Ah that would explain why you were so jumpy. Well, I'm sure you saw them off my dear, but again leather armour is easy to come by. Some styles are bound to be replicated now and then."

"Your telling me that it's just coincidence then. That Cerberus here is just keeping up with what ever is considered the in thing?" Cerberex asked heatedly. "Tell me brother when did you become such a patron of fashion? You, who spends so much of his time asking me the same question should I buy the newest trinket, bracelet, or ring to arrive by merchant or envoy."

Selwyn glanced at Cerberus. "You are perfectly right as usual dear niece. It seems too much of a co-incidence to be so. I will look into these bolts and armour styles you speak of and see if I can find anything unusual about them." Selwyn smiled at her but Cerberex's face remained irritated.

She sighed loudly. "Oh I'm sure you will. Very well, keep your secrets then but don't think I'm letting this drop." She turned on her heel and headed to the door.

"Sister!" Cerberex stopped as her hand touched the door. She turned back and looked at Cerberus. "You're reading too much into it. I know I have chastised you for your purchases in the past but this, well, it's for a girl." He stepped forward. "I know its shameful and you can taunt me about it later, but I commissioned it to impress."

Cerberex gave a laugh and smiled as he approached resting a finger under his chin. "Oh brother," she began leaning in to hug him. "How stupid do you think I am?" She whispered into his ear as they embraced.

Cerberus quickly pulled away. "Believe what you like then, but there's nothing to hide." He lied easily.

Cerberex pulled the door open a little. "That you so adamantly say so, tells me you have everything to hide little brother, and if you wont tell me, I guess I'll just have to investigate myself. After all I have a right to know why my house is being dragged through the mire." She left closing the door behind her.

The silence was heavy as Cerberex left. Cerberus listened as his sister's footsteps moved further and further away until they faded to nothing. For a moment he and Selwyn stared at the door of the library in stunned silence before Cerberus broke it, whistling low under his breath.

"That was close." He muttered to himself as he walked to the back of library.

Selwyn turned slowly his face a stern frown. "It was." He began to pace around the desk. "A trespasser she said." He stopped and glanced at Cerberus. "Who have you been sending out? Naturally, you know what this means. One of your crew has to put it delicately fucked up."

Cerberus's eyes were narrowed in thought. "No one. Excepting your assignment, there have been no hits in the last few weeks."

"Regardless, you need to find out who and more importantly why they revealed themselves." Selwyn sat in the chair behind the desk and steepled his fingers.

"Armour like this..." Cerberus rubbed his fingers on the thickness of the leather cuirass.

"Problem?" Selwyn asked.

Cerberus looked at him. "Far from it uncle, because there is only one person who wears leather quite this heavy that I know." His eyes drifted to the ceiling the room above of which he confidently knew to be his own.

Selwyn kneaded his forehead with his knuckles. "This is going to mean a conversation with your mother I fear and one that is going to make me rather unpopular." He sighed.

Cerberus looked at him. "No. She will never allow it."

Selwyn laughed. "Allow it? My dear nephew she doesn't have much of a choice. Blood will out and take it from me, there's only so long you'll be able to distract her for."

"She is my sister, not a tool uncle." Cerberus replied dangerously.

Selwyn folded his arms. "And you think that now her curiosity is peaked you will throw her off? Tell me boy, have you met the Watchers?"

"Yes." Cerberus replied sullenly.

"And you would say Cerberex is as good as those you have seen?" Selwyn continued.

Cerberus shrugged. "Better even."

Selwyn leaned forward. "Precisely."

Cerberus took in a deep breath. "What did you have in mind?"

Chapter 12:
Secrets

Cerberex plucked the petals from the tiny white flower one by one. A shout drifted from the house followed by another, then a male raised voice. Cerberus and mother she imagined. Served him right to finally be brought to heel. She looked down at crushed stalk in her palm.

"Feeling frustrated Cerberex?"

Cerberex looked up. A little less than five feet away her aunt stood, arms folded, her two tone hair pulled messily up onto her head. Cerberex swallowed her surprise and smiled. "Is it that obvious?"

Maleficent smiled. "Hard as it may be for you to believe my dear, there was once a time when I too had a brother that drove me a little wild."

Cerberex sniffed and walked to a small stone bench between them. "Cerberus is up to his neck in something." Maleficent sat down next to her, gliding across the ground in dark blue black velvet that draped across her form. Cerberex turned as she sat down. "I would do anything for my family aunt, you know I would." Something large smashed in the house, dragging her attention for a second. "Cerberus has always been a hot head but this - what ever this is." She paused. "He is going to get himself killed!"

Maleficent smiled and crossed her arms once more. "What if I told you that the reason they are fighting in there right now is because one wants to tell you everything and the other nothing." The corner of her mouth curled into a smile as Cerberex looked up.

"What do you mean?" Cerberex asked. "Aunt, you have that look about you that tells me you've been pulling strings. Please tell me that you are not responsible for Cerberus's recent behaviour?"

Maleficent's smile widened, her lips parting to reveal bright white teeth two of which were filed to fang-like sharpness. "While I'm delighted you think me capable of the task, Cerberus has always had a knack for getting himself into trouble. Let me ask you something first."

Cerberex's eyes narrowed in suspicion. "I... go on."

"How long have you known about Cerberus's nightly escapades? He's exceptionally discreet - well, usually." Cerberex's mouth opened but she held up a finger. "Bravo by the way on slipping away so quietly this time. It gave us quite a start to find you gone. Very little gets past your Uncle and I you see, " She leant in to Cerberex's ear. "And we've had many years of practice." She smiled. "Oh, your cousins were far from angelic."

Cerberex glanced at her. "He's my brother, I make it my business to know where he is. He and Lida especially. The lady has an ability to tempt him like no other. I overheard talking on the roof. Then saw him leave with another, so I followed."

"That's really quite impressive. Why?" Maleficent prompted.

"Because it's as if Cerberus wears two faces. The one everyone sees during the day and the one that stirs when he thinks he is alone. I follow because I worry that he thinks himself something special and what that might do to the rest of us." Cerberex looked at Maleficent expectantly.

"Ah yes. Well, your mother, your brother, and your uncle are currently in heated debate about your involvement." Maleficent looked up listening intently to the silence. "I would say its currently fifty fifty as to which is winning." She turned back. "You said to your uncle something about a trespasser?"

"In black. Fast and skilled. I found him hanging around the standing stone." Cerberex replied quickly.

"What were you doing there?" Maleficent asked with sudden directness.

Cerberex waved her finger. "Your turn."

Maleficent sighed. "Really Cerberex?" She replied, a pained expression covering her face. "I spent years tutoring you before you chose the Watchers. We've covered the family tradition did you really believe it was nothing but history? I respect you want to protect Cerberus but honestly my dear, who did you imagine would take that mantle?" She watched Cerberex's head snap up.

"No..." Cerberex looked at her aunt sideways imagining some jest.

Maleficent returned her look. "Did you really believe that all those years you were away, your brother sat and did nothing? Oh he plays the play boy lordling very well, I grant you."

"No." Cerberex repeated. "It's... I would know. That's not us. "

Maleficent ignored her but her eyes glistened with glee. "Oh yes my dear." She replied matter-of-factly and listened for a moment. "Twenty-five to seventy five I reckon," Something heavy hit a window and thankfully bounced. Maleficent looked at Cerberex's shocked face. "Or not."

Cerberex looked at the crushed stalk. "You're not serious?! We stepped away. The family stepped away from all of that. No wonder they're arguing."

"Oh its not him they are arguing about. It's about whether you should know my dear - or at least, what you should know." Maleficent leaned in whispering. "Of course your uncle is very persuasive." She shrugged. "But then your mother can be very stubborn. There's only really one way to truly influence..." Maleficent didn't finish her sentence. Cerberex was already stood, across lawn, and halfway up the trellis that lead to the stained glass windows of the her mother's study on the second floor.

Maleficent dusted herself down and stood. "Whoops." She whispered to herself. A second later the garden was empty.

Cerberex pulled the stained glass window open and leaped through, drawing herself back up fluidly. "How dare you attempt keep me in the dark!"

The room before her was relatively small, filled with comfortable chairs, a small leather trimmed desk and shelves upon shelves of books - her mother's personal library. Her mother, uncle, and brother, all sat, looked in shock and surprise at her explosive entrance.

"Cerberex!" Her mother was the first to regain composure. "That is not how a young lady enters a room." Her eyes were wide as she slowly stood from behind the desk.

"That's how this one enters." Cerberex replied petulantly. "How could you not tell me?" The question now aimed at Cerberus sitting opposite in a deep red armchair.

"My dear..." Selwyn began.

"And you, organising everything behind the scenes. Excitement? Wasn't that what you referred to us as? You have known all this time and played me like some human half-wit. Tell me, are you part of this shady underbelly to our house too?" Cerberex rounded on him before he could so much as provide an answer, verbally forcing him to take a seat.

"What are you babbling about Cerberex? How dare you speak to your uncle like that." Her mother stalked out from behind the desk. Her hands held loosely behind her back.

"You are a consummate liar mother, but its not working this time." Cerberex hissed.

Selwyn kneaded his forehead. "Maleficent my darling, this is clearly your work." He whispered to himself. He looked up at Cerberex with a weighted stare. "Sit." He instructed, "and get a hold of yourself." The tone brooked no argument and Cerberex perched on the window sill sullenly silent. He steepled his fingers and her mother, Elryia, scowled at him. "Don't look at me Elryia. You made it plain that you had no intention of talking to Cerberex about this. Did you seriously believe that you could hide from it forever? You lied to her. Told her that the family had no interest in outside engagements, all to shelter her from the business of her own house. It is no wonder she is furious."

"I had hoped there would be no need." Elryia muttered through gritted teeth. "I had hoped that at least one of my children might be spared. That I might be permitted to have one free of the burden, one to live a long life in peace."

"Every time, you told me that Cerberus was just a tear away. All that time you made me believe it was Cerberus's fault that the name Dhal-Marrah was nothing but a joke." Cerberex snarled.

"Because it is!" Elryia shouted. "You're brother should never have taken you're father's place. Look where it has got us. We are reviled by the other houses. Why else would I look to arrange a match for you if not to protect you from the indelible scar that being Dhal-Marrah brings."

Cerberex recoiled for a moment. "But I am the heir to this house. You can't take that away from me." She whispered defensively.

"Then behave like it." Elryia replied before turning back to Selwyn.

"You can't deny it now Elryia" The sudden tension was cut by Selwyn's calm, quiet voice. "You must let her..."

"You have no say here." Elryia replied immediately.

Selwyn stood angrily. "I am not the one driving your children away Elryia. I understand your concerns I really do, but this is not something you can control like everything else in this house." He turned and paced behind the chair for a moment. "You know this ... why are we even having this debate?" He slammed his hands down on the back of the chair. "She is a Dhal-Marrah."

Cerberex glanced over to Cerberus catching his eye. He sat, his arms folded, a sliver of white hair hanging across his cheek. He took in a deep breath and raised his eyebrows looking at her. She narrowed her eyes and caught sight of the familiar looking armour carefully folded on his lap. Cerberus watched her gaze as it flicked to the armour then back at him and grinned. "Fancy a set of your own do you sister?" He whispered.

"One more word out of you Cerberus and I will ensure that you don't talk for the rest of the week." Elryia didn't even turn but her hand shot back wreathed in faintly violet sparks.

"Well that hardly seems fair." The door opened seemingly of its own volition as Maleficent entered. "He's done rather well at keeping out of your personal feud." She waved her hand and a third arm chair ground its way across the floor. Maleficent arranged the skirt of her dress and sat between Cerberus and Selwyn. "Now," She pointed at a decanter of red wine on a side table and the crystal glass along side began filling. "let's desist in the shouting contest. I'm growing rather tired of it and" she gestured to the smashed vase in the corner. "It's beginning to have quite a cost." She snapped her fingers and the filled glass floated gently into her extended hand. She took a long sip and sighed. "Elryia darling, stop postulating and take a seat will you? You're beginning to look like one of my experiments that's been on the burner to long." She took another sip, savouring it with her eyes closed. Silence.

"Much better." Maleficent sighed.

"Dendrion would..." Elryia began again.

Maleficent cut her off. "If anyone here knows my dead brother's mind it's going to be me. I spent centuries living in this house with him - far more than your paltry marriage." She finished the glass. "Not that it matters much. There is only one person here who can ultimately make a decision about this."

"And who is that Aunt Mal?" Cerberus asked looking up with a smile of success.

"Do wipe that ridiculous grin from your face Cerberus. Your sister." Maleficent bent and peered around to Cerberex. "Cerberex darling?"

Cerberex's mouth opened and closed as all eyes in the room turned to her.

"Mal my sweet, I understand that you think it should be entirely Cerberex's decision but realistically with all things considered, what she's been up to, there really can only be one option." Selwyn interrupted.

"What rubbish! Her mother and I do very well knowing almost everything and yet remain blissfully unaware of the exact details." Maleficent replied.

"A slightly different scenario in your case my dear." Selwyn continued.

"Semantics Selwyn." Maleficent brushed him off. She returned her gaze and smiled, her fangs peaking just slightly over her bottom lip. "You are an incredibly talented and intelligent young lady Cerberex. You will someday be head of this house. So you have a right to know all the details. It is your choice and many before you have lived in happy ignorance. That said hundreds of years of Dhal-Marrah leadership has stemmed from..."

"I want to see it." Cerberex could feel the breath catch in her throat as Maleficent's voice faded to silence. Her heart thumped in her chest with excitement and terror at the same time. "I want to see it for myself."

Maleficent nodded. "Then that decides it."

"You would let a girl no older than..." Elryia began, rising to her feet.

Maleficent's head snapped back to her. "You were planning to wed my niece to a ranking member of house Valouris. I think that renders your coming objection rather obsolete don't you?" She took a deep breath. "Cerberus, would you be a good host and introduce your sister to the 'family'. Your mother and I have some things we need to discuss." She looked miserably at the empty glass in her hand. "Something I feel will require a lot more wine."

Cerberex caught the eyes of her aunt on one side of the desk meet those of her mother on the other and watched the contest of wills.

"You do not get to judge this issue Maleficent." Elryia whispered, her voice filled with passion. "Keep to your little experiments and leave the governing of my family to me."

Maleficent smiled and examined her finger nails lacquered in the colour of nightshade. "Once upon a time Elryia, you and I were such good friends." She sighed. "No in this I do get to place some semblance of order. This persistent argument has gone far enough. You are not the only Lady Dhal-Marrah in this house, you are the second." She spoke the last four words quietly under her breath. Turning to Cerberus and Cerberex, she raised her eyebrows and gestured to the door. "Well? What are you two waiting for? Have at it."

Cerberex looked at her brother then back to Aunt Mal. "You have some family secrets to divulge brother."

Cerberus stood slowly and backed towards the door, his eyes firmly fixed on his mother as if retreating from a cornered bear. He turned and held it open looking at Cerberex with expectation. Cerberex stepped past him and Cerberus closed the door behind them. They both waited for the inevitable screaming match only to be greeted by silence then - "I can still see your feet!" Cerberex concealed a laugh and moved down towards the main landing.

Cerberus caught her from behind and pulled her to a stop. "You know I don't like this idea." His face was sullen.

Cerberex smiled as she turned and folded her arms pouting. "Oh don't you want to share your toys little brother?" She snorted a laugh of derision and turned her back on him. "Lighten up, you look almost as upset as when mother refused to let you keep that Turatee you fished out of the lake."

"You have no idea what you are getting into Cerberex." Cerberus called after her.

" Oh I have a pretty good idea. You see while you were having daddy time with father, I was sat in that room back there listening to the pair of them drone on and on about this house." She turned, her hands placed on her hips. "Dhal-Marrah. The black dragon. The menace that isn't seen. The death, and oh I'm sure there were others but my personal favourite was The Silent Execution."

Cerberus smirked and shook his head. "You are way off."

"Am I? Enlighten me." Cerberex mused.

Cerberus stalked towards her with a predator's grace. "You're not going to be able to un-see it afterwards."

"Are you trying to put me off?" Cerberex purred.

"I'm advising you that it's all or nothing - there is no in-between ground." Cerberus stood barely a foot from her now.

"Aunt Mal seems to disagree with you on that point." She replied, watching him circle around her and continue to the stairs the other side of the landing.

"Relics of a different system." Cerberus's voice echoed back to her.

Cerberex laughed as she jogged to catch him up. "I wouldn't let Aunt Mal hear you call her a relic, nor mother for that matter."

Cerberus smiled taking the stairs slowly. "Wouldn't dream of it."

Cerberex caught his arm halfway down, coasting him to stop. "Seriously Cerberus. I know you want to play the dashing dark knight, riding the rooftops of the city, righting wrongs and slaying monsters. I can only imagine how tedious life must be cooped up with the pair of them, but you almost got yourself killed. I find it sweet you've taken to keeping old traditions alive, but still."

Cerberus looked at her with a mixture of irritation and glee. "You seriously under-estimate my abilities sister." He pulled away and headed in the direction of the dinning hall.

"I wasn't the one that needed to be rescued from prison." Cerberex muttered.

Cerberus opened the dining hall's door and stepped within checking the room for unwanted eyes. "I had it in hand."

Cerberex raised an eyebrow as she followed him to the blank wall space further down the room, running her hand along the smooth surface of the table. "Sure you did. That's why I had to murder five people to get to you."

Cerberus paused. "Yes I've been meaning to ask you about that. Are you," he paused looking for the right word, "alright?"

Cerberex looked at him awkwardly. "What? Of course I'm alright." She snapped at him.

"But how do you, how did it feel?" He pushed.

"I ... I didn't feel anything. I did what needed to be done to stop you making an arse out of yourself." She gave him a slight push. "This isn't about delving into my secrets its about yours."

Cerberus smiled coolly but there was a glint of mischief in his eyes. "You're going to regret that statement in a minute."

"What makes you think that?" Cerberex asked, her patience thinning.

Cerberus turned back to the wall. "Because I was much like you the first time I entered the route." He laughed quietly under his breath and smiled at the wall.

Cerberex watched in surprise as a portion of the solid stonework in front of them faded before her eyes revealing a narrow path outlined in faintly glowing red.

"Welcome to the route sister. There's no going back now." Cerberus whispered as he passed within.

Chapter 13:
The House of Assassins

The corridor beyond extended for only a short distance in almost pitch blackness, before suddenly dropping down a steep flight of what presumably were stone stairs. Cerberex's vision was well honed to seeing through even the darkest night, yet this was a darkness so complete she could feel the sense of vertigo rise from her stomach.

"Keep up with me and follow each of my steps." Cerberus's disembodied voice seemed hollow in the strange blackness.

"If I could see anything that wouldn't be so difficult." She replied in annoyance as her foot skidded on a chipped stair.

Cerberus's hand grabbed her by the waist to prevent her moving further as a snapping sound of tiny metal fragments echoed from below. As the noise subsided Cerberus let go of his breath. "You're going to need to be a lot lighter on your feet from now on."

"Then may be you should consider installing some lighting." Cerberex replied sarcastically. She ran her left hand along the wall to steady herself, feeling the smooth stone of the house's foundations.

"This was a terrible idea." Cerberus sighed. "Come on not far now." He guided her by the hand, taking the steps one by one until the stone beneath Cerberex's finger tips changed to rough compacted soil and rubble and they emerged through a narrow archway into a wide room dimly lit. Black and white stone tiles covered the floor as she stepped on to it mirroring Cerberus's footwork and she took in the ancient stonework.

"Eroth's teeth!" Cerberex muttered as her eyes adjusted to the haze of stirred dust. The far end of the wall was carved from the very bedrock into the semblance of an enormous dragon, wings unfurled as it swooped. A single unassuming wooden door in the centre of its mouth amidst dozens of carved, sharp teeth. She caught sight of two dark silhouettes move along the edge of her vision either side. Her hands instinctively wandering to the knives at her sides.

"They wont harm you because you're with me." Cerberus whispered back to her.

"Do I look worried?" She returned.

Cerberus smirked. "You should be."

Cerberex let the comment slide as she followed him along an unmarked path across the tiled floor right up to the maw of the beast. Tentatively, she stretched out a hand and touched the curve of a tooth. Catching Cerberus's grin out of the corner of her eye. "What?"

Cerberus held his hands up in mock surrender. "Oh nothing." He continued to grin as he watched, placing his hand on the door's latch. "Shall we?"

Cerberex looked up and shielded her eyes as Cerberus pushed the door wide revealing the bright gold of torchlight. When her eyes adjusted, she peered through the door. Figures dressed in black leather armour or sparring wraps walked along the hallway beyond, moving in and out of doorways on either side. She looked at Cerberus. Cerberus looked back and nodded to the hallway. Lightly Cerberex stepped through and felt Cerberus follow behind, closing the door with a gentle click.

"Welcome sister." Cerberus whispered as he took her hand and steered her away from the door like a scared horse likely to bolt.

"Who are all these..." Cerberex began as she felt the suspiciously appraising look from those who walked past.

"Well you are a born Dhal-Marrah, House of the Assassin. You tell me who you think they are. Consider them the extended family." Cerberus replied barely able to contain his enjoyment at the discomfort she was feeling.

"They're all..." Cerberex allowed herself to slowly be guided further. She peered through a single doorway, nudging the door open further with her foot. Beyond a room at least twice that of the dining hall stretched out filled with plain wooden bunks. Most looked like they had not been touched in sometime but those nearest the door had seen recent activity.

"They're assassin's," Cerberus finished for her, "or at least most of them are."

"Most?" Cerberex asked, allowing herself to be pulled away.

"Well some of them are still just training." He replied absently as they passed a small mess room prepared for the next meal. "Ah, you'll like this one I think." He paused at a door and removed a set of keys from his pocket, carefully inserting them into the lock and taking a torch from its sconce in the wall nearby to light the way within.

Cerberex looked at him questioningly as she entered. "Oh my!" She gasped at the scene in the dim torchlight. The room beyond was the size of a large closet and every wall was covered in shelves and rows of weapons. Without even thinking Cerberex's hand stretched out and seized a small crossbow attached to a heavy wrist-guard, dislodged the bolt within and held it up accusingly.

Cerberus nodded. "Yes, you've seen it before." He sighed with irritation but the smile refused to leave his face. "You can have one if you want. It's not like I don't have many spare." He sniggered.

Cerberex put it down. "I'll pass." She leaned in as she passed back through the doorway. "My bow could out shoot your little pea-shooters any day."

"Oh you think so?" Cerberus scoffed as he re-locked the door and placed the torch back on the wall sconce. He turned and beckoned her to follow. "Come with me."

Cerberex followed him intrigued. Passing other similar doors as the hallway became darker till it was only lit by the residual light of a large single arch at the far end. The closer they came the more Cerberex was sure she could hear the sounds of combat. "Do you hear that?"

Cerberus smiled. "Of course." He continued towards the lit archway at the far end. Silhouettes, many of them, danced against the opposite wall.

As they approached Cerberex was confronted with a black clad group. Cerberus placed his hands on her shoulders and pressed through to the front where two female Drau traded blows in a circle of sand indented into the floor. She could feel the looks of irritation. As Cerberus followed, these looks retracted to ones of slight respect and those blocking the path made way as he passed through. Cerberex raised an eyebrow.

"What?" Cerberus grinned.

"You..." Cerberex began accusingly before her sentence was cut short by a jolt to the shoulder as a hooded figure moved passed her and Cerberus without comment. "Was it something I said?" She turned on Cerberus, the indignation writ large upon her face.

Cerberus watched the figure move into the darkness beyond the arch and disappear. "No one you should worry about." He muttered before returning his gaze back to the fight all charm and smiles.

Cerberex cocked her head to one side questioningly before a heavy thud from the pit followed by a roar of approval from the small crowd, drowned anything she might have said. She watched as coin exchanged hands quietly between the group and the older looking female in the pit held out a hand to the other now prone on the ground. Cerberus was tutting.

"Negari knows not to get so close." He shook his head.

Cerberex turned her gaze, analysing Negari's opponent. "Who is the other?"

Cerberus shrugged. "Another assassin."

Cerberex narrowed her eyes as she caught the barest flash of metal disappear into the winner's palm. "She cheated." She hissed into Cerberus's ear.

"What did you expect? We don't fight fair." Cerberus laughed at his sister's look of outrage.

"We?" Cerberex repeated, scowling as the female stalked the pit to cries of approval.

"Yes, 'we', as in me - they, " he paused and gestured around the room. "Us."

Cerberex sneered as the female noticed them and stepped up.

"Cerberus! Darling! Enjoy the performance did you?" She purred.

Cerberus inclined his head fractionally. "Meera."

Meera smiled turning her gaze to Cerberex. "And who is this ... this unmarked stranger in our midst." The words were laced with curiosity.

Cerberex met the challenge of her gaze without blinking. Cerberus laid a hand on her shoulder as if sensing her irritation.

"Allow me to introduce Cerberex Dhal-Marrah, my sister, Meera." Cerberus replied quietly.

Meera's eyes lit up. "The Cerberex Dhal-Marrah?" He face split into a wide smile of bright white teeth.

"Do you know of any others?" Cerberex asked as she held herself to her full height.

Meera giggled and gave an over accentuated bow.

Cerberus gave her shoulder a slight squeeze. "You'll have to excuse Meera. She has a habit of tending towards the dramatic."

Cerberex nodded in understanding. "Of course brother. I'd expect no less of a cheat." She winced as her brother's nails dug into her shoulder.

"Play nice sister." Cerberus whispered in her ear.

Meera held up a hand. "No, no, Cerberus darling, her candour is - refreshing." Her gaze switched to Cerberex. "Your new here so I'll forgive the slight." She smiled but her eyes were like knives. "Especially when the one in question is a pampered noble lady."

Cerberex snorted and brushed off Cerberus's hand, feeling the press of his nails once more in her shoulder. "Pampered?"

"Let it go Cerberex." Cerberus warned.

Cerberex took a step forward as Meera turned to leave. "Pampered am I? Would you like to see how well a pampered lady can do?"

Meera turned laughing. "Oh you can't be serious? What do you think this is? A tavern brawl? Come and find me when you've been blooded."

"Technically she has." Cerberus replied before Cerberex could respond. His mouth curled at the corners as Meera looked at him in genuine surprise. "She's killed no less than five which, I think is more than you did on your first run?" He boasted and folded his arms.

Meera turned back to Cerberex the surprise mixed with the slightest suggestion of respect. "Well," She placed her hands behind her back looking up and down, taking in Cerberex's posture, stance, and capabilities. "If she has your leave master, I'll happily demonstrate my capabilities once more."

Cerberex took a step forward but Cerberus stopped her. "What? Do I need approval now?" She muttered dangerously, under her breath, suddenly aware of the silence in the room, the ten or so pairs of eyes on them, and the sudden sense of being out of place that lurched in her stomach.

"Meera?" Cerberus called and held out his hand. Meera looked at it. Cerberus sighed. "The knuckles?"

Meera clicked her tongue in annoyance then after a moments pause handed them over. "As you wish."

Cerberus smiled and turned to Cerberex. "Knives." He didn't need to ask twice. Cerberex had already unbuckled the twin harnesses that bound them to her upper legs and waist. The blades clattered on stone. Cerberus grabbed her by the hand and pulled her in as if to embrace her. "Do not let her get too close for too long. Her left side is marginally weaker than the right."

"You don't think I'm capable brother?" Cerberex sniffed.

"Far from it." He pushed her away, "but so is she." He clapped a hand against her arm and smiled. She smiled back.

Cerberex landed lightly in the sand to the sound of clinking coins as those around them began to wager on the outcome. Within the small arena, Meera paced the perimeter like a caged lion. Cerberex stood still as the sounds of the crowd dulled into background static. Slowly she took in a deep breath, feeling the steady beat of her heart in her chest, the thrum of adrenaline in her veins and let it go. Her vision crystallized as instincts trained through years of hunting with Agrellon's finest came rushing to the fore. She blinked and when her eyes opened again Meera's fist came rushing towards her face. Instinctually, she moved left. Returning with a swift punch designed to wind her opponent. Meera spun around her arm, grabbing it and forcing it behind her back. Cerberex could hear the crowd laugh. Gritting her teeth she threw Meera bodily over her head, spinning out with a kick that should have sent her flying into the sand. Impossibly, Meera moved just beyond the kicks reach.

"Is that the best that you can do?" Meera chuckled. A second later, and she was at Cerberex's throat.

Cerberex gasped at the speed as the fingers pushed into the jugular. She raised her hand to bring it down on Meera's arms. Meera caught it mid-air. Feeling spots of black begin to collect at the edges of her vision, Cerberex stamped down hard against Meera's foot. For a split second the grip loosened. Cerberex twisted away sucking in lungfuls of air, contorting beneath the swing of a fist, and spinning a kick into the back of Meera's knee, forcing her down for a moment. As Meera turned, she hit down hard with her fist. It connected.

Cerberex could feel the intake of breath from the crowd as the crack of the hit reverberated around the room.

Meera leaped to her feet, sweeping her hair from her eyes with one hand. Muttering and whispers followed as she brought her hand up to her lip, pulling it away to see her own blood upon her fingers. Her eyes flicked up to Cerberex and a smile pulled at her cheeks. "Now that's more like it." She purred.

The two circled each other slowly. Meera licking the blood from her lip and Cerberex feeling her breathing come more rapidly than she would like. Silence hung in the room like a suffocating blanket. Cerberex's ears thundered with the sound of her own heart beat. Meera took a quick step forward and she darted backwards in response.

"You know you're very good for a pampered noble." Meera paced steadily back and forth before sighing. "But I'm better."

Cerberex had no time to dodge, no time to assess, she barely saw her opponent move. The sudden roar of the crowd was the only indication that Meera had disappeared from one spot only to re-appear in another. The fist smacked into her ribs forcing her to bend double. Followed by a sickening crack as Meera's knee collided with her nose. Cerberex could feel the blood begin to pour as she lurched forward, swinging wildly. Unimaginably, Meera was suddenly behind her. A skid that made the sand flick outwards and Cerberex felt her legs go out from beneath her.

"Enough." A voice commanded above the din.

A fist slammed into Cerberex's right temple. She caught a blur of black movement before another smacked painfully into her left. She fell forward bracing herself on her arms and coughed a wad of blood and phlegm onto the sand.

"Enough!" The voice shouted louder. Cerberus's voice.

Cerberex felt cool air brush behind her. She reached back grabbing at nothing as her head snapped back with Meera's arm wrapped around her throat.

"You could yield?" Meera's whisper was hot against her neck.

"Dhal-Marrahs" Cerberex gripped the arm with both hands. "Don't..." She pulled with all her strength. "Yield." She felt the arm move just fractionally.

"Pity." The word felt like a shard of ice had slipped down Cerberex's spine. Then with a sudden taught click, her world turned to black.

Cerberex rolled over coughing congealed blood as she wrenched her head away from the acrid smell. The right half of her face was coated in a layer of sand and her head felt like a dozen northern mammoths had just passed their summer migration inside it. A pair of firm hands circled under her arms pulling her up into sitting position and dragging her across to the lip of the circles edge. Cerberex blinked, one eye slightly swollen. For a moment she saw only a black shadow. She blinked twice more, picking out the details of a heavily hooded individual.

"Take it easy." The voice under the hood was soft and quiet. "You're quite the firecracker!"

Cerberex winced as her neck gave a resounding crack. "Did I win?" She grimaced.

"No." The voice chuckled. "But I'll give you credit for having the balls to try!"

"Did my brother tell you to keep an eye on me?" She leaned forward daring to peer beneath the hood, only for the figure to stand and take a step back. The sound of oncoming footsteps and voices met her ears, dragging her attention away. When she looked back the figure was gone.

"Cerberex!"

She tried to stand as Cerberus's voice carried through the air.

"Eroth! My dear niece you look like you've gone five rounds with an angry wildborn!" Selwyn placed an arm beneath her as she wobbled. "What in all the hells did you do Cerberus?"

Cerberex raised a hand. "I'm fine uncle." She looked up to see Selwyn's worried face.

"You and I have a very different understanding of the word 'Fine' young lady." He reached into his pocket and pulled a vial of gently pulsating amber liquid. "Luckily for you, so does your aunt."

"How reassuring." Cerberex joked, seizing it and knocking back the contents in a single gulp. For a second she felt a sudden surge of heartburn, then a slow warming sensation crept along her muscles, forcing them to relax. The pain in her head cleared and the blur of her vision slowly merged back into one cohesive picture as the swelling of her eye receded.

"Apparently I didn't win." Cerberex sat on the lip of the pit and folded her arms.

"Did you honestly expect to my dear?" Selwyn perched to one side of her as Cerberus took the other.

"Are they all that rude and conceited or just that one?" She rounded on Cerberus who raised his hands in mock surrender.

"Hey, you challenged." Cerberus laughed. "You should have seen her face when you squared that punch - worth it!" He lowered his hands. "Meera can be intensive at times."

Cerberex looked Cerberus up and down a few times. He'd changed. His torso armoured in interlocking black leather that she had seen him holding what seemed only moments before, her father's rapier was belted to his waist. Her eyes drifted to where her knives would have been.

"It's all right." Cerberus began, sensing the question. "They're safe."

"Safe is not here." Cerberex replied curtly and then turned to Selwyn. "But you are." She turned back to her brother. "I thought this club of yours was fairly exclusive."

"It's not a club." Cerberus corrected almost immediately. "And Uncle Selwyn is technically already a member - has been for years."

Selwyn waved a hand as Cerberex looked at him with a raised eyebrow. "Retired - thankfully."

"Then why are you - wait..." Cerberex began and then looked back at her brother's attire. "He's here to collect me isn't he?"

Cerberus knuckled her hair as he stood up and simply smiled.

"And where are you going? Last time you ended up in prison and you're hardly healed. If you tell me now it will save me the leg work when I need to save your sorry arse again." Cerberex added, stiffly rising to her feet.

"Your hardly in any shape to be doing that yourself." Cerberus laughed.

"Children!" They both stopped as Selwyn held his hands out sighing. "Cerberex, if it's important that you know, I'm merely a liaison. Typically I follow up on the things your brother wants..." he searched for the word and smiled. "Researched. Your brother is working on a pet project of mine."

"Research?" Cerberex repeated. "How long was I out?"

Cerberus and Selwyn exchanged a look. "It's nothing, a little run that's all. Just keeping tabs on the houses and I'm taking some friends with me." Cerberus explained. "I'll be perfectly safe."

"How lovely. When are we leaving?" Cerberex asked expectantly.

"The deal was I would show you the route. Nothing was said about you joining in with me on my night-time walks." Cerberus countered.

"Cerberus." Cerberex stood a foot away. "It has been barely a day since I hauled you unconscious to the doors of this house. If you think that I am letting you out of my sight again so soon little brother, you're in need of some serious cranial readjustment." She sighed. "Why are you doing this anyway? You've got what you wanted, Lida is presumably somewhere in the house. What more could you possibly want from the palace?"

Not for the first time was Cerberus thankful that his skin tone was dark enough to cover the heat he felt in his face as she mentioned Lida's name. He sucked his teeth for a moment as he thought.

"You invited her in, you can't stop her from being inquisitive." Selwyn chuckled quietly.

"I wasn't given a choice." Cerberus almost whispered. "I do not want her involved in this." He hissed.

Cerberex bristled. "Well, too late now brother. I'm knee deep in this hole of yours, so you better show me just how far it all goes."

Cerberus drew himself up. There was a dangerous belligerence to his sister's voice. "Very well." He said suddenly breaking the tension. "You'll find your knives in the armoury." He threw her a bundle of keys. "Go and get them, help yourself to anything else you think you could use. Let's see just how far your willing to go."

Cerberex caught the keys with one hand a smile plastered across her face. "I'll need my bow."

Cerberus shrugged. "I'm not leaving for a few hours yet, there's time."

"Not quite what I was getting at." Cerberex replied.

"Ah, of course." Selwyn smiled at her. "Allow me my dear niece, to escort you back to home turf when your ready." Selwyn nodded to Cerberus and then followed Cerberex who had it not been for the twinge in her joints, looked like she could have skipped all the way to the armoury.

Cerberus waited until their foot steps had faded down the hallway beyond before in a blur of movement he was across the room dragging a hooded figure from the shadows of the room's equipment stands and slamming it into the nearby wall. The shadow gave a grunt at the force of the impact, knocking back his hood to reveal the palest blonde hair. Cerberus tore down the scarf that masked his face.

"Good Evening Kane." Cerberus smiled, with all the congeniality of a devil.

Chapter 14:
Wild-born

Cerberus waited. He was rapidly realising he had become unaccustomed to waiting. The three others nearby we similarly irritable at the delay. Meera paced like an angry cat. She'd taken the news of Cerberex joining this run surprisingly well. Cerberus hated to think what it meant if having his sister around actually improved Meera's attitude. Maybe that one hit had knocked some sense that Cerberus had failed to teach in years of trying - that was a hideous thought! Kane stood in the shadows hood and scarf up. Cerberus smirked, even in this light he could still see the shiny purple bruise beneath his right eye. He'd confessed to accidentally bumping into Cerberex fairly quickly. He'd also insisted that he'd had no idea who she was and that she definitely didn't know who or what he was. That alone had saved him from Cerberus knocking him clean out. He wasn't sure if he believed him, realistically he'd been too pissed off that all this had happened because of one sloppy move. He watched Kane intently noting the stiffness to his pose, the new oil sheen of recently cleaned armour - preening are we Kane? No he thought, No. There was going to be another conversation dependent on tonight's activities. His eyes flickered to the third. Seska, sat cross-legged with perfect balance on the branch just above Kane tossing a knife and catching it again. Her muttering was too low even for Cerberus to discern but he could guess nonetheless.

A twig cracked. In a second each of the other three assassins were on alert weapons drawn. Cerberus didn't bother turning around. He smiled. "You're late." He watched as a crushed twig fell to the ground in front of him followed by a gentle thud as Cerberex dropped from the next tree.

"I've never been late a day in my life dear brother. You are simply early." Cerberex purred.

Cerberus looked to his left. It occurred to him that he had never seen Cerberex fully armed since the day she had returned home. She cut quite the imposing figure. She wore little in the way of actual armour. Only around her middle and up to her chest, protecting her vital organs, did she have anything that might stop a blade. The rest was hide or fur. In comparison to the other assassins she looked - what was the word? Feral?

Meera stepped forward nodding at the two knives strapped to Cerberex's thighs. "I take it you know how to use those?" The words left her mouth and the tip of one blade immediately touched her chin.

"Would you like to test me?" Cerberex's voice whispered.

Meera smiled and pushed the knife away with a finger. "I'll trust you."

"Enough." Cerberus whispered. "Get on or get out."

Cerberex's eyes narrowed for a moment. She inclined her head.

The corners of Cerberus's mouth curled. "I hope you can keep up." A blur of motion and he scaled the outer wall and disappeared towards the city.

Meera grinned at Cerberex. "Well this should be most entertaining." She gave a mock bow before her form seemed to shift smoke-like up and over the wall in persuite of Cerberus.

Suddenly finding herself alone Cerberex launched herself up the wall and over. By the time her feet lightly touched the ground the other side, Meera, Cerberus and those that had stood with him were already beginning to scale the buildings on the city's outskirts. Eroth's fangs they were fast! Cerberex sprinted towards the block-like overhang of the nearest house. Using a stack of discarded wooden crates to boost her leap. A strong hand reached out and grabbed her arm as she pulled herself up. The individual was tall, and heavier built than Cerberus. "Do you need help my lady?" The voice was muffled behind a black scarf but Cerberex caught the indulgent politeness in his voice and bristled. Snatching her arm away and running across the rooftop as fast as her legs would carry her.

Under the covering shadow of a partially eroded gargoyle, Cerberus watched his sister run by. He'd also watched Kane stop. Of course he could have told him that Cerberex would never accept any help but then where would be the fun in that. Cerberex jumped past, oblivious to him, with all the speed and grace of a cat. Fast, but she would never be able to keep pace with them long distance. Cerberus sighed as he shifted from his hiding spot to the other side of the roof top in a heartbeat. "Shame. Selwyn was right. She'd have made an excellent candidate were she half a century younger.

Cerberex sensed the shimmer of movement to her left as she made the next leap. So Cerberus wanted to see what she was capable of did he? She smiled to herself. "Well little brother, if you are in search of a show, then a show you shall have." She slowed her pace. Inhaling deeply of the night air, feeling its cool touch against her cheek. The slight scent of smoke carried across the current of the breeze, rising from the city as the lanterns burned. She could sense the crawl of those to brave the night on the streets like the drum of tiny insects in the back of her head. She could hear ... the whisper of fabric, the patter of light feet speeding across tile and stone, the imperceptible squeak of leather. Her eyes shot open. "You're not the only one with a few tricks." Without breaking her stride she shifted her direction, slithered down a drainage pipe, and headed east towards The Vaults.

Shattered structures jutted from the ground like titanic rib-cages. A fine mist coiled around them. Cerberus stopped and perched on the ledge of a fractured wall. A moment later Meera joined him from above, then Kane, and finally Seska. He waited patiently for a fourth set of expectant footsteps. Minutes passed.

"You didn't loose her already did you?" Meera whispered so close that Cerberus could again feel her breath on his neck. "I thought you said she was good enough."

Cerberus hissed at her through his teeth. His eyes darting to every shadow across the titan graveyard of buildings. Once these structures had been part of the ever growing outskirts of Everfall. Dedicated to the Goddess Eroth, they held the final remains of Drau heroes. Ancient family lines had been laid to rest within these mighty stone palaces to the dead. All gone. Nothing but ash and dust, and shattered ruins made long before his time. Eradicated by the machines of the Dwentar nation. Within this labyrinth Cerberex may never find them and he had not the luxury of time to wait.

"Double back and find her." Cerberus muttered.

"What?" Meera recoiled in surprise. "You can't be serious."

"You heard me Meera." Cerberus growled.

"I'll go." Kane's voice cut in.

"Looking for someone?" A female voice, immeasurably loud against the quiet. Cerberex stepped across the thin parapet of what once had been a knife like tower opposite. She stood stark black against the pale sliver of the moon.

Cerberus stood as Meera chuckled, "Oh, I take it back."

Freeing a deep breath of frustration. Cerberus smiled before appearing at her side a moment later.

Cerberex disguised her surprise at the sudden speed of Cerberus. "Did you think that trick would loose me so easily?"

Cerberus was taken by the brightness of her eyes. "No." He replied.

Cerberex leaned in. He could smell the faint perfume of her hair. "I've tracked animals with more stealth." Cerberex dropped form the building.

Cerberus felt the hush of fabric as Meera appeared at his side watching Cerberex stalk the shadows. "You know, I think I might like your sister after all." There was a resonant tone of respect within her voice that Cerberus found surprising.

Cerberus dropped catching up to his sister with ease. "Do you want me to apologise because my friends are good at what they do?" He asked keeping pace with her.

"Don't test me again Cerberus." Cerberex stopped, standing in front of him.

"I was a hunter before you'd leaned to walk."

Their eyes locked for a moment. To Cerberex's surprise, Cerberus blinked first. He smiled. "Well then let's find you some prey."

"Are you two going to talk all night?" Meera's voice from above made the pair of them look up. Meera pointed to where a man-made ridge overlooked a cracked road intersecting the ruins and aching back on itself towards the city.

"What do you see?" Cerberus called up to her.

Meera craned her neck before looking back. "Lights." She replied.

Forgetting Cerberex for a moment, Cerberus ran lightly for the ridge. Darting through the cracked doorway set in a single standing wall and balancing on the sheer edge of a jutting spike embedded into the ridge itself.

Kane and Seska moved in the shadow of a crumbling statue. They nodded to Cerberus as he looked in their direction, then returned their gaze to the cluster of lamplights casually making their way down from further up the road.

Cerberex clambered atop a broken window ledge above her brother for a better look. The ridge dropped twenty feet straight down but was pockmarked with stone doorways. Gnarled, hooded figures kept a silent vigil over the crypt entrances. To Cerberex they looked more like crows than guardians of the honoured fallen. She sniffed distastefully before her eyes snapped back to Cerberus. He caught something vaguely metallic hurled from the darkness a short way off.

Cerberus caught the spyglass and held it up to his eyes. Focussing the lens on the lights ahead. He pulled it back suddenly, his eyes sliding sideways in sudden thought, before returning it to his gaze.

Meera landed next to Cerberex with a light thud. She smiled at him briefly and looked down. "Do we let this one pass then?"

Cerberus held up a finger as he continued to work the lens.

Cerberex felt a soft breeze against her cheek and turned as Meera held a leather cuff attached to which was a miniature crossbow. Judging by the bare wrist on her left arm, she had removed it recently. Cerberex simply stared at it then looked at Meera who continued to smile at her.

"I'm... well let's say that my specialism requires me to be a bit closer." Meera murmured pushing the contraption into Cerberex's hands.

"And what am I supposed to do with this?" Cerberex asked guardedly.

"Well shoot with it darling! I mean I doubt Cerberus would want his precious sister too involved."

Cerberex looked at it and pushed it back. A snort of laughter made her and Meera look up at Seska balanced above them. "She thinks she'll get the jump with that." Seska laughed, quietly pointing to the bow on Cerberex's back.

Meera looked back at Cerberex and smiled like an indulgent mother. "Oh trust me darling, this is much faster."

Cerberex smiled sweetly. "Then you haven't seen someone use one of these very well."

The smile wavered on Meera's face. "As you wish." She re-attached the cuff onto her wrist. "What's the verdict Cerberus?" She asked without her eyes leaving Cerberex for a moment.

"This one gets no closer." Cerberus's voice called to them.

Meera smiled and looked over her shoulder to a moving shadow then up to Seska.

"Well I'm not looking after her." Seska announced flatly.

"Excuse me?" Cerberex looked up in surprise.

"She's with me." Cerberus's voice brooked no argument as he climbed up to them.

Meera and Seska inclined their heads, looked down at the rapidly advancing lights, and dropped. Cerberex gasped and looked over the edge with relief to see two shadows hopping down the ridge from statue to statue.

Cerberus looked at Cerberex and then around her as a humanoid silhouette disappeared over the edge of the ridge some ten feet away. His eyes returned to hers. "Follow me."

Cerberex opened her mouth to respond but Cerberus didn't wait for her reply and set off jogging along the ridge. Cerberex pursed her lips in irritation, took a deep breath, and followed him.

Cerberus couldn't help but enjoy the irritation his sister must be feeling at this point as he vaulted atop of huge stone edifice that might once have been an aqueduct shorn to rubble as it traversed the chasm below. The ridge was crumbling under the weight of the stone. slopes of fallen debris, the evidence of landslides, made the structure grumble under his feet.

Cerberex caught him up feeling the stone shift beneath their combined weight. Tentatively she looked down. The road sloped gently upwards towards the top of the ridge further on. Flanked on both sides it would have nowhere to go. The perfect place for an ambush. She gave her brother a sideways glance.

Cerberus watched as the lights rushed towards them. It was clear now that it was a wagon of some kind and moving at a good speed.

"Are you really as good as you say with that thing?" Cerberus asked nodding at Cerberex's bow.

Cerberex unslung it. "The best." She replied with a note of hesitation. There was a fanatical look to him that rang alarm bells in her head.

"Shoot the driver." Cerberus nodded as the wagon came within range.

"What?" Cerberex looked at him in surprise.

Cerberus looked at her nodding at the wagon. "Shoot the driver."

"Cerberus, this is banditry..." Cerberex began.

Cerberus laid a hand on her bow and tugged but Cerberex would not let go. "Do you trust me?"

"Well, yes obviously." Cerberex replied, pulling the bow out of his grasp.

"At this speed, can you shoot him?" Cerberus pressed.

"You know I can, but at least tell me why I must." Cerberex forced herself not to shout at him.

"Then shoot him." Cerberus repeated and watched as Cerberex slowly notched an arrow and paused. Pulling back the mechanism on his own miniature crossbow, Cerberus aimed it roughly at the wagon. At this range he knew that the bolt would lack the punch to kill outright. "For Eroth's sake Cerberex! Shoot him or I will."

Cerberex scowled at him. She could hear the sound of horse hooves coming closer and watched as Cerberus clicked the bolt into place on his crossbow. A moment more and it would be too late even for one with her skill.

For half a second Cerberus genuinely thought that his sister would refuse. He wouldn't have blamed her, she wasn't part of this world. Suddenly, Cerberex twisted back and fired with a speed that surprised even him.

The arrow hissed through the air with barely a whisper before slamming into the neck of the driver, piercing the jugular and emerging the other side. It was nothing short of a superb shot.

In a moment that felt like an hour, the driver seemed to slide from his seat. The reins came with him as the wagon trampled over his body, catching in the wheel and careening the pair of horses suddenly to one side. Cerberex watched the wagon tip dragging the the horses with it.

Pinpricks of light flickered on the opposite embankment. Cerberus blinked and pulled back. "What the..." He could see Meera and Seska speeding towards the wagon as another, possibly a survivor, pulled itself from the wreckage. Immediately the pinpricks of light began to converge on them. Cerberus watched them attaching the grapple head to his crossbow. Meera and Seska were both accomplished, they could handle a few extra he told himself.

The ground below lit in a wash of white light so bright that Cerberex and Cerberus had to shield their eyes. A short scream cut the silence as they watched Seska caught up and tossed like a rag doll into a stone doorway, cracking it before crumpling as she hit the floor.

"Shit!" Cerberus ran across to the edge and jumped - turning and firing the crossbow head at the stone edge as he fell.

Cerberex leapt for him before he could fall catching only his cloak which tore away in her grasp. She watched angrily as her brother plummeted down the zip-line, landing heavily on an approaching lantern below. Cerberex blinked and quickly notched another arrow, firing a second later not to kill but dissuade another approaching Cerberus from behind. She watched as Cerberus dodged something silver and fired again this time killing out right. "Some people can't take a hint." She muttered to herself.

The light flashed again and Cerberex couldn't help but turn her head away. When she looked back Cerberus was running almost inhumanly fast towards an individual swathed head to foot in heavy robes. Even at this distance Cerberex could see the light dancing in the figures hands. She looked for Meera and found her trading blows with a stubby sized humanoid unable to take notice of the wagon's occupant. She notched another arrow and aimed. The loosed shot should have skewered it through the head, but as the arrow came close she watched as it held out a hand shattering the projectile as if it were nothing but matchwood before pointing a finger at Cerberus.

Cerberex realised a fraction too late what was about to unfurl. Shouting a warning to Cerberus, she launched herself from the precipice and skidded down the side of the ridge with an avalanche of small stones. A flash of light again and Cerberus was thrown back with a smell of burning flesh. Cerberex launched herself forward to him, landing heavily at his side, the thud of her landing echoed by another.

Cerberex looked up. A thrill of surprise and recognition jumped through her. The other crouched opposite and looked at her eye to eye. The face was angular framed by pale, almost white, blonde hair. Silver-like eyes held a look of concern mixed with a touch of fear. In a heartbeat the image of her trespasser came unbidden to her mind. "You!" She cried out, unable to stop herself. The stranger opened his mouth to speak as Cerberus moved and groaned, cutting off any words he might have formed. A second later and a flash sent him soaring to the other side of the road and out of sight.

Cerberus's eyes flickered and then went wide. Cerberex felt rather than saw her attacker from behind. She tore the two hunting knives from their scabbards, bringing them up in a cross to trap the long curved blade headed for her back. She felt her arms buckle at the strength behind the weapon and kicked out, hoping to knock her opponent to his knees. He recoiled in surprise more than pain, the heavy wrap about his head falling away to reveal serpentine-esque features that were almost draconic in shape. Cerberex stood, keeping herself between her brother and this new comer. She had seen his kind before but not here, not this far south.

Wild born they called them. It was a colloquial term for all humanoids of more animalistic visage. They came originally from the Wildlands of Kurth but many could be found in the northern lands of the Drau by choice or by bond. Cerberex had encountered only two in her life but both had been furry, diminutive creatures. The scales of the Wild born shone black-blue with an oily sheen. Sharp bone jutted above the eye ridges and along the snout, leading to a mouth filled with thin, needle like teeth. Lightening sparks jumped between each tooth, building in intensity. Cerberex flattened herself over Cerberus rejoicing to feel his steady breathing beneath her armour. The discharge from the beast's maw made the hairs on the back of her neck stand on end and left a lingering smell of ozone.

As the wash of electricity receded, Cerberex sprang to her feet slicing with both hands at the Wild Born's face. It ducked low beneath her strike, hissing like an angry serpent before bringing its own blade down in a hacking motion that would have parted her at the shoulder a moment earlier. Cerberex pushed for the advantage. The hunters blades singing through the air in a whirlwind of movements the echoed loudly against its scaled hide with little or no avail. She breathed hard, leaning back from another wild swing trapping the blade and yanking with all her might to pull it from it's clawed grasp. With a yell of exertion, the scimitar skittered across the cracked paving and came to rest on the doorstep of some ancient mausoleum.

The Wild Born's head twisted to watch it's weapon hit the ground too far out of its reach. It turned hissing and spitting something Cerberex could be fairly confident, were probably curses. She spun her knives expecting the next attack, she did not have to wait long. The creature sprang at her with tooth and claw. Cerberex gave a yell as she felt hot, white pain pierce her side and stumbled against it's weight. Dropping one knife she raised a hand, pushing the creature's neck as it's jaws snapped at her face. Eye's closed, she could feel the sting of sparks against her cheek. The Wild born snapped again, it's breath smelled of carrion and old blood. Its spittle flecked at her. Cerberex gasped again as the claw tore itself free from her side. Taking another stumbling step backwards, she could feel hot liquid begin to seep into her clothes.

Breathing as much as she could through the pain, Cerberex watched her foe. "Why doesn't he simply blast me to ash?" she wondered, gripping her remaining knife so tight her knuckles turned white. "It doesn't want to harm itself!" The realisation came to her like a slap in the face. "It is not immune to it's own weapon." It was true. The Wild born stood before her growling through its fangs but though its mouth glowed with bright energy, it would not discharge it against her. For a moment the pair of them stood at an impasse. Each waited for the other to make the next move. Cerberex shifted first and the Wild born flew towards her, making it with barely two strides of its muscled legs. Cerberex gave a short shriek and the creature fell upon her, bracing against the impact with her back leg. The creature squealed and wheezed. She felt her right hand suddenly sticky. Though it's mouth was barely an inch from her face, Cerberex dared to glance down, seeing her knife pushed to the hilt between the leathery scales and into the creature's chest. Cerberex looked back up and met it's glare. She watched as it's eyes flickered. Then with a sudden burst of vigour she had not thought possible, the Wild born pushed against the blade. The jaw opened. Cerberex felt the sudden chill, the brightness building and building as the Wild born prepared to turn them both to bloody, scorched, corpses. A soft click punctuated the terror that had turned her ability to think to ice. A second later a heavy 'thunk' resonated from the back of the creatures skull, snapping its face away.

The full force of the Wild Born's considerable weight fell against Cerberex, toppling her like a stone. She winced at the stab of fresh pain running through her side as she landed with the creature cold dead atop. A black bolt protruded from the base of its skull. Cerberex craned her neck beyond the scaled shoulder to see Cerberus a short way off, his crossbow arm outstretched. Slowly he lowered it. Took a step and staggered, nearly falling against the cart and swearing loudly.

Chapter 15:
A Pound of Flesh

It took both Meera and Seska to pull the Wild borne corpse from atop Cerberex. Cerberus watched them prize the beast from her with a welter of blood as its chest slipped from her knife. Neither of the two had been left unscathed by the skirmish. Meera's coat had been turned to ragged ruin and she sported several thin cuts across her cheek and chin. Seska's arm hung limp, dislocated at the shoulder. She winced with every breath - tell tale signs of a broken rib. Of them all Kane appeared to have come off the lightest. His hair was matted with blood from a heavy gash at his fringe line. All in all not the best showcase. Cerberus swore again under his breath. He'd meant to prove to his sister the capabilities of but a few of his most trusted individuals - well excluding Kane currently. Somewhat childishly he had to admit, he had also wanted to shock if not ultimately scare, his sister out of the notion that she wanted any involvement in his affairs what-so-ever. Failing that, to at least demonstrate that he had no need of her 'help'.

Cerberus straightened as his sister approached, disguising the searing heat of the pain it took to stand upon his own feet. Wham! The fist connected with his lower jaw with enough force to almost knock him down.

"What did you think you were doing?" Cerberex shrieked, flying at him like a harpy till Meera and Seska pulled her off.

"Easy darling, you might break him and we can't be having that now." Meera murmured with veiled delight.

Cerberus looked back rubbing his jaw. Cerberex was a mess. Her hair stood out at odd angles and blood spray coated her face and front. Her hands too were slick with it. She sucked in heavy breaths and rubbed her nose with the back of her hand, smearing the viscera across her face. Seeming to calm down, Meera relinquished her grip and handed Cerberex back both her knives. Cerberex snatched them away. Ramming them into their sheaths with barely a thought to the meat still hanging on one of them. He glanced away at the wagon. Kane, hood and scarf replaced, grunted as he pulled two long wooden boxes for teak and iron from the wreckage. He frowned at them and looked up at Cerberus.

"What is it?" Cerberus asked breathily as he limped away from the women. The pain. Eroth! Cerberus would have taken his own leg if he thought it would have made it stop. Instead he gritted his teeth.

Kane looked up at him a flicker of concern as Cerberus approached. He reached back to a pouch behind him and drew an vial of amber liquid.

"Do you need a pick me up?" He proffered it in Cerberus's direction.

Cerberus waved it away. "It's nothing." He lied. "Old wound. What's this?" He pointed at the boxes, diverting the course of the conversation.

"Post." Kane replied assessing the locks of each box.

"Post?" Cerberus repeated. "No, that's not right. Selwyn told me this was from Darktide. A special order for our new Lord Vor'ran." He took another painful step towards the boxes and peered at them.

Kane shook his head. "Not this Cerberus, this has the marks of Night-moth Vale."

"Night-moth?" Cerberus repeated back at Kane again, his eyes narrowed thoughtfully. "Kane, who is this delivery for?"

Kane stood and ran back to the fallen body of the driver in search of a manifest.

"So? What's the bounty darling?" Meera slinked up to Cerberus and draped herself across his shoulder. Cerberus gasped in pain and she recoiled as if burned. "Your hurt." It was not a question.

Cerberus winced as he adjusted his weight, leaning as casually as he could against the wagon and took a deep breath. He looked past Meera. Seska seemed to have calmed Cerberex to a level of barely concealed rage, a step down from her full fury. He allowed himself a private smile for a second before Kane's footsteps returned. "Well?" He asked, turning towards Kane expectantly.

Kane unfolded the parchment and glanced along it before glancing back at Cerberus with a look of surprise. "Us." He replied simply. "Or rather, your family."

"What?" Cerberus snatched the paper away to look himself. The ink did not lie. He folded the paper again. "Night-moth." He whispered to himself and rubbed the still red mark on his jawline. "There are Dhal-Marrah lands stretching right across the Night-moth Vale. Silk, spice, medicinals. Most of my family's wealth is stretched across those plains." He pushed the paper into his belt pouch. "Open it." He commanded.

"Cerberus these locks - they could be trapped." Kane knelt down pulling a short dagger from his belt and poking the lock of one gingerly.

"He has a point Cerberus." Meera agreed.

"Who does?" Cerberex chimed in darkly as she and Seska joined them.

Cerberus pushed Meera away. "Open it." He repeated forcefully.

Kane looked at Meera with a raised eyebrow. She took a step back and gently guided Cerberex to do the same as Kane stood and unsheathed the larger sword he had strapped across his back. Carefully he placed the tip between the frame of the lock and the polished wood of the first. Taking a deep breath he pushed down with all his weight. There was a sound of splintering wood, followed by a sudden 'ping' as the lock tore away. A deafening silence drowned all sense of time. Kane let go of his breath and performed the same exercise to the second box.

Cerberus leant forward slightly. Sweat was beading on his forehead. "Open them."

Gingerly, Kane wedged the tip of the blade in the gap between the lid and the box itself. Flipping it open as if expecting a live wildcat to come springing out.

The groan of distaste echoed around the group. Meera forcibly turned Cerberex around.

"Well, that's just unpleasant." Meera commented, swallowing hard.

Angrily Cerberex shoved away Seska and Meera's controlling arms and turned to look. She stared blinking. "Are... are those ears?" Cerberex stared at the fleshy cargo of the open container unable to draw her eyes away. Maybe twenty pairs of elegantly pointed ears bereft of their owners, lay across the red silk padding of the box. Some were no bigger than her thumb, others had meaty scraps or strands of hair still attached. She fought the wave of nausea that threatened to overwhelm her.

"And the other one." Cerberus growled.

"I think we can guess what's inside Cerberus." Kane replied.

"I said open!" Cerberus shouted, the sound of his voice echoing through the darkness.

Kane swallowed and opened the second smaller box. Inside a severed hand lay atop a scrap of parchment. Kane nudged the dismembered limb aside and picked up the note. "It's for you." He muttered holding it out to Cerberus.

Cerberex leaned towards the box for a closer look. The hand was rough and pinkish grey. The dark purple stain of an old tattoo marked the wrist. She grimaced and reached out to it, feeling the cold waxy texture of dead skin. Stretching it out, Cerberex cocked her head to one side trying to make out the pattern. Her eyes widened in surprise. "It's a dragon!" She cried out. Dropping the severed hand quickly and her eyes flicking up to to Cerberus. "It's the mark of our house." Her voice uncommonly high pitched.

Meera helped her up. "Some of your house's retainers indulge in a little ink-work. It's like a mark of loyalty." She whispered quietly.

Cerberus looked down at the note in his hand. The word 'Cerberus' had been cursively written in an elegant hand. Gently, he unfolded the paper and scanned the contents grinding his teeth as he read.

"What is it?" Cerberex demanded.

Cerberus closed the note after he finished and crushed it in his palm. After he moment he cleared his throat. "You have my Queen. I have your lands. For each day she does not return I shall exact a pound of flesh from those you think to protect. This time it is ears, the next shall be tongues, can they work without their eyes?" He recited.

A call echoed further down the road. Instinctually, Meera, Kane, and Seska ducked low. A little way off the dancing lights of lamps glittered against the shadows.

"They knew we would be here." Seska cursed. "The wagon was bait."

Cerberus looked out at the lights. Ten maybe more? "Leave the boxes. We can't fight in this state."

Meera nodded. "Leave and live to fight again." Her eyes never once leaving the lamps.

Cerberus nodded back and turned. His form seemed to shift one moment before the next there was a painful yell and Cerberus was on the ground gasping.

Cerberex was at his side first. Her eyes darting to find the cause of her brothers sudden agony. Carefully feeling for any wound she ran her hand down his leg pulling it away quickly when it came back wet with his blood. With a quick intake of breath she ripped the seam apart with her fingers. Meera ran to her side, a lantern prised from the wagon swinging in her grip as she knelt. The wound looked to be as if it had been healing but was now torn afresh. Black veins pulsated beneath the skin up past the knee and down to the ankle. Cerberus screamed as she probed it and the veins spread further.

"Shit Cerberus!" Meera pulled back from the acridly sweet smell of necrosis. "The hell did you think you were doing coming out with a wound like this?"

Cerberex pulled one of her knives and cut the sleeve from her left arm. Shearing it into two thick strips she balled one, ramming it into Cerberus's mouth. Quickly, she looked over her shoulder. The lights were much closer now - it wouldn't be long. Turning back she pushed at the wound. Cerberus writhed against her until a heavy boot pushed down onto his chest.

Kane bore his weight down on Cerberus enough to keep him still and looked down watching as Cerberex pushed at the wound eliciting a spurt of puss-like ichor. Dodging the spray, Cerberex quickly tore her way further up Cerberus's leg. Gently at first, she fed the other strip of fabric under his leg to where the poison in his veins had yet to reach. Then with a quick glance at Cerberus, she knotted the fabric and tied it down hard. Cerberus bucked so hard that Seska had to practically lie over him to prevent him from moving as Cerberex finished wrapping around the rest of the cloth.

"What are you doing?" Meera stood up in alarm as she heard the sudden series of shouts coming towards them.

Cerberex looked up at her. "If I do not tourniquet the wound, the poison will continue to rise up his leg." She pointed to the cloth. "With this he might lose a leg. Without it he will most surely die. Which would you prefer." Meera opened her mouth and closed it again. "That's what I thought."

Seska sat up looking around Cerberex at the coming lights. "We need to disappear."

Cerberex grabbed hold of Cerberus's arm and hauled him to his feet pulling the cloth strip out of his mouth. "I'm not leaving him here." She stated matter-of-factly.

Meera placed a hand on her shoulder. "Oh darling, whoever said we would."

"I can still walk." The sound of Cerberus's breathless voice startled the group.

"The hell you can! At present you can barely stand." Meera retorted. She looked at Cerberex her hands open. "Let me take him back."

Cerberex clutched Cerberus's arm. "He's my brother." She muttered childishly.

"Your not fast enough." The friendly politeness in Meera's voice was gone in a second as her face began to crease into a scowl.

"She's Dhal-Marrah Meera. Know your place." Kane's voice was low.

"Know yours." Meera hissed swiping at him.

A heavy crossbow bolt smacked into the wood frame of the wagon. Seska and Kane both ducked and clicked their own into place.

"We don't have time for this." Seska called out, ignoring the volume of her voice as three more bolts splintered the wagon's shell. "And we cannot win this fight. There are too many."

Meera turned to Cerberex already dragging Cerberus out of the line of fire, and sighed. "Seska and I will draw them off as best we can. Look for that one." She pointed to the heavy silhouette of Kane. "He will be your eyes." She turned looking over her shoulder and the other two who stood and gave a short nod.

Kane stepped towards them and slung Cerberus's other arm over his shoulder. "This way." He muttered, keeping his voice as low as possible. Cerberus could be heard grinding his teeth closed as even with help, he could only just walk.

They weaved through the ruins as fast as they dared with Cerberus making as little noise as was possible. Unable to climb the ridge, they were forced to keep as much to the shadows as possible while still following the cracked road leading back to the city proper. Kane kept an unrelenting pace between crumbling walls and sundered statues till they paused in the shelter of a shorn pillar for Cerberus to catch his breath. The city's east gate wasn't far and was rarely patrolled. Beyond it lay some of the poorer districts of Everfall where they could disappear, or so her guide told her. Cerberex had other ideas. Her sense of direction was unparalleled. South West, somewhere among the glitter of city lamps was the perimeter wall of the Dhal-Marrah estate. To get there they would have to cut back across the The Vaults but it would be quicker than navigating the warrens of the downtrodden in the city. Even without seeing his face Cerberex could tell that her guide disliked the idea.

"Cerberex is right." Cerberus croaked while panting for breath. He propped against the column. "The house is safer."

"Cer ... Master, we don't have means to get you across the perimeter wall." Kane pressed.

Cerberus managed a pained look. "I'll manage. We've been set up. They'll be expecting us to try the gate."

Kane sighed. "As you wish." He glanced at Cerberex. "I will keep a little way's ahead. If something should go wrong, keep going. Do not look back." With that he pulled Cerberus upright and swung his arm over his shoulder again. Cerberex nodded doing the same as they began moving back towards the scattered ruins.

As the shattered structures grew larger Kane departed, leaping up into the empty window frame of a faintly familiar mausoleum. Cerberex continued forging forwards, stumbling with the unfamiliar extra weight. Her internal compass told her that the edge of the wilderness that bordered the perimeter of the house should not be far. From here the ruins would be more dispersed. Open ground covered the distance between the city and The Vaults, there would be little to cover them from seeing eyes.

Suddenly out of nowhere a bolt slammed into the stonework of a far wall. Cerberex almost toppled over a loose rock trying to avoid the sound. Cerberus grunted and he tried to steady himself, but his leg was past obeying any command. A second and a third bolt hissed through the air above their heads. Cerberex dared to look back. Shapes were shifting through the shadows. Cerberex caught her breath and unslung her bow from her back. Notching an arrow she fired into the darkness. A volley of bolts answered her. Rolling backwards she hid behind the stone block, dragging Cerberus with. More bolts rapidly followed the first, clicking as they ricocheted from her cover. By now the sound was accompanied by the drum of heavy feet. How they had caught up so fast or what had become of Meera and Seska - Cerberex didn't know. As she lurched up from her hiding spot to return fire, a cry cut the quiet. A ghost of midnight jumped down as the first interloper came into view, disembowelling him with a wide sword. Cerberex fired, adjusting the aim to the group following behind. A gargle and light thud told her she had struck true. She stood, reaching for another arrow.

Kane turned and pulled down the scarf muffling his voice. Flicking his sword he picked out Cerberex reaching for her quiver. "Go!" He yelled at her, giving her pause. "Go now! I'll hold them off."

Cerberex didn't need to be told twice. She slung her bow back over her shoulder and reached down for Cerberus. He no longer growled or grunted. All feeling of his leg had disappeared. That her brother felt no pain was a blessing but Cerberex knew it was no more than a timer whose grains of sand were rapidly running away. With the tourniquet cutting off the blood supply to his leg it had become numb, but if the tourniquet was not removed soon Cerberus would loose his leg entirely. Remove the tourniquet and the poison in his blood would surely spread.

"Can you run?" Cerberex asked as she pulled Cerberus on with renewed vigour.

Cerberus stopped, pulling his sister back and tested the weight on his leg. He gave her a quick nod.

Cerberex nodded in return. "As we did when we were children then. Ready?"

Cerberus prepared himself.

"Left first. Go!" Cerberex whispered and began to run, Cerberus keeping in step beside her while she supported the bulk of his weight.

Chapter 16:
Gloom-flower

Cerberus's leg crumpled beneath him as they hit the perimeter wall. Cerberex was forced to scale up six feet of thick stone and drag Cerberus up by herself. Her muscles burned as if on fire as they both landed heavily the other side. Cerberex rolled over first and reached out to Cerberus. Carefully pulled back the cloth of his trousers. With Cerberus' skin colour it was difficult to tell in the poor light but Cerberex was convinced there was a blotchy discolouration to it. She glanced towards the towering silhouette of the house outlined in silver by the moon. It was still a good twenty minutes away. She looked back at the wound then up at Cerberus's face. "I'm loosening the bind. If I don't you'll lose everything below the knee."

Cerberus looked at her and buried his fingers into the damp earth and grass for grip. He took a deep breath. "Now." He hissed.

"This is going to hurt." Cerberex added and began to undo the tourniquet.

Cerberus cried out in pain for a second then clenched his mouth shut. The wound on his leg pulsed. Blood filled the gash and dripped down into the ground. Slowly the blotchy purple receded from his skin. His entire leg throbbed with pain.

As Cerberus's natural skin tone returned, Cerberex tied back off the tourniquet once more eliciting another short cry. With any luck, her brother's protests would be heard by a patrolling house guard and aid would be on the way. Carefully, she helped Cerberus onto his good leg. Though her back protested, she once more shouldered him and began to slowly hobble to the house.

Cerberus pulled back. "No. That way." He pointed towards what once might have been some form of outhouse for storage long since in disrepair.

"Brother, you need this seen to sooner rather than later. We don't have time for your little excursions now." Cerberex muttered.

A curl of a smile cornered Cerberus's mouth. "Trust me. There's another way in."

Cerberex looked at the pained but determined look on her brother's face. Hissing through her teeth she veered towards the outhouse. "You better be right."

The roof of the part stone part wood structure had collapsed partly such that Cerberex had to kick in the door to force Cerberus and herself through. Cerberus motioned to a pile of bags stuffed with Eroth knew what. "Behind them." He winced as she propped him up.

Exhausted, Cerberex shifted the heavy sacks revealing a passage that had been crudely boarded up. Behind the planks the faintest glow came from much further down a set of rough steps that seemed to have been carved simply from the earth itself. Pushing her fingers between the planks, she tried to prize them away. The wood creaked but would not move. "It's stuck." Cerberex huffed trying a different panel.

Cerberus limped over and leaned against a fallen wooden beam next to her, pulling off his arm bracer with his teeth, while his other arm supported his weight. Once free he held it out towards the boarded entrance. A soft click resonated and the panels collectively swung inwards.

"How did you do that?" Cerberex murmured, peering into the dust and dark of the path beyond.

Cerberus managed a grin and wiggled the fingers of his left hand. "Magic."

Cerberex gave him a disapproving look as she turned back to help support his weight. She could barely see beyond the first few steps, save the pinprick of flickering light she took to be some kind of torch. Cerberus and Cerberex had to stoop as the gentle slope of the steps and the passage evened out.

"Where does this lead?" Cerberex whispered. Her instincts told her that unseen eyes were watching their progress.

"The far end of the assassin's route. We don't have need of it too much these days." Cerberus replied.

"A back door?" Cerberex smiled. She did not smile for long. The prod of a blade end under her chin was the first she knew that they had been found. The glow further down grew brighter illuminating the two black clad figures in front of them.

"This one is unmarked and unknown." The voice was muffled that Cerberex couldn't tell if it was male or female. The press of the blade began to dimple her skin. Moments later a torch came moving at speed down the tunnel. Cerberus leant against his sister and held a hand up to his face.

"Put your blades down you fools!" Cerberex felt the knife immediately retract from her throat and breathed out in relief at the sound of Meera's voice. "This one might not be known but tell me you don't know the other." Angrily, Meera shoved the heavily masked individual aside, holding the torch out to examine them. "Eroth, you've taken a beating." She smirked but Cerberex thought there was a flicker of concern in those eyes before it was gone.

"He needs healing and something stronger than those little amber vials you've got." Cerberex caught Meera's arm.

Meera pulled it away and looked at Cerberex. "Where is Kane?"

"Who?" Cerberex asked, frustrated by the question.

"Your guide. Where is he?" Meera looked past them into the shadows and saw nothing.

"I don't know. He stopped to draw others off us." Cerberex replied impatiently. "I need to get my brother to either my aunt or my mother now."

Meera's eyes flicked back to Cerberex. "Alright darling." There was a snarl to her voice. She whispered something to the masked figure now behind her and the individual disappeared down the tunnel like smoke. "I'll take you through. Follow me."

Meera cut a winding path at a fast pace. "She's worried." Cerberus groaned as compacted earth turned to stone floor and more torches lined the walls.

"That makes two of us then." Cerberex muttered keeping her eyes on Meera.

Cerberus coughed a laugh. "No. She's worried about you."

Cerberex almost stopped in surprise. "Why?"

Cerberus shook his head and almost fell as Meera stood by a wall. A dead end. Cerberex watched as Meera nicked herself on a small dagger and a bead of blood welled up on the thumb. Roughly she dotted a seemingly random allocation of stone blocks. Cerberex took a step back as a dull red glow ran along the bricks and a grinding vibration knocked dust from the ceiling.

"It is opened one way only." Meera replied before Cerberex could ask. "So don't try using it to get back in darling."

"More entrances?" Cerberex whispered to her brother,

Cerberus nodded. "Mother is rather good at what she does."

Cerberex raised an eyebrow in surprise.

Golden light spilled from the thin opening before them. Beyond Cerberex could make out the dark wood of the library's shelves, then Meera was pushing them through. "Fix him up. The route is nothing without a master. I have a guide to find."

Cerberex stepped through with Cerberus giving a yelp of pain as his leg caught on the change in flooring between the two rooms. Cerberex looked back just in time to watch the bookcase shift back with a click. Finally Cerberus hobbled to a plush red armchair a few feet away and collapsed into it with a sigh.

Cerberex moved for the door. "Don't move."

"As if I could." Cerberus breathed, stretching his leg.

Cerberex gave him a murderous look. "Do you want me to let mother see you like this?"

"Hell's no." Cerberus replied almost immediately.

"Then shut up." Cerberex opened the door and slipped through.

Aunt Mal's laboratory door had been something of a forbidden territory when Cerberus and Cerberex had been children - in many ways it still was to anyone not wishing to invite an explosive death. It lay at the far end of the hall way and extended down into the basement beneath the kitchen. Feeling much like a child again as she checked the coast was clear, Cerberex fled down that hallway now as if the hounds of the abyss were on her tail. She hammered on the door with enough force to shake the wood on its hinges. The imprints of the studded exterior left welts in her hands.

"Aunt!" Cerberus called when no immediate answer came. Gingerly she tested the handle. The door swung inward noiselessly. She took a single step inside. "Aunt?" She called again.

"Lady Cerberex?" The voice almost made Cerberex jump out of her skin. She turned to see Lida dressed in a simple pale cream and blue dress. "Hells breath, you look terrible!"

Cerberex dipped into a quick bow enough not to appear rude. "Your majesty, have you seen Lady Dhal-Marrah?"

"Your mother?" Lida asked.

"Well either of them right now will do." Cerberex replied slowly closing the door again behind her with a soft click.

"She left a moment ago." Lida replied.

"At this hour - and my aunt?" Cerberex continued her eyes widening.

"Lord Charnite too with Lady Maleficent." Lida added her tone laced with concern. "Cerberex, what is wrong? You look like you've disembowelled a bear with your hands!"

"We were attacked." Cerberex surprised herself how easily that rolled off the tongue. Concern mixed with a touch of fear washed Lida's face of any remaining colour but Cerberex continued. "The King is not unaware of your location. I was hoping we might have another day or two but he's clearly a cunning bastard. My brother's wound is reopened and it looks vicious." She could hear herself babbling but seemed to be unable to prevent the words from coming out. It was like a broken dam.

Lida took a step forward and placed a hand on Cerberex's shoulder. "Show me." The voice was commanding yet soft. "Show me." She repeated as Cerberex recoiled from her.

Cerberex looked at her. "I apologise but I don't think Cerberus would forgive me if I did. He, how can I put it? Has an inflated opinion about you." She made to step past but Lida's grip suddenly turned into a vice-like hold.

"Lady Cerberex, we've had our differences and I know what you think about me yet its you who comes yelling for help, covered in blood that seems not to be your own, implying that the King has attacked you and your brother is wounded." She took a deep breath.

"I never said Cerberus..." Cerberex began meekly.

"It was implied." Lida cut her off. She relinquished her hold. "Cerberex, just show me for Eroth's sake!"

The tension lasted for but a moment but it was Cerberex who gave first. She moved past and gestured towards the library.

"Did he not take any of his 'friends' with him bar you?" Lida asked as they moved briskly.

Cerberex looked back in surprise. "You know?"

"You didn't?" Lida's face seemed more surprised than hers.

"I.." Cerberex began. "I knew Cerberus had been paying the palace night time visits. I believed that we - the family were well, passed all that."

"But you're a Dhal-Marrah Cerberex. Surely you were aware that your house has been known to train assassins and buy spies for generations." Lida's voice lowered to a whisper as they approached the library door.

Cerberex felt stupid. She had known in a way. She had been barely a spark in her father's eye when the Dwentar War had ended but her mother and aunt had talked about it about the Great House Alliance, like it was just yesterday. She felt ashamed that she had been too absorbed in the attentions she received from would be suitors to take much notice. Now it was coming back to haunt her. She opened the door to the library in silence.

"Well where..." Lida began. Cerberus sat with his head slumped. The tie around his leg had loosened. Blood pooled on the floor. "Eroth!" Lida swore as she and Cerberex ran over to him.

"He's loosened the tourniquet." Cerberex stated the obvious.

"What in the hells did he do that for?" Lida muttered. Looking around she noticed the desk and with a single brusque motion shoved the charts and books atop it unceremoniously onto the floor. "Help me Cerberex. Lie him on the desk."

Between them they heaved Cerberus onto the desk. Cerberex was surprised by how much he weighed fully kitted out in armour even if it was leather. She watched as Lida took it all in. "What have you done?" Lida muttered. Cerberex was unsure if it was to herself or as a question expecting an answer. "Do you know how to take any of this off?"

Cerberex looked over the number of buckles and sections. She'd not had the time to study it enough to work out which took off what. Sliding a knife from one of its sheaths, she slid it under the chest piece and sawed her way through the side until the last piece of leather gave and the entire chest piece folded back and away.

Quickly Lida began to unlace the shirt and pull it back to reveal his torso. Lida stretched out a hand and placed one against Cerberus' chest. "He's still with us at least." She spoke to herself quietly. Carefully she began to inspect the wound.

Cerberex looked down at her brother lying like a slab of meat on a butchers counter. Motionless. She took in the criss-cross of thin scars across his torso. She'd always known that their father had had the propensity to be cruel, but this? She leaned forward her eyes narrowing as she picked out soft dark marks almost unnoticeable with Cerberus's complexion. "Does he...?"

"Have a tattoo? Several actually. Not one of your brother's most well considered life choices." Lida's face did not change as she anticipated the question. "This is the wound he suffered in the prison." She stood shaking her head. "It's re-opened and heavy with necrosis." She scratched her head. "I don't understand it. Your mother and I healed this before. It shouldn't be..." She paused thoughtfully. "Unless... Unless he was poisoned or the wound was reinfected before he left." She looked at Cerberex. "Find me some gloom-flower. I need to counter the infection before I can heal it closed."

Cerberex straightened and left with a surge of speed she didn't know her tired legs still possessed. She had no idea where in the house she might find gloom-flower or even what exactly it was but if there was one place in the house she might bet on it was Aunt Mal's laboratory. Without a thought Cerberex pulled back on the heavy laboratory door and darted down the steps two at a time. There was a dim light coming off a shelf filled with jars with some form of luminescent fungi in various shades. A table of alchemical alembics and flasks glinted across the room, and row upon row specimen drawers ran the rest of the length. Cerberex grabbed the first drawer she could get her hands on and began going through the labelled items within.

"Cerberex Dhal-Marrah, what precisely do you think you are doing?"

Cerberex froze like a child caught in the act of raiding the sugar jar. The voice was calm, collected, measured. Slowly she pushed the drawer closed and turned around.

Maleficent stood her hands by her side, in a floor length gown decorated in sparkling silver beads against black velvet. "What is the meaning of this?"

"Gloom-flower?" Cerberex stuttered as she tried to regain her composure.

Maleficent narrowed her eyes and brushed an errant strand of hair back from her face. She made her way slowly to Cerberex and took a jar from the shelf above, unscrewed the top, reached in, and pulled out a trio of shrivelled black petals. For a moment she held them out but as Cerberex reached for them, she wrenched them out of her reach. "Since when did you have interests in herbology Cerberex?"

Cerberex reached out for them impatiently. "Her majesty is asking for them."

Maleficent held them out again and Cerberex snatched them out of her grasp. There was the tiniest movement and Maleficent had her by the wrist. A moment later the door to the laboratory opened again.

"Really Maleficent, we are going to be late and more than fashionably." Selwyn took two steps down the stairs and stopped. "Well now this is interesting."

"I told you, someone was in my laboratory." Maleficent smiled at him and held up Cerberex's arm as if brandishing the culprit to make a point.

Selwyn held up both hands. "I take it back." His head turned inquisitively to Cerberex.

"So, what has your brother done this time?" Maleficent asked, turning back to Cerberex. Her eyes glistened at Cerberex's look of surprise. "Oh come now niece, you of all people should know that I do not care for people to come into my laboratory. My guess is that something has happened and given that your covered in blood and looking for gloom-flower, my hunch is that something has gone very wrong indeed."

"Lida wants the gloom-flower." She muttered trying to prize her wrist from her aunt's hand.

"Cerberex." Maleficent's grip tightened.

"Alright, alright. She needs it for Cerberus. The wound on his leg has got infected." Cerberex answered quickly.

Maleficent let go. "Well let's go take it to her then. It would be rude to keep the Queen waiting after all." The slight curl of a smile at her lips. She turned almost marching Cerberex back up the stairs. "I believe you owe me some coin." Cerberex heard her whisper as they passed Selwyn on the stairs. She turned giving her aunt an appraising look. "Well go on." Maleficent encouraged, shooing Cerberex out of the laboratory.

"What in Eroth's name took you so long?" Lida's voice called out as Cerberex opened the door to the library. There was a static to the air that had not been their before. As Cerberex approached, softly followed by Aunt Mal, she saw Lida arms stretched out. One hand precisely placed just above Cerberus's sternum and the other stretched out towards his leg. A haze of pale light enveloped him. "I can't exactly keep this..." Lida looked up for a second and stopped as the two came near. "Ah, you ... Lady Maleficent."

Maleficent took a step forward. "Your majesty, your doing a lovely job but may I?" She stepped forward rubbing her hands together and examined the wound. It oozed thick congealing blood. She looked up encouragingly, wiping her hands down the priceless gown as if it was nothing but casual-wear. "If I may?"

The brightness curling from Lida's fingertips diminished. Cerberus twitched. "I'm fairly proficient in..."

Maleficent waved a hand without looking at her. "Oh I know you are my dear, but don't worry I've got this. Would you be so kind as to give me some space? Cerberex just put the Gloom-flower down on the desk for me if you please."

Lida looked at Maleficent in bewilderment as she moved around the desk and came to stand next to Cerberex. "She does know who I am doesn't she?" She whispered, leaning in close to Cerberex's ear.

Cerberex smiled. "Yes. She just doesn't care."

"Ladies!" Maleficent looked up with annoyance.

Lida raised an eyebrow at the outburst and opened her mouth to say something.

"Best not. Aunt Mal doesn't like being disturbed but she is the best." Cerberex cut in before Lida could get a word out.

"While I appreciate the compliment, I need quiet." Maleficent glanced up. "Cerberex will you please sort yourself out. You're in polite company and you look an absolute disaster."

Cerberex looked up with a flush of unexpected embarrassment and backed away towards the door, gently pulling Lida along with.

Chapter 17:
Hearts & Minds

Mid-morning sun crept across the sky streaking it with hues of pink. Cerberex hovered by the windows of the dining hall, masked by the stained glass. Uncle Selwyn and Lida were in the small courtyard beyond and she was doing her best to discretely listen in to their conversation with little success. She could see them clear enough peeking past the curtain. Lida sat in a dark green dress with silver beads that had been lent by Cerberex and appeared to be listening intently to Uncle Selwyn. Selwyn in a navy blue long coat was speaking at length and yet no matter how close Cerberex pushed herself to the glass she could hear ... nothing.

"It's a simple concealment spell." Maleficent's voice was heavy with exhaustion, lacking it's usual hint of mischief.

Cerberex turned to see Maleficent sipping a fluted glass of wine, her hand quivering with a slight shake.

"How is Cerberus?" She asked. It had been a full day since their abortive mission and Aunt Mal had refused entrance to his room by anyone excepting herself.

"Irritated." Maleficent replied in a word. " He can either use the walking stick or spend the time to heal properly laid up in his room - it matters not to me."

"And mother?" Cerberex asked taking a seat the opposite side of the table.

"She has been informed that Cerberus's wound was more persistent than we thought and that you found him in the house passed out." Maleficent replied. "I think it would be safe to say that your little excursion should not be divulged to her." Cerberex nodded straightening the plain black cotton of her dress uncomfortably. Maleficent put the crystal glass down on the table and steepled her fingers. "What is wrong Cerberex? You have that look about you."

"We need to send her back." Cerberex stated simply.

A tired smile curled the corners of Maleficent's mouth. "I see. Well Cerberus would disagree I think."

"Unsurprisingly. He always does when 'she' is involved." Cerberex helped herself to a little wine.

Maleficent's smile widened slightly. "Is this by chance, about the box?" Her eyes glinted as Cerberex looked up and over-filled a glass, spilling claret in a small puddle. "Cerberus talks in his sleep - didn't you know?"

"The note was very clear. If she is not returned, worse would follow." Cerberex took a sip from the glass.

"So you would rather hand over the Queen into the hands of an evident sadist?" Maleficent watched Cerberex down the glass, stand, and wander back to the window. "It was a disgusting find but you don't actually have proof that our wards in Night-moth have been touched."

Cerberex listened to the silent window in frustration for a moment before looking back. "There was a hand with our symbol upon it."

"Grave robbery perhaps." Maleficent suggested.

Cerberex's face creased with annoyance at the flippant remark. "Some of those ears were from children. Quite frankly I couldn't care less if their owners were wards of the Gal-Serreks themselves. It's beyond barbaric."

"It is politics." Maleficent added simply.

Cerberex made a face. "Politics? This is far from the polite verbal backstabbing of politics." She returned her gaze. Lida was now pacing like a angry cat.

"It is politics under this King. " Maleficent sat back in her chair. "He is looking for us to rise to his challenge. He is anticipating that Cerberus will act out of anger. Luckily for us he clearly remains unaware of Cerberus's condition or there would most likely be Gal-Serrek forces here already."

"Why? Dhal-Marrah has no quarrel with the Gal-Serreks. If my half-wit of a brother hadn't been at that party none of this would have ever happened."

Maleficent's eyebrows almost shot off the top of her head. "No quarrel?" She snapped suddenly making Cerberex jump. "My dear niece you are half orphaned because of that bastard family!" Cerberex recoiled back into the wall at Maleficent's sudden burst of anger. "Did you merely imagine that your father's death was an accident? The Gal-Serrek's and the Dhal-Marrah's have allied once and the result killed a King. Thankfully they only slaughtered themselves, though they blame us entirely for their misfortune." Maleficent's stood and clasped the back of her chair. "The Gal-Serreks breed only ignorant delinquents. They rattle their sabres and expect the world to kneel. Rest assured niece, had the blade been in Dhal-Marrah hands we would not have simply sent ears as a message." Maleficent took a deep breath and the fervour drifted from her eyes as swiftly as it had come. "It's a touchy subject. You should have more tact."

Cerberex exhaled a breath she hadn't known she'd been holding. "I meant no offence Aunt."

Maleficent waved away the apology. "Queen Lida cannot return skulking back to the palace pretending nothing has happened and we cannot pretend that she is not here."

"Then you're suggesting we should just let our lands burn and those in our care be tortured?" Cerberex fought to keep her frustration in check but couldn't help the sarcasm that came unbidden to her voice.

"Absolutely not." Maleficent walked over to the window. Selwyn and Lida were now making their way into the garden proper. Judging by the smile on his face, whatever the conversation had been, Selwyn evidently felt he had acquired the upper hand in it. "We simply play a smarter game."

The cane tapped on the stone slabs with a soft click. Cerberus chewed on his tongue with irritation as he limped across the garden. His armour, rapier, knives, crossbow, even his hair tie, had been confiscated by Aunt Mal who despite his protest, flatly refused to return them. The cane was a short staff of ebony lacquered to a glossy sheen and topped with a silver handle shaped into the head of a dragon. Cerberus guessed that it must have belonged to some great uncle. Certainly neither of his parents would have been caught dead with one!

"Brooding doesn't suit you Lord Dhal-Marrah."

Cerberus turned quickly, suddenly torn from his thoughts by the voice. Lida walked purposefully across the lawn. The green of the dress shifted hue as she walked but it fitted poorly. Cerberus guessed it probably belonged to his sister. Regaining his composure, he attempted a modest bow. Lida waved him up with a flick of her wrist.

"I can't say I'm not relieved to see you walking about all things considered." Lida gestured to his legs. "That's twice now I believe."

"I'm sorry?" Cerberus raised an eyebrow as he caught the smug note in Lida's voice.

"You seem to need rescuing a lot these days." Lida continued. "It's becoming a habit."

"Twice in a century is hardly a habit Lida." Cerberus retorted.

"It's 'your Majesty'." Lida corrected with a flash of irritation. "Honestly, does no one in this house observe basic etiquette?"

Cerberus snorted a small laugh. "Very well ... your Majesty." He bowed again as deep as his leg would allow. "And yes we understand courtly etiquette."

"You seem to be out of practice then." Lida retorted.

Cerberus looked around at the empty gardens. "Oh we understand it, we're just not bothered by it."

"And why's that?" Lida asked following Cerberus as he began to walk away.

Cerberus turned back and leaned on the cane with both hands, feeling the wood flex slightly. "Because you're not going to be called anything when your dead." He grinned. "Your Majesty."

"The only person who appears to be intent on dying would seem to be you." Lida countered easily keeping pace with him.

Cerberus glanced sideways at her. "Well death and I have an understanding."

"He doesn't appear to be keeping to his side of the bargain very well." Lida laughed.

Cerberus laughed. "Yes, someone should really talk to him about that." He stepped under a small stone archway into a well tended walled garden centred around a gnarled tree devoid of all leaf or greenery. To all intents and purposes it seemed utterly dead.

"I must say, I do prefer you this way?" Lida broke the sudden silence between them first.

"Limping?" Cerberus teased.

"No. Appropriately dressed." Lida replied.

Cerberus looked down at his clothes. A black shirt and trousers, soft boots - not exactly his best. "Ah, you mean without armour."

Lida stepped away towards the tree and laid a hand on it, peering up through the branches. "Well, you seem more at ease." She patted the tree softly. "Quite dead."

"What?" Cerberus asked confused.

"The tree Cerberus. It's definitely dead." Lida repeated.

"Oh are we back on first names already?" Cerberus asked sarcastically, earning him a stern look from Lida. He grinned and looked up at the tree. "Didn't you get stuck up there once?"

Lida blushed, her face pricking with colour. "I think that might be an exaggeration."

Cerberus ignored her and continued. "On that branch just there." He pointed to a thick branch that overhung the flowerbed of tiny white blooms. He could feel her gaze but continued relentlessly. "My father had to come out and 'rescue' you because you were howling so much."

"And whose fault was it that I was there in the first place?" Lida folded her arms.

"Well in my defence, I did tell you that girls can't climb." Cerberus's eyes glinted cheekily.

"Oh can't we?" Lida replied, rising magnificently to the challenge. "How exactly did I get up there then?"

"I didn't say you couldn't get up there now, but you certainly can't get back down. At least, not all dressed up like that." Cerberus nodded to the long dress trailing in the grass.

"You always were very good at getting me into trouble Cerberus." She paused. "You still are." Lida stroked the grey bark with her hand before lounging against it.

Cerberus gave a look of mock anguish. "Me? Surely not."

Lida placed her hands behind her back. "My mother used to tell me you were a terrible influence." She tipped her head back slightly. "You don't appear to have grown out of it." She sighed. "I still owe you an apology I suppose."

Cerberus looked at her in sudden surprise. "What for?"

"Firstly for my out burst that night you visited my personal chambers. Secondly, for all the disruption my presence here is causing." Cerberus opened his mouth to reply but Lida cut him off. "And I am aware of this box you've found."

Cerberus's face dropped. "I gather Selwyn informed you?"

"Lady Maleficent actually." Lida replied.

Cerberus sighed with annoyance and turned away. He took a few steps before suddenly turning back around. "What do you see in him?" Lida stepped away from the tree with sudden alarm as Cerberus took a step back towards her. "He's twice your age. He's cruel. He does nothing bar eat and drink his way into oblivion." He took another step. "He's torn away every friend you owned and punished anyone who sought to come to your aid." He stopped. "Do you love that?"

Lida closed her eyes and drew herself up. "You know I don't Cerberus, but what choice did I have. My mother and father dead. My brother left without so much as a goodbye. The Trileris were rabble rousing against House Charnite, Estalia were engaged in corporate war with Valouris; If I had done nothing there would have been civil war. I was barely in my first century for Eroth's sake!" She took a deep breath. "I had to make an alliance to a major house or risk loosing everything my family had worked so hard to create."

"You were, you are Queen. You should have crushed their squabbling." Cerberus muttered.

Lida stepped up to him her hands outstretched. "I was a girl on the throne. Crushed? I barely knew how to hold an argument."

"You seemed to do so well enough against me." Cerberus countered petulantly.

"I had to ally with a major house that could protect the kingdom from itself." Lida continued imperiously, ignoring him.

"You could have allied with Dhal-Marrah." Cerberus replied curtly.

A long pause stretched out like a blanket, smothering all sound with a strange static. The tree creaked in the gentle breeze. "I waited but you never came." The words crept from Lida's mouth, barely a whisper. She straightened the dress and fiddled with a loose bit of hair as she turned to leave. She let out a strangulated cry as Cerberus grabbed her wrist.

Cerberus let her go as she wrenched her arm away. Carefully her leaned the cane against the tree and looked up into its branches stretching towards the sky like a gnarled hand. "Girls can't climb." He spoke quietly and looked back at her.

"I beg your pardon?" Lida looked at him with a mixture of surprise and alarm.

Wincing as a stab of pain shot up his leg Cerberus placed a foot against the tree. "I said, girls can't climb."

Lida looked at the tree and then at Cerberus. "You cannot be serious." She looked back at the tree again. "Cerberus your injured."

"Good, you'll get a head start then." Cerberus reached out and grabbed the first branch beginning to pull himself up onto it. He looked back to see Lida's face simply staring at him. "If it makes you feel any better you're welcome to stop me." He made a show of wobbling as he stretched for the next branch. "Whoops! Any time you're ready."

"Eroth's teeth you're going to break your neck!" Lida gathered the skirt of the dress up into one hand and began to climb with a dexterity that surprised even her.

Cerberus paused halfway up, leaning against a branch as he waited for Lida to catch up. He grinned as she reached him. "Well, ladies first." He gestured towards the top.

Lida looked at Cerberus like he had inexplicably gone mad. "I'll fall." She protested.

"I'm going to push you if you don't." Cerberus gave her a gentle nudge.

"You wouldn't dare." Lida clutched to the branch like it was a lifeline.

Cerberus raised an eyebrow. "You seriously underestimate what I will do when bated by the prospect of a dare." He flashed a grin and shunted her again.

Lida stretched and grabbed the next branch feeling it bend as she pulled herself up. Suddenly her feet were no longer on the branch beneath her as Cerberus grabbed her with one hand and began to push her up. "Eroth! When did you get so heavy?" He huffed.

"I... what?!" Lida called below her at the insult. A tearing sound made her look back as the back of the dress caught on the sharp stump of a snapped branch.

Cerberus moved beside her and then over took, hooking one arm around the last branch while holding the other down towards Lida. She grasped it around the wrist and he pulled her up towards him. The pair of them wrested on the branch and looked out. From here the west side of the house only just blocked their view ahead. To the left the city lay like a dark smudge towards the horizon, the towers of the palace jutting out like shards of black glass. To the right patches of woodland and abandoned towers dotted the landscape and far away the ghostly peaks of mountains bled against the sky like a watermark.

"Girls still can't climb." Cerberus whispered into Lida's ear.

Lida gave him a gentle shove. "What's this then?"

Cerberus smiled. "Ah well, I don't think I mentioned anything about Queens."

Lida gave a laugh. "You really are a piece of work Cerberus." She looked down at the ground. The white flowers of the bed below looked like fresh snow. "Getting down might be more tricky."

Cerberus closed his eyes, feeling the breeze against his skin. "My mother says all Dhal-Marrah men should come with a warning notice." He smiled and looked down. "Get down? Easy."

"You can't possibly be suggesting I jump." Lida looked to him with a whisper of fear in her voice.

Cerberus's eyes lit up. "Oh you can't tell me now that your afraid of heights." An evil smile curled his mouth. "After all this time. That's why you got stuck?"

Lida refused to respond. She looked back squinting to make out a swift moving object hurrying along the path to the front of the house. "You have visitors." She announced and raised a hand to her eyes. "Charnite colours it looks to be." Cerberus's twisted his head to see. "Who are you expecting?"

"I wasn't." The smile wavered from Cerberus's face. "Selwyn... I mean Lord Charnite, sent a guard envoy to Night-moth Vale. Six men to look in on our holdings and validate the claim that was made." His eyes traced the black speck. "There is no way that any of them could be back by now." He looked at Lida. "I should get you down I suppose."

"That might be easier said than done." Lida gingerly attempted to crouch down and reach the branch below.

"Not really." With one healthy push Cerberus sent Lida off the branch and tumbling towards the ground.

Lida gave a single short scream as the ground came rising rapidly up towards her. Bracing herself against the pain of the impact, she heard the light thud of boots reaching the ground before Cerberus caught her, holding her for a second before his leg gave way and sent them both toppling into the flowers.

Lida sucked in deep breaths in an attempt to stop her furiously thudding heart, slapping Cerberus across the face the second he sat up.

"Worth it!" Cerberus laughed as he rubbed his cheek. Pain throbbed in his leg, angry at the sudden activity. Cerberus shuffled to the cane still leaned against the tree's base, using it to pull himself up as Lida began to pull bits of leaf litter from her hair. He extended a gentlemanly hand. Lida ignored it.

A light lunch was being served as Cerberus and Lida returned to the house. There was a wet tickling sensation down Cerberus's leg and he was fairly sure that he had at least partially re-opened the wound. He tried to sit straighter and not let it show as the pair of them sat at opposite sides of the table. Aunt Mal and Cerberex were already helping themselves to cooked meats and slices of some brightly coloured root vegetable that was evidently in season.

Aunt Mal leaned slightly in her chair and proffered a carafe of wine. "May I tempt you Majesty?" She asked. "Nothing as exquisite as what your used to I expect, but it has a nice bouquet."

Cerberus laughed into his own glass at Maleficent's friendliness.

Cerberex sitting two spaces away to Cerberus's right, screwed her nose up. "I can smell blood." She turned to Cerberus with a look of distaste. "Cerberus, is that you?"

Cerberus opened his mouth to deny it only for a high pitched scream to echo through the house. Immediately all attention to him was lost as with a series of scraps and the crash of a toppled chair, each of them rose from the table. Cerberus was first to dash for the door, absently leaving the walking cane behind him still rocking slightly on the floor. Cerberex was not far behind leaving Aunt Mal to reassure the Queen. The pair of them rushed down the corridor beyond the dining hall's doors and into the entrance hall. Two Dhal-Marrah house guard stood looking as if they had rushed from one side of the estate to the other.

"We tried to stop him and wait for Lord Charnite but he insisted that he see the Lord of the house immediately." One announced as Cerberus rounded the corner into the entrance hall.

"What in all the hells was that?" Shouted Cerberex as she appeared at Cerberus's side, finally followed by Maleficent a whisper behind. "Oh hell no!" Cerberex continued as they took in the view ahead of them.

A shattered china plate cover the ground from where a serving woman had dropped it, one hand now clutched over her mouth, the other on a small table. In the middle of the entrance hall an armoured guard in the deep blue of house Charnite stood. The silver of his plate was dappled in blood and he clutched at his eyes.

"What is the meaning of this?" Cerberus asked. His breath caught in his throat as the guard pulled away his hands, revealing that his eyes had been pulled out and crudely carved into the skin of his forehead were the words "she's mine."

Silence suffocated the air from the room, smothering them.

Chapter 18:
Calm Before the Storm

Cerberus walked with purpose. Events were moving fast. To his mind it was no longer a case of if the Gal-Serreks would move against them - but when. The cane tapped against the stone. Assassins moved out of the way as he passed as if sensing the mood of their master. He passed the armoury. Aunt Mal had seen fit to return his rapier under the assurance he would continue with the cane for at least another day.

"So the cripple walks among us." Meera laughed as Cerberus rounded the corner into the bunk room.

In a second Cerberus flicked the cane up, levelling the silvered end into Meera's clavicle and pushing her against the open door. "This 'cripple' can still beat you Meera and don't you forget it."

Meera gave a strangulated laugh as she looked around the bunk room. Five pairs of eyes watched them. "I wouldn't have said you couldn't darling."

Cerberus withdrew the cane. "Did you receive my warning?"

Meera straightened. "I did." She motioned for him to follow her to the back of the room. "You can't possibly believe that the house would actually..."

"I've just sent a man with no eyes back to his family for no other reason than he was loosely affiliated. The man wasn't even a Dhal-Marrah - and all this was done in broad day light. At this point I'd not put anything past them." Cerberus interjected.

Meera pursed her lips. "And all this because you gate crashed a party?" Cerberus shifted uncomfortably. Meera's eyes narrowed. "What aren't you telling me?" She glanced around. "Cerberus, how can I deploy our forces best if you don't tell me what I'm missing?"

"As much as it pains me to say it, we may have something of his." Cerberus muttered.

"Of his?" Meera glanced over at the others in the room. "What did you take?" She hissed.

Cerberus walked to the far wall. "The Queen is in house Dhal-Marrah." He whispered.

"Still?" Meera's face turned pale in shock. "Are you mad? We do not have the forces required to take on whatever the Gal-Serreks can throw and the King's guard!" She paused as her rising voice attracted the others attention.

"Selwyn seems to think that they wont want to make this public. We're expecting a raiding party not an army." Cerberus replied.

"Selwyn Charnite." Meera spat. "It's his fault we are in this mess in the first place."

Cerberus looked her in the eye. "Careful Meera."

"Of what? I'm not the one that needs to be careful. You're putting your personal feelings before the job Cerberus and it's going to get you killed."

Cerberus took a deep breath. "Meera, you are my best, you are my friend, and you are my first. We may be few but we will be enough." He held out his hand.

Meera looked at it as if it was a coiled snake. "When?"

"That's what you're going to find out for me. Take a couple with you and keep an eye out. I want to know the second that anything changes." Cerberus smiled still holding out his hand.

She looked at him and clasped his hand in hers. "I hope your right about this Cerberus, I really do." Meera turned to the five remaining assassin's in the room. "Seska! Pick one of the newly blooded and suit up. We have work to do."

The heads of the other assassin's snapped up as Meera called over to them. Seska in the midst of playing a hand of cards with Kane looked up, locked eyes with Meera, and gave a curt nod before laying her cards upon the makeshift table and scooping her wins. She looked to her left, giving the young male drau next to her a nudge and the pair of them walked out.

Meera turned back to Cerberus. "You've been making some very poor decisions Master. As your First it's my duty to remind you to start thinking with your head and less with your heart." She did not give Cerberus the chance to reply, turning heel and marching towards and out the door of the bunk room.

Cerberus took in a deep breath and slowly walked to where Seska's seat had now been taken by a much younger occupant carefully shuffling the deck of well-worn cards. They looked up at him as he drew near with expectation. "No time for games." He said quietly. "Those of you marked, get your weapons and join the patrols. No one walks alone tonight." His eye caught the young dealer. "For those of you not, rest up. You're going to need it." He heard the slight groan as the cards were put down. Kane stood up to follow the other older assassins. Cerberus put a hand on his shoulder, holding him back. Kane looked. "Not you." Cerberus spoke quietly. "You and I need to talk Kane." Cerberus let go and moved past. For a moment Kane didn't move but then slowly he picked up his torso armour from the end of the bunk and followed Cerberus out and down the hallway.

The small study was dusty with an essence of fallen grandeur. Cerberus gestured to a pair of worn looking chairs in the corner as Kane followed him in. Cerberus rarely used the study, preferring to be out among them rather than cloistered away with books and paper. Kane sat heavily, disturbing a fine layer of dust from a nearby shelf and looked at Cerberus with thinly veiled intrigue. Cerberus shut the door without a sound and took the other seat opposite.

"Well you're walking at least." Kane began lightly in an attempt to break the oppressive silence between them.

Cerberus looked at the cane and snorted a laugh. "Don't worry, I wont need this for long. Just long enough to appease the family and drive me slightly mad in the process." He looked at Kane with glinting eyes.

Kane smiled with relief at the joke, relaxing back into the chair. "And there I was thinking we had achieved that already. You do realise that your sister is almost entirely responsible for you still having that leg." He grinned.

Cerberus's lips curled slightly at the corners. " Her and you as I understand it. You're lucky to still be with us too I believe."

Kane shrugged. "Nothing I couldn't handle." Unconsciously he rubbed his side just below the ribs. "Bastard shot a bolt and cracked a rib. It's healing nicely though. Why? Did you want to see the scar?"

Cerberus gave a short laugh. "Far from it." He leaned forward. "Question is whether you're field worthy."

Kane's eyes went cold. "Cerberus please tell me that you did not ask me here to tell me I'm on light duties." He paused and looked at Cerberus's wounded leg stretched out between them. "Because it doesn't appear to be stopping you." He added pointedly.

Cerberus's smile didn't waver. "Far from it but Cerberex isn't here to patch us all up as a field medic." He tapped his fingers against his knee.

Kane raised an eyebrow. "Would you rather we had left you?"

"That's what you are supposed to do." Cerberus replied.

"Your sister would never have forgiven us if we had. She's already rescued you once. If you'd been captured again or worse she would likely have..."

"refused to leave?" Cerberus cut in sarcastically. "Mourned my passing?"

"I was going to go with killed us but sure why not." Kane smirked.

"Oh I highly doubt that she could have taken out two chosen and an assassin by herself." Cerberus laughed.

"I think you doubt her capabilities." Kane began quietly.

Cerberus leaned forward. "Do I?" He watched Kane carefully as their eyes met.

Kane sat back in the chair, his eyes narrowing with suspicion "Where are you going with this Cerberus?" He began tentatively.

Cerberus raised an eyebrow and sat back folding his arms. "Kane I'm going to make an educated guess that you rather like my sister."

"I... what?" Kane looked in surprise. Caught off by the sudden bluntness of the statement. "No! Not like ... Cerberus don't you think that having your sister around might actually be a benefit with her particular talents?"

"Oh come off it Kane you're a terrible liar!" He paused. "And I should have figured it out faster."

Kane rubbed his eyes. "Cerberus even if I was - and I'm telling you it's not like that - do you honestly think that I would make any move? I rather like my neck where it is and without any extra breathing holes."

Cerberus laughed. "Your making excuses to patrol her haunts. You stopped to help her on the way to The Vaults. If you can't see it yourself I guarantee you that everyone else can."

Kane's brow furrowed with annoyance. "Ridiculous! We were shadow walking. She would never have kept up." He stood. "If this is what you want to talk about then I'm not continuing this conversation. Your sister is talented I grant you, but..."

"Oh calm down and sit." Cerberus waved him down. "I'm not here to push a confession." He watched Kane sit back down. "Cerberex is skilled and she knows about all of this now, but let's be clear, she is not one of us. The Gal-Serreks will come to retrieve Lida one way or another and they will do it in the only way Gal-Serreks know how - with brute force. If they can destroy what's left of Dhal-Marrah in the process so much the better. Cerberex is heir to this house. Without her Dhal-Marrah fades into obscurity."

"You don't think the King might be more interested in you than your sister?" Kane interjected.

Cerberus grinned. "Oh I'm counting on it, but my guess is he will want to deal with me personally. Cerberex is collateral in ensuring there aren't any loose ends." He paused. "So I want you to watch her."

Kane almost jumped up from his chair in surprise. "You want me to what?"

"I want you to watch her. She's aware of you now, so go, feel free to introduce yourself although I'd advise not telling her everything we've spoken of." Cerberus's eyes glittered with glee at Kane's shock.

"You've been very clear about keeping out of sight of the house above, and now you want me to go and introduce myself to your sister." Kane rubbed his temple.

"If the going gets rough it will be your job to ensure that she's not caught up in it. Her protection if you like." Cerberus added.

"I hardly think she needs protection." Kane muttered.

Cerberus smirked. "You might not think so." He paused. "She's in the library I think this evening. No prior entertainment plans." He stood and opened the door. "Why don't you liven up her evening."

Kane looked at him with distaste. "You send me like some penniless entertainer?!" He stood again taking a deep breath. "Fine. I'll check in on her." He made his way to the door but stopped just ahead of Cerberus. "I'm doing this because you ask and because we all owe her a favour after last time. It's professional not personal."

Cerberus nodded smiling. "Of course." He held the door open in expectation.

Cerberex wrested her head against her hand as she idly flipped the pages of the large leather bound book. Smaller tombs and sheaves of paper covered the desk, precariously close to the naked candle. She closed her eyes against the words of the pages as they blurred. She could still see the empty eye sockets of the Charnite guard in her mind. Upon closer inspection, they had discovered the eyeballs in a pouch attached to his neck but as skilled healers as both her aunt and mother were, there was no possible way the guard would see again. Of the others he had been sent with there was no sign. Uncle Selwyn seemed fairly resigned to the notion that they had never made it to Night-moth Vale.

She turned the page again. House Gal-Serrek was not as old as that of Dhal-Marrah. It had risen to prominence a little before the Dwentar War. Cerberus seemed convinced that they were coming and had responded in the only way Cerberus ever did, by stamping his feet and making a lot of noise. Cerberex sighed. The Gal-Serreks must have heralded from an older probably extinct house. Considering that House Dhal-Marrah seemed to still play host to a coterie of assassins in the basement, it now seemed reasonable to believe that the other major houses might also quietly continue the old ways. So what would that be in the case of the Gal-Serreks? She flipped past a dozen or so pages in the hope that the information might jump out at her.

"Are you looking for something in particular or do you simply enjoy the sound of turning paper?"

Cerberex almost knocked the naked candle onto the floor as she jumped at the sudden sound of the voice. She looked behind her around the back of the chair. Its owner leaned nonchalantly against a bookcase. The recognisable dark leather armour was now unbuckled casually at the top. No hood or mask covered the stormy colour of his skin and pale silver-blonde hair was pulled into a tight knot at the back of his head. He studied her with silver flecked eyes that held just a hint of violet.

"It's you again." Cerberex stood, turning away from her studying.

"It's me again." The stranger smiled and rolled his eyes dramatically.

Cerberex looked around suddenly drawn by the silence of the room. "How long have you been standing there?"

His smile widened. "About fifteen minutes."

"Fifteen minutes! How?" Cerberex demanded unsure if he was lying.

"Well, I'm pretty good at what I do." He took a step forward. "We keep bumping into each other it seems, so maybe its time for proper introductions."

Cerberex placed her hands on her hips. "Well I think I introduced myself quiet clearly the first time."

He gave a quiet laugh and put a hand on his shoulder. "Yes, you rather made your point."

Cerberex couldn't help herself but laugh a little at the pun. She performed a small mock-curtsey. "Lady Cerberex of House Dhal-Marrah."

He made an overly exaggerated bow in response. "Kane."

"Kane? Is there a house or name that goes with that?" Cerberex asked.

He shrugged and shook his head. "Just Kane."

"Well 'just Kane', it's a pleasure." She smiled sarcastically.

He dipped his head a fraction. "The pleasures all mine." He replied and walked to the desk scanning over the books lying open upon it. "So what are you looking for?"

"Well I learned recently that I'm harbouring a host of bloodthirsty murderers beneath the floors of this house." She watched his nose wrinkle at the description. "Oh don't worry it's something the Dhal-Marrah's were once known for. Apparently." She gestured to the books. "But I'm beginning to wonder if we are the only ones still clinging to the old ways."

Kane chose to ignore the slight and flipped through a couple of pages. "You're looking for Gal-Serreks specialisms?"

Cerberex turned back to the books her arms folded in frustration. "Yes, but I can't find anything on the family let alone..."

"Fighters." Kane interrupted, looking at her with a grin. "Brute force shock troops and an exceptional mastery for smithing armour."

"How do you know that?" The words tumbled out of Cerberex's mouth before she could stop herself.

He stood up and gave her a sideways look. "You're the one who just called me a bloodthirsty murderer. Have a guess."

"Well I didn't mean..." Cerberex faltered. She raised an eyebrow. "Well 'just Kane' you are full of surprises."

"Would you like to know the others?" He asked politely sensing her piqued interest. He didn't wait for a response. "Lotheri are masters of the arcane. They train coteries of acanists not to mention healers. Charnite apart from being supreme diplomats and negotiators, also train law-keepers and lawyers. Quite possibly there is no secret in the city they do not know and so naturally spies also falls under their remit. Valouris are explorers. Their quite considerable wealth comes from the sea and ships. Estalia, well there's a shady house indeed. They'd like to think of themselves as assassins I'm sure, but they're really no better than slavers. Which of course brings us to Trileris, whose honour can be measured in coin. Their mercenary battalions have garrisoned the outer reaches of the kingdom for centuries."

Cerberex exhaled and slammed the book shut. "Where did you learn this?"

"We like to keep up to date on what our targets' capabilities might be." Kane replied cryptically.

"Targets? You mean those you're assigned to kill." She perched on the table.

Kane took a respectful step back. "The clue is in the name."

Cerberex looked at him her eyes darting over his armour.

Kane grinned. "Oh your quite safe. I'm not carrying any weapons with me." He paused. "Or at least, not ones you'll find easily." He stretched his arms out as if allowing her to check.

Cerberex didn't fall for what seemed an obvious trick. "You don't seem... I mean you don't talk like the type."

"Not enough 'killer' for you?" Kane asked with a laugh.

Cerberex smirked. "Not quite." She paused. "Have you killed?"

Kane looked at her puzzled. "You saw me."

"Not like that. I meant contracted." Cerberex clarified.

"Yes." He replied simply.

"How many?" Cerberex continued, folding her arms.

"Some." Kane returned.

"Does it pay well."

"Enough." Kane mirrored her folding his own. "You know, you ask a lot of questions."

Cerberex caught herself. "Oh, I'm sorry."

Kane laughed. "No no, it's quite alright." He put up a hand. "Actually it's quite refreshing." He watched her eyes flicker with surprise. "Well I mean I get asked questions but usually it's the same one over and over again."

"What's that?" Cerberex looked at him amused.

"Why?" Kane replied and the pair of them laughed.

Cerberex opened the drawer of the desk and pulled out a bottle of cherry brandy. She uncorked it and offered it to Kane first. "You know contrary to my brother's other acquaintances over the years, I think I might actually be able to tolerate you 'just Kane'."

Kane took the bottle and swigged. "I feel honoured." He coughed.

Chapter 19:
The Dead of Night

Cerberex woke. Her mouth tasted like ash. She pulled her head achingly from the desk and massaged it with one hand. The library was dark but not quite light-less. Slivers of silver cut past the curtains at the back of the room. She stretched almost knocking over the empty bottle on the edge of the desk. Her head was throbbing. She felt around as her eyes adjusted but found only the one. Carefully she sniffed the bottle in her hand. The lingering aroma of alcohol made her stomach turn, mixed with ... something else?

"Bastard." She swore putting the bottle heavily down on the table. "How could you have been so stupid to let him drug you so easily." Cerberex chastised herself, pushing up from the chair. A heavy thud from beyond the library door made her freeze for a moment. Silence followed. Her eyes narrowed. Quietly she made her way towards the window and shifted the curtain. The moon was hanging low in a soft teal sky that seemed to render everything like a charcoal sketch. She drew the curtain back. It was maybe four in the morning. How long had she been out? She rubbed her eyes. Her memory seemed to be shattered into thousands of tiny fragments. The faint sound of something shattering echoed in the silence. Her head snapped back to the door again. "What the?" She spoke to herself making her way unsteadily to the door. It was too early for the day servants to have begun and none so far as she knew, would dare make such a noise at this hour.

Cerberex steadied herself against the solid wood of the door, closed her eyes, and listened. Silence once more seemed to stretch out timelessly, then just as she was about to turn the handle, a series of soft thuds - footsteps, out of sequence, heavy, definitely more than more pair. Each thought crystallized painfully in her brain. Cerberex took a deep breath and gently twisted the handle, inching the door open with a soft creak. She jumped back in surprise at the pale figure in the hallway beyond. The serving girl sat sleeping on a chaise long. Her grey dress made her look spectre-like against the studded velvet. Cerberex glanced down the hallway and quietly made her way over towards the sleeping human. Gently she shook her. She felt wet. Cerberex's eyes narrowed and she withdrew her hand. It seemed sticky, she brought it to her face and sniffed, taking two steps back in alarm as the iron tang of blood filled her nose. Hushed murmurs of conversation drifted down the corridor. Cerberex rubbed her hand against her clothes. She had no weapons. Her knives safely locked away in her room alongside her bow and arrows. Flattening herself against the wall, she began to make her way towards the voices.

There was no mistaking it. The voices were male. Two maybe three of them? It was hard to say from the echo of the house. She neared the end of the corridor. She had half expected whoever it was to round a corner on her at any moment. She doubled up into a crouch as she approached the entrance hall.

"I don't care if you have to behead everyone in this house - find her!" One voice raised louder than the others.

Cerberex moved up against a small side table and peered round. She could make out the shapes of four individuals. One stood ahead of the others. Another heavier humanoid shadow stood between two more.

"What of this one?" Another male voice asked and Cerberex watched the middle individual nudge forward.

There was a heavy sneer. "He won't talk. Dhal-Marrah puppets always stay quiet." The first voice murmured. Its owner took a step forward. Cerberex saw the reflective shimmer of a dagger too late as it sank into the central individual. They gave a muffled yell before slumping forward and Cerberex realised they had been gagged. The dagger sank into them a second, then a third, till the body fell heavily to the floor. Cerberex shifted back against the table her breath caught in her throat.

The small ceramic bowl atop the table wobbled with her sudden movement. It hit the floor but didn't break, rolling out into the middle of the room. Cerberex tried to make herself as small as possible. She dared a second peek, watching as the bowl rolled till it was stopped by the heavy leather of an armoured boot. Cerberex pressed herself back against the table again.

"We're not alone gentlemen." The first voice muttered.

"Sir, the orders are specific. We are..." A second voice interrupted.

"It's probably nothing." A third added.

"I'm well aware of our orders." The first again. Then the soft pad of foot falls growing closer. Cerberex held her breath. "Bowls don't just fall over." The first began again. He was close now, much closer. Cerberex could almost sense his shadow looming over her. "I've heard things about this place." The edge of a boot came into view. Cerberex shut her eyes tight expecting discovery at any moment.

"Sir, the orders..." The second voice came again, the urgency of it more profound than before.

"Yes, yes..." The first grumbled turning away.

Cerberex let go of her breath. She waited for a moment and listened for any sound of the trespassers. Silence gathered once more. She stood fluidly in a bid to run for the stairs and shrieked as firm hand grabbed her arms.

"And what do we have here?"

Cerberex caught the face of a male Drau flanked by a second. Their light scale armour was edged in red and both were heavily built. She snapped her arm free of the grip restraining her and twisted a few feet away almost knocking over the table she had used as her hiding spot.

"Evening gentlemen." Cerberex began breathlessly, her voice sounded stupidly loud. "I don't believe we were expecting guests."

The sound of low laughter echoed between the pair of them. The taller of them nodded at the second. "Take the Dhal-Marrah bitch down but keep her alive. She might be useful if we run into difficulties."

Cerberex watched as the second inched towards her. The soft hiss of a sword or knife leaving its scabbard reached her ears. She dodged to one side as it swung towards her, delivering her elbow into it's owners face and twisting to follow with a low punch to the gut. A warm smugness fell over her as she felt the fist connect and the drau double up.

"I think your difficulties are just beginning." Cerberex smiled dangerously.

"Cerberex Dhal-Marrah is it then?" The taller and Cerberex assumed mastermind of this operation, unsheathed a heavy sword from his back. The edge of the blade notched for maximum pain with minimum damage.

Cerberex took a calculated step back. "You sir have a hint of breeding about you. So I'll make you a deal."

The drau took a step towards her, watching her every move. "You have nothing to offer me Dhal-Marrah besides your pretty little head." His grip on the blade tightened. "Your miserable excuse of a house might have been left to disappear into inevitable extinction but you've taken something that doesn't belong to you and my lord can't be having that." He sneered. "Really I just needed the excuse." He leaped forward.

Cerberex darted to one side as the blade shattered the small table into matchwood. "In my defence." She replied trying to keep to his side. "It was actually my brother that did the taking." She clenched a fist and hammered it into the Drau's ribs. Her knuckles cracked and pain burst up her arm as she discovered the metal panel that lay beneath. She gasped and withdrew her arm.

The drau laughed. "Oh your going to need something better than your little hands to get through me girl."

Cerberex felt the bruising begin to swell across her knuckles. She gave a cry as arms suddenly encircled her from behind. She pushed against the restraint, glancing over her shoulder and catching the face of the second drau - nose lodged at a peculiar angle and leaking a trickle of blood.

"Put some restraints on this one, maybe we'll make an example of her." The first drau began as he leaned in to peer at her.

"Take your hands off my niece." Cerberex glanced up at the overhanging landing of the first floor as the sound of Aunt Mal's voice.

Maleficent stood surrounded by floating globules of gently pulsating lights. Her face was a mask of rage despite the dangerous calm of her voice. "How dare you enter this house without invite or warrant." She moved to the bannister. "Where are your manners?"

Cerberex felt the arms around her tighten as she tried to use the distraction to her advantage. The drau looked at her and then at Maleficent.

"Well as you appear to have rendered yourself mute, I suppose that leaves me to take out the trash myself." Maleficent brought up her hands. Cerberex had a second to suddenly coil in and throw her restrainer over her shoulders with a grunt of effort, before Aunt Mal brought them together with the sound of a thunderclap. The two drau slammed backwards colliding into a set of shelves that buckled, tipping the contents of two shelves on top of them. Cerberex looked up, Maleficent's arms were outstretched and her unbound hair whipped about her as if caught in the grip of a hurricane.

"Hurry my dear, I'd hate for you to get caught up in what happens next." Maleficent called down to her.

Cerberex needed no provocation. She sprinted for the stairs taking them two at a time. Nearing first her brother's bedroom, she barged the door open and glanced around. A lantern flickered almost to guttering. The room was in disarray. Wherever her brother had gone he had left in a hurry. She turned and jogged the few feet to her own room, flying into it as if the very demons of hell were behind her. In the entrance below she could hear the sound of thundering feet. She hadn't believed they were alone but the sound of so many. As she pushed the door closed she could hear her aunt retreating into the house calling Selwyn's name.

Cerberex looked around and laid her hands against a wooden dresser, dragging across the tiled floor and across the door. Muffled by the wood, she could hear the heavy footsteps coming closer. She heard the door of her brother's room slam. The dismayed voices as they too found nothing but an empty bed. She stood listening as they tore Cerberus's room apart, rooted to the spot. Suddenly her own door gave a loud bang, shocking her back to her senses. The dresser rocked but did not budge. Shouts came from the other side. Brought to her senses, she glanced about the room. Her light armour, recently cleaned and oiled since last use, hung on a mannequin nearby. She dropped down and dragged a trunk from beneath the bed. Twisting the key in the lock she pushed open the lid and pulled her bow, knives and arrows from within. The door gave another bang. Cerberex stood and drew one of the knives from its sheath. The silvered edge of the blade seemed to shimmer. Careful not to cut herself, Cerberex sheared through the skirt of the dress, tearing it to just below her waist. She dropped the knife to the bed and grabbed the light armour. Another bang and the dresser by the door was shunted a few inches, the polished wood of its surface splintering. She slipped into the trousers. They were soft with over lapping leather strips designed to protect against the thorns and bracken of the wilds but not a sword. Hands reached around the small opening in the door and the dresser began the grate across the tiles. Cerberex grabbed the top half, buckling it once, twice, three times, around her breast and waist like an over sized belt. The dresser toppled. Cerberex reached for her bow.

The door slammed open with a loud bang against the adjoining wall. Cerberex watched a drau in heavy leather and plate tinted black and red in alternating layers cautiously enter the room and look at her arrow drawn a matter of maybe six feet from his face. Cerberex smiled. "Good morning." She fired. The drau toppled backwards as the arrow protruded from his left eye. A series of shouts came from the landing beyond in response. Cerberex slung the bow onto her shoulder and grabbed the knives from the bed, sliding them into their sheaths either side. Bright torchlight flickered towards the room from outside the doorway, casting several dark shadows. She looked around and moved toward the window pushing it open. There was movement below. Shouts and curses reached her ears but it was impossible if they belonged to those fighting for or against the house. She twisted looking up. A window ledge of the room above jutted a few inches out and beyond that a supposedly decorative gargoyle glared down from the roof.

"Seize her!" Voices shouted.

Cerberex made the decision and grabbed onto the window frame, pulling herself out onto the ledge. She reached up and felt the her fingernails break as she hauled herself onto the ledge above. Looking down, her room below was now filled with light and dark shapes. She grabbed the jaw of the gargoyle, balancing on her tip toes precariously. The gargoyle thankfully didn't move. She hooked a foot up onto it's neck and hung upside down for a moment before pulling herself up onto its back and shimmying between its wings onto the roof.

For the first time in what felt like hours but could only be measured in minutes, Cerberex stopped to take stock of the situation. Evidently, Cerberus had taken care of the Queen, removing her she hoped, to a safe house or hiding spot or ideally as far from the Dhal-Marrah manor as possible. That left the house itself and those within, her priority. She stalked across the rooftop watching the movements below. The sky above her was slowly beginning to turn a grey blue, bleeding colour back into her surroundings. She could see more clearly now that those enemies within the grounds themselves and from the sounds of things in the house also, were more pre-occupied with searching more than murder.

Cerberex skittered down the other side of the roof. Jutting from the floor below, a small balcony lay atop what might be the dining hall below that. She jumped and rolled as she landed on it. Peering over the ornate balustrade, the walled courtyard lay below. Four figures stood in the pre-dawn light with their backs pressed against each other. Their black armour was becoming more familiar. Cerberex felt sure that one of the females had been the one she'd seen fighting Meera on her tour with Cerberus, the other could be Seska judging by the twin daggers but she couldn't be certain from this angle. For a moment she watched confused by their cautious moves. Then she noticed the six other plate armoured shapes gradually encircling them from various sides.

"Your house is taken." Cerberex ground her teeth as she recognised the voice. From beneath her walking into the courtyard, sword once more across his back, the same drau that had sought to capture her what seemed only moments ago. "And you are surrounded." Cerberex quietly slid an arrow from her quiver and unslung her bow waiting for the assassins' inevitable attack as she notched ready.

"You break the covenant of hearth and home sir." Seska seemed to spit the words from her mouth. Though a hood covered her head, Cerberex knew her voice.

The drau laughed dryly. "Someone should tell your master that. Don't cite the law to me bitch. The covenant doesn't protect traitors and criminals." He took a step forward. "But maybe you need a better incentive." He turned and gestured behind him and a second drau in heavy plate armour stepped into the courtyard shoving a young black clad man in front of him.

Cerberex withdrew the arrow in her bow as the prisoner stumbled onto the stone slabs in front of the other assassins. He had short pale grey hair against alabaster skin and was young. Cerberex guessed that this unknown male was less than a century. She re-notched the arrow and waited.

A murmur rippled through the circle of assassins. One by one they sheathed their weapons and knelt placing their hands on the back of their necks. The drau laughed again as he approached. "Common sense prevails."

"We claim..." Seska's voice can again.

Cerberex flinched as she watched the drau backhand her across the face. "Oh do shut up you common slut." He stepped over her. Cerberex willed the others to stand as she tracked him with her bow. The drau spat at the prone form in front of him. He waved a hand as he turned away. "Take the pretty ones. The King can always use more entertainment."

"And the boy sir?" The voice was muffled behind the helmet of the plate armoured drau.

"Kill him. I'm not a babysitter for bastard whelps." The drau sneered.

Cerberex looked as her target began to move, torn between him or the other assailants now closing in. She waited for a moment, silently praying that the remaining three assassins would take up arms. Yet they stood meek as lambs in the slaughterhouse. The click of a heavy crossbow being loaded and Cerberex hissed in frustration as she switched targets while the drau moved out of sight back into the house. She waited as the armoured drau wrenched the boy to his feet and reached for a sword and fired. The arrow soared punching into the back of the plate and staggering him enough for the boy to twist from his grasp. Lightening quick she notched another and fired again. The attention of the assassins was now on her. From the corner of her eye she could see the surprise across their faces. The arrow embedded itself between the vembrace and shoulder guard illiciting a cry of pain. Suddenly a hail of heavy bolts whistled towards her. Cerberex ducked, just missing them by barely an inch. She cursed quietly under her breath. "Why do you not fight?" She hissed to no-one under her breath. Slinging back her bow she waited for the sound of reloading and vaulted over the top.

The landing was heavy as she dropped from the floor above. She grunted as she landed but had no time to check for injury. Spinning her knives from their scabbards she ploughed both into the abdomen of a surprised crossbowman, kicking him away and spinning under the sword swing of the armoured drau. She turned to the assassins only now beginning to rise from the ground. "Get up." She shouted at them. "Get up you idiots and get after that one." Cerberex gestured to the drau who had earlier called for them to yield. "And prey to Eroth that I don't tell Cerberus what I just witnessed!" She parried the next heavy sword blow.

"Do not let them get away." The muffled shout of her opponent called to the others as the assassins shot passed her like chasing shadows.

Cerberex glanced the next blow off the sides of her knives hearing them scream against the metal before a heavy boot slammed into her stomach and sent her winded, across the paving. She coughed and looked up at the faceless suit of armour looming over her. She tried to move but her stomach rebelled. The sword rose and Cerberex waited for the slice.

It did not come. The helmeted head snapped back suddenly as a cord spun around his throat. Cerberex shifted and saw the initiate pull the two ends of a wire garotte with all his might. Gripping her right-hand knife, Cerberex forced herself to her feet and dragged the blade across the bared throat of the armoured figure. Hot blood sprayed against her armour as he dropped.

The pair of them watched thick crimson spilled across the stone paving breathing hard. They eyed each other warily.

"Lady Cerberex..." The initiate began, slowly crossing his arms against his chest and lowering to an awkward bow.

"Wha- what is your name?" Cerberex caught her breath.

"I er, they call me Clogaen." He replied.

Cerberex stood and held up a hand. "Let me guess, just Clogaen?"

Clogaen nodded.

Cerberex forced a smile. "Can you shoot Clogaen?"

"I... well yes, I can actually." Clogaen replied tentatively.

Cerberex swung her bow off her shoulders and unbuckled the quiver. Taking a step forward, she handed it to him, watching as he looked at her like she was offering him a vial of poison. "Well take it, it wont bite!" She shoved a quiver into his hands. Clogaen took it and held it clumsily. Cerberex rolled her eyes. "I'm not about to let my home be overrun by these bastards and I doubt my brother will either. So when these fools regret trespassing on House Dhal-Marrah and believe me they are about to regret doing that, you are going to harry them with arrows from the roof just to push the point home got it?" Clogaen's face lit up slightly and nodded. Cerberex put a hand on his shoulder. "Go." She watched as he raced towards the house and began to climb the trellis. "Try not to break it." She muttered out of earshot.

Reflexively spinning her knives, Cerberex stalked back into the house through the dining hall's garden doors. The house was alive with the sound of combat. She moved quickly avoiding the fallen chairs and destroyed tableware that littered the floor. Standing by memory with her back against the wall, she tried to press her way through it. The wall felt solid. "Come on, open!" She muttered to it but it did not budge. A yell echoed somewhere in the house. She turned and placed her palms against the cool stone and pushed for all she could muster and nothing. "For the love of Eroth, open up you bloody thing!" Cerberex insisted and struck at it with a knife illiciting a few sparks off the blade. Suddenly the outline of the doorway flashed red and the illusion of the wall melted away. Cerberex gave a cry of success before having to take a step back as a black shadow passed through the door and suddenly stopped.

Kane stood in the doorway looking at her with as much surprise as she stood looking at him. Cerberex recovered first, sheathing a knife and punching him straight to the face.

"Ow!" Kane recoiled slightly. "What in all the hells?"

"You drugged me." Cerberex shouted at him and took another punch.

Kane dodged effortlessly out of the way. "You pretty much asked for it!"

Cerberex prepared a third punch and paused before she could throw it. "I what?"

Kane straightened. "Well specifically you questioned my abilities and I think at one point possibly stated that you were and don't quote me on this, too quick to meet your end on the tip of an assassin's blade."

"So you drugged me?" Cerberex's eyes flashed with anger.

"Well more to the point, I could have poisoned you," He dodged again as she punched. "But I feel Cerberus might have frowned on that." He gave her a quick grin.

A banshee shriek resonated through the house. Cerberex stopped glaring and snapped her head around to the door at the far end of the dining hall. "Are the other's safe?" She asked turning back.

"Safe?" Kane repeated. "If by 'safe' you mean out defending your house, then yes."

Something heavy thumped to the floor of the room above. Cerberex wrinkled her nose. "Time to round this rabble up."

Kane pulled the sword out from its sheath between his shoulders with one hand and brought up his scarf to mask his face with the other. "I couldn't agree more."

Chapter 20:
Messenger Boy

Cerberus backed up towards the wall of the visitor's chambers. Three drau stepped forward in a semi circle, the same stupid smile copied on each of their faces. Each was clearly imagining the reward for bringing down Lord Dahl-Marrah. Cerberus shifted in the plain assassins armour. It felt a little tight but his own was in need of significant repair.

"Gentlemen, I believe you were expecting someone else." He spun the rapier and grinned.

"As you say little lord, but we'll take Cerberus Dhal-Marrah as a conciliation prize." The left one sniggered. His voice was rough, uncouth, farming stock maybe.

"Ay and by the time we've finished with you, you'll be dying to tell us where the sweet little Lotheri lady is hiding." The middle one added with all the bravado of a thug.

Cerberus shook his head. "Well unfortunately I have other things that require my attention rather than deal with you but you're here, you've pissed me off, so welcome to the top of the shit list!"

Dependably the three immediately rushed forward, blades bared in a profuse of weaponry. Cerberus sighed and stepped lightly to one side. Grabbing the first he slammed the drau into the wall with a pleasing crack as the idiot's nose broke under the impact of his face. The scream made his comrade stagger for the only second Cerberus needed to grab his head between his palms and twist. He fell limp in Cerberus's arms and Cerberus dropped him unceremoniously to the floor. The whistle of metal through the air made him duck and turn bringing up the rapier to parry a heavy downward strike. He pushed the blade aside and swung to open his stomach. A heavy thwack resonated as a black fletched bolt slammed into his opponents neck. The drau attacker grasped at his throat as he sank to his knees, blood beading on his lips. Cerberus looked to the other side of the room and saw Meera in the doorway arm outstretched her finger wrapped around the trigger of her crossbow.

"Sorry I'm late to the party darling." She purred, casually stepping over the twitching man. She walked with poise but Cerberus could see she was breathing heavily and a slight limp hampered her gait. "Got into a spot of mischief. I sent Seska back ahead. Did she reach you?"

Cerberus shook his head and nudged the now dead miscreant with the toe of his boot. "I've seen no one bar Gal-Serrek scum for at least an hour."

Meera paced the room, swinging open a wardrobe and finding it empty. "So where is she?" Meera turned and placed her hands on her hips.

Cerberus smiled. "In the safest place I know. Though she didn't go quietly." His face changed to one of slight concern.

"Did she not. Well the sooner we evict the squatters, the sooner she can get out of our hair and return to more comfortable quarters." Meera reloaded a bolt into her crossbow and pulled two small daggers from her belt.

Cerberus stepped over the bodies to the door and glanced down the corridor beyond. Movement made him snap back to the wall. Meera looked up and shadow walked to the opposite side of the door as a thunder of feet ran passed.

"How many?" Cerberus mouthed at her.

Meera shrugged. "I only saw the last ones leave. Nearly didn't make it in time to see anything." She whispered back.

Cerberus waited for the tremor of feet to fade and nodded to Meera. One after the other they silently slid from the doorway into the corridor beyond. The house thrummed to the sound of skirmishes taking place between Dhal-Marrah house guard and the intruders from all angles. Cerberus had last seen his uncle brutally decapitate one just outside the bathing room with a sword Cerberus could only guess, had been liberated from one of the archaic suits of armour that decorated the house. His mother had appeared from her own rooms like a banshee, hurling another over the bannisters of the first floor landing with enough force to crack tiles. Her hands had been bursting with arcane light. The heaven's only knew how Aunt Mal fared but Cerberus wagered that whoever found her would likely regret it. That left Cerberex. Where was his sister? He had gone back to the library as soon as he had made Lida safe and found nothing.

They rounded the corner. A dark shape lay dumped against the wall. Cerberus almost tripped over the outstretched legs. The black leather armour too familiar. Cerberus knelt and tugged down the scarf. She was young. He looked her over. A massive wound to her side was slick with slowly congealing blood. He grabbed her right arm pushing up the sleeve.

"She's an initiate." Cerberus stated grimly. He looked over his shoulder at Meera and stood looking back angrily at the dead girl. "I thought I was clear, they were to stay behind, a final defence."

Meera placed a hand lightly on his shoulder. "Darling, don't be so upset. Your house was under attack. They were never going to simply sit on their hands and wait for the action to come to them."

"Do you know this one?" Cerberus asked.

Meera leaned forward and peered at the face. "Maybe." She shook her head. "Not a name to put to a face though. She must have been quite new."

"Barely out of training and already dead." Cerberus ground his teeth. "If one's here then the rest of them will be out too."

"They are trained for this Cerberus." Meera coaxed. "They just wanted to prove themselves. We both know how that feels."

"How it feels got this one dead." Cerberus replied and knelt once again, crossing the dead girl's arms across her chest and placing his forehead gently against hers.

Meera huffed impatiently as Cerberus tended the dead initiates rites. "We should get a move on." She muttered. "The longer this pack of dogs stay, the stronger their hold will be and more likely they'll call to reinforce their position." She stalked around Cerberus and peered down the corridor lit in half-light. "They're looking for the Queen." She turned back. "Out of curiosity whereabouts did you detain our foremost guest in the route?"

Cerberus muttered the last words of the rites and stood. "In the armoury naturally. Doors are a magic null. Can't be opened without the key or a decent skill at lock picking."

Meera muffled a laugh. "Oh she is going to be pissed with you darling."

Cerberus shrugged. "Guess I'll have to beg the Queen's forgiveness."

A loud explosion rattled the pictures on the walls. Meera steadied herself as the house rocked. "What in all the hells was that?"

Cerberus started moving down the remaining corridor to the far stairs. "No idea, but my family would rather raise the house to the ground than hand it over to the Gal-Serreks." He replied, speeding up into a gentle jog.

They sprinted down the skinny staircase and out to the first floor landing. Rounding the corner Cerberus ducked as a sword came flying at him out of nowhere. It narrowly missed his head. Trained reflex saved him, but only just. He swung out with his sword and kissed through the deep red leather jerkin of the swordsman but not enough to sufficiently injure him. In his periphery he could make out a cluster of six making their way into the entrance hall below.

Meera stepped out behind Cerberus and vaulted the wooden banister of the landing into morass of soldierly want-to-bes. Cerberus heard the yells and smiled, leaping sideways and running the wall to get behind his attacker. He stepped up behind him before the swordsman could get a move on him and with a delicate precision drove his rapier through the back of the ribs and up into the heart. Cerberus had turned and descended the first stair before the body crumpled to the floor leaving an ugly red smear along the wall.

Two more in Gal-Serrek's colours greeted him as he slid down the bannister of the stairs. A crude mace slammed just a little ahead of him, tearing through the wood like it was made of straw. Cerberus jumped to the next step and reached to the front of his leather cuirass, pulling free a small blade secreted within. With practiced aim he flicked it towards one while tearing through the cheek of the other with the rapier. They recoiled from him simultaneously cursing, one clasping the rent in his face while the other screamed over the gash through his eye. With remarkable insight, they retreated down the stairs almost tripping over the body of a fallen friendly dispatched by Meera only moments earlier. Cerberus stopped, grinned, and winked at them. They turned and fled for the front door.

A scream suddenly pulled silence to the room. Three remained. Cerberus made sure to catch their eye as he descended the last step. He paused as his gaze filtered to the final figure. Meera stood still against him one arm forced behind her back and a barbed blade laid gently against the pale skin of her neck. Her face was a mask of undiluted rage.

"That's far enough." The Drau's voice was commanding.

Cerberus paused. "I'd consider your next words more carefully." His voice was barely above a whisper. "They might be your last."

"You should listen to him. 'Might' implies that you could get out of this alive." Meera hissed against the sword pressed to her throat. "For the short amount of time it takes me to hunt you and any of your remaining whore-sons down"

The drau laughed and pulled her arm further up behind her back, the blade nicking the skin of her throat enough to draw a drop of blood. "Such a vulgar tongue to rest inside such a pretty little mouth. Keep it tied down lest I rip it out." Meera shifted her weight sending her boot directly into the Drau's groin. He groaned and spat a curse, wrenching her arm up till she gave a scream and her arm gave an audible crack.

Cerberus's eye's narrowed. "I'm going to enjoy taking you apart."

Cold laughter filled the entrance hall. "Oh I've heard of the fabled skill of the Dhal-Marrah's little lord. Your sister squealed like a stuck pig when I found her."

"That was a mistake." Cerberus growled. He spun the rapier in his hand, feeling it's lightness as it cut the air.

"Come on then little lord. I've waited a long time to test my blade-work against someone with actual skill, lets see how if you disappoint." With a heavy shove, the drau threw Meera to the wall. She bounced off it to the floor with a shriek of pain, clasping her right arm as she sank to the floor.

Steel rang. Cerberus shadow walked across the space between them, not giving his opponent a moment's notice to do more than react on instinct. He barely masked the surprise as the blade of the rapier bounced off.

"You'll need to do much better than that." The drau sneered as they drew close across blades.

Cerberus was done with talking. He pushed away and began to circle. analysing. His opponent was well armoured even if it didn't immediately show. There was trained skill behind the use of his sword but the weapon itself was a heavy blade meant to inflict pain and suffering rather than kill.

They clashed again. Cerberus dodged and weaved, glancing the barbed sword away and twisted almost dancing as the rapier sliced under the Drau's arm. The softer leather parted. The drau pulled away pushing a few fingers into the hole, assessing the damage. Circling, his eyes pinned as Cerberus copied his movements. With a yell he swung in a downward arc. Cerberus backed up bringing up his rapier to glance the blow and stumbled as he knocked into a table. The blade slammed against the rapier and its barbs pierced into his shoulder. Cerberus hissed as he felt the barbs bite and pushed against his opponents strength for all he was worth.

A whisper of air brushed the room as a door banged from the direction of dining hall. Kane flew through the air, a long, elegant, drau blade keening as he seemed to suddenly appear from nowhere. Cerberus's opponent pulled the barbs from his shoulder with a tear to meet the sudden threat. He watched as Kane exchanged a flurry of beautifully executed blows. Steel screamed. Across the other side of the room the patter of feet. Cerberex burst into the entrance hall a moment later, careening to a halt at the sight of Kane engaged with the drau interloper. Her eyes narrowed in recognition. Cerberus breathed a sigh of relief.

A cry and a clatter of metal on stone tiles snapped Cerberus's attention back to the present issue. Kane withdrew clutching an arm to his chest. His leather armour was rent from collar to hip. He pulled back his hand and Cerberus saw the blood smeared across it.

"Shouldn't have got in the way boy." The drau snorted as he kicked Kane's sword away. He raised his own. Kane prepared to dodge. The blade fell.

Silver skittered across the barbs like a xylophone. Three blades crossed. Cerberus, Cerberex, and the drau all looked at each other. Cerberex pulled her second hunters knife up, pressing it's point at the Drau's chest. "Move. I dare you!"

The drau tried to pull back the blade, hearing it only ring against metal as it's barbs now lodged it against the other two. The sound of footsteps across the landing above triggered Cerberus to check for incoming combatants. Selwyn appeared on the landing with their mother. Elryia gave a shriek at the sight of Cerberus and Cerberex engaged at blade point.

"Calm Elryia. I think the children have it under control." Selwyn began but Elryia was already moving her hands. Sparks flared as she focussed its energies on the drau between them, blowing him off his feet. His sword whined as it slid down Cerberus's blade inert without its owner. Cerberus let it clatter to the floor. Turning, he slowly stalked towards the drau now moaning as he tried to pick himself up from the floor.

A rustle of movement and Aunt Mal appeared from the other corridor into the entrance hall. She cocked her head to one side at the sight of the drau. "You're a stubborn little bastard aren't you! Didn't you quite get the message last time?" Her hands sparked.

The drau looked around him. Suddenly aware of the significant change in odds. "The house of Dhal-Marrah is nought but a den of thieves and murderers." He grimaced as he stood dusting himself off.

"Murderers?" Maleficent stepped forward. "You would talk about murderers." Her voice was bitterly quiet.

"This shit hole of a house is done. You could have let it fade. Disappeared into mediocrity. The King will no longer be so merciful." His eyes met Maleficent's and then Cerberus's with equal disdain.

Cerberus stood barely three feet from him. Without warning he slammed his empty fist clean into the Drau's jaw, knocking him back. "Any parting words scum, before I send you to the great beyond?" He pushed the rapier up under his chin.

"Cerberus..." Selwyn's voice echoed with caution.

"Be rid of him Cerberus." Elryia cut him off. "No son of the Gal-Serreks is welcome in this house."

Cerberus pushed the tip of the rapier up, the soft flesh parting from its razor edge.

"Cerberus, no!"

He paused as Cerberex's hand wrested on his shoulder. "Give me one good reason why not." Cerberus muttered murderously through gritted teeth.

The drau hissed a laugh. "Stopped by a little girl. Do it boy. Do it, and watch as all hell comes down upon you and your pathetic excuse of a house."

"He wants you to kill him Cerberus. Can't you see? He can't go back with nothing but the bodies of his own men." Cerberex moved her hand and brushed passed him. "As terrifying as you may be little brother, he fears his own superiors far more."

The Drau's eyes flared and he grinned. "Ever get to the Night-moth Vale little lord? Did you enjoy the view?" His eyes drifted to Cerberex. "They welcomed us like heroes. All dressed as we were in black and silver. What fun a little chalk and charcoal can do when applied to skin and hair eh? Master even welcomed us into his hovel of a home. Of course the game was up pretty quick after we dashed his brains out against the wall. His mongrel woman screamed and screamed..." His voice trailed off as the rapier slid further into the skin, blood beginning to run down the length of the blade.

"He's bating you Cerberus." Cerberex continued but her voice was laced with hate. She took a deep breath. "You're not... This house, we are not like them."

Cerberus felt the tension in the room stretch taught. His eyes never leaving the madly grinning expression in front of him. With a yell of exasperation he withdrew the rapier and walked away towards Kane.

"I always knew Cerberus Dhal-Marrah was a weak little runt." The drau spat blood on the floor.

Cerberex stepped in front of him as he tried to continue to goad Cerberus. "There's a smell about you that reeks of breeding." Cerberex cut in. "So what is your name?"

A flicker of pride beat across the Drau's face for a second. "Velek Selolan."

"You're a knight then. No actual royal relation. Just an underling." Cerberex filled in the blank. "A knight who enjoys sending messages?"

"What can I say? Why send a body when a finger will do?" He leaned towards Cerberex the blood running along his chin and down his neck. "Leaves you the rest to play with."

Cerberus helped Kane up and turned listening to Cerberex's conversation. Her calm tone barely concealed the fury that shook from her form.

Cerberex leaned in with gritted teeth, beckoning him as if to whisper a secret. "My sentiments exactly." With a speed that made Kane start back in surprise. Cerberex spun her knife and in a blur of motion held two flaps of skin between her fingers. Blood dripped from her hand as the drau desperately pushed away with a shout. For a second Cerberus couldn't quite figure out what she had done till he saw the bloody tips of the Drau's ears.

Cerberex's voice was quiet and deadly. "Run. Run back little man. Run back to which ever cesspit spawned you." She flicked the flaps of skin down to him. "You don't deserve the tips that mark you as kin. Let's see how long you last without them." Cerberex turned on her heel and stalked to Cerberus. "Get someone to dump him at the edge of Gal-Serrek territory. If they want a message they shall have one"

Cerberus raised an eyebrow. "And here I was thinking you were about to be the diplomatic one."

Cerberex grabbed Cerberus's shoulder pulling him close. "Don't test me. This is you're fault. You brought this down upon us." Cerberus could feel the vibration of her rage trembling down her arm. "Where have you hidden her?"

"Who?" Cerberus replied.

Cerberex shook him slightly and watched him wince. "Do not play me for an idiot!"

"She's safe. I left her in the route." Cerberus replied keeping his voice low.

Cerberex glanced over at Kane. "Can you walk?" She nodded to the tear in his armour.

"It's a scratch. I'll live. Thanks for asking." Kane winced as he stepped forward.

"Will you let me in or must I sit and hammer at the wall all day?" Cerberex asked sarcastically.

Kane looked at Cerberus and waited for the slight nod. "Right this way." He gestured and winced again.

Cerberus watched the pair of them return back in the direction of the dining hall. Kane's wound was more than just a scratch he knew, it would need seeing to, probably some stitches. He glanced over at Meera to see Aunt Mal hanging over her and gently moving her arm. He watched her hands begin to emit a subtle golden glow and the strain on Meera's face begin to relax. Slowly his eyes drifted back to the drau still sitting on the floor. He sheathed his rapier and took a step towards him. "Let's play a little game." He smiled coldly as the Drau's eyes met his. "Tell me, how fond are you of hide and seek?" The smile spread across his face yet never quite reaching his eyes.

Chapter 21:
The Butcher's Bill

It was as if the lights of the assassin's route were somehow dimmer, though no torches had been doused. The air stank like a slaughter house. Blood seemed to cling it. Cerberex looked around as Kane followed her in. He pulled down his scarf. "I think it goes without saying you've not caught us at our best."

Cerberex didn't respond weaving around groups of assassins. Her eyes drifted to the smear of blood across the floor. "What..."

Kane stepped ahead of her blocking her path. "You don't need to see this." He glanced behind him. "It wont be... pretty." He put a hand out, stopping her as she tried to walk past. "The Gal-Serreks - they're a brutal bunch."

"I am Lady Cerberex in case you had forgotten. Get out of my way!" Her voice was hushed. Cerberex's eyes darted around at the few assassins glancing at them. For a moment she thought he would refuse, but after a moment Kane stepped aside. A trickle of blood spattered the tiles. She looked Kane in the face. "Your wound needs seeing to." She said simply as she passed, following the trail to the bunk room.

Cerberex's legs dragged at her as she approached the door. Her heart felt like it had died in her chest. Suddenly it seemed like she couldn't breath. She put a hand on the wooden frame of the doorway and held herself there. Several of the bunks had been shoved up next to each other to make space. At first she heard only the moans. Forcing her head up she saw a half naked figure on a bunk bleeding from two stab wounds one in stomach, the other in the shoulder. The wounds had been roughly plugged to staunch the bleeding but Cerberex knew that without proper healing, he would surely die. Another in the next bunk wheezed as he desperately tried to suck air in and out of his lungs. Cerberex would have described him as a living pin cushion had she been able to summon the words to her mouth. Three heavy crossbow bolts stuck in his arm and chest. At best he'd cracked a few ribs, at worst a perforated lung. The more she looked the more she saw. Her eyes refused to blink, staring till they ran. Broken bones, nasty lacerations, it was no wonder the room smelt like an apothecary. Poultices and potions seemed to flow like bread and wine.

Slowly her eye's drifted to the created space in the middle of the room. Four black forms lay as if sleeping. Their arms brought up to cross their chests. She took a step forward, then another, ignoring the glances of those trying to tend to their wounded friends. The first had been a clean death. A single congealing wound to the temple caused undoubtedly by a single bolt. She lay unmarked save for this single fatal blow. Cerberex could hear Kane behind her whisper something inaudible. "You know her?" She asked without turning.

Kane sighed. "Her name was Seilie. She joined a little before me. We received our mark at the same time."

"I'm sorry." Cerberex whispered, glancing back.

Kane stood with his arms folded and shook his head. "Don't be she would not have wanted it any other way. We all knew what we were getting into when we joined. Few assassins die comfortably in their beds."

Cerberex turned back. "Do you know the others?"

Kane took a step forward, his breathing was heavy and he clutched an arm to his chest. He shook his head. They're not marked. They're initial training would have been overseen by the Chosen directly."

Cerberex looked at them. They were so young. One, a female, was rent with holes. The second was male, with a gash so heavy to his neck it was a wonder he still had a head. The third made the heat of anger ignite in Cerberex's chest. He was torn from neck to navel. No clean blade had made that wound, it was like claws had torn through him. No easy death. The boy had died from extreme blood loss in undoubted agony. She felt herself be roughly pushed aside as two assassins brushed past carrying another limp figure. She watched as they laid her down gently and folded her arms like the others.

"Cerberus will kill me if he knows you saw all this. Come away." Kane tried to pull her back, she turned and shoved him away then looked at her hands streaked in blood.

"That's not a scratch." She folded her arms. "You need to see someone about that. Do you have healers?"

Kane held the arm back to his chest and nodded. "There are a few of us with those particular skills."

Cerberex looked around. Taking in the faces. "Where are they then?"

"Well I imagine there rather busy." Kane tried to laugh but it turned into a cough. "Seska's one..."

Cerberex looked at him in surprise. "Seska? She doesn't seem the type."

Kane raised and eyebrow. "You know some of us did have lives other than this once upon a time. We weren't born assassins. Well not in most cases." He nodded down the hall. "Either way Seska's how shall I say ... picky. She's probably seeing to the other Chosen." He slid down the nearby wall and sat on the tiles.

"You need a healer or there will be another name to add to the butcher's bill." Cerberex looked in the direction Kane had nodded.

"Are these Chosen that important?" The question was more directed to herself.

"They are my foremost assassins." Cerberus's sudden voice made Cerberex jump. Her nose wrinkled in anger.

"I hope you're happy." She snarled.

"Happy about what?" Cerberus reached down and pulled Kane back onto his feet.

"This is all your fault Cerberus. Their blood is on your hands." It was all she could do not to shout at him.

Cerberus handed Kane to another assassin. "You want to do this? Now?"

"The attack on this house, the murder of the ones on that floor, this is all because you got yourself involved all over again with that..."

Cerberus took a step towards her. "Think very carefully about how you finish that sentence."

"Touch a nerve did I brother?" Cerberex spat.

The hand came across her face out of nowhere. "Snap out of it! This is what we do. Sometimes people die. As for my personal feelings, the Gal-Serrek's have been waiting for a reason to slaughter the rest of us for years."

"That's not what I meant." Cerberex interjected.

"Oh I know what you meant so perhaps I should remind you that if you hadn't tried to jailbreak me, she wouldn't be here in the first place." Cerberus hissed. He took a deep breath and rubbed his hand across his face. "I don't have time for this. I have last rites to perform for five and then check I still have four Chosen."

"Four?" Cerberex called after him. "Three girls and a boy, Seska included?"

Cerberus looked up at the ceiling. "Yes. They're responsible for the initiates so at least one would have been there when these ones died and I'd like to be able to write something positive to their families" He pushed passed her.

"Oh your Chosen were out." Cerberex whispered as she waited for Cerberus to move far enough away he couldn't be heard.

"My lady?" A soft tap on the shoulder made her spin around in surprise and reach for her knives. "Whoa easy!"

Cerberex looked at the young drau, his features cleaned up a bit yet still recognisable. "It's Clogaen isn't it?"

A smile spread across his face. He made a bow and crossed his arms over his chest bowing sombrely. "I should have thanked you."

Cerberex took the bow and examined it for any damage. "You shouldn't have been there."

Clogaen's eyes studied the floor. "Apologies my Lady, I overheard your conversation with the Master." He paused and glanced up at her. "I would never say the Master was wrong..."

Cerberex gave a mad laugh. "Oh take it from me Cerberus is wrong most of the time. He just doesn't like owning up to it." She growled, resting the bow satisfied on her shoulder.

Clogaen straightened. "Um, not my place to agree... but he is misinformed."

Cerberex's eyes narrowed. "What are you saying?"

Clogaen looked around and gestured for Cerberex to follow down the hallway towards the training room. He stopped between lamps keeping to the dark. "When the attack on the house came, our scouts told us of their arrival first. The Chosen are in command if the First and the Master are engaged, so it was them that heard the Gal-Serrek's were coming. They whispered something. I didn't hear all of it, only Sylas saying that we should wait for them to get closer."

Cerberex scowled. "Sylas is the male? Is he in charge of them?"

Clogaen muffled a laugh. "He wishes! No that honour falls to Meera as First."

"Did they say why? Was there a plan, some form of trap they hoped to spring?" Cerberex pressed.

"I wouldn't know my lady, initiates aren't usually given missions till their ready to receive their mark, but..." He faltered as another assassin walked by.

"What is it you don't want anyone to hear?" Cerberex whispered.

"Seska returned minutes before, saying something about others arriving. I thought maybe the battle had already taken place but when I looked around most of the assassins were still here." Clogaen replied.

"Clogaen are you telling me that there were attackers in the house and your commanders kept the bulk of your forces back?" Cerberex could feel her heart miss a beat.

"No, no, not at all my lady. They were sent almost immediately afterwards, then a short while later the initiates were told to make ready also. Sylas's actual words were it was time to prove ourselves." He paused.

"Let me get this straight, these four knew that the attack was coming, knew when they had entered the house even, and then committed you all to routing a prepared force?" Cerberex was doing her best not to show the anger in her face.

"We were told the Master would meet with us. Watch to see which made the grade." He muttered, seemingly ashamed. "I..."

"You little snitch!"

Clogaen yelled and Cerberex stepped back in surprise as suddenly a tall, male drau with a fine scar across his left cheek, seemed to almost materialize behind Clogaen, grabbing him and pushing him against the wall all but oblivious to Cerberex.

"Sylas!" Clogaen breathed as he looked up into the Drau's face.

"You spied on us and now you divulge secrets to those outside the route?" Sylas's face was creased with rage. "You little shit! So initiate, you think you know better than the Chosen do you?" Clogaen tried to speak but Sylas tutted and put a finger to Clogaen's lips. "Think you could have done it better? Well boy, come, I'm sure our council would love to hear your wisdom. Show us what you would have been capable of." Without evening deigning to look at Cerberex, Sylas put both hands on the younger Drau's shoulders and then seemed to melt into shadow leaving only Clogaen's stifled cry behind.

Cerberex looked around initially too startled to speak. She heard a yell from the training room, saw the glint of a shadow through the light from its archway. Clogaen's defensive voice then a shout of pain. She looked back at the bunk room deliberating on fetching Cerberus. Another cry made her mind up for her. Cerberex turned to the dark and ran towards the training room.

"Well come on then runt? Where's you're fighting spirit?" Cerberex peeked around the archway to see Sylas nudge Clogaen with his boot. The other three wandered towards the pit like big cats taking interest in the torture of a mouse. Cerberex couldn't help but notice that none of these apparent Chosen seemed to have taken a scratch in the attack on the house.

"What's all this Sylas?" Seska looked down at Clogaen who seemed to have the sense to stay down.

"Little shit's been listening in to us haven't you?" He kicked Clogaen and the boy rolled across the sand. "Telling tales weren't you?"

"Sylas, I never said anything but the best..." Clogaen pleaded between breaths. "I was just..."

"Lying bastard." Sylas spat stalking towards him.

"Relax Sylas. Who has he got to tell?" Another female drau, Cerberex didn't recognise her, interjected. She was small but sharp faced and wiry. "You poor boy." She crooned as she approached Clogaen

"Dichta..." Clogaen looked at her as if beholding an angel.

"Ssssh." Dichta helped Clogaen to his feet. "If you have concerns, of course you should be permitted to voice them."

"Thank you, I... of course, no concerns just..." Clogaen began.

"To your superiors." Dichta finished. "How dare you spill the routes secrets to an outsider. It's bad enough that the Master hangs on the old man's word every time he comes down here!" She spun around Clogaen pulling his arms his back and knocking out his legs. She leaned down to him. "I don't think you understand the gravity of your decision."

Clogaen writhed to no avail and his face hardened. "An assassin regrets no decision."

Sylas laughed. "True, but your not an assassin so you will."

As Sylas leaned in Clogaen knocked back his head and then slammed it into Sylas's nose. Sylas gave a cry and stepped back clutching his face.

"Oh, you little..." Sylas muttered murderously and brought his fist clean across Clogaen's face.

Cerberex could feel the force of the blow from her hiding place. She winced as Clogaen brought back up his head, his nose dripping with blood before whack! Another blow, this time to the stomach with a well aimed foot. Clogaen doubled forward but Dechta pulled him back. Thwack! Another fist. Smack! And again.

"That's enough!" Cerberex roared as she stepped through the archway, her bow clattering to the ground. She watched as another fist collided with Clogaen's face and the boy lolled, blood spilling from between his teeth. He looked over at her barely concious, through a busted eye. "I said enough!" Cerberex's voice dropped to a growl.

Dichta looked up with mild surprise and unceremoniously dropped Clogaen into the sand. "Well, well look who it is." She looked down at Clogaen then back at Cerberex. "Sweet on this one?" She smiled. "Maybe you and I aren't so different. Like to break them in young?"

"I am Lady Cerberex Dhal-Marrah..." Cerberex began drawing herself up.

Dichta flicked a hand. "Oh we all know who you are love." She stalked around Clogaen who could do nothing but breath heavily on the floor. "Your name just doesn't really hold any power down here." She giggled.

Seska stepped ahead of her. "Meaning you should leave."

"I'm not leaving except with the boy." Cerberex held her ground. She could sense the burst of adrenaline rushing through her veins as her heart beat faster. Cerberex did not feel fear in the conventional sense. She had that emotion drilled out of her by the Watchers in the most part. Still, she had to admit, the four of them dressed in black leather armour that had seemed to gleam like oil on water, cut imposing figures.

"We have every right to discipline our own." Dichta pouted.

"Funny, what I saw looked more like a pack of rabid hounds set on a fox." Cerberex replied, forcing a smile onto her face. "I expected more finesse." She looked around them, seeing Clogaen shift an arm to push himself up.

"You're getting involved in things that do not concern you."

The third female was up into her face, though Cerberex hadn't seen her move. "Step away."

"Take Negari's advice." Seska added.

Cerberex took a small step around Negari's short frame. "Perhaps I didn't make myself clear." She let her voice carry to fill the room. "Let the boy go."

"Intervening in this acts as a challenge little Watcher. You have no idea what we are capable of." Sylas wiped the blood from his knuckles.

Cerberex placed her hands on her hips. "If challenging you is all it takes to free Clogaen, you'll pardon me if I'm not quaking in my boots. You say this is how your clique deals with transgressions. Well I can't wait to see the hell my brother unleashes on you when I tell him that you surrendered to a couple of Gal-Serrek louts and all because you didn't want to get your pretty armour damaged." Cerberex caught the flash of anger ripple across each of their faces. She looked directly at Seska. "And to think I actually thought well of you."

Sylas flexed his hand. "You dare speak to us about the intricacies of combat? You, who does nothing but fuck her way up the nobility tree!" Cerberex almost recoiled as if she'd been slapped in the face. She could feel the anger begin to rise.

"Oh that's right!" Dichta clapped her hands excitedly.

Sylas waved her quiet as he strode up to her face to face. "You're nothing but a prize whore when it comes to face to face. What are you going to do? Shag the lot of us for the boy's freedom?" He took a step back. "I'd do it but unlike some I like a bit of privacy" He glanced at Dichta.

Cerberex took a deep breath and stepped down the short step looking at the sand. "Darling," She slinked towards him. "You wouldn't even get past the foreplay." Like a viper, she coiled in on herself and unleashed a kick so hard it sent Sylas flying back a full five feet away into the sand.

A gasp emitted from Clogaen's lips but it was drowned by Dichta's sudden clapping. "Now you've done it." She giggled.

Cerberex watched, her fists clenched, as the three females moved, dispersing themselves around her. "Ladies, I have no quarrel with you... yet."

"Oh it's too late for that Watcher. You may have no right to challenge but we'll accept it nonetheless, if purely for the amusement of taking you down a peg or two." Negari smirked as Sylas picked himself up and joined them in a heartbeat.

Cerberex looked at Clogaen stumbling to the pit's edge. He was looking at her, a painful, torn expression on his face. "Get out of here Clogaen." Cerberex called her eyes drifting back to the four slowly surrounding her. "Don't try anything stupid."

Clogaen gave her a nod. It was difficult to tell through his swollen face but she thought she saw him mouth the word "Luck" as he lurched towards the archway as fast as he could physically muster.

Cerberex waited for the sound of Clogaen's footsteps to fade down the passage beyond. "You know he's going to tell everyone what's happened here."

Dichta smiled. "Let him. A challenge is a challenge. We run by our own laws down here."

Cerberex kept watching, never letting any of them out of her sight. "Four against one? Hardly seems fair."

Sylas grinned. "Something you should learn about us. Assassin's don't play fair."

Cerberex flexed her fists. "Well then." She licked her lips. "Let the games begin." The words left her lips and before she had time to blink, the four of them moved like smoke in the wind.

Chapter 22:
Clicked

Cerberus was watching as the last stitch was pulled tight closing the wound across Kane's chest when the initiate burst into the bunk room as if the hounds of hell were on his tail.

"Eroth's fangs!" An initiate holding a cold press to his head stood up as he entered the room. "What the hell happened to you?" Despite a hand encouraging him to sit he dropped the pack and moved to grab his friend before he could stumble.

"Tharn." Clogaen grabbed the older boys shoulder and wheezed.

"Alright, easy does it. Why the hell didn't you queue up for a healer? You're a mess!" Tharn wrapped an arm under him and ushered Clogaen into the bunk room.

Kane downed the vial of amber that had been shoved at him and reached out for Cerberus to help him sit up in the bunk as the female assassin put away the surgical kit.

Cerberus helped move Kane and sat up, craning his head for a better view.

"Tharn... the Master..." Clogaen stuttered.

"I'm right here." Cerberus stood up as Tharn brought him up to them. A number of heads looked out from over bunks as he did. Cerberus shifted uncomfortably under the scrutiny. He took in the boy's busted lip and bruised face.

"Master." Clogaen tried to cross his arms over his chest and bow.

Cerberus motioned for him to stop. "Don't. What happened?"

"Lady Cerberex," He wheezed. "She's challenged... Chosen."

"Which one?" Kane and Cerberus asked simultaneously and then looked at each other in surprise.

"That didn't take long." Kane added with a weak smile.

Clogaen coughed. "All of them." He managed.

There was a flurry of movement. Suddenly any assassin capable of standing under their own will threw away whatever he or she was doing and made for the door.

Cerberus looked at Kane's freshly stitched wound. "Stay here. You'll open it back up if you don't give it time."

"The hell I am!" retorted Kane swinging his legs over the bunk onto the floor. "And you'll have to knock me out to make me."

"Tempting." Cerberus muttered before helping Kane up.

Kane shove him off, grabbed a questionably clean shirt from under the bunk, and jogged to the door, shrugging it on as he went. Cerberus shook his head and followed, catching him up with ease.

The press of bodies at the arch of the training room bubbled with barely contained excitement. Assassin's began placing wagers between each other before they could even see the action. Cerberus understood their sentiment, there had never been a challenge since before his father Dendrion Dhal-Marrah, had been Master. He tried to smile as he pushed his way through. Tried to keep the fact that his stomach was knotting so tight he felt sick to the core. Cerberex was accomplished of that there was no question. Her skill with a bow - exemplary even. Against one of the Chosen she might win, Dichta maybe, but against four well even that might give him pause for thought.

Assassins stood shoulder to shoulder with initiates right up against the edge of the pit. Cerberus muscled his way up to just before the front line perched upon its lip. Kane stood just behind him. Through the gap between shoulders, Cerberus could make out Cerberex dancing with shadow's across the sand. She had an ugly welt to her face already. Cerberus took in the situation within a handful of seconds. Cerberex was moving this way and that. So far as he could tell none of the other four had taken any real damage.

"They're toying with her." Cerberus muttered over his shoulder. "They were waiting for enough of a crowd so she'll be humiliated."

"What ever your sister did, she pissed them right off." Kane agreed.

Cerberus tracked the moving shadows with his eyes. He could just make out Dichta and Negari shadow walking the perimeter, waiting for their turn to strike. Sylas span past like a blur knocking into Cerberex's shoulder to take her off guard, then Seska came across knocking out a leg from under her, forcing her onto one knee. Cerberex stood back up and wailed with her firsts at opponent's she could barely see.

A gap in the front row allowed Cerberus to step up to the edge of the pit. Cerberex seemed so far unaware of him. A good thing, she didn't need a distraction. He saw Sylas drift to a pause and his head slowly turn in Cerberus's direction. He didn't acknowledge but Cerberus felt sure that Sylas knew he was there and so would the rest of them, now the challenge would really start.

As if on cue, Dichta struck forward. Pirouetting out of Cerberex's wild punches and sending one of her own in to Cerberex's stomach. Cerberex seemed to wince but somehow managed to stay standing till Negari came from behind and wrapped an arm around her throat, throwing her over her shoulder. Sylas shifted across the sand placing a kick that made her roll across the sand. Cerberex stood panting and used the momentum to catch the punch Dichta aimed for her head, knocking it back into Dichta's own face. Out of luck the sprawl of Dechta on the ground threw off the attack Seska had planned. Forcing her to continue to circle. Sylas's blow came out of nowhere though. He had always been fast, there was no way that Cerberex could have seen the fist coming. The crack of it snapped Cerberex's neck back as it collided with her cheek. She spun away, wiping the blood from her lip. A mistake. Negari used Dechta as a springboard and leaped bringing her elbow snapping down between the shoulder blades of Cerberex's neck. The crowd groaned as Cerberex stumbled.

"Hell's fire! Cerberus do something." Kane hissed in Cerberus's ear.

"Do what?" Cerberus watched as Cerberex scored a hit on Seska, taking out her feet to the delight of the crowd. Her minor victory was short lived though as Dechta grabbed her arm pulling it back so far that Cerberex issued a short scream.

"Shit Cerberus they'll kill her!" Kane added agitated.

"You can't get involved - Right of Challenge." Cerberus replied.

"She's not one of us - your sister isn't beholden to our rules." Kane looked around frantically.

Cerberex flew across the pit and hit the sand hard issuing another groan from the crowd. A shadow flitted across from the far side and Sylas leaped. Cerberex saw him rise into the air, front foot poised to smash into her face, she rolled and barely avoided the impact. Pushing herself up onto her feet. The other foot spun in a high kick as she rose connecting with the back of her head and forcing her back into the sand.

"What the... What the hell is this?!" Meera appeared at Cerberus's side.

"It's a challenge." Kane called over to her. He was frantically lacing up a crossbow mounted wrist guard he'd purloined from an unwatching comrade.

"Cerberus, stop this madness!" Meera shouted shrilly over the din.

Cerberus watched as his sister rocked back on her knees, her eyes closed, panting. "Get up." He whispered to himself. "Come on, get up."

"What's come over him?" Meera called to Kane.

Kane shrugged. "They're going to kill her in there." He finished lacing the wrist guard.

Meera looked at him as he out stretched his arm. "Don't you dare! Don't you dare shoot one of my Chosen!"

Kane gave her a murderous look. "Got any other bright ideas?"

Cerberex hadn't moved. Cerberus watched the four circle the pit like vultures. This was it. They were sizing her up for the final blow. He caught the nod from Seska to Sylas. He felt the brush as Kane levelled the crossbow and...

Sylas whispered across the sand, shadow walking so fast that Cerberus could barely keep a lock on him. His fist came back and... missed. Cerberus blinked. It shouldn't have been possible. His target wasn't even moving and yet somehow faster than the blink of an eye Cerberex had shifted her position that the hit glided harmlessly past her shoulder.

Cerberus grabbed Kane's arm and forced it down. "Wait."

"What the..." Kane's arm came down to his side.

Sylas scraped to a halt on the opposite side of the pit, a look of confusion writ large across his face. The crowd drew quiet, not quite understanding what had happened. Sylas looked at Dichta who rolled her eyes but no one saw. No one was watching them. All eyes rested on the kneeling form in the centre of the pit.

Cerberex came to a stop against the sand. Her mouth tasted of blood. Her body shook under the force of will it took just to remain concious. Her heart thrummed in her chest as she closed her eyes against the sand, rocking back onto her knees. She could still feel the echo of the last hit pulsing through her. She sucked in air into her lungs. The sound of the crowd had diminished into a low drone of white noise. She could not win. The thought was calm but alien. She could not win. They would make her an example. The anger boiled in her like a volcano but it was nothing in comparison to the exhaustion she was feeling. She reached down and felt the sand between her fingers. "No". A small voice somewhere in the back of her head whispered. "No, not today." Louder this time. She was Cerberex Dhal-Marrah and hell be damned she was going to let this bunch of upstart brats humiliate her in this way.

Something ice cold seemed to slide into Cerberex's head. She felt her heart slowing. Thump-thump... thump-thump........thump-thump. As if obeying some primal instinct she shifted her body ever so slightly to the left. Thump-thump........ thump-thump. A brush of wind blew her cheek as the fist passed over her shoulder and its owner spun away. Thump......thump, thump......thump. She opened her eyes. Each grain of sand on the ground seemed to sparkle like a field of diamonds, picked out in spectacular clarity. Thump....... thump. The chill floated from her head, down her neck, past her shoulders, across her chest. Thump.... The pain of her bruises turned to numbness. Thump......... thump. Slowly, first one leg then the other, she rose from the sand. A detached part of her said that somewhere the crowds were cheering even if all she could hear was the sound of her own heart beating. Thump .....thump.

Cerberex took in long breaths as she studied the four of them arrayed around the perimeter. She could see their forms flickering from one point to another. There was a rush of movement. Without call her body seemed to react of it's own volition. Time seemed to slow for a moment. Seska's arm appeared over her shoulder. Cerberex grabbed it, spinning the weight of Seska's body into the oncoming Dichta and sending both sprawling into the sand. She ducked as Sylas ran at her with a leap designed to crush his knee into her face. Taking him off balance. She twisted back into almost a flip and felt her fist connect with his jaw so hard she was sure he must break a tooth, a second later her knee smacked neatly under his chin. Something definitely cracked in his mouth. Dichta disentangled herself from Seska and her and Negari came from both sides. Cerberex rolled backwards clasping a hand on both of their heads. Unable to stop in time the pair smacked into each other with the dull crack of meeting foreheads and fell to the floor... lights out. Seska's arm snaked out from behind and wrapped around her throat. Cerberex felt the tightness, knew she could not breath, and yet the ice in her brain made it impossible for her to recognise any problem. She reached back grabbing Seska by the hair and pulling her over her shoulder as she spun. Seska flew off her back and rolled across the pit hitting her head on the side. She rolled onto her back, gasping on the sand but she stayed down. Now there was only Sylas. Gone was the cocky look of self-assurance. The tables had turned and he was being careful. They circled each other. Cerberex waited with the patience of one who time had lost meaning. Eventually, Sylas struck, he darted forward aiming to glance her head with his elbow as he came past. Cerberex stuck out a leg knocking him off balance. She grabbed his arm as he lurched, twisting back until she felt a pop followed by a shout of pain. Sylas lay sprawled on the floor, his left arm limp and definitely dislocated.

It was done. Her brain still filled with an icy fog that banished her thoughts, told her body to stand tall and it obeyed. She surveyed the scene blankly. Faces pressed in at her from the edge. Some overjoyed, a few suspicious, but most simply shocked. She felt the adrenaline begin to wane. Her limbs felt suddenly heavy. Darkness crawled at the corners of her vision. She took a step forward and the world spun.

Sylas cried out as his shoulder popped from its socket. Cerberus winced but he couldn't tear his eyes away. "Eroth!" He breathed as Cerberex straightened. The room silenced and then roared approvingly. Most had no understanding of the significance of the spectacle, simply delighted by the show. He watched her take a step and stumble. Without thinking he was at her side in a flash. His arm wrapped around her waist. "Oh no you don't." Cerberus whispered to her.

Cerberex grabbed his shoulder. "I... I don't feel so good." She slurred.

Cerberus could have kissed her for talking. "Come on. You need to walk out of here on your own steam. Once we are out of sight I can carry you."

Slowly Cerberex focused all her efforts into putting one foot in front of the other. Cerberus helped her up the lip of the pit as hands reached out to pat Cerberex's shoulder. Cerberus leaned into Meera as they passed. "I want their badges on my desk."

Meera's impassive face looked at him in shock. "What? No! This was... I have no idea what this was, but..."

"Badges. My Desk." Cerberus cut her off. His tone brooked no argument.

The assassins and initiates parted to let them pass. Cerberex stumbled passed them drunkenly and as they rounded the corner of the archway and stepped out of sight Cerberus felt her leg's collapse under her own weight. Swinging her up into his arms he watched her go limp and her eyes flutter shut. With but a thought, Cerberus shadow walked to the bunk room and carefully laid her down on a spare bunk. A few moments later he felt the approach of Kane suddenly appearing at his side he glanced at him. A coupled of the top stitches had pulled, leaving a small blood mark on the shirt he wore.

Kane stared for a moment at Cerberex's prostrated form before looking back at Cerberus. "Well what now?"

Cerberus looked down at Cerberex. "You keep what you beat." He muttered quietly.

Kane's eyebrows flew up. "You cannot be serious. You're going to strip them of rank and give it to her?"

"That's the rule." Cerberex replied flatly.

Kane spun Cerberus to face him. "She's not one of us Cerberus. The others. They may not accept it. Eroth knows, that should never have taken place!"

A brush against his sleeve and Meera appeared next to Cerberus. "Well I hope you're satisfied?" She spat.

"Is it done?" Cerberus asked, ignoring her tone.

"Badges on your desk as requested." The outrage in her voice was palpable. "As I understand it, your sister challenged them. I see no reason for them to be punished or humiliated like this."

"As I have just said to Kane. The rule on this is clear. You know our ways. You keep what you beat." Cerberus turned back to Cerberex. His voice calm and impassive.

Meera's face flushed with anger. "You'd humiliate my Chosen further by giving their honour to someone not even part of our organisation?"

"Nothing to say that only an assassin may challenge." Cerberus replied.

"It's implied Cerberus!" Meera gave a heavy sigh of exasperation. "She is not one of us. She cannot challenge."

"Isn't she?" Cerberus pressed a finger to his lips in thought.

"Cerberus, darling, you can't break the rules simply because they inconvenience you." Meera tried to persuade him.

"Then take my sister out of the subject." Cerberus folded his arms. "I'll tell you what I just saw shall I? I saw the four foremost assassins of the route go into a fight against a single adversary and lose."

"It means..." Meera began.

"It means everything." Cerberus countered. "Cerberex just beat all four of the Chosen in hand to hand combat in front of every assassin in the route."

"She's too old to be an initiate." Meera tried a different tactic.

"I'm not making her an initiate." Cerberus argued back.

The three of them paused looking at each other. At last Kane took a deep breath. "Well if no one is going to ask then I will. What in all the hells just happened in there? No one, and I mean no one in this route would dare step into the ring with Sylas let alone with the ladies present as well! What are the Watchers teaching these days? I have never in my entire life ever seen one move like that." Meera and Cerberus looked at him. "I'll tell you what I saw. I saw something change. If this wasn't Cerberex, if this was just another assassin hell even an initiate, I would have said I saw them click."

"That's not possible." Meera replied flippantly. "The switch needs to be vigorously trained. It takes months for some of our newest to even access it."

Kane shrugged. "Tell me you saw something different then."

"The switch doesn't need to be trained in everyone." Cerberus whispered.

"What are you talking about?" Meera rounded on him.

"The switch. Kane's right. If we were talking about a fellow assassin we'd all say we saw them activate their switch. It's true we train the initiates to find theirs and how to press it, but my father only mentioned it to me in passing. Mine was already developed before I started training." Cerberus explained.

"You're trying to tell me that your sister has suddenly developed a kill switch?" Meera raised an eyebrow. "Unlikely."

"Meera has a point Cerberus. If that was the case, surely your father would have insisted on training her." Kane added.

"Finally some common sense." Meera hissed.

"I don't think he knew about it." Cerberus nodded at Cerberex. "In fact, I'd go so far as to say this is the first time she's clicked." He paused. "We need to keep an eye on her - we need to be sure, because if she does, she may just be the biggest danger to us all."

Chapter 22:
Changing Winds

Cerberus sat in a high back chair, legs up upon the end of the bed, rapier untied leaning against the arm. His arms were folded and a dishevelled strand of hair hung over one cheek. In a feat that might well cost him dearly from one or both parties, Cerberus had procured a relaxant from Aunt Mal's laboratory and administered it to Cerberex shortly after he'd got her to her room. Since then he had sat unmoving save for the occasional flicker of his eyes beneath their lids.

A quiet murmur, barely more than an escaping breath, came from the other end of the bed. One red eye slid open followed by the other as Cerberus looked over. The sheets moved and an arm moved with them. Cerberus pushed the hair out of his face and sat a little straighter.

Cerberex blinked and rubbed her face. The swelling had gone down but as feeling returned her body reminded her of the punishments it had endured. She let out a more audible groan.

Cerberus let the thrill of relief run through him and grinned. "I'd like to say good morning but it is in fact the afternoon."

Cerberex sat straight up at the sound of her brother's voice and let out a squeal as pain seared across her left side. Gasping she breathed through it.

Cerberus took his legs off the bed and stood. "Might I congratulate you on your first broken rib." He gestured to the bandages wrapped around her middle two bone splints had been inserted to reinforce, significantly impeding the amount of movement Cerberex could make.

Cerberex looked at the bandages then raised a free hand to her face again, feeling the split lip that was almost healed. Her eyes glanced up as a sudden memory flickered in her head. "There was a boy..." She began.

"Clogaen." Cerberus nodded. "All patched up. He might feel a bit stiff for longer than you will." He walked over and adjusted the pillows before dragging the chair closer so they could both talk at eye level. "I'd ask how you feel but I think that's a little redundant."

Cerberex narrowed her eyes. "Why are you here Cerberus?"

Cerberus glanced at her. His face contorting into an exaggerated look of surprise. "Can't I be concerned?"

"You aren't normally." Cerberex winced as she adjusted her position.

Cerberus smiled and brought a finger to his lips as he pondered the phrasing of his next sentence. "True, but I credited you with more intelligence than to start a brawl with a bunch of trained killers."

Cerberex swung at him but it was devoid of real strength and Cerberus moved his head easily out of the way. "The boy..." She began again.

"Yes, we've had a rather interesting conversation." Cerberus cut her off again.

"Then you know. You know why they were beating the snot of him." Cerberex replied sternly.

"Oh I've rather got the idea." Cerberus paused. "I might have dealt with the four differently however." He caught Cerberex's look. "Oh alright I would have dealt with it exactly the same!" He laughed. "Still I probably wouldn't have needed to - if you'd called me." He raised an eyebrow as he looked at her.

Cerberex remained impassive. "They were going to kill him."

Cerberus shook his head. "No they weren't." He sat back and refolded his arms. "Sylas." He began changing the topic quickly before Cerberex could say another word. "He trains those assassins who specialise in swordplay - fighters if you like. Negari is spectacular at unarmed combat. Seska's gift lets her throw daggers with an unnerving accuracy; and Dichta? Dichta could surprise a ghost with her speed and silence." He watched Cerberex's face. "I would be hard pressed to find anyone bar maybe Meera, willing to step into the ring with one of them. You decided to step into the ring with all four at once. Do you have any idea how lucky you are right now?"

Cerberex shrugged. "Have you come to berate me on my lack of judgement?" She replied sarcastically.

Cerberus sighed. "I applaud your valour in standing up for one of my initiates, I really do." His face fell as he looked at her seriously. "But they should have pulled you to pieces."

Cerberex met his gaze. "Well next time I'll remember to..." She stopped and cocked her head to one side. "Should?"

Cerberus licked his lips and nodded. "Should." He rubbed his face. "How much do you remember?"

Cerberex's brow furrowed. "I remember Sylas's face as he beat that boy and stepping into the pit. I remember the first few hits and I couldn't even keep track of them. They moved... they moved faster then anything I've ever encountered." Her brow creased further. "I felt cold and then..." She tried to pull more fragments together before shaking her head. "No that's it."

Cerberus clicked his tongue. "Well, you have the gist of it. They, the four of them together are what the route call Chosen. That means they are the best assassins in the route. Now the only way to become a Chosen is to evict one from their spot by challenging them to a fight. Not just any fight. All the safeties off - oh they wont kill each other, but they might come close." He paused and steepled his fingers. "You challenged all of them."

Cerberex looked at him defiantly. "I couldn't exactly go running back after you now could I?"

"That sister is precisely what you should have done." A curl of a smile wavered on Cerberus's face. "But you didn't. You took them all on - at once." He paused. "And you won." The smile wouldn't be hidden any longer and crept to both corners of his mouth. He blinked and his eyes met hers. "There's no handbook, no Assassins Codex 101 - but you challenged all of them and in one round, beat all four with nothing but a handful of bruises and a broken rib." He reached into his pocket and withdrew a small circular item no bigger than a coin. On one side the symbol of House Dhal-Marrah was embossed on the dull metal.

Cerberex glanced at it curiously. "Brother, I'm not one of your assassins." Her words drifted warily from her lips.

Cerberus looked at the object as he ran it across his knuckles. "No you are not." With a flick he knocked it over to her.

Cerberex looked at it, turning it over in her hands. On the reverse a pin allowed it to be attached to clothing or light armour and her name lay engraved beneath. "What is it?"

"The route can't run without Chosen. Simply, I cannot be in more than one place at once." He began.

Cerberex looked up at him quickly. "Cerberus I am not..."

Cerberus waved her comment away. "Whatever your planning on saying is irrelevant. The second Sylas hit the sand the choice was out of my hands." He took a breath. "If anything, over the last few days you may have proven to me that having a few individuals around with a semblance of your skills at tracking and archery might not be a bad thing. Truth be told, if they come for the Queen again, we will need every ounce of advantage we can get."

"You want me to train them? They'll never listen to me." Cerberex replied.

"They will with one of those pinned to your chest." He nodded at Cerberex's clenched hand. "Though I don't think you'd need it. You're not an assassin sister, but you've made quite the impact." He paused and studied her. "Consider it a temporary contract. If you decide not to you can always hand me the pin back." He pulled a tiny glass bottled from a pouch at his waist and drew a tiny dagger.

"Wait, what are you..." She yelped as he pulled the blade across her thumb. Blood welled up from the wound and dripped into the bottle. "What the hell did you do that for!" She yelled at him, snatching her hand away.

Cerberus corked the bottle and replaced the dagger.

"Relax it's just a few drops." He shook the bottle with interest. "Besides, we're going to need to modify the enchantment if you're to be able to get in unaided." He smiled. "Give it some thought. You can pick who you want - within reason, whenever you're ready." He made his way over to the door and gave her a curt nod before leaving, closing it with a gentle click behind him.

As the door closed Cerberus let go of a breath he'd not known he'd been holding. He gestured to a passing servant, a human male with a mop of dirty blonde curls. Wrapping the bottle in a handkerchief he handed it to him. "Don't drop it." He said slowly. "Take it straight to my aunt and tell her that Lady Cerberex was most obliging. She'll know what it means." He watched as the servant bowed and immediately turned away on the errand.

"How is your sister?"

Cerberus straightened at the sound of the voice behind him. He turned slowly. Lida leaned against the bannister of the landing a little ways off, watching the a trio of servants cleaning the entrance hall below. He glanced around assessing the number of eyes in the vicinity and then finally, gave a low bow. "My Queen."

A flicker of a smile seemed to shimmer across her face for a moment. She turned her head to look at him. "I take it, it's not life threatening."

Cerberus wandered around to her and leaned against the bannister at her side. "A fractured rib, some bruising, a split lip." He replied. "My sister will be up and chastising me for my lack of manners again before long."

"Lord Charnite tells me that you lost eight house guard and a number of ... other unorthodox fighters." Lida didn't look at him. She lowered her voice. "He also says that you suffered losses to your household staff too."

Cerberus shrugged. "We will replace them in time and Cerberex's injuries were..." He paused. "Self inflicted."

Lida choked on a laugh. "Well that's a callous way of looking at it." She studied her hands and watched as a scattering of tiny sparks darted from one finger to the other. "You should have let me..."

Cerberus sighed. "Oh Eroth! Don't start this again." He rubbed a finger along the bridge of his nose. "It would have been tantamount to giving them exactly what they wanted."

"I'm not a push over Cerberus. Take it from me, I'm well versed in taking care of myself." She stood straighter placing both hands against the wooden surface in front of them. "And if it had got to that, they would have left and you would not have suffered the losses you did."

Cerberus let out a laugh. "You can't honestly tell me that you believe that?" He turned and saw her face devoid of mirth. He stood up staring at her straight in the eye. "They would have taken you back, and then they would have attacked us regardless. We would have lost more not less."

Lida tried to smile. "Lord Dhal-Marrah I'm going to thank you for your hospitality."

Cerberus's face dropped. "Lida." He began dangerously.

Lida raised a finger. "You and your family have been a gracious host but I've overstayed my welcome here too long."

Cerberus ran his hand along the banister as he took a step forward. It recoiled as it touched hers. "You can't go back." He could feel the rage building in his chest. "Tell me you are not going back."

Lida took a step back. "I can't stay here any longer Cerberus. Aelnar will tear down this house stone by stone if he has to. My leaving here will ensure that his wrath has only one direction in which to vent." She laced her fingers in front of her, holding herself with a regal grace.

"Lida... My Queen, he will murder you. He's planned to ever since you bound yourself to him." Cerberus could hear the passion in his voice but the words would not be checked. "He might not be able to execute you, but he will take no issue with torturing you day by day until life becomes unbearable." He took a deep breath. "Please. Tell me you will not go back. I give you my word, I will rid you of him if you ask. Nothing would give me greater pleasure - but do not force my hand, we are not ready."

"Cerberus you always were the dramatist." Lida chuckled. "Do you not think it has been tried? No. I will make the preparations. Don't think me a fool, I'll not be heading to the palace alone. I intend to stop by the Temple of Eroth on the way. I'll arrive with a contingent of Matrons and none will gainsay me. They will let me pass as if nothing is amiss." A flame of intent burned in her eyes. She brushed her fingers against Cerberus's. "I would rather spend the long years of my life in torment, than see House Dhal-Marrah brought to ruin. I will not be the thing the destroys you." She whispered and turned, walking away towards the next flight of stairs and the guest quarters.

Cerberus stood statue still for a moment breathing as if he'd just run from one side of the city to the other. The silence stretched on before Cerberus gave a frustrated yell and hammered his fist down on the bannister's railing, storming away. He did not notice the singed imprint of his fist on the wood, nor the creak of hinges and wisp of white hair from Cerberex's bedroom door.

Cerberex changed into simple shirt and trousers. Her wardrobe was rife with fitted dresses and beautiful lace-ware kindly commissioned by her mother in some hope that her beautiful daughter would one day turn in to a proper lady. That day had not yet arrived.

The house was tense. As she slipped silently down the staircase, she could feel it like an off vibration. Servants avoided her gaze as she passed. Gently she collared one. "Something is wrong." It was not a question.

The pale skinned girl averted her eyes. "The pale lady has had a frightful row with Lord Charnite my lady." Her voice was barely above a whisper.

"The pale lady?" Cerberex looked away puzzled. "Ah, you mean the Queen?"

The girl nodded. "She made several threats."

Cerberex placed her thumb and forefinger beneath the girls chin and forced her to look up. "What were they arguing about?"

"I couldn't hear properly my lady." Her eyes widened as Cerberex raised an eyebrow. "Lord Charnite wouldn't let her do something. He said he'd lock her in if she so much as tried."

Cerberex let go. "So Uncle has still got some fight in him then." She looked back at the girl. "One more thing. Did the pale lady leave or is she still in the house?"

"I believe she is in the gardens my lady." Her eyes darted to the direction of the dining hall. "Can't say if she'll stay here much longer though. She was very insistent."

Cerberex reached into a small pouch tied to the belt at her waist and withdrew three black florins, holding them in front of the girl's waist. She waited for the girl to hold out her hand expectantly before pulling them back. "The pale lady, you know where she is sleeping and where she keeps her things?" The girl nodded and Cerberex smiled. "Go into her quarters and find something of value. Remove it and bring it to my quarters."

"Steal it my lady?" The girl asked, suddenly unsure. "My lady, if I am caught..."

"Five then." Cerberex cut her off and reached into the pouch again withdrawing two more. "And if you are caught then this conversation never happened." She held out the coins, making sure they jingled in her palm.

For a moment the girl simply stared at them. Then suddenly, she snatched them up and dashed for the stairs. Cerberex smiled to herself. The Queen would be going nowhere today. She turned down the corridor to the dining hall and tried to disguise the pain it cost her to move.

Selwyn paced up and down like a caged animal. He paused and looked up at her as she entered. She could see the anger boiling beneath the calmness of his face. "Niece!" He forced the smile across his face. "Cerberus says you are feeling under the weather. Can I get you a drink? Something to eat?"

Cerberex waved away his offers and sat, dragging the chair back far enough she could rest her feet on the table. Languidly, she draped an arm across the back of the chair. "I hear that our guest has finally tired of our company."

Selwyn folded his arms. "I'm hardly surprised Cerberex. I imagine the entire house probably heard it."

Cerberex nodded. "I see that you didn't take it that well."

Selwyn scowled. "Evidently. She's stubborn. Seems to think that the Matrons will somehow shield her from the King's displeasure."

Cerberex nodded. "She had a similar conversation with Cerberus - a quite enlightening conversation I would add, but it amounted to something very much the same." She sighed and drew in her arms and legs, to sit more comfortably.

"Niece, why do I get the impression that you have done something." Selwyn took a step forward and rested his hands, leaning on the table.

Cerberex smiled. "She's not leaving today Uncle."

Selwyn closed his eyes and pinched the ridge of his nose. "Don't tell me - I feel it would be safer to simply remain ignorant."

Cerberex's smile broadened. "As you wish." She paused and then rolled her eyes. "Would you like me to talk to her lady to lady?"

"I appreciate your stalling technique my dear, but perhaps not this time." Selwyn replied.

Cerberex's hand drifted to the arm of the chair. "Uncle, there seems to be a lot of effort to keep Lida somewhere she clearly doesn't wish to be. Surely it would actually improve our circumstances if she were to leave."

Selwyn's eyes flicked open. "Improve? Absolutely not! It would make things far worse."

Cerberex twisted a coil of her hair around her finger. "So Cerberus also said."

Selwyn cocked his head to one side. "What are you getting at Cerberex?"

Cerberex stood from the table. "I'm feeling that Lida still being here is very engineered Uncle."

"If you're implying something niece, then you are much mistaken." Selwyn replied slowly.

Cerberex shrugged. "I imply nothing." She stood and stalked around the table and past him. The bare wall the other side seemed to almost shimmer as she approached. Tentatively, she stretched out a hand. At first all she felt was cold stone brush the ends of her finger tips. She frowned, then she felt a sudden pull and the illusion stuttered and faded. Cerberex stepped into the darkness of the route and Selwyn watched without comment.

Chapter 23:
The Stuff of Stories

She expected a challenge, questions, some one at least. The quiet was disconcerting. As she entered the wide space before the route, the shadows shifted along the unfurled wings of the dragon relief. They shuddered to a standstill as her feet echoed with each step, but they did not detain her though she could feel their eyes. Within its mouth, the small unassuming, wooden door lay slightly ajar, a thin shaft of golden light lit the floor. Gently she pushed it further.

The corridor beyond was for the most part empty. A single black clad figure lounged in an alcove nearby. With their scarf up, Cerberex could not tell if it was a he or she that marked her passing. Only that they stood a little straighter as she did and their watch bored into her back as she move on. Whispers pricked her ears as two more stalked by from the bunk room. The silenced as they saw her, pressing against the wall to let her pass. She noticed their curious look as she approached. "Cerberus?" She asked simple.

They looked at each other. "The Master is busy." One of them replied.

"Busy?" She repeated. "Or out?" She watched as they looked at each other again and sighed. "Never mind, I'll find him myself." Her hand drifted to the painful broken rib in her side. "He might have made himself available for his own sister you know." She watched as the two simply looked at each other and then her unsure how to continue.

She sighed and brushed passed them her fingers touching the pocket that held the round pin. Her ears caught the mutter of her name as she made her way to the bunk room. She turned but they were already moving on. Cerberex frowned. She tried to pull herself a little straighter and walked towards the bunk room's open doors.

A sudden burst of self conciousness shot through her as her hand touched the wood of the door frame. Cautiously she peered around the corner suddenly unsure of what she might see. The bunk room was busy. Some sat reading, others played cards or tended equipment, while the odd pair stood simply talking. Cerberex's eyes darted across the faces. None were that of her brother. A polite cough behind her made her jump. Cerberex stood and spun around. The unmistakable shape of Sylas accompanied by Dichta sauntered passed.

"Do you need help looking for something?" Dichta pouted dramatically placing her foot to trip her. "The floor perhaps?" She giggled locking arms with Sylas before sauntering passed.

"No, I found it with your face if memory serves." Cerberex muttered as they moved down the corridor. Her voice had been barely audible but the slight pause in Dichta's footfalls told her that she'd heard it.

Gritting her teeth against the stab of pain as she took a deep breath, Cerberex stepped into the doorway of the bunk room. She cleared her throat quietly and stepped passed the threshold. The first pair of bunks on either side seemed to belong to initiates. Two younger Drau, a male and female, stopped mid-conversation as she passed and watched her with a look of surprise and not a little admiration. The same muttering of her name seemed to shadow her as she passed till those beyond now stopped and stared before she even got to them and stood to get a look at her. Cerberex felt her heart begin to pound in her chest. Her mouth felt dry. The urge to turn back clawed at the back of her mind. She stopped and swallowed again, seeing the sea of onlookers.

"I... I'm..." She stuttered feeling her fingers begin to twitch.

A shunt of movement echoed throughout the room. A shift that radiated from her like a miniature earthquake. Cerberex watched as first those directly in front of her clasped their hands into fists before crossing them across their chest and bowed, swiftly followed by the next, then the ones after them, till the entire rooms occupants now stood before her their eyes lowered to the floor. Well, not all of them. A black clad individual with palest blonde hair pulled back into a tight knot at the back of his head stood leaning against the post of a bunk three rows back.

Kane lounged, his black armoured jacket unbuckled. He looked back at her as her eyes caught him across the crowd. His mouth curled into a half smile. Cerberex's face creased with confusion and then caught the glint of a small metal disk on his collar. His smile broadened as she noticed it. He placed an open palmed hand upon his chest and inclined his head slightly.

Cerberex opened her mouth trying to form an intelligent sentence.

"My lady, I would like to petition to specialise under your tutorship." Cerberex was taken aback at the sudden disturbance of the silence. A male drau easily as tall as herself pushed towards her. "Tye." He crossed his arms across his chest again and lowered his eyes.

"I will also petition!" Another voice, female, shouted from across the room.

"I too!" Another called.

"What criteria do you ask for my lady?" Cerberex's head snapped around as another voice called from behind her.

Kane's eyebrow raised as the room began to vibrate with sudden requests then the questions began to flow thick and fast: Why did you challenge? How did you anticipate them? Do all Watchers train to be like that? Did the Master teach you?

Kane chuckled. "It can be a bit strong when you aren't used to it." He sauntered forward and guided her from the bunks, towards the training room.

"And you didn't see fit to warn me about that first?" Cerberex managed.

"Well you wouldn't have taken it if I had." He laughed.

Cerberex coughed. Though she didn't like to admit it the pain was better. It wasn't that it wasn't there, more that she could no longer feel it. "I see you got one too." She nodded at Kane's collar.

"About the same time you got yours I imagine." Kane replied. "So where is it?"

"I haven't agreed to accept it." Cerberex explained.

Kane looked at her in genuine surprise. "Accept it? Why in Eroth's name wouldn't you? It's the greatest honour. Cerberus must think very well of you."

Cerberex withdrew the pin from her pocket. "It's... I'm not..." She tried struggling to find the right way to explain her feelings. "I'm not one of his..."

"Assassins?" Kane finished.

Cerberex shrugged. "I was going to go with groupies, but your wording sounds better." She gave him an evil smile as they entered.

Kane laughed. "Groupies? Oh I'm not sure that I like that Cerberex."

"Really? What happened to 'my lady' or did you suddenly leave you manners on the table?" Cerberex nodded to the table behind him

Kane looked at the table and then back at her. "You're a Chosen, so am I. In this room we're equal."

"Oh and who did you floor to earn yours?" Cerberex pressed.

Kane looked over at the pit. "Nobody but if you think you can do the job of four people..." He unpinned the badge and placed it on the table before looking back. "Be my guest."

Cerberex raised a hand. "A jest." She folded her arms. "I've not agreed to anything yet."

"Oh well when you have come to a decision do please let us know." Kane clenched his fists and crossed his arms to his chest bowing low. "My lady."

"What is that?" Cerberex asked, suddenly changing the subject.

Kane snapped his head up. "What is what?"

Cerberex mimicked the pose of his arms and then refolded them. "That."

Kane relaxed and stood. "Oh, ah well ... it's a sign of respect really."

"So I gather but why the arms?" Cerberex continued.

Kane laughed. "You really want to know?" Cerberex nodded. Kane grinned. "Because it's really difficult to pull a blade on someone like that." He chuckled as a flicker of alarm crossed Cerberex's face. "I don't believe anyone's had that problem in a while though." He added in a conspiratorial whisper.

Cerberex turned in alarm as the calls and shouts returned. A coterie of petitioners entered the training room in search of her.

"HEY!" Kane's voice rose above the racket and the shouts diminished back to silence. "I'm pretty sure that if Lady Cerberex was taking petitions right now, she'd have asked, so go and get back to what you were doing."

A groan reverberated around the room. Cerberex felt the crowd retreat. Tye snatched her hand up suddenly. "My petition still stands my lady, I'd be honoured if you'd accept me."

"Tye!" Kane's voice shouted.

Tye let go of Cerberex's hand and he turned heel back to the bunk room.

Cerberex let go of the breath she'd been holding as Kane reached her. He brushed passed her shoulder to shoulder. "Follow me." He whispered as he passed.

Cerberex counted his footfalls once, twice, on the third she turned and moved away in the same direction. She stopped in the doorway puzzled for a moment by his sudden disappearance before making out his silhouette down the far end of the corridor, illuminated by a wall sconce. She moved briskly to catch him up. He turned into a small side room before she'd reached him.

Slowing her pace she edged to the threshold. Kane leant against a dusty desk, arms folded, gesturing to a pair of moth eaten chairs. "What in all the hells was that?" Cerberex blurted as words returned to her mouth.

Kane laughed as he sat. "What? You thought your little run in with Sylas and his friends would remain a secret? The entire route watched you hand it to them - my lady. Take it from me, that's not something that happens everyday." He laughed at the look on Cerberex's face and shrugged. "Sometimes we can get a bit... over excited." He straightened. "Right now you're the stuff stories are made of." His eyes glanced over her. "So?" He asked. "Where is it?"

"Where's what?" Cerberex looked around puzzled.

Kane rolled his eyes. Cerberex blinked and he was suddenly a foot away. Reflexively she jumped back hitting the door. "Hey, hey!" Kane held his hands up, palms open. "I'm not Sylas." Cerberex gave a wince as the pain lanced up her side as her body relaxed. Kane put one hand down and reached behind him. "Didn't get out unscathed I take it?" He drew a small vial of amber liquid from one of the numerous pouches at his waist and held it out. "Here." Cerberex looked at it speculatively for a moment and took it. "It'll numb the pain. Makes it easier to heal up after you've taken a beating."

Cerberex took it and flicked off the silver cap. Glancing back at him she knocked back it's contents. It felt like she'd swallowed fire. She leaned against the door coughing.

An awkward silence thickened between them.

"You should take it." Kane broke the silence first. When Cerberex said nothing he continued. "It's rare for even an assassin to see one of those." He paused. "Is that why you're down here? Are you looking for Cerberus so you can give it back?" Cerberex's eyes looked away. Kane's eyes narrowed. "You are aren't you?" He paused. "You know pin or no those ' groupies' out there won't accept that. As far as they're concerned you defended one of their own against those they considered the best in the field." Cerberex's eyes shot back. "Oh what they were up to is the worst kept secret in the route." He smirked. "Cerberus may have accidentally let it slip after his little chat with Clogaen." He shrugged. "So that said, whether you like it or not, your story is being told by candlelight - you're a living legend in their eyes." He shifted, giving her some space. "Look I should probably check in on that lot but think about it. Cerberus is in the garden." He paused as if thinking. "Main courtyard."

Cerberex moved out of his way and watched him leave in surprise. "How do you know that?" She called after him.

Kane paused and glanced back. "A question for another time." He laughed at the disappointment on her face. "What? I've got to keep a few secrets. Especially if you aren't sure about whether you're going to work with me or not."

"Work with you?" Cerberex moved through the door and spun around expecting to catch him but Kane was nowhere to be seen.

Cerberus moved quickly. No intended destination called to him. He moved for the sake of moving - to cool the heat he could feel boiling inside. On the edge of wide expanse of grasses and flowers he came to a stop. The horizon was lit as if it was on fire yet a cold wind blew from the tops of the mountains. He glared even as the chill brought water to his eyes. He could hear Lida's voice in his head. Cool, calm, collected. Like a Queen's should be. A light patter of rain began to fall and her voice melted into a younger rendition. Laughter like shattering glass. He closed his eyes.

"Stop, you'll make me fall!" The voice made his heart stop for a second.

"You wont, I'm not letting go." An echo of his own drifted a moment later.

"Pining does not suit you brother." The crystal clarity of Cerberex's voice made him turn. He saw her flinch for a second at his glare.

"I'm not." He watched her slink the remaining distance. "You seem much better."

"Help from an unseen quarter." Cerberex replied cryptically. She placed a hand on his shoulder. "You can't make her stay Cerberus."

Cerberus shook her off. "He will destroy her." His voice was a growl. "He will take her apart piece by piece until there is nothing left. Even now she meekly patters back to him."

"Duty makes a person do strange things." Cerberex coaxed. "Point in case, I'm here."

"Duty." Cerberus spat the word like a curse.

Cerberex took his hand. "And she isn't yours." She added quietly. Cerberus gave her a murderous look. Cerberex gave his hand a squeeze. "Did you think I didn't know?"

"Sister." Cerberus's voice was filled with menace. "You are choosing to talk about something you know nothing about." His hand touched the pommel of the rapier at his waist.

"Give it up brother. What will you do? Stab me in the middle of the garden?" Cerberex took a step back, her arms stretched out.

A fluttering of feathers and chatter of birds erupted from somewhere in the garden. Cerberus turned towards it, the sound just touching the edges of his senses.

"Go on then brother if it will help..." Cerberex continued.

Cerberus tried to close off her voice as the dark shapes of the birds swooped and soared to the east. "Quiet." He breathed.

"Vent if you need to..." Cerberex prattled on.

"Shut up Cerberex!" Cerberus reached up and put a hand over her mouth to silence her. A rustle of leaves and snap of dead twigs made both of them look around suddenly. Cerberus glanced at his right hand then back. Movement, not here, past the stone wall. His hand wrapped around the hilt of the rapier.

A shift of a shadow passed the opening in the wall. A brush of cloth over dead twigs. The eyes slightly reddened around the edges either by rage or tears. Cerberex relaxed. "It's just Lida." She whispered.

Cerberus watched with suspicion.

Lida looked at the pair of them as if surprised to see them thick as thieves.

A soft click. Almost imperceptible.

Cerberus sprinted.

Cerberex raced after him. Oblivious to his reason.

Cerberus watched in slow motion as the tiny silver flash darted through the air. Leaping a bed of small purple flowers in a cascade of petals, Cerberus launched himself forward, grabbing Lida's waist. A shout, an abrupt scream. Another silver flash passed over his head as he landed heavily, pressing his body over hers.

Cerberex caught up panting and gingerly touching her side with one hand. "What now?!"

Cerberus pushed himself up. Lida looked up at him, her eyes wide with shock. She sucked in a breath. He pulled his hand away from her waist and watched in a moment of confusion at the patch of deep crimson that smudged his palm. "No." The words escaped him as he looked back and watched a dark patch begin to expand from her side where a sliver of silver jutted out eliciting another sharp scream. Quickly he clasped his hand across the wound and held the tiny bolt end to his face between his thumb and forefinger. A shattered glass end dripped with some form of clear liquid. "No." He repeated.

"Eroth!" Cerberex cursed as she too saw the liquid drip and hiss as it hit the ground. Deftly she prized the object from Cerberus's fingers. Bringing it to her face she sniffed the shattered end and looked at Lida. Veins bulged along her neck turning blue then purple. The acrid scent of bile brought tears to her eyes. "Basilisk." She whispered.

Cerberus looked at her. "Will she live? How do I cure her?"

"I... I don't know!" Cerberex stammered staring at the shard.

Cerberus hammered the ground with his free fist. "Damn it Cerberex, think!"

"It's Basilisk Venom brother." She whispered. "There is no cure."

Lida's lip flecked with blood as she coughed. Cerberus cradled her to him. "How do you know this?" He whole body seemed to shake. "No, I don't believe it. Your wrong."

Cerberex studied the tip of the shard her eyes picking out fine striations on the tip. "Because I have some myself." She muttered.

"There must be something." Cerberus wiped the blood from Lida's face as it took on a chalk white pallor. "I'm here." He whispered.

Cerberex looked at him puzzled before she realised he was not talking to her. "Only if it has been diluted."

Cerberus looked at her. His eyes were like bright embers. "Diluted?"

Cerberex held the shard in front of her. "Basilisk is thick, oily. If this was meant to inject it must be thinned with alcohol but that can change the venom's properties." She watched a tear seem to sizzle down Cerberus's face. "Aunt Mal, she would know how to begin a transfusion."

Cerberus nodded and placed a hand on her shoulder, pushing Lida into her lap. He felt like fire. "Do it."

"Alone? I'll never get her there in time." Cerberex retorted.

Cerberus nodded across the grass. "Well thank Eroth you have a following." He stood up nodded to a couple of black smudges coming towards them before scanning for the attacker. "Wherever they are, they aren't seeing another dawn."

"Cerberus!" Cerberex called as he took a step forward. She watched him pause and look over his shoulder. She held up the shard. "The markings. They are Dwentari. Watch you back."

Cerberus raised an eyebrow in surprise but nodded.

Cerberex heard the footfalls of help racing across the lawn. Her eyes traced Cerberus across the garden path, then he was nothing but a blur.

She looked back at Lida. Froth was building on her lips, and her extremities twitched. A terrible thought occurred to her. If the Queen died here, now, in House Dhal-Marrah, every house would believe them to be responsible. Worse, the Temple of Eroth could well excommunicate them for the death of Eroth's chosen daughter. Cerberus would never forgive himself for letting it happen and she would never be able to forgive herself if her actions to detain the Queen had single handedly allowed her murder.

Chapter 24:
Waking the Dragon

Cerberus saw nothing but red as he approached the far perimeter wall. He shuddered to a stop. Part of his head said he should call for reinforcements. That this was too dangerous to take on alone. That he had no idea how many he would find. The heat of his breath seemed to mist the air as he stooped and examined the boot print perfectly preserved by the earth. "Not light on your feet are you." Cerberus muttered. He looked up at the tree line ahead. So they sought to throw him off - big mistake.

Cerberus shadow walked across the intervening gap. The ferns were bent and crumpled. He smiled. "Run if you must but you're only going to die tired." He whispered to himself. This was Cerberex's domain but he was no slouch and he had the advantage of home territory. He stepped beyond the first line of trees, every sense on edge, every thought bent towards some trap or ambush. Part of him felt guilty for leaving Lida's side. Not to matter, he would deliver her the head of her attacker when he returned. She was going to live he told himself, because the thought of the alternative made his vision spin. He would bring her the head if not before he had squeezed every iota of information from it before hand. He smiled and made no move to cover the sound of his feet. He wanted this one to know he was coming.

Shafts of pale sunlight filtered through the tall canopy at intervals, dappling the air. The snap of a fallen branch grabbed Cerberus's attention as something darted through the undergrowth to his left. Cerberus twisted his body side on at the familiar click. Two heavy yet small bolts hammered into the base of a tree where moment's before his head had been. "Come on out and play then." He called out. The hammer of heavy feet replied to him and disappeared deeper into trees. "Coward!" Cerberus shouted after the sound, shadow walking across the glade. A low chuckle of laughter made him turn.

"Coward?" A pale individual in mismatched clothes and shorn head, stepped between two large ferns where Cerberus had previously stood. He clapped his hands slowly. He was too short to be Drau, to tall to be something else. Cerberus's eyes narrowed. Human then. "Truth be told my contract extends only so far as to kill the lady." He raised a small hand crossbow. "But your head has a tidy reward all of it's own."

Cerberus smirked and stepped towards him. "Many have tried to take it, many have failed."

The human laughed. "That's the problem with you Drau. You're too filled up with honour to get anything done." He nodded and ropes descended from the trees. Cerberus watched four more slide down to the ground.

"Which one of you pulled the trigger?" Cerberus asked, surprised at the level of calm he did not feel.

The shaven man increased the strength of his smile as a thick set figure only four feet tall moved in from the other side.

Cerberus did not need to guess. There was no mistaking the outline of a Dwentari. He stretched out his rapier and pointed at it. "You die last."

Bolts fired from all angles at once. Cerberus was already a blur but even he was admittedly surprised by their co-ordination. Cerberus dodged as best he could but even with his preternatural skill, numbers could still overwhelm. He let out a cry as the edge of one bolt tore through the top of his shoulder. It's shooter gargled as Cerberus rammed his blade up and out of the man's throat severing his vocal chords. He tore the blade back leaving a ragged wound and a spray of blood that spattered his face. He felt the liquid hiss on his skin but he was already moving to truly notice it. Heavy arms wrapped around him from behind, thick as winter logs, squeezing the air from him. A skinny individual barely more than a boy judging by his height, barrelled into him a short curved blade aimed to gut him. Using his restrainer as a counter-weight, Cerberus pushed up and kicked out. His boot connected with the skull and with a dull crack, the boy sprawled to the floor. Cerberus watched with strange delight as blood pooled from his nose, the bone jutting at an unnatural angle into his face. He rolled screaming and the noise was music to Cerberus's ears.

Cerberus panted. He felt hot. He felt on fire. He felt... alive. The smell of burning drifted to his nose and the arms around him threw him forwards with a yell. He turned taking a step back as a small hand axe parted the air a hair's breadth from his nose. The second blow knocked the rapier out of his grip but Cerberus came at him regardless. Cursing as he dodged and ducked, beneath the Dwentari's strikes. His hands reached up and clasped around the rough skinned face. Thumbs found eyes and pressed. A yell turning into a scream only served to fuel the furnace that seemed to burn where Cerberus's heart had once been. He felt a burst beneath his thumb tips and pushed the Dwentari to the ground. "Don't fret I'll come back for you." He whispered in it's ear as he skidded around, scooping up his rapier as a heavy short sword came down with enough strength to watch the blade of his weapon bend slightly under the strain.

"Niklaus, leave it. We're paid for the woman. Don't get greedy on me." Cerberus caught the shaved man out of the corner of his eye. He hissed in frustration as he watched him head back into the trees again. With a deft swing he tore a rip in the flesh of his new attackers abdomen.

Blood filled the air. Cerberus breathed it in, letting the heady scent fuel him. The air warped as he breathed out. He wandered towards the slumped form of the Dwentari. Kicking him with a boot, it's limp form toppled to one side. Cerberus reached down and pulled it up by its thick hair. Its face was caked in blood from its burst eyes. A look of agony mixed with a smile of grim finality masked its face. Cerberus looked the Dwentari up and down, finally noticing the runic blade gripped into its chest. Cerberus groaned and ripped it out. It was only four inches long, solid silver with brutal barbs, and every surface of it was covered in intricate script. Cerberus had not studied the languages of other lands like his sister, yet he felt sure that he knew what this was. He watched the blood run down it as if studying a master work. A pact blade. Used for no other reason than to end ones life in the event of capture or worse. Strange the creature carried such an item. Mercenaries were usually such fearful folk.

Cerberus looked in the direction he had last seen the fleeing man. He twisted his neck to one side feeling it crack. Then he was gone. From standing to sprinting the world seemed to blur as he passed, shadow walking from clearing to clearing, stopping only to leap a fallen tree or rotten branch. The branches pressed in at him, clawing his face like a crone's fingers. He urged himself to go faster, hearing the pounding of his quarry's feet ahead. Ferns curled in as he passed. Briar's charred at his touch. Ahead the ground suddenly dove directly down. Cerberus leaped a tree stump and landed on a rocky outcrop five feet away from his prey.

The man gave a cry as he first looked down at the bowl in the earth and then at Cerberus inching slowly towards him. Cerberus could only guess at the terror going through the man's head. He could feel it in the air and it tasted divine. He took another step forward and the outcrop rocked under the weight of them. The man gave a short shout of alarm, unintentionally taking a step back where his foot met nothing but air. He toppled like some form of gangly flightless bird. Turning end over end into the bowl's bottom below. Cerberus sighed and jumped. His shadow form bounced from rock to thick root to leafy mound as he made his own way to the floor, landing in a crouch with one hand gently touching the damp earth. He stood fluidly, taking in his new surrounding. A tall shard of glass-like rock pierced the earth at the centre and only a few feet away the shaven man scrabbled in the dirt, tearing up leaves and clumps of moss.

Cerberus strode over to him, grabbing him by the back of his collar and dragging him yelling to the stone shard at the centre. He slammed the man heavily against its perfectly polished surface, taking in the wide eyed terror that seemed to radiate off him. One side of the man's face was bleeding heavily from a long gash in his temple he must have sustained on his way down and his arm hung limply dislocated at the shoulder, while the other scratched at Cerberus's hand clasped firmly about his throat.

"Talk." Cerberus's voice came out as a low growl. His eyes unblinking, seemed to bore into the man.

The man reached out to his face, struggling to breath. Cerberus relinquished his grip a fraction. "Please... Please." The words were breathy and pleading.

Cerberus sneered and tightened his grip slightly. "Talk." He repeated. Then skewered the ground with his rapier. "Or I shall cut it from you." He drew a small throwing knife from the small of his back.

"It was only a job." The man babbled at the sight of the blade. "Take the pretty woman out of the picture."

"By who?" Cerberus pressed the knife against the man's cheek just below the eye.

"I don't know." The man blurted.

Cerberus dug the tip of the knife into the cheek. The man squealed like a stuck pig.

"I don't know - I don't know! The contract isn't given to me, just the details." The man's chest rose and fell fit to burst. "Take out the lady to that description."

"The bolt. Talk to me about the bolt." Cerberus drew the point away again. Gritting his teeth against the pain as his whole body seemed to want to tear its way out from the inside.

"Part of the deal. Death had to be dealt a particular way. We were paid extra to acquire it." Tears ran down the man's face. "Please... please don't..."

"Who are you?" Cerberus spat the question.

"Tomas of the Head Hunters." The man slurred the words in his rush to answer. "Please, I beg you... They'll pay you! Gold, Florin, whatever you ask its yours if you let me live."

"Pay me?" Cerberus snarled a hideous smile. "You have no idea who it was you shot. Who gave you this order?"

"Some lady." Cerberus shook him. "Alright, alright! Lady Trileris - it was Trileris."

"Trileris." Cerberus repeated and heard himself laugh hollowly "I should have known." His eyes shot back to Tomas, the very look making the human shrink from him. "And what about me?"

Tomas nodded so hard his head cracked back against the stone. "D...d...Dhal-Marrah." He stammered.

Cerberus felt something leap inside him. He glanced to see the skin of his hands beginning to peel and char black. The veins in his wrists pulsing as if aflame. His gaze rested upon Tomas. "The woman you were sent after is Lida of the house of Lotheri. To scum like you that might not mean much. To those of us with even a hint of Drau blood in our veins, she is our Queen. The essence of a goddess made manifest. A conduit of Eroth herself." He watched the man flinch at every statement. "And you thought to murder her."

"I... I... her name was not given to us!" Tomas begged, shifting to his knees.

Cerberus measured his breathing. The pain was pushing through his skull now, he could feel it behind his eyes.

"You've made a poor choice of friends Tomas." Cerberus heard the words but the voice was not his own. "No matter. You'll now serve a greater purpose." It growled Cerberus clutched at his head. He couldn't swallow. With stark realization he found he couldn't breath. "What... magic...is...." He found his own voice again for a moment as he reached out at Tomas. Tomas screamed as flames encased him. Cerberus screamed too.

Cerberex felt a sharp pain stab in the back of her head. For a second it seemed her head was aflame. She blinked and it subsided to a murmuring discomfit. Lida's quarters hummed. Siphon's, filters, pumps, and more rattled, hissed and bubbled. Tables had been brought from across the house and arranged around the bed and a veritable influx of servants came to and fro bringing what ever the fraught Maleficent asked for next. Yet it had all come down to a quiet waiting game. Cerberex watched as blood writhed around twisting tubes into quietly thrumming alembics. Lida lay pierced by hollow needles at various intervals. Her breathing came short and erratic. Her skin still the colour of a corpse. For once Cerberex was pleased that her brother was nowhere to be found.

Maleficent sat the other side of the bed leaning as if to watch for even the slightest movement. She glanced at Cerberex as if about to speak then returned her gaze back to Lida.

"Will she make it aunt?" Cerberex's voice was barely above a whisper.

Maleficent didn't look up. "Well it would not do for her to die on Dhal-Marrah lands." She paused and her voice dropped. "So we should consider where she should be found if she doesn't."

Cerberex look horrified. "You can't tell me we'll dump her body somewhere."

"I'm not sure we'd have a lot of choice my dear. Do you have any idea of what it would do for the Queen to die in our care?" Maleficent replied. "It would ruin us."

Maleficent glanced at Cerberex. "Oh don't fret. Your Uncle will come up with something - he usually does."

Cerberex let the silence stretch out. "Aunt?"

Maleficent's face creased with irritation. "Mhmm."

"You realise this is the second attack in as many days." Cerberex added quickly.

"Yes, they're getting sneaky aren't they." Maleficent murmured. Cerberex wasn't entirely sure that she was talking to her until Maleficent looked up at her. "Funny don't you think? That they spend all of their energy despising us and then only go and botch up this attack when the first was so close." She paused. "Now if only they had some professionals they could count on hmm?" She whispered conspiratorially. She sat back. "And where is your brother?"

Cerberex thought about the question then replied, "Hunting."

Maleficent raised her eyebrows. "Ah, so we wont expect much left then." She sighed. "Oh I do hope he remembers to clean up."

"You sound disappointed." Cerberex snorted.

"I am." Maleficent replied. "I have so many questions I'd dearly like to have answered." Cerberex looked at her. "Well," Maleficent began. "Such as where this ingenious piece of equipment was procured? Also, where exactly one has obtained Basilisk Venom - not exactly something that you ask an apothecary for."

"I have some." Cerberex began.

Maleficent sat up in surprise. "Hell's teeth! What ever for and more precisely, where did you get it?"

Cerberex shrugged. "I brought it home with me when I came back from Agrellon."

"Watchers are handing that stuff out?" Maleficent shook her head. "The world is definitely changing."

"Yes it is." Cerberex thought privately. "Aunt? How would you proceed?"

"At what Niece?" Maleficent lowered her jaw onto her steepled fingers. Resuming her watch when Cerberex didn't answer she looked up again. "This?" She sighed. "Oh my dear Cerberex, this is but the beginning."

"The beginning?" Cerberex almost shouted before clamping a hand over her mouth.

Maleficent looked at her disapprovingly. "He wont stop until she is delivered to him. Be that in a box or under her own steam appears to matter little." She sat back and smiled gently. "My dear, sweet girl. Never lose that little spark. The belief that you have - that somehow everyone will play by the rules." She leant forward. "The rules are a lie. They exist because Drau do not play well with each other. We tear each other's throats out like wolves in the night for the right to dominate and we are not beneath indulging in a little trickery to force matters. There is no fair play, no status quo to rely on. It is simple survival by whoever can wield the biggest sword."

"I cannot believe that." Cerberex replied.

Maleficent gave her a cold smile. "Choose not to then. You are young Cerberex. Perhaps you will prove to me otherwise." She stood and stepped to the door. "But I doubt it." She murmured before she left.

Cerberex slouched in her chair silent for a long while listening to Lida's stuttered breathing. Her brow furrowed. Reaching to a stack of notes on a nearby table, she pulled away an empty piece of parchment. Taking up the abandoned quill nearby she began to write feverishly. An hour ticked by and as the sun began to shift to the horizon, she stopped and re-read what she had written. She brushed the quill end under her chin and considered the wording. With any luck Lida would wake and read it before her aunt did or perhaps worse, her mother.

It was time to end this. She felt that the words should shock her somehow, but in reality she felt very little. The letter laid out her plans if a little scant on the detail. Oh she was aware that others had tried what she was about to do with little success - Cerberus for one. She folded the parchment in half, then half again. Her eyes looked at Lida. "If I do not then Cerberus will." She whispered. "And if I know my brother, he'll not be so subtle and that alone will get him killed because he cannot get as close as I might." She tucked the parchment underneath Lida's hand so it would be the first thing she felt when she woke. Sisterly, she brushed an errant heir away from her face then straightened and folded her arms. "Now there's no need to look at me like that your Majesty, I'm well aware of the risks but I'm afraid you have bound yourself to an animal - a monster no less, and that my Lady simply wont do." She smirked fully appreciating how mad she must sound. "Look after my little brother Lida. After all, he just can't seem to help himself when it comes to you." She lowered her tone to just above a whisper. "The Dhal-Marrah's aren't in the habit of giving second chances. So when you wake for him, do try not to screw it up this time!"

Lida's face remained unmoving.

Cerberex smiled and rubbed her side. "Well, I'm glad we had this little chat. Now if you'll excuse me." She performed a small curtsey. "I have some important matters to attend to." She giggled madly.

Chapter 25:
The Beast in Velvet

Cerberex made all speed to her room with an aura of purpose. Looked both ways and closed the door quietly behind her. She stopped and held her breath waiting for something to jump from the shadows. Nothing. Upon a small side table a gold ring lay upon a white handkerchief. She smiled. The girl had done well. Had Lida not been more permanently detained, she'd have certainly been concerned about the misplacement of her own house signet! Cerberex scooped it up and opened a small pouch at her waist, dropping it within. It wouldn't do to have evidence of her theft simply lying about for when the next person entered her room.

The deed done, now the real preparations were to begin. Cerberex darted about the room. First flinging wide her wardrobe she rummaged around the old clothes and winter wear flung in the bottom. At the far back, coated in a fine layer of dust, she withdrew a dark brown leather bag. Quickly she gave it a shake and emptied its current contents onto the floor. An empty water flask rolled under the bed as she dumped the bag on the floor. Unceremoniously she began to pour through the gowns hanging up unworn. Black, blue, Russet Red, and many more. Some beaded, some stitched with fine metallic threads, some with spider-like lace. Her hands glided over their fine textures, till she at last paused on one. She ran her hands down the brushed velvet the colour of charcoal. Tiny satin ribbons laced the sleeves to the bodice and the front was finished in delicate white pearls. A moment of fond memories stretched on, before she yanked it from the cupboard and with an action that would have horrified or her mother, shoved it into the bottom of the bag.

Placing her hands on her hips she nodded and moved to the bed, retrieving a small ebony trunk from beneath. The brass-work of the clasps gleamed and well oiled hinges barely murmured as she lifted the lid. Within her blades, bow, and arrows lay encased in soft green velvet. Gently she pulled out one of the knives and slowly unsheathed it. One of a pair, she had worn no other since their acquisition. They had accompanied her on hunt after hunt. Gutted beasts and monsters in her Watchering days. Hunters blades they were called. Silvered along the edge, they never dulled nor lost their lustre. They had never failed her. "Once more unto the hunt my friends." She whispered as she picked up the other and along with their scabbards added them to the bag. Mournfully she looked at the bow. It seemed forlorn without the knives to keep it company but she had no way of disguising it and it would surely not fit within the bag. She lifted it gently onto the bed and lifted away the velvet cushion. Beneath the false bottom lay a plethora of tiny instruments and glass flasks. They tinkled against each other without the cushion to hold them still. Her hand reached down for a black pouch and tipped the contents onto her hand. A dozen thin, three inch long pins lay against her hand. She put them to one side. Reaching back into the box she began to lift the flasks one by one examining the labels. Dibella Berry, Nightshade, Gorse Bite, Amber-leaf, Corpse-bloom, Basilisk. Her hand snatched up the Basilisk and she shrugged - it seemed only fitting. Two empty flasks lay next to the assorted poisons and irritants. placing them on the floor, Cerberex opened the flask of Basilisk Venom. The oily substance oozed from it's container in a bile-like stream. Carefully she measured half a flask and quickly replaced the venom back in its slot. Next she brought out two more flasks. Amber-leaf to sooth the sudden pain and dull the senses - he'd feel nothing till it was too late; and Dibella Berry to thin the mixture and mask the scent. One drop of Amber-leaf to four of Dibella was added before she sealed the concoction and gave it a sudden shake. Studying the pale oily mixture she once more opened it and one by one inserted the thin needles within, before placing them on the table. She needed each needle evenly coated.

"While her tools brewed. She walked across the room to a large dish of water and washed her hands, running them damp through her hair till she looked like she had walked for an hour in light rain. She glanced at the stone fire place on the far wall. It had not been lit in a couple of days but Eroth willing, there should still be soot within the catch underneath. Dhal-Marrahs had a unique and easily noticed colouring. The lightening white hair and red eyes were a dead give away. Something would need to be done about that. She stalked over to the fire and knelt, dragging open the catch. Soot plumed as she dislodged it just as she had hoped and she buried her hands into the soft black powder before running it through her hair. Thirty or so minutes later she looked like a different person. A raven haired female - if a little streaky in places. She twisted her hair up and wandered to the table. With extreme care to not cut, scratch, or so much as prick her skin, Cerberex pushed the pins into her hair, holding it in place.

She stood in front of the mirror and took in the reflection as she slung the bag over her shoulder. She steadied herself with a hand against the glass eyes closed as if in prayer. "Fear not this night." She whispered the mantra. "For I am the hunter and the dark holds no terrors." She opened her eyes and the reflection stared back. Grabbing a plain cloak, she swept from the room.

The city bathed in twilight as Cerberex darted hood up from street to street.

A chill wind kept all but the dangerous inside. None took a second glance at the quiet form slipping between alleys. Looming above her even at this distance, like a massive multi-eyed gargoyle, the palace glinted and glimmered. In the light of a thousand lamps its spires appeared to pierce the sky - impossibly tall. Perhaps under normal circumstances it could be considered a thing of beauty, to Cerberex it seemed to glare at her - ever more foreboding the closer she came till she stood barely a street away from its gates.

Heavy armed guards stood upon the threshold. They had upgraded since last time. She looked down at her hands - perfectly steady. Cerberex took a deep breath, adjusted her hold upon her bag and crossed the street. Ten feet away, six feet, at three feet the great pole-arms of the central pair levelled at her. She stopped bowing low as heavily armoured feet approached her.

"The palace is closed to civilians for the evening. Go peddle your wares elsewhere." The voice echoed behind the plume helmet of the guard captain.

"I am not a civilian good sir." She replied. Doing her best to mask her voice into a gentle wheedle.

"Sure you aren't." He turned and clicked his fingers.

Cerberex took a step back as the pole-arms advanced on her. "I have information."

The captain laughed coarsely. "There is no information that could interest me. Get out of here."

"Not even if it concerned the death of the Queen?" She added hurriedly keeping her eyes low.

Another click and the pole-arms turned away. "That information is extremely dangerous." The captain's voice was low. He stopped a foot from her, so close she could smell the sweat beneath his armour. "Who are you?"

At first Cerberex did not reply. She had not thought of an alias. "My name is unimportant." Slowly she reached behind her and withdrew the ring. "I bring proof that the deed is done." She watched as the captain reached out but closed her fist around it. "Their is more but not for your eyes."

The captain hissed in irritation. "So the Trileris come through with their mongrel hounds." Through the top of hood she watched him look back. "Take this one to see Lord Vor'ran." He called. One guard handed his pole-arm to a comrade and stepped forward. Cerberex smiled beneath her hood and made to move passed. The captain's hand arrested her, holding firm to her shoulder. "You were told to meet in three days." He leaned towards her. "This had better be important to break that."

"Lady Trileris was insistent." Cerberex replied, hoping that the leading lady of that house had indeed had a hand in Lida's currently attempted assassination.

The captain smirked. "She has always had ideas above her station." He let go. "Weapons up! Let her in."

Cerberex stepped between the guards and beyond the gate. She heard the pole-arms crack as they crossed back behind her. A gauntleted hand rested on her back. "Keep going. This way." Cerberex allowed herself to be lead up the stone stairs, through the great doors, and into the belly of the beast.

Raucous laughter and the echo of music hit her as the doors groaned to a close. Judging from the smells and sounds that assaulted her, King Aelnar was not loosing any time while his Queen was away. As expected she was lead down a small corridor, a servant's aisle that ran with only a wall between them and the great hall. Light dimmed. Cerberex counted her footsteps, slowing them a fraction allowing the space between the guard behind her and herself to diminish.

"Pick up the pace." The guard gave her a shove.

Cerberex sprawled elaborately across the floor. Swinging her bag across her front. She bite down on a whelp of pain as she landed on her cracked rib.

"Get up." The guard ordered.

Cerberex pushed her hand into the bag, wrapping her hand around the hilt of one of her knives. "Mind your hands sir. I'd hate to explain to Lord Vor'ran why the goods I bring have been damaged."

"Why you..." A heavy hand dragged her back up to her feet.

The blade sang as she turned to him and plunged it to the hilt under his metal cuirass. She clamped her hand over his mouth as he attempted to yell and twisted the blade, rupturing organs. He sagged like a sack of stones. Cerberex dropped him carefully to the floor. Pulling the leather bag towards them she replaced the knife just as footsteps hurried towards them.

"Hey!" An elderly Drau, well dressed, holding a thick ledger with ink stained finger tips caught up to them. "What is this?"

Cerberex kept her hood up. "Help me. He's been at the wine a little too long."

The elderly Drau grunted in annoyance. "Imbecile! Put him in one of the food cellars until her sobers up. I shall be having words with Captain Sillonir."

Cerberex pulled the guard's arm over her shoulder. She cursed quietly at the weight of his armour, before dragging him in the direction the elderly Drau gesticulated wildly. She could hear him muttering irritably under his breath as disappeared in the opposite direction. She waited for the patter of his feet to fade before she looked up. Her eyes darted around noticing a heavy wooden door. Dragging the guard with her she tried the latch. It swung with surprising ease to reveal a set of solid stone stairs. Unceremoniously, she dumped the body forwards allowing it to rag doll down the steps. Quietly she tiptoed after it.

Looking around she appeared to be in some form of water closet. Cerberex smiled at the the fortune of it. Positioning the guard so he seemed to have fallen into a stupor with his head slooped towards a barrel. She froze as the sound of footsteps echoed past the door and waited. The footsteps faded and She let out the breath she had been holding. Quickly she dropped the brown leather bag and dragged out its contents. Hastily she undressed, slipping on the gown and brushing herself down. Pushing everything else back into the bag. She headed back up the stairs and opened the door a fraction, just enough to check what lay beyond. Quietly Cerberex slipped passed the door, an oddly beautiful figure carrying a strange brown bag. She held herself with as much poise as she could muster while walking with as much speed as the gown's restrictions would allow.

The corridor ended abruptly onto a busy hallway somewhere between the private chambers and the great hall. "You." Cerberex froze. Another guard across the hallway called out to her. "I don't know you."

Cerberex performed her best courtly curtsey a little off-balance with the weight of the bag. Demure was not her natural demeanour but she did her best to pull it off.

The guard looked her up and down. "Lady?" He asked cautiously.

"Not by title sir, but yes, Queen's lady," She replied.

"What is this?" The guard pointed to the bag.

Cerberex looked at the bag and then glanced up at the guard. "I... I'm sure I don't know. I have been told to take it to the private chambers of his majesty. Truth be told I dare not ask." She whispered the final words.

The guard looked her questioningly. He was not as armoured as those she had previously come across but he had a look about him that brains were definitely trumping brawn in his case. He stepped back, assessing her again. "You are new? They were quick to gain a replacement."

"Replacement sir?" Cerberex tried to ask innocently.

"Replacement." He replied and his eyes narrowed. "Strange that you are not aware."

Cerberex could have kicked herself for her stupidity. A Queen's lady did not ask questions. Why would she? Living within the palace she would be privy to every little going on.

"I'll take you to the queen's quarters - if another can vouch for you then we needn't ask further questions." He offered an arm.

"He isn't sure." Cerberex thought to herself. "He doesn't want to directly call me out if he is wrong." She took his arm. Allowing him to carry the bag. All the while her head ran with what to do next. She knew none of the Queen's ladies particularly. How would one vouch for her?

Grey stone walls slowly transcended into softer almost homely décor. She did her best to appear as if she knew where she was going. She could feel his eyes glance down at her every few feet yet she kept her own focused on the path ahead. A pair of simple doors lacquered white with a motif of twin crossed staves inlaid with silver seemed too simple to be their destination. Regardless the guard pushed open one ushering her gently inside.

Cerberex stepped through into a large communal room. Couches and high-backed chairs clustered together. A table of assorted dishes and beverages stood to one side. She could feel the press of many pairs of eyes stare at her as she entered, blinking without a sign of recognition.

"Good evening ladies." The guard gave a shallow bow as he followed her. "Have I found a lost friend?"

Silence. It rose up against her like a tsunami. She opened her mouth about to attempt to protest.

"There you are!" A bright face Drau draped in crystals approached them beaming. "Oh my dear, did no one tell you? His majesty hates the colour black. No that wont do at all."

The guard stepped away. "You know this one lady?"

The Queen's lady looked at him baffled. "Of course sir, this is..." She glanced at Cerberex.

"Nethlae." Cerberex interrupted quickly choosing the name of a cousin.

"Of course, Nethlae." The Queen's lady looked at the guard with expectation.

For a moment Cerberex couldn't tell if he bought it. "My apologies Lady Nethlae." He offered her a slight bow. "I believe you were delivering..."

"Oh don't worry about that - we'll ensure it's done." The Queen's lady interrupted. "We couldn't possibly send Nethlae dressed as she is. It would be completely remiss of me." Cerberex watched with surprise as the guard was ushered from the room as pleasant as if he had meant to leave the entire time.

When she returned she pushed the bag into Cerberex's arms and half dragged her across the room into another that appeared to be little more than a walk-in wardrobe.

"Let us be clear. I know not who you are, but you are courting death." The lady rounded on Cerberex her smiles suddenly turned to frowns at the flick of a switch.

Cerberex took a step back. "Thank you for vouching me."

The lady waved her hand. "Enough. Why do you come here Nethlae?"

Cerberex smiled. "First my name is not Nethlae."

"I had already surmised as much." The lady placed her hands upon her hips.

"It's Cerberex." Cerberex added.

The lady blinked. "Cerberex?" She repeated. "Lady Cerberex?" Cerberex nodded. "Hells teeth! We must get you out of here at once." The lady glanced around nervously as if the very walls had suddenly grown ears. "If the King knows you are here he'll kill you on sight. What in Eroth's name are you doing here? Do you bring news of the Queen? Is she returning?"

Cerberex laid a hand on her shoulder and looked her eye to eye. "I'm going nowhere." She replied. "When the bells toll for the King's passing or news of my execution spreads through the city - then I shall have left. Tell me your name."

"Cynthia" The lady whispered. "My lady you can't!"

Cerberex raised an eyebrow. "What makes you say that?"

"So many have tried, even your lord brother if the stories are true. None have been successful. It is impossible." Cynthia stumbled over her words.

"Calm yourself. No one is immune to death - so he's cheating it. How?" Cerberex guided her over to a small stool and sat her down.

"The Queen has spent nights trying to answer that question." Cynthia replied still staring at Cerberex. "Forgive me, you're... you don't look as I expected."

Cerberex smiled. "In this case I'll take that as a compliment." She crouched to Cynthia's level. "Has the king received gifts? Does he do anything special in his normal routine?"

Cynthia shook her head. "He receives many gifts but his most treasured possession is an amulet gifted to him by his cousin. He will go nowhere without it."

Cerberex raised an eyebrow. "Tell me of this amulet?"

Cynthia furrowed her brow recalling its shape. "A hollow disk of intricate lines and weaves. It has a tiny gem at the centre that changes colour."

Cerberex paused in thought. "But he doesn't wear it all the time does he Cynthia?"

Cynthia looked at her wide eyed. "I cannot tell you this!"

Cerberex looked at her. "Cynthia, I'm right aren't I? He does take it off doesn't he?"

Cynthia sighed and nodded. "I have seen him do this." She looked up. "You must swear that you will not tell the Queen. She will return and his rage will be murderous."

"If you know because of why I think you do, her rage is going to be pretty incandescent." Cerberex replied. She paused but Cynthia would not continue. "Very well, you have my word."

"It is the last thing he removes before... before he...meets anyone in his private quarters. " Cynthia began diplomatically.

"You mean before he fucks something." Cerberex abbreviated. Cynthia looked up at her shocked. "Don't give me that look. You're not as innocent as you look - I just watched you swear blind I was Nethlae five minutes ago to a royal guard." She continued. "So where's the problem. It wouldn't be the first time a King has taken a mistress. Whose the lucky lady this time?"

Cynthia looked up at her. Her expression hardened to anger. "Lucky? No one who enters that room is lucky Lady Cerberex.He will take it off and place it upon the small table on his side of the bed." She pointed an accusing finger at the wall in what Cerberex assumed was the general direction of the King's quarters.

Cerberex stood up taken aback by the vehemence of Cynthia words. "What..." She did not have time to finish the sentence as Cynthia stood and turned unlacing the back of her dress and pulling it open with one hand. Cerberex couldn't prevent the gasp. "What in the..." Cynthia's skin was a master-work of cuts, healing burns, and purple welts.

Cynthia turned back around and re-laced. "And I am lucky." She whispered.

Cerberex could not think of the words. Suddenly her skin felt cold, her heart felt like lead. Intense fury simmered under her skin. She forced herself to breath. "How long has this gone on for?"

"Every night since the Queen's disappearance." Cynthia replied.

"He will pick someone tonight?" Cerberex growled.

"Once he has tired of the fawning lords and ladies downstairs? Yes, he'll ask to be brought some 'entertainment' as he puts it." Cynthia nodded.

Cerberex sniffed. "Entertainment is it? An easy way in at least." There was no question. She held Cynthia's chin. "No more. You will send no more to that fate do you understand."

Cynthia nodded then shook her head. "If we do not send anyone ... I don't know what will happen next."

Cerberex pulled her into a gentle hug. "Nothing, because the bastard's not seeing another dawn so long as I live. He has to be stopped."

Cynthia pulled away her eyes wide. "Lady Cerberex you can't, you mustn't!"

Cerberex gave her a cold smile. "My mother gave up telling me what I can and cannot do a long time ago - I strongly recommend that you do the same." She took a step back. "Although, I may need a little help."

Chapter 26:
Goodnight

Cerberex sat and listened till the candles grew dim. Cynthia did her best to dissuade her but her mind was already made up. In truth, she heard little of anything the lady said, lost in her own thoughts till she looked up to find the lady had stopped.

"Would it make you feel better if I knocked you out?" Cerberex asked. Her voice was chillingly exact.

Cynthia looked up shocked. "Why would you do that?"

Cerberex shrugged. "It seems you'd prefer it almost if you didn't know what was happening."

Cynthia opened and closed her mouth twice, unsure of what to say next. A quiet knock on the door saved her from formulating a response. "Lady Cynthia it's time again." A muffled voice called from the other side.

Cerberex looked at Cynthia with a raised eyebrow. "It was your turn wasn't it?" Cynthia simply stared at the door. Pushed her tongue into her cheek and nodded, turning to face the door. "Lady Cynthia has been taken ill." She called out. "Tell whoever it is that Lady Nethlae will attend in her place tonight."

Cynthia looked at Cerberex. "You can't do this."

Cerberex looked around the walls of the room, lined with clothes. She wandered to one in deep red. "Do you think he'd like this?" She asked ignoring the question.

"You can't." Cynthia repeated.

Cerberex nodded. "I'll take that as a yes." She stripped down and began redressing, feeling it a little tight. "Will you hide this for me, somewhere where I can get back to it easily enough."

Cynthia took the dress out of habit. "Don't speak." She began, helping Cerberex with the long row clips. "It only prolongs it." She brushed away the lint from the skirt. "Eroth willing, he will be too drunk for it to be too long." She tucked away a showing hemline. "Just remember it isn't you - if you realise it's you you'll go mad."

Cerberex nodded. She handed Cynthia her bag. "These are worth more to me than silver or gold." She paused. "If... if the worst should happen. See they are returned to house Dhal-Marrah."

Cynthia took the back and peeked within. "You're going unarmed?"

Cerberex smiled grimly. "Oh I'm never unarmed. I'm going to tear his throat out with my teeth if it comes to it." She turned and opened the door.

She recognised her chaperone almost immediately. He looked tired to the soul yet still managed to maintain a soldierly pose.

"Lady Nethlae." His eyes looked her up and down. "We meet again."

Cerberex curtsied. "So it would seem sir, though you've yet to give me a name."

The guard appeared to suppress a smile. "Lieutenant Falda, officer of the Queen's Guard." He held out a hand. "I understand that Lady Cynthia isn't available this evening."

Cerberex nodded. "She is unwell sir."

Falda pulled a face. "Unfortunate." He held out his arm. "Shall we? The King does not like waiting."

Cerberex stepped forward and took it. "Let us not detain him then." They stepped from the Queen's quarters.

Falda's pace doubled as they moved down corridors and across walkways, passed rooms adorned with portraits, till the subtle regality turned into an almost overbearing sumptuousness that bordered on the obscene. Walls were lined with silk, golden gilt filigree seemed to flow across the ceilings the value of which may have made a dragon wince. Chandeliers of coloured crystal glinted at every intersection. "Does he fancy himself a god?" Cerberex caught herself thinking as she passed.

They stopped almost as abruptly as they had started before a mighty pair of engraved doors in a deep polished redwood. She went to step forward but Falda caught her arm. "I hope Lady Cynthia isn't... too unwell." He stated.

Cerberex's brow furrowed at the strange statement till it dawned. "You're sweet on her." She thought before regaining her composure. "Lady Cynthia will be absolutely fine." She patted his arm. "Nothing a nights uninterrupted rest can't cure." She gave a half smile and tried to pull away but Falda held on.

"It isn't my place to say." He began and paused. "I, I know that the King can be heavy handed." He closed his eyes for a moment. "If it is too much, I wanted to tell you that I will be just by this door."

Cerberex looked at him surprised. "I... appreciate the sentiment." She replied slowly. "But take it from me, I know what I'm doing."

Falda blinked at her boldness. "Then I wish you luck Lady Nethlae."

She watched him turn and cross his arms. Cerberex faced the door feeling the coolness of the metal handle in her grip. She took a breath and pushed the door ajar, slipping through into the room beyond.

Cerberex wasn't sure what to expect as she entered the room but what a room! Every surface, from the walls to the ceiling was lavished in shades of red and gold - Gal-Serrek, she realised. It was a take on the colours of house Gal-Serrek. The door closed soundlessly behind her. She rubbed her arms though the room was plenty warm enough, in fact despite the space, it was almost stifling.

"Last time I checked, I asked for Lady Cynthia. You are not her." The voice made her jump.

Cerberex went down to one knee spreading the skirt of her dress around her as much as was possible. "Lady Cynthia is unwell your majesty." She felt rather than heard his footsteps across the carpeted floor. Then the touch of his hands as they glided down the clips along her back. Her skin crawled beneath. She kept her head down and for a moment worried he would see the pins secreted in her hair.

"I've not seen you before I think." He murmured circling her like a hound on a fox.

"No, your majesty." Cerberex kept her answers soft and simple but her eyes were darting in search of anything that could be useful.

"Breaking in the new blood then?" There was a smirk to his voice. She felt him lean to her. She could smell the wine on his breath. "Don't worry breaking in is something I excel at." He paused. "Stand, my little raven haired beauty. Let's have look at you."

Slowly she rose to her feet. Normally she would have held her face proud and tall, but these were not normal circumstances. She felt the steady thump of her heart and checked her hands. Steady. His hand wrapped around her waist. It suddenly occurred to her how tall he was, there was muscle in that grip. True most of it had wasted but the linger of it remained. The grip still held power. She felt the fingers trace upwards around her curves and gritted her teeth at the tiny screaming part of her brain. The hand slid down the neckline. She closed her eyes and focused on her breath entering and leaving her lungs. Fingers plunged and grabbed almost painfully. She risked a glance to his pudgy neck. A silver chain hung around it decorated with a single pendant of gold wire wrapped around a single jewel that changed hue in the light..

"I think you will do nicely." He breathed forcing Cerberex to focus every atom of her being into not twisting and sending her elbow straight into his face.

"Whatever pleases your majesty." She whispered.

She heard him laugh under his breath. "It pleases me very much."

Cerberex opened her eyes as the screaming in her head became a roar. She refused to turn away. "Fear not the night." She told herself.

Her body stiffened as he tore the clasps away. "Spirited, Excellent. You'll want to keep that in mind." Fabric tore beneath his grip as he pulled the dress away.

Cerberex stood motionless, refusing be ashamed of her naked form. The tinkling of metal echoed behind her. She twisted to see the talisman dropped by a silver tray and turned back before he could look at her.

"We'll start with these, and lets see how we progress." His voice seemed distant in her head.

Cerberex was unprepared for the force of the impact. It sent her sprawling forcing the air out of her lungs. When the second came she had to bite down so hard her tongue bled in her mouth. The sweet iron taste of it was enough to keep her mind off the pain across her back. Clawing at a chair she pulled herself up to her feet.

The third impact illicited a squeak from her vocal chords before she clamped her mouth shut. She felt tiny shards impact along her back and then tear away. A trickle of what surely was blood. Her heart was thundering and she felt herself waver. She had imagined he might hit but this?

"Oh don't light out on me now my little raven. The fun is just beginning." He hiccoughed.

Cerberex steadied herself and remembered the ears, the blinded guard, Lida's corpse-like form. The next hit hammered against her fractured rib and white pain coursed across her body. Darkness threatened the edge of her vision. "Get up." A voice that seemed to be hers but wasn't called softly in her head. She grabbed the arm of the chair. "Get up." She pulled her weight forcing her knees to lock even as they shook. "Get up". Suddenly heat blossomed on her shoulder, the smell of burning flesh, and then there was only ice.

It dropped into her skull like sweet relief. Her body was no longer hers. She felt it stand and in a strange detached way, knew the punishment it took, but it was not her. The cold travelled along her with an electric surge that carried away the pain and locked it somewhere to be processed later. She felt the hand about her throat drag her across the room. Knew that she could not breath as it threw her on the bed, but it was not her. The ice grew till she could not recall her name or what was happening to her and as her ears popped with the pressure of it, she allowed it to carry her safely away.

Cerberex blinked. Under breath her voice counted "Three-hundred and forty-two." There was only darkness. The sheets of the bed were wet - by sweat or blood she couldn't tell. Her body screamed at the slightest movement, yet her head still seemed to hold an icy numbness. In disgust she pushed away the fat arm that hung over her and rolled off the edge of the bed expecting her legs to obey. They did not. She hit the carpet with a dull thud and allowed herself a a small groan. Cerberex touched her back wincing. The skin was shredded with tiny lacerations. She felt disgust rise in her. Cerberus could never know she had allowed that - that thing to defile her. He would never understand why she had paid this price. Gingerly she touched her hair and felt the end of a pin still hidden there. She looked up at the edge of the bed and grabbed it, pulling herself up despite the shrieking of her bruised limbs.

Quietly she limped to the other side of the bed and withdrew the first needle. Carefully she pushed it into the skin around his belly leaving it in place before she withdrew it cleanly away. The king murmured and stretched but did not move. She inserted the second, then the third, until all but the last had been used. As she inserted the final needle the muscle convulsed. She leant in, holding it in place. "Compliment's of House Dhal-Marrah you bastard!" She spat horsely. With a speed mustered from some forgotten part of her. Cerberex made to leave. The ice in her head made everything little more than a fuzzy outline. She almost head-butted the door. Her hand wrapped around the cold handle and as the last burst of strength left her body she hefted it open. Blinding light hit her. She raised a hand and stumbled through the gap hitting the cold stone floor.

"Eroth's fangs!" She heard the curse seemingly too loudly. "Lady Nethlae? Lady Nethlae!" The voice called but she did not know the person of which he spoke. A shadow loomed over her. "Falda." It came with a name.

Falda knelt over her naked form. "Yes lady, it's Falda." There was a hint of relief in his tone. Slowly his face became clearer as Cerberex squinted at it. Had he stood there all that time? She could see purple-black circles around his eyes.

She shivered. Falda quickly removed his blue and white uniform coat. She felt the soft material against her skin. Then the sensation of gently being picked up. Lights flashed past for what seemed like forever. Then the sound of a door and the gentle moonlit glow. Whispering. Male then female, then female again. Then soft cushions. Then nothing.

Cerberex woke with a start, sitting bolt upright and immediately wishing she hadn't. She wore a soft white night gown that hung a fraction too big. She lay back again and looked around in the the soft pre-light of dawn. The Queen's common room. She recognised it as if from a terrible dream. She was lying on one of the large sofas. Glancing about, she saw Cynthia her head resting to one side asleep. A bowl of bloody water rested on the floor near her feet. Her eyes opened at Cerberex's stirrings.

"Eroth be praised! you're awake." Cynthia whispered, suddenly shifting to a straighter position.

Cerberex reached for Cynthia who knelt on the floor next to her. "Have the bells tolled? What time is it?" She murmured.

"No my lady." Cynthia replied.

Cerberex nodded. "I need to get up."

"You need rest my lady." Cynthia insisted trying to gently ease Cerberex back against the cushions.

Cerberex had not the will to disagree. "How bad is it?" She asked instead.

Cynthia looked away. "I wasn't even sure it was you when my brother brought you back."

Cerberex looked at her in surprise. "Falda's your brother? I thought... That monster did that to you and made your brother listen?" Cynthia looked away ashamed. Cerberex grabbed her arm. "I didn't mean to shame you." She paused. "Please will you bring me my things? I need to clean up and look the part before the show starts."

Cynthia gave her a pained look but nodded. "Your clothes have been pressed ready for you. I will see if I can find something to ease the pain."

Cerberex watched her wander away and turned back to face the window. If luck was smiling, her family might still be in the dark, there was a slim chance she'd be home again before anyone had any idea what she had been up to. Slim, but it was there. A thin beam of sunlight filtered to the floor. Time to see this through. She looked up to a patter of footsteps. Cynthia returned with a pile of freshly folded clothes, a leather bag, and a small tin.

"This will help numb the worst of it. I would have found something faster acting but I felt too many questions might be asked." Cynthia held the tin out to her.

Cerberex popped off the lid and looked inside at the wax-like cream. Carefully she began to apply it to her shoulder, wincing as she did. "Surely the entire palace is aware of what the King has been up to."

Cynthia shrugged. "Possibly, but one does not go around confessing it the day after." She helped Cerberex stand and offered her the clothes.

"Knives first." Cerberex pointed to the bag.

Cynthia held out the bag and watched as Cerberex strapped them to her thighs before taking the dress and gently easing it on.

"What is the King's schedule today?" She asked drawing Cynthia's attention from the bruises and cuts.

"He will first eat, then change to begin daily duties." Cynthia began.

"And those daily duties are..." prompted Cerberex.

It will usually include some civilian cases but there are rumours that today he has something important to unveil." Cynthia began to help with some of the lacing.

"Do you know what?" Cerberex asked.

Cynthia shook her head. "No, he has told no one save maybe a handful of members of his own family." She stood back and produced a small mirror.

Cerberex peered at her reflection. Most of the soot from her hair had fallen out leaving it a dirty white. Unattractive but it would have to do. She smiled at Cynthia. "Will you come and watch the show?"

Cynthia shook her head. "Without the Queen we are not permitted within the grand hall."

Cerberex tried to grin. "Trust me, no one is going to notice."

No one did notice the silent arrival of Cerberex as she emerged from the servant's passage. Hiding behind a pillar that supported a heavy over-hanging landing, she straightened herself, held her head high, and did her best to act every inch the lady. The hall was a sea of reds and teal greens mixed with clusters of ivory and blue. Other colours dappled between them. Every so often the massive doors at the far end of the hall would shudder and another family group would arrive to various greetings of those nearby. Occasionally the names of particular families would be shouted across the din of too many voices. Cerberex recognised none of them though she knew of their houses well enough, after a while she began to ignore it much like the others.

Cerberex felt the heavy doors open again. "Welcoming to the court - delegates of House of Dhal-Marrah." Cerberex froze in surprise. Her mother had not been present at court in years. Dhal-Marrah had been represented by elements from House Charnite. A tight knot formed in the pit of her stomach. "Don't let her be dead. Eroth! Don't let it be so". She craned her neck.

For a moment it seemed as if the room suddenly turned chill. Loud voices reduced to hushed whispers as a the doors opened to reveal three lines of tall Drau almost all with the tell-tale lightening white hair that had ever been a genetic family trait. Against the back light, Cerberex couldn't tell who lead the house. She didn't have long to find out. As the doors closed once more the sound of trumpets filled the hall and onto the balcony at the far end the Royal House, the House of Lotheri filed silently passed, followed by the close family of the King and then finally, by the King himself.

"All hail King Aelnar." The call came and was repeated. Cerberex remained stoically silent.

Aelnar stepped passed towards the balcony's edge. "Great Houses of the

Draurhegar, before we begin on more common matters..." He paused and rubbed his chest as if experiencing a sudden burst of heart burn, before clearing his throat. "Before we begin on common matters, I have some distressing news." A murmur filtered through the crowd. Cerberex watched as his eyes alighted on the black smudge of Dhal-Marrah's representatives. A look of glee passed his face. "Today it has been brought to my attention that our beloved Queen, my beautiful wife, upon embarking on diplomatic talks with a house within this room..." He coughed.

Cerberex stared unblinking. On the edge of her hearing she could just make out the sound of a deep bell tolling. "Come on." She thought desperately.

"As I said, while in diplomatic talks with a noble house - has been murdered by an assassins weapon." The room erupted in a mixture of shock and anger. Heads turned to look at the Dhal-Marrah representatives. "Yes my lords and ladies, I too find it more than a co-incidence that co-insiding with this terrible news, the House of Dhal-Marrah have seen fit to grace us with their presence."

Cerberex felt cold. "Come on." She thought again frantically as the bells continued to toll outside.

"I call..." Suddenly the King bent double coughing furiously.

"King Aelnar is mistaken." Cerberex knew that voice and suddenly shrank against the nearest column. Elryia's voice was clarion clear.

"You dare contradict the King?" A voice shouted from within the crowd. "Queen Lida has not been seen since rumours..."

"Because I am right here." The voice was weak but it was heard.

A shift of movement vibrated through the crowd as the Dhal-Marrah's parted. Though the Dhal-Marrah contingent was only maybe a dozen strong - whatever her mother had managed to muster at such short notice, their presence reverberated from every corner of the room. Lida made her way from the centre her arm locked around that of Selwyn Charnite. Suddenly it was as if the great hall had been sapped of all oxygen. The tension seemed fit to burst. Cerberex glanced up at the Aelnar upon the balcony. He was looking pale, almost ill. This was not the turn of events she had imagined.

"What is wrong Aelnar?" The Queen called up to him. "Surprised to see me in something other than a box?"

Cerberex shrank back to the shadow of the pillar as Lida and her uncle passed. Again she glanced at the king. Aelnar had began coughing into a handkerchief. Even at this distance she could see a bloodshot look to his eyes. "What...is..." Aelnar reached under his clothes and pulled out an amulet glancing at it. "What..." He tried again between coughs. "How have you..."

"How have I what?" The Queen spat. "I am as you see, right in front of you and the entire court. You wish to accuse me of something?" Though she clung to Selwyn like she might slip and fall, her voice alone was enough to force the crowd to recoil from her.

Aelnar looked behind him to the red and black Gal-Serrek retainers. "Vor'ran?" He croaked, desperate for breath. Cerberex watched as a thin, red robed figure pushed his way to the front. Catching the King as Aelnar stumbled.

"What is this witchery?" Vor'ran asked more to himself than the hall at large. He pulled down the lower Aelnar's eye lid and cursed. "You imbecile! When did you take of this amulet?"

Lida patted Selwyn's arm and Cerberex watched her uncle bow his head with a slight smile and withdraw, allowing Lida to stand alone. The Queen pulled herself as tall as she possibly could. "You would dare send mercenaries and traitors to kill me Aelnar? Has it come to this?" She stretched out a hand and a bolt shot from it slamming into the hanging banner of the Gal-Serrek coat-of-arms and setting it ablaze.

A cool pair of arms wrapped around Cerberex's mouth and waist, pulling her back with a sharp jerk. Cerberex clawed at them to no avail against the thick leather. Desperately she tried to thrash as she felt herself get pulled further back into the shadows of the room.

"Quiet!"

Cerberex stopped in surprise as she recognised the voice.

"We need to leave - now." There was no room for argument in Kane's voice.

Cerberex stilled and Kane moved his hand from her mouth and grabbed her arm instead, pulling her insistently. "Come on."

Cerberex turned and then twisted back at the sudden rattling wheeze that burst from the balcony. "Wait, wait!" She whispered, the undertone of morbid excitement just squeezing through.

"This is beyond my ability to heal cousin." Vor'ran said just loud enough for those below to here. Aelnar grimaced a snarl and pushed him away, standing to grasp the edge of the balcony.

"We don't have time for this." Kane continued more urgently but Cerberex would not budge.

"You try to poison me? Me! I am... I am..." Aelnar gasped for breath. "I am... your King!"

"I have done nothing Aelnar. You accuse me in a court composed of those who have noticed the lack of my presence. No I have done nothing to touch you." Lida took a step forward and almost fell. Cerberex watched Selwyn almost run to her aid and only just stop himself. "No Aelnar, your end is as it should be, ordained by the Goddess herself. I am her anointed and none but

Eroth may end me." She paused watching Aelnar clutch at his throat as foam spilled from his lips. "I have endured you too long. I have watched you terrorize the houses into submission but I am not without allies of my own you hell forged traitor." She spat. Cerberex's eyebrows almost raised off her head. She had never seen this side to Lida. Gone was the girl. Here stood a Queen.

Cerberex watched as Aelnar leant over the balcony. His face a mask of rage. He reached out as if to claw Lida from existence, over stretching just too far. She watched as if in slow motion as the King fell from the balcony hitting the stone floor with a sickening crack. Only she knew that he was dead before he hit the floor.

Muttering and cries of alarm echoed around the great hall at the sight of the King's death. Lida turned and looked at them, fury flaring in her eyes. "What has become of you all?" She almost screamed, bringing the entire hall to silence.

Cerberex could hear the breath catch in Kane's throat.

Lida glared with the look of one half-crazed. "I am Lida of the House of Lotheri. Anointed of Eroth. Queen of the Draurhegar by the blood that runs through my veins and you will kneel!"

Cerberex looked on in stunned silence as slowly at first, the compliment of the hall seemed to sink to one knee in an expanding circle till on the floor, only the black clothed and white haired delegation of Dhal-Marrah still stood. She watched for a moment more till with a flourish her mother, uncle and then the rest of them knelt.

Lida stood and turned, looking at the balcony. Her eye's locked with Vor'ran and for a moment Cerberex worried that he might dare attack the Queen. Her fingers touched the slight lumps of her blades beneath her dress in anticipation. Stiffly, Vor'ran went to one knee and clenched his jaw shut as he lowered his head. The Gal-Serreks had already done the same.

"It is done." Cerberex whispered. A beautific smile unfolded across her face as she let Kane lead her quietly away. Somewhere the last echo of a bell still rang and as it died Cerberex felt an unimaginable weight lift from her.

Chapter 27:
Flames & Forgiveness

Kane dragged her while weaving between the sudden onslaught of running servants as news of the King spread quickly. A heavy black carriage waited just within the courtyard entrance. The door flew open as they approached and Kane pushed Cerberex inside. The door shut immediately behind and a scrabbling on the outside told her that Kane was most likely sat on the roof. She looked around, blinking in the darkness as the Carriage lurched forward.

"Niece." Maleficent's voice acknowledged. Cerberex opened her mouth, a slew of sudden protestations immediately manifesting without her bidding. Maleficent held up a hand and silenced her. "As much as I am so looking forward to what ever excuses for your behaviour you have dreamt up this time. We are on a tight schedule." She knocked three times on the roof and the carriage picked up the pace, pushing Cerberex backwards into a seat.

Silence thickened between them until Cerberex could stand it no more. "What is wrong?" She asked slowly. "I am entitled to attend the court if I wish."

Maleficent levelled her with a long stare. "Have you any idea how paranoid the house has been the second we discovered your departure? This is the second time niece. Must I attach a bell around your neck!"

Cerberex did not respond. Her aunt's voice was dangerously low and she had no wish to spend the next week or more as a fish, cat, or other non-verbal creature. Not that she had actually seen her aunt perform such magic but she did feel that such a feat was entirely within the realms of her aunt's capabilities.

Maleficent huffed. "You are not your brother Cerberex Dhal-Marrah. Simply because you have been allowed to see what the house's true wealth is, does not mean that you can go gallivanting about in the same way that he does." She steepled her fingers. "More to the point, when we need you and cannot find you anywhere within the house, it does tend to raise some alarms."

Cerberex raised an eyebrow. "Need me?"

Maleficent ignored the question, peering out through the blinds of the carriage to see how far they had got.

"Need me?" Cerberex asked again her suspicions rousing. "Aunt, what has happened since I left." She looked at Maleficent. "What has he done?" She asked slowly.

Maleficent's head twitched. "You're brother has always had a bit of a temper." She replied tactically.

"Meaning what exactly?" Cerberex continued. She had felt the carriage stop. A knock at the door made them both jump.

"There's a parade my lady, the carriage cannot get through." Kane's voice partly muffled, could be heard from the outside.

Maleficent hissed with irritation. She leaned to the window and pulled up the blind, leaning out into the street. "Get Lady Cerberex back to the house - quick as you can." She called looking up. She pulled her head back in and looked at Cerberex. "I trust that you will do as I ask?"

Cerberex nodded before the door next to her flew open again and a hand grabbed hold and yanked her through.

Once again Cerberex was temporarily blinded by the sudden light. There was the sound of drums, music, and the pounding of feet all around them. "How fast can you move in that?" Kane asked through the scarf pulled up over his mouth and chin.

"Are you joking?" Cerberex laughed. "How fast does it look like I can move?"

Kane rolled his eyes and reached behind him, drawing a small throwing knife. Taking hold of Cerberex's arm he spun her around to a slight tearing sound as one third of the skirt was sliced away.

Cerberex gave a slight shriek and desperately tried to pull the remaining skirt down further.

"Run then." Kane prompted and began to dart through the crowd.

Cerberex followed after him suddenly very concious of just how many people might see her like this.

They moved through the crowd like strange shadows. Cerberex found herself barely able to keep up. One moment Kane was only a few paces away the next he was the other side of the street. It was all she could do to keep enough of a bead on him until she turned the corner and was confronted with nothing. She stopped. A cackle of laughter erupted from two children standing on the corner as they pointed at her strange attire. She looked around for a sign of Kane, seeing nothing until an arm reached down and grabbed the back of her clothing. She looked up and saw two silhouettes standing atop a tall wall. Cerberex blinked and saw them now stood looking down from the roof of the building itself.

The wounds across her body stung as she began to climb up. It took her several minutes to reach the edge of the roof and a hand reached down to give her the extra purchase to ascend. Cerberex looked up and immediately wished she hadn't.

"Well, well. Aren't we a sight darling." Meera let go of Cerberex and stood, folding her arms. "They did say you have a unique sense of dress."

Cerberex stood and pain lanced from her shoulder, swiftly followed by a tickling sensation. She looked down and watched drops of blood ran along her hand and dripped from her finger tip.

"You're bleeding." Kane pointed out the obvious with a tone of concern.

"It's nothing." Cerberex replied hastily and tried to smear it away on what was left of her dress.

Kane removed the throwing knife once more and approached her. Cerberex took a step back forgetting for a moment the edge of the rooftop and wobbling precariously before Kane made a grab for her and pulled her back from the precipice.

"If she says it's nothing leave it Kane. I'm sure Cerberus's Chosen Watcher can take care of herself." Meera yawned.

Kane ignored her and though Cerberex tried to pull away from his grip carefully cut away at the stitching of the sleeve and gently tease it from her arm. The flayed patch of her shoulder was welling with blood.

Kane recoiled as he saw it. "What the hell have you been up to?"

Cerberex tried to pull away but Kane's grip was like a vice.

Meera's eyes narrowed and she gave a low whistle. "This little Watcher has a story to tell." Her eye's danced across Cerberex's legs noticing the cuts that had barely begun to scab, and the small burn marks at the backs of the knees. "Someone, has done a number on you darling." Her eyes locked with Cerberex and her head twitched to one side.

Kane reached back into a pocket and withdrew a familiar vial of amber liquid before he began slicing the sleeve seam, turning it into a long strip of fabric. Gingerly he began to wind it under Cerberex's arm, wrapping the wound up and staunching the blood for the time being. Cerberex winced as he knotted the ends.

"It'll do." He grunted and watched her down the vial. "You're going to need some proper medical attention on that though." He looked at Meera and nodded. "We've spent to long. Let's go."

Meera nodded and looked back. "Do try to keep up darling, we wouldn't want Cerberus to burn the whole house down."

The pair of them ran along the roof and leaped onto the ledge of the adjacent building before continuing. Cerberex jogged and leaped, only just making the jump as she tried to catch them.

Their pace was relentless. Though they paused every four or five buildings to allow Cerberex to catch up she never seemed to be able to get any closer to them; a point she was certain, Meera would enjoy pointing out to her later. By the time they began to near House Dhal-Marrah Cerberex began to see what Meera was referring to. The large front doors lay wide open and a thin trail of black smoke curled its way towards the sky.

Kane and Meera seemed to almost slide down to the ground as they approached the front gates. Meera passed them uncomfortably, looking back to check for Cerberex who lowered herself down to the ground with all the grace of a flightless bird. She sighed and shook her head.

Cerberex ran passed them heading for the house with all the speed she could muster as the smoke from within seemed to billow at intervals. None stopped her as she took the three steps up to the front door in one neat leap. Within she could hear screaming, the shouts of many voices, but one unmistakeably the sound of Cerberus. Her mind suddenly surged with panic as she flew inside.

At first she thought that the entrance hall was ablaze. The heat hit her like a furnace and she instinctively recoiled, shielding her face with her hand. Bright fire-like light brought spots of colour to her eyes, and the smoke and smell of smouldering wood made her choke and blink away tears. Somewhere within the inferno she could hear Cerberus yell. She tried to step forward until two pairs of hands pulled her back.

"Whoa there - you'll fry!" Kane's voice shouted above the crackling.

"My brother is in there." Cerberex writhed from their grip. "Who started the fire?"

"Darling, I don't know how to tell you this but Cerberus is the fire." Meera coughed, letting go and bringing a hand to her face.

Cerberex looked at her puzzled for a moment before looking back, trying to shield her eyes from the brightness. She squinted as the epicentre of the flames seemed to writhe and then with a scream Cerberus's face flickered in the flames. Cerberex started back in surprise. "Eroth!" She swore watching as Cerberus seemed to roll in the flames. "Cerberus!" Once again she started forwards only to be held back. "No! I can't just let him burn."

"The flames aren't natural." Meera soothed. "They might not be burning him but they will burn everyone else." She held out a hand to reveal a large burn to her palm. "When we found him he was almost too hot to even touch. His armour was almost melted to him. When we tried to get him away he broke into a rage and by the time we got him to the house he was physically smoking."

"Then this happened." Kane interrupted.

Cerberex looked back. "If he continues like this, he'll burn the entire house to the ground." She muttered.

Kane and Meera nodded.

"Is the house evacuated?" Cerberex asked without turning back. Her gaze was transfixed on her brother. It was true. In part his cries did not seem to be filled with pain so much as anguish and rage in equal parts.

"What could be. We cannot leave the run unattended." Meera replied her grip on Cerberex loosening.

Embers began to coil as the shelves began to catch alight. Cerberex looked at them in alarm. "The hell you can't! Go, get everyone out of there now!" She shouted at Meera. "We need water, buckets of water."

"Water isn't going to stop that." Meera pointed out gesturing to the white hot flames encasing Cerberus.

"You said that he was angry?" Cerberex asked feeling the sting of hot ash against her face. She looked back as Kane nodded. Cerberex looked forwards. "Get water." She instructed and sidestepped towards the flames.

The heat was intense. Cerberex was sure that she would catch alight herself, still she forced a hand out towards Cerberus stealing herself against the burning she was sure she would feel. "Cerberus!" She called as she inched towards him.

"You would dare steal onto these lands, these lands, Dhal-Marrah lands?"

The voice was lower than what Cerberex knew of Cerberus. It growled and roared like the flames themselves. "Brother?" She called feeling the ends of her hair begin the frazzle in the heat.

"A hundred years and you have taken everything from me but you will not harm the ones I love. You will not take that.""

She could see him now. Flames poured from a dozen old scars as if he had somehow turned molten from within. "Cerberus." She whispered, choking. "Cerberus, it's done. He will not be taking anything any more."

Cerberus's white hot face turned towards her. He opened his mouth eliciting a yell of anger. A rush of heat ignited the air.

Cerberex's skin began to peel but she pushed herself forward and grabbed Cerberus's arm. The pain did not come. As they touched it was as if the flames cooled though they burned around her much the same. She took hold of her brother with both arms. "Brother, it is done. He is dead. The King is dead. I have seen it with my own eyes."

"I will not rest until I have had vengeance for every drop of blood." Cerberus looked at her with unreasoned hatred.

Cerberex began to feel tears roll down her face. "Eroth! Cerberus please! You're going to burn down the house." She embraced him. "Lida needs you." She whispered as the flames roared higher. She held him tight. "We'll have our revenge. We'll see the name of Dhal-Marrah restored. I will be here to see it with you. I'll accept your pin or badge or whatever you want to call it. " She paused. "I will be there - till hell freezes." She whispered half waiting for the flames to consume them both. A chill ran through Cerberus's body and the flames stuttered. "I can't lose you."

"I... I..." Cerberus coughed and his face suddenly creased with pain.

Cerberex pulled back slightly wiping away the tears on her cheeks. "Cerberus?"

The flames began to lower. "I... I..." Cerberus repeated over and over again like a stuck mechanism. The flames ebbed. "I know." He finally managed. His voice returning back to its usual if exhausted cadence.

Cerberex tried to catch him as his legs seemed to give from under him. Water splashed around them as suddenly those nearby began to desperately try and put out the burning furniture.

Kane leaned forward helping Cerberex back to her feet as Meera began checking over Cerberus's wounds. Several old looking scars had burst open as if the cuts that had made them had only been made yesterday.

"Are you alright, are you burned." Kane pulled her about looking for any sense she had harmed herself, his face suddenly panicked. Cerberex winced as she snagged her shoulder against Kane's armour. Gently he edged her away as the sound of wheels and horse hooves could be heard outside.

She glanced back with a wave of fear. "Hell's teeth! She can't see me like this, there'll be murder!"

Kane glanced back as Maleficent's form stepped from the carriage and then back at Cerberex. "We could fix you up in the route but you might not like it." He whispered as he moved away.

Cerberex glanced at the oncoming silhouette of her aunt for minute more and then followed limping in the direction of the route.

Cerberus moaned as Maleficent, her face creased with exhaustion, held her hands in place. Faint strands of pale gold moved along her arms and hands and into Cerberus's body. Scratches and small cuts healed. The body could be mended, the mind well it would take time for it to trust that the pain no longer existed.

He opened an eye as Maleficent removed her hands and collapsed back into the chair.

"Tell me again Cerberus?" Maleficent sighed.

Cerberus shifted against the cushions. "I can't. I don't know. If I did I would tell you. I don't know how it happened."

"People do not generally spontaneously burst into flame." Maleficent replied her eyes partly closed. "I can't. Whatever you're doing is resisting my magic."

Cerberus felt guilty. Over only a handful of days they had bled his aunt's healing magic dry. He only needed to look at her to know that she was rapidly reaching her limits. "I'm sorry." He mumbled.

Maleficent opened her eyes. "What?"

"I said, I'm sorry. None of this would be happening if I had simply sent Meera or Kane or someone else to check in at that party." Cerberus explained.

"My dear nephew. You have always been rash to act." The words passed from Maleficent's mouth barely more than a whisper. She took a deep breath and shook her head, beginning to stand and failing. "Now the real work begins."

Cerberus gave her a sideways look. "Real work?"

Maleficent nodded and smiled. "Oh your going to have to reign in that temper now my dear. The King maybe dead but there's a much more dangerous game afoot." She glanced at Cerberus. "Politics."

Cerberus groaned and squeezed his eyes shut.

Maleficent laughed. "Oh Cerberus, don't be like that. Just think of how much more time you'll get to spend with Queen Lida - who I must say, from first person accounts, acquitted herself most admirably given the circumstances." She paused. "The incineration of the Gal-Serrek standard? A nice touch I think." Her smile widened to reveal the two fang-like canines.

"Almost wish I was there to see it." Cerberus winced as he shifted position.

Maleficent waved a hand. "Well I'm sure she'll come by again. Especially since she's declared to be quite concerned with your sister." She looked at Cerberus and looked for a response. "Who come to think of it, has been very keen to avoid me."

"What has she done?" Cerberus asked very slowly.

"That my dear nephew, is something I should very much like to know." Maleficent steepled her fingers and her face grew dark for a moment before it brushed away and she looked up with a smile. "I think the fortunes of the Dhal-Marrah's are about to change." She clapped her hands with a sudden burst of excitement. "I shall summon the tailor for a visit."

Cerberus rolled his eyes.

"Of course I don't suppose you have seen your sister?" Maleficent gave him a long side ways look, her almost purple eyes twinkling.

Cerberus shook his head and watched her leave. "But I'm sure I can guess." He muttered under his breath once he was sure she was out of earshot.

Cerberex hissed and twitched as the needle pierced the skin.

"Stay still." Kane insisted, sitting behind her with a surgical kit open at his side.

"Then stop hurting me." Cerberex spat through gritted teeth.

"I did warn you." Kane replied irritated. "Hold your breath."

"What? Why?" Cerberex glanced back.

Kane knotted the thread and snapped the end away. Cerberex gave a shriek as the skin pulled tight.

"Remind me never to ask for medical help from you again." She panted. She glanced down at the bloodied and torn dress on the floor and then wrapped the blanket of the bunk they were sat on around her like a towel.

Kane looked at her and raised an eyebrow. "You know I share this room with a number of other ladies right?" His eyes glanced up and down as she pulled the blanket further around till everything was obscured. "Seriously, I've seen far worse!"

Cerberex's head snapped up in irritation.

Kane laughed and put his hands up in mock surrender. "Relax. I saw nothing." He pushed the surgical kit under the bed. "Surprised you of all people would blush though." He muttered.

"Why would you say that?" Cerberex snapped.

Now it was Kane's turn to look away. "I... well..."

"What?" Cerberex asked dangerously.

"Your brother... Well, I was told you had a reputation." He scratched his head and glanced up at her.

"Cerberus tell you this did he? Or maybe you simply watched." Cerberex knew he meant nothing by it but he had caught a nerve that would not be dropped so easily.

Kane looked around and put a finger to his lips. "It was a slip of the tongue." He replied meekly checking to see how many ears were listening.

An awkward silence thickened between them, until Kane reached back underneath the bed and pulled out a long wooden case, opening it and handing her a shirt. "It might be a little big." He offered her a smile.

Cerberex's eyes narrowed but she took it with one hand still holding the blanket in another.

Kane sighed. "I'll um, I'll see if I can find you some trousers or something from the armoury." He stood and turned away.

Cerberex watched him walk through the door before sniffing the shirt. It smelt of soap and also faintly of leather oil. She slipped it over her head. It was far too large on her, given a belt she might have been able to wear it as a very short dress. Light footsteps sounded behind her and Kane handed her a pair of black, partly armoured trousers along with a belt thread with a number of pouches.

"We don't really have that many among us as err, petite as you." Kane chose his words carefully as he turned away while she put them on. He looked down as the blanket fell to the floor and counted to ten before tentatively peeking over his shoulder.

Cerberex pulled the buckle of the belt tight. She looked ridiculous and she knew it. She huffed and looked at Kane with arms folded. "Well?"

Kane sat back on the bunk. "You want to tell me what you were doing?"

Cerberex remained stoically silent. Kane shrugged. "Very well, let's try a different one. Who beat the hell out of you?"

There was a long pause before Cerberex opened her mouth. "I don't see why I have to explain myself to you." She replied. "Or any of my brother's lackeys for that matter."

Kane's eyes turned cold. "Right." He stood up and picked up the blanket folding it and throwing it onto the bunk. "You're going to come with me."

Cerberex stayed, bracing herself.

Kane leaned against the bunk. "I'll carry you if I have to but it might be a little undignified."

Cerberex sniffed. "Chance would be a fine thing."

Kane sucked on his teeth. "Scared then?"

Cerberex's eyes narrowed but Kane simply turned and strolled out the door. She moved briskly to follow and looked into the corridor beyond half expecting him to have disappeared, only to see him slowly making his way down towards the training room. Cerberex followed, her curiosity getting the better of her. She reached the arch and peered in. Kane pulled off his shirt and dumped it on the small table. He wandered around to a wrack of wooden training blades selected a fairly long piece out of routine and turned, hopping into the training pit.

Kane pointed to the wrack as Cerberex slowly entered. "Pick one."

She sauntered to the wrack and glanced over the wooden replicas. Then back at Kane. "If I use any of these I'll snap them."

Kane snorted and kicked the sand. "Just pick one." He watched as she selected a wooden short sword, spinning it a couple of times to get a feel for the weight.

Cerberex stepped down feeling the strange skid of the sand. "What now?"

Kane paced around. "You need to blow off steam and this is the best way I know." He flicked the sword up onto his shoulder.

Cerberex looked down at the wooden blade then back. "I'll batter you." She spoke matter-of-factly.

Kane's eyes narrowed as he held her gaze. He could see the slight concern wave across her features and smirked. "Oh really?"

"Did you see what I did to Sylas and the others?" Cerberex paced opposite him.

Kane stopped. "You'll have to hit me first." He could barely suppress the smile and waved her forward. "Ladies first." He whispered.

Cerberex spun across the sand, striking out at him with a wide swing. For a moment it seemed that Kane wasn't going to move until with a blur he was gone. Cerberex looked over her shoulder to see him behind her, wooden sword still lazily resting against his shoulder. She let go of a long breath. "This isn't fair. I'm the walking wounded. If I move any faster I'll pull open stitches."

Kane shrugged. "Guess I'll have to stitch you back up then."

Irritation bubbled up inside Cerberex. She breathed in and felt the pull of the wound on her shoulder as she flexed it gently.

"Oh come on. I know you've got more than that." Kane goaded.

Cerberex flipped back and stretched out a leg hoping to knock his feet out from underneath him. Once again Kane moved just out of reach but Cerberex didn't stop. She twisted as far as she could and swung again. Strike and then strike again.

Moments turned to minutes. Sweat poured from Cerberex's forehead as she felt the pull of every tiny wound. With a final bust of energy she leaped using the edge of the pit to gain a modicum of height advantage. The crack of both wooden blades resounded across the room and she looked up to see Kane motionless, holding back her attack one hand on the hilt and the other on the flat of what would have been the blade. Suddenly with surprising strength, he pushed her back. Cerberex moved, mis-stepped, and fell back onto the sand. The short sword fell with a dull thud shortly after. She glanced up.

Kane spun the blade back onto his shoulder. He looked down at her. "Feel better?"

"No." Cerberex hissed.

"Maybe we should go again then." Kane took a step back and kicked the wooden sword back over to Cerberex.

Cerberex stared at it. "Enough."

Kane nodded and dropped down onto the sand. "So who's responsible for the this then?"

Cerberex looked away. "It doesn't matter."

Kane shuffled closer. "Cerberex I've seen my fair share of wounds. So I'll tell you what it looks like to me because none of these wounds were designed to kill. They weren't inflicted while fighting for your life and they sure as hell aren't an accident." He paused. "I know how to cause wounds that look like that Cerberex." He continued quietly. "Not that I'm proud of that." He added quickly as Cerberex shot him an angry look. He waited, expecting her to lash out but she looked back to the sand again. "Cerberex... they look like torture. You're right you don't have to tell me but Cerberus is going to kill me if he finds out that you've been hurt."

Cerberex picked up a fistful of sand and let it run between her fingers. "They're dead. It's done now."

Kane straightened. "Whose dead?" He asked slowly.

Cerberex shut her eyes and the memories of the night flashed before her. She opened them again quickly feeling her heart begin to race.

Kane looked to one side thoughtfully for a moment. "Oh Cerberex you didn't." He whispered as he began to join the dots.

Cerberex felt the air catch in her lungs. "I was gone before dusk. I did it for Dhal-Marrah and for Cerberus. There would have never been an end without one of them dead. I couldn't let them find a way to kill him and had they killed Lida he would never have been the same. I wanted him to be happy." She tried to look up but couldn't meet his gaze. "I..." Tears began to flow down her cheeks. "I can still smell him." Miserably, she forced the words to come. "I remember everything now in perfect clarity. The knives, the needles, the way he wanted me to scream." She sobbed. "but I wouldn't let him know he was breaking me." She whispered. "I can still feel him on me." She looked up at Kane her face a mask of terror. "Please don't tell Cerberus that he broke me!"

Kane shifted onto his knees in front of her. "Oh hell Cerberex!" Suddenly he grabbed and hugged her. Cerberex's eyes widened in surprise at the embrace. "You're not broken." He muttered and pulled back keeping his hands on her shoulders. "You should have told us. We would never have let you be subjugated to that." He raised her chin. "You are Chosen. I don't care that you weren't trained an assassin and neither does anyone else. You are one. You are a Dhal-Marrah. There isn't a soul in the route who wouldn't walk into the mouth of hell at your side if you asked. You wouldn't have been alone to face that demon."

Cerberex hiccoughed a mad laugh. She leaned against her knees. "What can I say? I like being independent."

Kane laughed and moved around to wrap an arm around her shoulders. "In that, you and your brother are not so dissimilar."

Cerberex narrowed her eyes and jabbed him in the ribs.

"Ow! What was that for?" Kane rubbed the skin.

"For saying I am anything like my brother." Cerberex replied.

Kane laughed and then looked at her seriously. "I wont tell Cerberus." He watched a look of relief pass over her face. "But you should." He continued. "Take it from me. Your brother is very well informed on all goings on. He will find out one way or another. You will want to tell him before that happens."

Cerberex wrinkled her nose. "He'll never forgive me."

"He will." Kane stated with absolute conviction. He stood and picked up both training blades. "One thing's for certain though." He continued.

"What's that?" Cerberex asked still sitting.

Kane smiled and looked back at her. "Meera is completely wrong about you. You should absolutely be here."

Chapter 28:
Caught in the Crossfire

"No, no, no, no!" Cerberex shouted, frustrated as a flurry of arrows disappeared into the undergrowth.

Rain pattered softly like a fine mist. Cerberus ignored it, watching with immense pleasure as his sister attempted to turn two assassins and two initiates into Watcher material. Of the entire route she had only asked to select four. Cerberus had no idea what her criteria had been but the selection were clearly performing far below Cerberex's expectation if her irritation was anything to go by.

Cerberex wandered down the line to the older boy still struggling to load another arrow. "Tye it is a piece of wood, not a wild animal. It is not going to bite you, so stop wrestling with it!"

"So you've finally set her to work then?"

Cerberus stiffened though he had known of Meera's approach long before she slinked up to his shoulder.

"I didn't think she was the type to take to it so quickly." The venom on Meera's words was barely concealed.

"Cerberex might surprise you about a lot of things." Cerberus smiled.

"Your surprisingly cordial about her today." Meera looked at him in surprise.

Cerberus shrugged. "She may have saved my life. I at least owe her respect." He ducked as one of the initiates misfired and the arrow hissed past his head. "They couldn't hit the side of a barn." He muttered to himself.

Meera snorted. "I'd say I told you so but ... oh wait I did tell you so." She sighed. "Assassin's are not Watchers."

"They should at least be able to shoot at something and hit it." Cerberus replied and grabbed her arm before Meera could leave. "I'm guessing you have information or you wouldn't be here."

Meera tore her arm away with a look of irritation. "Your flames?" She watched Cerberus nod curtly. "No one has anything like it. I have spoken to every arcanist in the city, even applied coin where necessary. The best I can account for is that your pent up emotion caused you to use magic where you should not have been able to." She laughed quietly. "So you're either emotionally repressed or Eroth saw fit to play with you for her amusement. Take your pick of those extremes as you wish."

Cerberus did not laugh but turned to face her as Cerberex continued her efforts. "Meera, my aunt will confirm that there is absolutely no arcane ability in my soul capable of setting a candle let alone myself alight." He walked slowly by her side.

"And there I was believing that there was nothing you couldn't do." Meera replied although the sarcasm was curbed. "Does this really scare you that much?"

Cerberus coughed a laugh. "Scare me?" He paused and placed a hand on her shoulder. "Meera, it terrifies me!" He replied quietly.

Meera's eyes lit with concern. "Then I will keep looking for the answer."

Cerberus looked across towards where the house rose like a dark gargoyle. "I felt pain but it wasn't... burning. I felt it like a sting across my back." He whispered and glanced at Meera. "Cerberex has a limp, she treats herself with an unnatural care." He turned and gestured to the group continuing their practice. "Do you see it? She carries her bow on the wrong shoulder. Her footfalls are heavier on one leg than the other. I know she's hurt and yet she has told me nothing. Tell me that I am not the cause Meera?"

Meera placed her hands on his shoulders and turned him away. "I saw Cerberex walk into the flames and bring you out unscathed Cerberus. Unscathed save injuries she already had when Kane and I sought her out." She smiled and placed a hand on his cheek. "Darling, you should worry less. The source of Cerberex's injuries were not caused by you." She ran a thumb along the cheek line. "We've known each other too long. Perhaps, there are simply some hidden depths you weren't aware of - new talents." She watched Cerberus's eyes narrow. "Cerberex is a big girl. She can take care of herself." She smiled and leaned in just touching his nose.

Cerberus recoiled as if Meera had just uttered a curse. "What... what do you think you're doing?" He checked his voice from crying out as he brushed her hand away.

Meera stepped back as if stung. "I thought... You've asked to run with me and only me the last three days straight!"

"What did you think?" Cerberus asked. "We've been down that road Meera and neither of us can say the memories of it are kind."

"I have fond memories Cerberus. I remember when you would not let me out of your sight." Meera hissed, her body automatically moving as if ready to strike.

"I have three small scars on my shoulder blades from your knives. They are all the reminder I need." Cerberus hissed.

"And I still have claw marks - I don't remember you complaining at the time!" Meera retaliated her face flushing with embarrassment at the situation.

"I wasn't there the next morning to compliment you." Cerberus looked at her then looked away clenching his jaw.

Meera chocked on a bitter laugh. "So it's true then. You're heart is set on someone else."

"Just because I won't go there doesn't mean..." Cerberus began slowly, regretting some of his previous comments.

"She's not yours, she's never going to be yours. Why would she? She has the best of everything at her fingertips. You think she'll decide to tarnish that pretty skin with a quick romp with you?" Meera's voice began to raise.

"Careful." Cerberus growled.

"Oh I'm not half done darling. You think you can use me and toss me aside like some servile dog? Well Cerberus, I am no ones pet to be used." She snarled.

"No, you're an assassin under my command." Cerberus replied forcing himself to maintain composure.

"So you say." Meera hissed. "But I'm not your plaything." She turned and began to stalk away.

"Meera!" Cerberus called after her but she did not turn though he could hear her voice still.

"And to think I loved you - would have done anything for you. You want answers Cerberus? Go find them yourself. I'm done doing your dirty work."

Cerberus watched her silhouette flicker and disappear towards the house like a ghost. His heart was thundering inside his chest but his outward expression remained stoic.

"Well that looked... fraught." Cerberex whispered in his ear.

Cerberus physically jumped. His attention had been so focused on Meera's unexpected advance, he hadn't even heard Cerberex finish her session. "Finished destroying the confidence of my assassins sister?" He asked, pulling himself together.

Cerberex shrugged. "Only two of them as I understand it. Honestly, their useless. What do you teach them?" She smirked at him.

"To not die." Cerberus replied quietly.

"Oh I think I touched a nerve." Cerberex pressed. "Relax Cerberus, at least Clogaen shows promising talent and there's not been a sight of a single intruder since the black banners raised for the kings unfortunate passing. I think I might call that a win. It would seem your... our, Queen Lida has rather got a hold of things - finally"

"If you knew anything about the Gal Serreks sister, you'd know that they're at their most dangerous when you can't see or hear them." Cerberus retorted.

Cerberex stepped back with a look of mock terror. "Oh Eroth no! Tell me that besides becoming a living lantern, you've not developed precognostic capabilities!" She laughed. A tinkling sound like small bells.

Cerberus eyes hardened. "Yes I saw the banners Cerberex. I sat on my windowsill and watched them rise. Sadly I was unable to witness the spectacle. You, you on the other hand had a front row seat if what I hear is correct."

Cerberex straightened. "Who told you that?"

Now it was Cerberus's turn to smile. "You did." His grin widened as Cerberex stepped back. "I only knew that Kane had to go and track you down but he was sketchy on the details - so nice to see the pair of you have become such firm friends."

"What ever he told you is clearly exaggerated." Cerberex replied coolly.

"Oh but sister I didn't ask. I might now though, now that you've peaked my interest." Cerberus stood and enjoyed the colour drain from Cerberex's skin. "Or perhaps you'd like to tell me what lead you to grace the palace with your presence?" He watched and waited as the silence drifted between them. He gave a cold laugh. "How about it sister?" He reached out and placed a hand on her shoulder. "Do we really need these secrets?" He gave it a sharp squeeze.

Cerberex yelped and pulled back retreating a few feet from Cerberus's grip. She glared at him but her eyes were darting for nearest point of retreat. "Oh please do try and run sister. Mother has had me cooped up like an invalid on and off for days now and I'm in need of the exercise." He could feel a heat beginning to build along his arms.

"Shut up Cerberus." The ice in Cerberex's voice was like a sudden stab wound to the chest. "How dare you try and intimidate me. Do I look like one of your lackeys?"

"I know you've been hurt. So tell me how?" Cerberus swallowed. "Was it me?"

Cerberex pushed past him. "I've been hurt a number of times before Cerberus. I don't remember you being this concerned about them then." Gingerly she touched her shoulder. "You know, have you ever stopped to consider that this paranoia is precisely the reason why you and Lida have never quite got there?" She straightened herself and brushed a strand of hair from her face.

"Was it me?" Cerberus called after her as she stalked away.

Cerberex paused. "No, it was not you." She replied quietly, jogging for the shelter of the house as the dying daylight gave way to a thunderclap and the rain began to pour.

Cerberex took a left at the house and disappeared down a set of old worn steps. The novelty of the various entrances in and out of the assassin's complex beneath the house had yet to loose its novelty. This she had assumed, had lead to some unused cellar. The ivy covered door opened soundlessly as she pressed against it, giving only a little resistance. Beyond age seemed to melt away to the familiar black and white paving of the route. The ability to come and go had yet to lose it's novelty and she doubted it ever would.

"You keep a lot of secrets Lady Cerberex."

Cerberex froze as the door gave a soft click behind her. She turned slightly and Meera stepped into the light coming to a stop a foot away. "Meera isn't it?" Cerberex asked though she had already taken the time to learn the names of those who carried influence down here.

Meera didn't smile. Cerberex couldn't be sure in the cast shadows but Meera's eyes glistened in the dark. "Have you... Meera are you crying?" Cerberex asked with barely concealed surprise.

Meera gave a snort of derision. "You know when I first met you, I thought 'now this one - this one shows some real promise. If only she was a little younger. This one could be something special'."

"Such a disappointment."

Cerberex felt a chill escape down her spine at the playful voice of Dichta echoed behind her. She let a long breath go and looked back to see four pairs of eyes and the door leading to the corridor beyond close pushing them into absolute darkness. Cerberex's eyes adjusted, barely making out the shadows in the room. "I thought we might get past this." Cerberex muttered.

Dichta's laugh sounded all too loud in the confines of the room. "Oh you're very funny."

"Shut it Dichta." Meera hissed and Dichta shrunk back like a scorned pet. "Can't you see that Lady Cerberex and I are having a girlie chat." The shine from Meera's eyes turned back to Cerberex. "Contrary to popular belief, I think you could do wonders down here. With the right tuition of course."

Cerberex felt the shunt as someone she was fairly confident was Sylas, brushed passed her. "I'm not sure that your friends here agree." She managed pushing down a wince of pain.

"What can I say darling, they're a little over reactive from time to time." Meera paused and leaned in till Cerberex could feel her breath on her cheek. "Comes with the job."

"I still say we should take her down a few pegs." Sylas cracked his knuckles just off to her left. "Make sure she truly appreciates just where she stands."

"Try it." Cerberex growled but the words were hollow.

Meera clapped twice. "Now, now. I'm sure that Lady Cerberex understands the situation here without any need for a repeat performance of last time."

"You've yet to tell me exactly what the situation is." Cerberex pointed out her eyes darting around trying to keep track of the shifting shadows.

"Why a change of leadership darling." Meera replied with surprise. "You see Cerberus and I, we've had a good run but anyone can see that he's just not - capable these days. For example how many times have you yourself had to drag him back now? Two?"

Cerberex coughed in surprise. "You seriously think I'm going to help you take on Cerberus?"

"Help? Darling you're going to jump at the chance." Meera replied smoothly. "I might even make you my first."

"What?" One of the shadows shunted to a stop as Seska's voice echoed through the gloom. "But you said..."

"Quiet. You'll get your pins - be satisfied with that after the piss poor show you made of yourselves." Meera hissed with infuriation.

"What in all of creation makes you think I would dethrone my own blood?" Cerberex gently fingered the pommel of the right hand hunting knife strapped to her thigh.

"I wouldn't recommend it." Negari's voice whispered in her ear.

"Is this a mutiny? You're going to cause a mutiny because Cerberus snubbed your advance?" Cerberex continued pulling her hand away from the weapon slowly.

Meera tutted quietly under her breath. "Of course not. I'm eternally grateful to Cerberus. He saved me. Gave me purpose. This is just business. Our ways might seem a little harsh but you didn't seem particularly adverse to that."

"Maybe we'll keep you're brother on - an administrative role perhaps." Sylas smirked.

"Fine. Challenge him then." Cerberex could hear the note of concern in her voice.

"Oh no no. Darling that wont do at all. Challenge him? Why certainly but I don't want to simply beat Cerberus. I want to humiliate him like he has me. I want to take something he cares about, like he took from me. I want him to know what that feels like." Meera's voice grew dark. "So I'm looking to pull on that endearing sibling rivalry your so good at engaging in." She continued suddenly light.

"No." Cerberex surprised herself by the sudden commitment in her tone. She shook her head. "No, I will not help you bate Cerberus." She continued cutting Meera off before she could argue. "Because it's madness Meera. You're feeling sore. I understand that. Cerberus is well let's be honest, blunt; but this" she gestured to the darkness. "This is pathetic. You're upset because Cerberus doesn't want you the way you want him. I know what I saw, but this is overreacting and I say this with all honesty Meera, you're going to have to get over it."

Cerberex heard the slight intake of breath. She felt the air seem to leave the room and for a moment wondered exactly how much of a mistake she had made. "Get over it." Meera repeated. Suddenly she reached up, grabbing Cerberex's chin, pinching it between her forefinger and thumb. "You're going to help me Cerberex Dhal-Marrah because you may be a great keeper of secrets but I, I am very very good at finding them out. You're going to help me because right now you are in a room with some of the most dangerous people in this kingdom - myself one of them which alone should be enough. You're going to help because when I'm done I will make life so unbearable for you, you will rue the day you so much as heard the word assassin. I will make you wonder about every shadow. I will make you need to check your back every time you look away. Finally, you'll help me because I know exactly to the minute detail what you were doing at the palace. I know the location of each of those wounds on your precious hide and all the details of how it got there; and I know just how much you would dearly like to keep that knowledge from the family upstairs. Think about how disappointed they'll be. What a naughty little girl you've been Cerberex. Tell me, did he give you a good work over? Was it a little more than you could handle? Are you going to 'get over it'?"

Cerberex smacked her hand away.

Meera laughed. "I think I may have salted a wound!"

Suddenly the door to the hallway creaked open and orange light flooded into the room forcing Cerberex to blink away stars as her eyes struggled to adjust so quickly to the brightness.

"Uh, hello?"

Cerberex could barely suppress the relief she felt at the sound of an unfamiliar voice.

"Well this doesn't smack of suspicious at all." The silhouette added sarcastically. "Having a private party are we?"

"Tharn darling, you're always so imaginative." Meera beamed a smile as she pushed past him with sudden speed, forcing herself out of the doorway. The other four following in her wake.

Tharn watched them and then gave Cerberex a sideways glance. Cerberex felt air rush back into her lungs.

"I'm not sure I want to know what's happening here." Tharn stated looking back down the corridor and then at Cerberex.

"Cerberus snubbed Meera." Cerberex replied and joined him in the doorway watching as the five of them chatted and laughed while they made their way towards the bunk room, as if nothing had ever happened. "I don't suppose you'd know if Meera and Cerberus... Did they ever?"

"Oh yeah." Tharn didn't even pause. Cerberex looked at him in surprise. "Trust me, everyone knows." He added not taking his eyes off them till they were out of sight, before giving a low whistle. "You should be more careful. Silas, Dichta, the rest of them, they're still pretty sore after what you did. They wont think twice at the moment of paying back the insult twice over."

"Meera's going to overthrow Cerberus." Cerberex stated.

Tharn looked at her taken aback. "No. Meera is Cerberus's First. They've been friends since... well long before I even arrived. They argue. It's normal and well, kind of her job as it happens." He opened the door wider and gestured for Cerberex to go through.

"This didn't sound like just an argument." Cerberex added looking down the empty hallway. "This feels personal."

Tharn gave her curious look. "You want me to get some eyes on this?"

Cerberex wrinkled her nose. Cerberus would doubtless take a dim view of her interference. "Could she take on Cerberus?"

Tharn raised an eyebrow. "You are joking right?" He coughed politely as Cerberex gave him a pointed look. "Well, the term 'Master' is given to the best of us. Technically, if and that's a big 'if', if Meera could best Cerberus then yes; but Cerberus and Meera have fought before and Meera's not won yet. If she actually challenged Cerberus and lost, that would be the end of her in the route. I doubt Cerberus would take a challenge lightly and that's assuming he let her escape with her life."

Cerberex felt the air in her chest tighten. "Challenges are to the death?"

Tharn shook his head. "First blood supposedly but a yield is more usual. Those two though? Let's face it, the Master would never back down and neither would she."

Chapter 29:
Nightmares

Pain burst across her back. She gritted her teeth. Refused to scream. There was already blood on the sheets. Her blood. She could hear his voice whisper in her ear. The touch of his fingers made her skin crawl. The smell of wine on his breath made her feel ill. The pain blossomed across her again and her muscles retracted arching her back. The air burnt in her lungs as she held her breath till blackness clawed at the edges of her vision. The sting of a sharp edge nicked into her shoulder and dug beneath the skin. Whispers. She couldn't hear, wouldn't listen to the words; they were poison to the mind. Then a wet tearing and she couldn't stop the screaming...

Cerberex sat up, sweat ran down the back of her neck sticking her hair to her like cobweb. She shivered and looked about the darkness, picking out the familiar furnishings of her room. Moonlight, filtered through the marginally opened window and struck strange shadows. She reached up and touched the pinched skin on her shoulder where the wound was slowly healing. The salt from her sweat made it sting. A side table the other side of the room held a water decanter of green glass set on a tray next to her hair brush and various bottles of perfume and scented oils - gifts from a number of suitors.

As her breathing steadied, she swung her legs out of bed and stepped lightly across the room in nothing but a white shirt. The cold of the stone beneath her feet felt reassuring. She poured the water into a tall glass left beside it and brought it to her lips, smelling it for anything out of the ordinary from habit rather than necessity. A shadow fell across the floor and Cerberex jumped as a humanoid shape seemed to appear from the corner of her eye. Water sloshed from the glass onto the floor. She turned and blinked at the mannequin draped in her own armoured pieces. Swallowing the sudden surge of fear she stepped towards it and caressed the soft leather. "You're being stupid Cerberex." She told herself. "There's nothing here but you." She took a sip of water and turned quickly as the moonlight caught a reflection in the floor length mirror. For a moment she saw Aelnar's face in the glass that same smile and wide lips. The glass slipped from her fingers and smashed against the floor. She took a step back and yelped as glass shards stabbed into her bare feet. When she looked back there was nothing but her own pale, horrified expression. Cerberex turned, scooped her discarded trousers from the floor, snapped up her bow lounging against the wall and began quickly dressed as Aelnar's laugh echoed around and around in her head.

Cerberex tiptoed across the threshold of her room still buckling the wide armoured belt across her waist. Silence greeted her. She glanced at Cerberus's door. No flicker of candlelight glowed from beneath it. For a hot second she considered running into his room and telling him everything, before she squashed the idea abruptly. Reaching behind she retrieved her bow and slung it gently across her back, tiptoeing towards the stairs and sliding down the bannister with a hushed whisper of brushed, heavy cotton on polished wood. The sound of whispers made her freeze. "Early rise servants." She told herself. "Just doing their jobs." Her heart continued to thunder in her chest.

"Keep it up my dear. You're doing so well."

The smell of rancid wine made Cerberex spin. A mechanical timer clicked loudly behind her. The echo reverberating within its long case. An empty glass stood on a shelf next to it yet to be cleared away. Cerberex gritted her teeth and stepped across the entrance hall.

"Go on."

She ignored the whisper. Each step made with exacting precision.

"Go on."

Her heart felt like it would burst as she entered the dining hall. The painted faces of ancestral likeness stared at her as if in silent rebuke.

"Scream for me."

The caress of his lips, the tug of her hair. The press of his hands.

Cerberex ran. She ran and leaped, sliding across the thornwood table and knocking over a candle stick. It clattered to the floor, it's echo drowned by the thunder of her feet. Skidding, she placed her hand against the wall. Glancing back with a sudden fear of what she might see. The illusion shifted and Cerberex almost fell through, her foot just catching the trap set upon the third step. A click echoed and Cerberex quickly shifted to avoid the bolt as it slammed into the stone the opposite side. Bracing herself for the pain of the bolt, she lost her footing and tumbled down the remaining stairs feeling the edge of each stone step as she fell. She landed with a heavy thud onto the crosswork panelling of the room beyond, her bow clattering after her a second later.

Gingerly, Cerberex picked herself up using her bow as a support. Nothing had broken but the metallic taste of blood filled her mouth. Cerberex reached in and dislodged the broken tooth, spitting blood onto the ground. Pocketing the piece of bone, she straightened herself out and stepped out towards the dragon mouth, barely looking to pick out the black shapes perched atop it's wings. Pushing open the door within, she expected the golden light of the route to banish away the shadows that seemed to haunt her steps.

The route lay in half light. At her sudden arrival, a figure wrapped in a heavy black wool cloak woke with a start from the stool he or she was evidently supposed to be keeping watch from. Cerberex stood still for a moment and then quietly closed the door. The individual sniffed and pulled the cloak further around, shifting their position. She'd never seen the route so empty - though ironically, she guessed that an assassin's work was probably better suited to the night.

Quietly, Cerberex moved down the hallway and glanced into the bunk room as she passed. The musky smell of sleeping bodies greeted her. A single lantern flickered at the far end and guttered as her shadow crept across the floor. Soundlessly, she continued down the thin hallway towards the training room. Only two assassin's passed her on her way. Their eyes betrayed how tired they were. They nodded as she passed but offered no further greeting. She stood under the arch of the training room and watched them till they disappeared from sight.

A spectral finger traced the back of her neck. "Scream."

Turning into the training room itself, Cerberex grabbed the nearest torch and lit every lantern and sconce in sight. The darkness fled from her till the room was filled with gold light. The gloating laugh faded. Cerberex slammed her hands down against the table jolting the wooden replicas that lay across it. She felt her nails scratch across the rough wooden surface and took in a deep breath. It came out in short, shuddering gasps.

"Welcome to hell my dear." The taste of blood in her mouth.

Cerberex squeezed her eyes shut. "Shut up." She whispered to herself. "Shut up, shut up, shut up!" She opened her eyes, blinking to adjust to the light.

Stalking across the room she opened every cupboard till she found a dusty quiver of arrows, iron tipped and blunt but still functional. She grabbed one, loaded it, turned, and fired in one fluid motion. The arrow gave a heavy thunk as it slammed into a wooden training dummy pushed into the middle of the pit for the morning. One after the other, Cerberex fired them with unerring accuracy. With every thud the whisper became quieter. The coldness in her muscles receded. One after the other, retrieve, and then again. The cold sweat of fear replaced with the hot of exertion. Again. The muscles in her arms burned from the repetition. Faster. She notched two, drawing and firing. Trading accuracy for volume. Faster. The wood of the dummy splintered under the abuse. Faster. The string taught until with an expected slap across the side of her face it snapped. The arrows disappeared into the dark corners and hit stone.

Cerberex looked at the slack string dangling from one end of her bow stupidly. Throwing it down with a loud crack on the floor. She skipped down the lip of the training pit and wandered over to the dummy. One by one she wrenched the other arrows from its solid wooden body, tracing her finger over each of the narrow, triangular, grooves in its once relatively smooth surface. She turned, took a step and stopped. Her bow lay on the pit's edge and paused. Furtively she glanced around, ensuring no one was about to see her next move. Cerberex crouched, placed the fistful of arrows she held down and dusting the sand off her hand on her leg. Slowly, she brought up a finger and tapped it thoughtfully against her lips as an idea began to crystallize in her mind. She closed her eyes. Reliving the moments Sylas, Dichta, Seska, and Negari had circled around her in this spot. Opening her eyes she could see the ghosts of the memory moving around her. She watched Sylas in slow motion as he sprinted from one location to another, his outline blurring with sudden speed. A blink and the spectres were banished. Cerberex glanced up at the bow again. Pursing her lips, she placed her hands onto the sand and pushed off sprinting the distance.

"Do you have any idea what time it is?"

Cerberex skidded in the sand and looked up to see Kane tiredly rubbing his eyes against the light.

"You do realise that assassins sleep right? We can hear everything your doing." Kane looked at her, then at the deep footprints in the sand and cocked his head to one side. "What are you doing?"

Cerberex grabbed the bow and angrily waved the slack string. "Snapped it." She muttered as if that answer solved everything.

"And you decided to jog a few laps of the training pit to work off your energy?" Kane asked the sarcasm all too obvious.

"No." Cerberex sulked and turned back to collect the arrows she'd placed. There was a whisper of movement and Kane stood in front of them, blocking them from her reach. She huffed and raised her arms in exasperation. "How?"

"What?" Kane blinked.

"How are you doing that?" Cerberex elaborated. "How is it that everyone can do that?"

Kane gave her a sideways look and shook his head. "That's not true. Almost all of the initiates can't." He watched her move around him and retrieve the arrows. "Would you rather I didn't?" He asked baffled.

Cerberex stood up and flicked hair out of her eyes. "Yes, I mean no!" Kane looked at her confused. "Just... just tell me how you're doing it."

"Are you jealous?" A smile twitched at Kane's cheeks and fluttered away at Cerberex's murderous look. He raised his hands in mock surrender. "Well as

I'm up at least." He paced around her. "It's called Shadow Walking."

Cerberex watched and then turned around as he suddenly stood behind her as if he had never moved.

"It lets you change from location to location with a speed that is difficult to track and more difficult to shoot." Kane continued blurring across the gap to a different spot each time.

Cerberex felt her head spin slightly as she tried to watch him. "What? How? Is it some form of teleportation magic?"

Kane paused. "Honestly, I've no idea." He glanced at Cerberex strangely. "Don't take this the wrong way but this may be a little out of your league."

"You just don't want to show me." Cerberex replied her eyes narrowing.

Kane shook his head. "It's more you don't have one of these." He shook his wrist, the faint, white imprint seemed to shift beneath his skin.

"So it is magic then." Cerberex muttered. "Never play fair. Isn't that what you lot always say?"

"Don't play fair." Kane corrected and paused. "Look, I'll try but just don't get your hopes up." He walked towards her and began to draw a line in the sand, indicating for her to stand at it. A moment later he stood at the other side of the pit and nodded. "Try not to think of it as if you're running towards me. Think of it as making it in one step."

Cerberex ran; and she ran again; and again. One hour, two hours, three. She slammed her hands against the side of the pit breathing heavily as her hair stuck to her face. "What am I getting wrong?" She yelled angrily, panting for breath. She turned and slid down the wall of the pit till her hands touched the sand.

Kane crouched down next to her rubbing the bridge of his nose. Dark circles lined his eyes. "Look, you're still healing, you're clearly emotional about this, and none of these things are making it any easier for you." He sighed at the irritated look Cerberex shot at him. "Why don't we try this again another time?" He tried to smile. "Preferably a time that's a little more... acceptable." He whispered under his breath.

Cerberex stared at the burred line still drawn in the sand for what felt like a long time and shook her head. "One more." She breathed and stood eyeing the line as if it's very presence insulted her.

"Cerberex..." Kane pleaded.

"One more." Cerberex cut him off and slowly made her way back to line with a slight wobble of exhaustion.

Kane pulled himself up and instead, opted to lean against the lip. He folded his arms. "You need to adjust your perspective." He began looking at the line by her feet. "Stop thinking about the distance." His eyes looked up and met hers. "Think about already being next to me." He locked his eyes with hers. "Imagine you are already here."

Cerberex nodded and took two steps back. Her eyes drifted to the line then to Kane. She felt the pang of expected failure shudder through her and gritted her teeth. She stared at Kane till it pricked tears to her eyes and her vision blurred. She pushed off. Her foot hit the sand. Disappointment. The second the same, then...

Kane slammed into the wall of the pit the air knocked out of him as Cerberex suddenly shifted across the divide and collided into him. He coughed and blinked in surprise.

Cerberex stood and suddenly stumbled as a wave of motion sickness hit her.

Kane laughed, his face swiftly shifting from shock to joy. "You did it!" He laughed again. "Though we might need to focus on your stopping next."

Cerberex shook the spinning from her head and looked up. Kane had his arms wrapped around her. She pushed back out of the sudden embrace. The world seemed to lean. She wobbled and stumbled onto the floor, feeling like she'd been stunned.

Kane was still laughing. "It does feel a little bit off the first time. You get used to it." He held his hand out. "Do you want to go again?" The tiredness seemed to melt from him. He grinned. "Let me go and get some kit." He jumped out and shadow walked to the arch before looking back. "And we're going to need a bigger space."

Meera watched through a chink concealed in the ceiling's crawl space above, as Cerberex took Kane's hand, to tired to bring herself up alone. She shifted keeping her eyes on them as Kane waited for Cerberex to catch him up at the archway. Her face was covered by a black scarf that muffled the sound of her breathing but her eyes told stories.

Chapter 30:
Passion's Fury

Pale sunlight filtered through stone grey clouds, barely lighting the room. Cerberus lay flat on his stomach still partly clothed in yesterdays ware, one leg hanging just off the bed. As the grey light bounced off of the small mirror recessed into the front of the wardrobe, a hand stretched out and grabbed the head of the bed. Cerberus groaned as his other hand pushed his hair out of his face. Six bottles of varying coloured glass, stood empty on a nearby table. Another groan escaped his lips and he rolled over.

It took him an hour to change and rise from his room stumbling, still slightly hung over. The subtle movement's in the house seemed terribly loud. His eyes drifted to his sister's room and he raised his arms to steady himself against the door frame behind him. Taking a shallow breath, he made his way towards it and knocked, wincing at the sound.

"Cerberex." He whispered placing his forehead against the door. "Sister?" He added when no one came to the door. He swallowed. "I know you're mad. Can I come in?" Only silence answered. Grasping the handle, Cerberus lifted the latch with a soft click and opened the door just enough to peer inside.

Cerberex's bedding was crumpled. Tentatively, Cerberus took a step inside. Glass crunched beneath him. He looked down and noticed the shattered glass. A lump rose in his stomach. "What have you gone and done now?" He asked the empty room. His eyes darted around looking for a clue that had prompted her to leave with such haste she had dropped the glass on the floor. Stepping over the glass, Cerberus approached the bed and placed a hand upon it. It was cold. He cursed quietly under his breath. Cerberex had been long gone.

Spying the half filled decanter of water, he drank some straight from the container. Taking a second swig, he swilled it around his mouth and spat it into a small dish. Two small sprigs of mint lay atop a selection of pale pink fruits. He plucked the green leaves and crunched down on them feeling his mouth burn slightly with the overpowering taste of the herb. Chewing, he began to feel the heavy fog in of over-indulgence begin to recede. He leaned against the table and only then noticed the discarded nightshirt. His eyes narrowed as he picked up small spots of blood marked across the floor, smudged with the speed of movement. A lump suddenly rose into his throat. The print of a barefoot stood barely three feet from him, slightly smudged. Another, same foot, a short distance from that.

Cerberus swallowed the leafy mush in his mouth and he knelt in examination.

Glancing between the two prints his mind worked feverishly to piece together the clues in front of him. Cerberex would never have been so careless. His sister was meticulous almost at keeping her bedroom in utmost order. He glanced at the bed, still wrinkled. "What woke you sister?" He asked quietly before he stood again.

Cerberus strode across the landing with a spur of speed and peered over the landing. "Cerberex?" He called out, startling a young servant boy, scuttling across the hall below. He turned and almost walked into a sleek wall of black velvet and silver-blue trim.

"What in Eroth's name are you doing nephew, standing on the landing screaming out for your sister?" Selwyn scorned with a twinkle in his eye. He looked - dishevelled.

Cerberus took in his uncle in a heartbeat and fumbled a backward step. "Have you seen her? She... We had a disagreement."

Selwyn's smile slipped. "She was up long before the house awoke. I glanced her slip down the stairs at some ungodly hour like the hounds of hell were behind her. I assumed she was after you." He put a hand out, steadying Cerberus. "How much did you have to drink last night? You reek of wine."

Cerberus shook him off. "Enough to sleep." He mumbled.

"So you didn't hear her then." Selwyn's eyes narrowed and an eyebrow arched. "Honestly, Cerberus." He sighed. "It's Cerberex, no doubt she couldn't sleep and felt like a night time hunt would take the edge off."

Cerberus gave his Uncle a look and headed for the stairs but Selwyn gripped his arm. "She's been off ever since she came back from her last excursion. What's going on?"

"Wish I knew." Cerberus growled and froze as a flurry of faint beats vibrated up his arm. He looked up at Selwyn, seeing him gripping his wrist.

"What the hell was that?" Selwyn asked darkly.

"Someone just rang the alarm." Cerberus managed as another painful flare from the mark on his wrist caused him to grip the bannister. "And another."

Selwyn masked the pain and pulled up his sleeve. A very faint sub-dermal tattoo seemed to pulse ever so slightly. He glanced up as door on the next landing flew open and Maleficent leaned over the bannister, barely dressed, looking down at them. "Would someone kindly like to tell me what all the talking is about? Some of us would like to get an extra five minutes peace."

Cerberus used the distraction to run for his room, reach behind the door, grab the rapier that lay behind it, and leap over the bannister landing quietly on the floor below. His hang-over fled as a third pain shot up his arm. Springing to his feet, he ran madly. Following the tattoo of fleeting signatures indicative that a number of assassins were on the move directly below his feet.

Cerberus flung wide the doors to the garden hearing them bang on their hinges. A flicker of shadow sped past him, Cerberus reached out and grabbed it. There was a soft tear of cloth but the figure stopped as it registered Cerberus. "What's happened?"

"I don't know? I felt..." The girl stiffened. "We have guests in the garden Master."

The girl was young, Cerberus suddenly realised. He grabbed her arm and pulled back the sleeve. The mark on her wrist was still a livid red. She'd had it maybe a week at most. She had no idea what was going on. "Get back inside." Cerberus grunted.

The girl paused. "Master..."

Cerberus met her gaze and stared back until she faltered and crossed her arms against her chest, a whisper of movement and she was gone. Cerberus rolled his eye's. Pain crawled up his arm for the fourth time, he barely flinched. "Cerberex!" He yelled across the garden and began to jog towards the far tree line. Out of the corner of his eye he could see three smoke-like outlines speeding back towards the house.

The tree's groaned as the wind caught them. Cerberus moved around them disturbing as much of the leaf litter as possible. "Cerberex!" He called out. A heartbeat later the wind brought back his echo. He looked around, anticipating some small clue. Spider-like crawling tickled down his spine and glanced backwards half expecting an arrow to come hissing towards him. A whisper of movement caught his attention before it passed a tall walled orchard. A familiar thrum vibrated along his mark. "Meera." He whispered hopefully. If anyone knew what was going on she at least would be on top of things. He winced at the thought. His behaviour to her had been, less than exemplary. Not entirely his fault, but he could - should have handled things better. There would be some bridges to build.

He rounded the opening in the wall. A cloaked figure hugged a gnarled sapling as if looking for some thing. Slowly Cerberus sidled up behind it, resting the point of the rapier at the base of the spine and watching as the cloaked figure stiffened. "Turn. Slowly." Cerberus intoned.

Inch by inch the figure turned and brought up its hands to pull back the heavy hood before a sharp flash of light made him blink and the figure disappeared before his very eyes. Lowering his rapier, Cerberus looked from side to side stunned for a moment. The cold touch of metal against his throat was definitely surprising.

"How do we keep getting into these situations?" The soft smell of violets crept through the air as the voice spoke.

Cerberus had never felt such relief. "A hundred years and I still don't know." He replied as the dagger moved away from his throat. He turned and stabbed the rapier into the soft earth, folding his arms. "You're the intruder." It was a statement rather than a question. "Every assassin under my roof is currently running around because you've shown up unannounced."

Lida slid the dagger into a belt. She wore a set of trousers and a shirt finely made but at least a size too large. Cerberus looked her up and down and then began to laugh.

Lida's eyebrows furrowed. "And what exactly is so funny?"

Cerberus tried to straighten his face. "Let's just say that House Dhal-Marrah is still a bit jumpy these days," he leaned in. "And maybe you should have just used the front door." He whispered.

"I felt that it would draw a lot of attention." The colour grew in Lida's cheeks.

Cerberus felt the hum of another group of assassins lope past. As gently as he could, he grabbed Lida's arm and pulled her toward the wall. "There are heaven knows how many lethally armed individuals hunting you right now." He replied to the unasked question he could see was beginning to form from her face.

Lida remained still and silent for a moment more, unsure if Cerberus was jesting or not. "It wasn't me." She stated.

Cerberus looked at her indulgently. "Trust me, as quiet as you think you may have snuck in, my people are very good." He moved away to retrieve his rapier. "Actually that's a good point." He turned his head back. "Why are you here?" He flicked the rapier up, lying it gently across his shoulder. "I could be wrong, but I thought you'd be..."

Lida held up a finger. "Don't." She met Cerberus's look eye for eye. "Don't." She repeated, the warning note in her voice insurmountably clear. She reached under the cloak's sleeve and withdrew a folded paper, stamped with the Lotheri seal and held it out.

Cerberus took it curiously and snapped the paper open. He glanced across the contents as his eyebrows rose higher. Slowly he looked up in shock. "Are you serious? You're re-instating us?"

Lida nodded laughing. "Well, your sister is a persuasive writer. The silver dragon has already returned to the great hall."

Cerberus folded the letter and place it in his pocket.

Lida drew herself up imperiously. "Of course you wont be able to get away with not showing up every once in a while."

Cerberus licked his lips. Then in a blur of motion he lifted her off her feet swung her around.

Lida shrieked at the surprise and grabbed his shoulders instinctively.

Cerberus felt her nails dig into his skin beneath his clothes and slowly put her down, feeling her grip loosen. "It's over." A voice in his head whispered so quietly it was as if his brain would not quite believe it. With his head reeling at the prospect, Cerberus didn't register the soft lips pressed gently against his cheek until they pulled away. He looked up in surprise.

Lida blushed. "I am so sorry. That, that was... I don't know what I was thinking." She looked away as the colour in her face continued to build.

Cerberus felt the ghost of the kiss on his cheek as if it was still there. He watched Lida stammer her apologies but could not hear the words amid the rush of blood to his head. A moment later and Cerberus could not remember moving across the dividing space or at what point he dropped the rapier and seized her arm; but he would remember the smell of violets. He would remember the softness of her touch, the silk-like texture of her hair, the way her lips seemed to quiver ever so slightly when they touched his. Most of all he would remember the sudden sense that the world had literally seemed to shift on its axis.

A slow clap snapped him back to the present. Cerberus pulled away, his look mirrored in Lida's eyes. Five black shadows perched atop the walls of the enclosed, abandoned garden at various junctures.

"Bravo." Meera's voice was mirthless.

"Meera this isn't because of you..." Cerberus began. "I know your hurting..." He tried to continue.

"Oh no Cerberus I'm so passed that now." Meera hopped down to the ground. "Couldn't be happier. I see you finally got the girl."

Cerberus raised an eyebrow surprised. "I'm pleased to hear it." He replied slowly as Meera approached all smiles.

Meera performed a slight bow towards Lida. "My Queen. Such an honour."

Cerberus watched as Silas, Dichta, Negari, and Seska walked along the top of the wall. It dawned on him he had not felt them arrive.

"It appears you've proved me wrong once again, Master." Meera smiled at Cerberus. Forcing his attention back at him. "Honestly, I had no idea you would stoop so low as to make a move while His Majesty still lies in state."

"What?" Cerberus's attention snapped back to Meera, catching only the final part of the sentence.

"Excuse me?" Lida's voice was crisp with anger.

"I held you to higher standards my Queen." Meera continued as if nothing had interrupted her. "Perhaps I should have known better."

A soft thump made Cerberus glance back. Silas stood in the intervening gap between him and the wall. An arm's stretch from Lida. "Meera..." He began, glancing for a moment where his mark lay beneath his sleeve and frowning.

As if in response Sylas held up his wrist wrapped in a bandage stained slightly with blood. Cerberus's eyes widened. "Down." He yelled. A flicker of movement later and Sylas squealed as Cerberus twisted his arm behind him, pulling a tiny knife from the back of his trousers. Lida shrieked and ducked with her hands over her head.

The world turned upside down as Dichta or Seska, or possibly both he wasn't sure which, spun him over. Seska wrapped an arm around Lida's throat dragging her to her feet.

"I dedicated a hundred and fifty years to you." Meera's voice was cool, calm, collected. "A hundred and fifty years." She repeated. "In that time you have only paid me in scorn." She waited for Cerberus's attention to be drawn. "You're not my Master any more Cerberus. You're nobody's Master. You're a traitor to this realm - a murderer a hundred times over. You used me and then threw me away. Day by day you stripped me of everything that I was. No more."

Behind him a hiss made him turn to watch a length of rope be thrown over the nearby tree branch.

"Well. Now it's my turn to return the favour." Meera's voice was suddenly by his ear.

Lida lifted from the ground. The noose around her neck pulled tight suddenly as Silas, injured wrist or no hauled on the other end with every ounce of strength. Cerberus felt his breath catch. His hand reflexively went to a bandoleer of throwing knives he knew were not there. He spun back to Meera, feeling a burst of heat course along his veins.

Pain shot through him. Cerberus looked down at the blade sunk to the hilt through his chest. Cold tried to freeze the fire within. Blackness crawled in spots across his vision. He stumbled slightly, still refusing to fall.

Meera leaned in her hand holding the knife and placed a kiss on his lips. "If I so much as twitch, this knife will sever the artery to your heart and your blood will pour into your chest. Of course you already know that so I wouldn't move." She patted his cheek.

Cerberus ground his teeth and blinked away pain. Remaining still by sheer force of will. "Cut her down." He panted feeling blood slide from the corner of his mouth.

"What's that? Oh no can do - all part of the contract. You understand contracts don't you Cerberus?" She pushed him to his knees, gripping the knife. Blood began to run over her hand. She smiled at him. "But while I have your attention." She twisted his head. Forcing him to watch Lida continue to scrabble at the rope around her neck. Twitching like a fish on a hook. "I wanted you to know it was me." Her voice seemed almost sad. "I want you to know I told the guard you were at the party. I sent the message saying that there would be a caravan incoming." She paused. "I even informed His Majesty of your sisters potential visit. She's so predictable!" She looked at his confused face in delight. "Oh he knew who was coming and who she was. Her pathetic disguise. He knew when he climbed onto her. When the stick came down, once, twice..." She made a face of mock distaste but the glee was clear to see. "Oh I didn't account for stupidity. Didn't think his Highness would fail to knock her off after he was done." She looked at the anger in Cerberus's eyes. "You couldn't save your sister from torture," She pulled his lolling head to look up at Lida. Her face was beginning to go blue. "And you can't save her." Meera shook Cerberus's head, keeping him awake. "You're a failure." She whispered

Cerberus's vision had blurred but he could still see Meera's gloating face. "When... When I... get out of this... I... I'm going to hunt you down... I'm going to watch the last breath leave your lungs... for... for the bitch you are!" He spat and pulled her with him as he reached down grabbing the rapier and slashing it wildly upwards.

Meera screeched. Clutching her cheek where and ugly slash began to well blood.

Cerberus grinned through bloodstained teeth as the sight of it made the heat rise within him like a furnace. "I'm coming... for..."

An arrow hissed through the air. Then a second. Then a third. Cerberus just caught the black and white fletching of one as it neatly severed the rope hanging Lida from the tree. She fell heavily and slumped coughing and pulling away the noose at her neck - sucking lungfuls of air. More arrows came.

Cerberus looked at Meera with a smile that was more of a grimace. "Seems... my sister... is a better teacher than you."

Meera scowled in irritation as an arrow threatened to take her eye out. "An inconvenience." She replied.

"Hey, bitch!" The voice was like a clarion call of hope to Cerberus's ears. "Take your hands off my... take them off Cerberus." Lida stood still choking. Her hands wreathed in blue flames. Her face beautifully murderous.

Seska, Dichta, and Negari moved up to Meera, the flicker of fear glinting in their eyes as another flurry of arrows fell.

Cerberus was sweating now. He could see the pommel of the rapier glowing under the heat of his hand. The skin around his fingers, blackening. It felt like something jolted inside him and with that acknowledgement, the flames burst from under his fingernails. Meera drew her hand away from the sudden heat.

"We are outnumbered." Seska whispered. "Leave and live. Be done with this Meera, there will be another time. We cannot take them all."

Meera growled as arrows rained. Negari caught one before it could sink into Meera's arm.

"Cerberus!" Cerberex shouted from his left as she ascended the wall.

Cerberus saw her appear on the wall's ledge. Kane leaped over the wall a second later. He wanted to call out but only smoke and ash would escape from his lungs when he opened his mouth.

Meera looked in the direction of Cerberex and smiled. Despite the insistent pulling of Seska, she grabbed the heated knife, looked at Cerberex, winked, and with one deft switch, twisted the blade.

Cerberus felt no pain, no tearing of flesh. He heard only the sudden, terrible, anguished scream of his sister. Then all was smoke and flames.

Chapter 31:
From Hell with Love

The scream escaped from Cerberex's lungs about the same time Cerberus buckled like the strings cut from a puppet. Time seemed to pause in that moment. Meera looked at her and smiled. Raising a hand coated in blood, she licked her tongue across the palm of it before bowing like a top-rated performer at a standing ovation. Cerberex notched an arrow and fired. Meera leaned casually to one side. The arrow burrowed into an unkempt flower bed. Meera waved an bloodied finger and... slammed into the earth five feet away!

Cerberex dropped from the wall and staggered back as Cerberus suddenly stood. Smoke pouring from mouth, ears, and nose. His eyes glared unblinking at Meera as his fist slammed into her with the force of a mammoth. An animalistic roar like nothing Cerberex had ever heard, bellowed from his mouth. Cerberex lowered her bow as Cerberus hunched onto all fours and seemed to grow. His skin already dark, cracked to reveal lines of flickering orange running from his eyes down his face like streams of lava. Cerberus grabbed the knife in his chest, yanking it free with an unearthly scream and a torrent of blood that hissed as soon as it touched the ground. In that scream Cerberex was sure she caught a single word - "Traitor!" As the sound echoed through the air, Cerberus convulsed as black wings tore from his back and is face seemed to elongate into a feral snout lined with razor sharp fangs. Cerberex retracted clawed at the ground as his nails elongated, turning into black claws. The molten rage in his eyes looked up, beheld Meera, and the thing that was Cerberus roared with all the wrath of the hells behind it.

Dichta looked at Seska and Negari and fled - a smokey blur that disappeared over the far wall. The other two looked at each other and slowly drew their weapons. Out of the corner of her eye, Cerberex could see Kane slam his elbow into Sylas's face with a crack that made her smile.

"What in Eroth's name is that?" Lida shrieked as Cerberex approached, gesticulating wildly as Cerberus and Meera circled each other akin to angry cats - though easily more dangerous.

Cerberex placed an arm almost protectively across Lida but her eyes would not leave Cerberus's new form. "Well madam, I'm no expert on the arcane, so you tell me!"

The last pieces of clothing tore away from Cerberus and with a sudden twitch, black scales encased his body in armoured hide not a moment too soon. Seska launched herself up and onto his back, stabbing down with short sword. The blade's edge screamed as it careened down the newly formed scales.

"Oh no you don't." Lida hissed and struck her hand out.

Seska fell from Cerberus's back with a short scream as she was launched into the air.

"Don't!" Cerberex turned the Lida. "You could hit Cerberus."

Lida nodded towards Seska and Cerberex suddenly understood as Seska stood confused but unscathed. "She's keeping them off him." She thought as realisation suddenly dawned.

Cerberus launched at Meera but she nimbly leaped away, hissing curses at him. Her eyes flickered to Cerberex then back to Cerberus. With the speed of lightening she turned and a moment later her blurred form dashed back up and over the rear wall.

A flurry of arrows skittered off Cerberus's scales, he turned and bellowed angrily at the four dark shapes across the near wall armed with bows - but he did not attack.

"He's still in there." Cerberex said out loud to herself. Bringing her fingers to her lips, she let forth a shrill high pitched whistle to attract their attention. "Stop!" She shouted.

A slight ripple of wind and Tye was at her side. His face was torn with confusion. "What... what is that thing?!"

Cerberex patted his shoulder. "Long story. Don't shoot it." She replied, her eyes widening as the Cerberus suddenly turned back in the direction Meera had gone and was suddenly pounding across the ground, heedless of tree or shrub alike. "Oh, boy..." Cerberex breathed slinging her bow across her back and sprinting after him.

Cerberex had hunted beasts. She'd run with the monsters of the wilds, but she could barely keep pace with the thing that Cerberus had become - not that he was hard to follow for all the carnage he left in his wake. She dropped from the perimeter wall just in time to watch Cerberus reach the edge of the city and with two heavy beats of the bat-like wings, take to the air. Cerberex doubled over to catch her breath and sprinted into the city's out limits, pulling herself up and on top of the first available building.

A blur of black slowed to her side as Kane caught up with her. "We can't keep up with him."

"We don't have a choice. The ballisters on the city's wall will shoot him out of the sky if we don't stop him." Cerberex shouted breathlessly.

Kane looked up as Cerberus's roar filled the air. A second later the sound of screams followed from the citizens below.

"Shit." Cerberex swore and forced her legs to go faster, leaping the gap between buildings while her eyes never left the winged outline of Cerberus in the sky.

"Take my hand." Kane reached out.

Cerberex looked at it.

"Take it!" Kane repeated.

Cerberex looked at Cerberus, then grabbed Kane's hand.

"Do not let go, keep your eyes up, and just keep running." Kane instructed.

Suddenly Cerberex felt her body lurch forwards impossibly fast - far faster than she thought was possible. Kane's hand felt slightly cool in her grip and though the world around her was a blur, she could hear Kane's panting as Cerberus's form grew closer, arching around the scaffolded, skeleton, of a freshly built tower.

Kane stopped a building away. "He's lost her." The note of bitterness wasn't even masked.

"How do you know?" Cerberex asked, watching her brother circle above them.

Cerberus roared with clear frustration and tore away a piece of scaffold like it were made of nothing but matchsticks, dropping it carelessly below.

Cerberex looked at Kane and then at the intervening gap. It would be a hell of a jump.

Kane looked at her. "No." He said flatly but Cerberex took a step back with her eyes locked on the nearest bit of scaffold. "You'll never make it. It's at least twelve feet. You're still injured."

Heedlessly Cerberex took another few steps back towards the far edge of the rooftop.

Kane shook his head and grabbed her arm, holding it firm as she tried to pull away. With his teeth he unlaced the wrist guard of the other arm and pushed it onto Cerberex's wrist. Cerberex looked at him with surprised. Kane tightened the guard as far as it would go but it still felt loose around her wrist.

"Pull the finger like this." Kane showed her and the wrist mounted bow clicked open. Kane folded it back. "If you fall..."

"I'm not going to fall." Cerberex told him bluntly.

"If you fall." Kane cut her off. "The bolt acts as a grapple. Aim for something and it will slow you down. Hold on with both hands or you'll snap your wrist." He sighed, let go and nodded at the building. "I'll follow you as best I can."

Cerberex looked at Kane and nodded. "He's my little brother." She replied as if it were the most logical answer. "I'm not letting him out of my sight."

Kane nodded and took a step back.

Cerberex took a deep breath and ran. She felt her feet pound along the roof, saw a handful of tiles slide and smash below her. Gritted her teeth as the edge came suddenly close and... It was like a dial suddenly clicked into place. The world around her blurred to nothing but coloured smudges. The off brown of the wood the only indicator that the scaffold was coming close. She felt more than saw it when she reached out and pushed up with a strange weightlessness to the next level up. "Keep Going." She told herself as the unfinished top of the tower came rising up to meet her.

Shuddering to a halt upon the shattered remains of the top most scaffold, a sudden lurch of motion sickness slammed into her. Cerberex swallowed the bile in the back of her throat only to look up to the sound of an angry whine muffled by the down-draft of Cerberus's wings.

A ballister bolt hurtled through the sky parting the wing membrane of Cerberus's left wing like it was nothing but paper. Cerberus roared in pain. A moment later a second slammed into the shoulder blade of the same wing. Cerberus screamed and reached back, tearing the bolt out with his teeth. Cerberex winced at the pain clearly evident in the sound then shrieked herself as Cerberus suddenly plummeted downwards. A moment later he rose again one wing beating feebly and Cerberex caught a brief glimpse of the joint dislocated from its socket before Cerberus turned to retreat.

Cerberex looked at the crossbow on the wrist guard and clicked it open as she had been shown. She looked up. "Sorry brother." She whispered before she fired.

The bolt flew upwards taking with it a line of silk rope. It hissed towards Cerberus only just snagging beneath two overlapping scales. Cerberex felt herself be pulled off her feet as Cerberus flew higher and began soaring back towards the outskirts. Holding on for dear life, Cerberex focussed all her efforts into bringing one hand over the other, slowly climbing upwards.

A third bolt flew passed. Cerberus banked sideways, almost falling out of the sky. "Stop bloody firing!" Cerberex shouted, her voice stolen by the rush of air. She glanced down, all too aware of the speed at which Cerberus was descending despite all efforts to the contrary.

A fourth ballister bolt sliced a second hole through the wing membrane the stretch of it shredding it to bloody ribbons. Suddenly the ground lurched towards them spectacularly fast. Cerberus let out a final roar as they skimmed a tall building and slammed into the scrub-land on the city's outer most perimeter. Cerberex dropped and rolled as bushes and trees simply shattered under the force of Cerberus's descent. With a thunderous shudder, Cerberus ploughed into the ground leaving a trench of charred earth as he landed.

Cerberex spat dead leaves and dirt. She pushed her self back onto her feet. The smell of charred wood filled the air. "Cerberus!" She yelled at the top of her lungs. Despite the protest of her muscles, she jogged and followed the trail of disaster. A rumbling groan made her pause.

In a slight recess in the surrounding terrain, a crater made from his own impact, Cerberus lay with his snout-like head resting on the ground. Eyes blinking with concussion. He lifted his head and bared his teeth as Cerberex approached. Slowly, she made her way down, ducking into a crouch as Cerberus issued a breath that felt like the hot air of a furnace. Step by step she inched forward till only a foot separated them. Cerberex had no idea of what the thing was that Cerberus had turned in to, but she knew the miserable rumble of a beast too exhausted to continue fighting. Swallowing, Cerberex reached out towards the nose of the beast, sidestepping closer till her fingers touched the small glossy black scales. She breathed a sigh of relief when Cerberus didn't immediately take her arm off and ran her hand up the nasal ridge.

Cerberus shuddered. Ash coughed from his mouth, the scales softened or fell off entirely. Cerberex took a step back as her brother seemed to shrivel back to a more normal size, the massive wings wrinkling into themselves with a hideous cracking sound. Bit by bit the rumbling and roaring became more and more like moans and cries of pain, till after a few moments the brother she knew lay curled up, naked on the ground.

A muffled movement stopped next to her and Kane pulled off the cloak and scarf he wore, draping it over Cerberus. "And you think you aren't one of us?" He whispered under his breath as they both knelt next to him.

Cerberex looked at him in surprise.

"You were amazing." Kane looked back and grinned. "Utterly mad." He added. "But amazing."

Cerberus groaned and Cerberex looked back quickly, peaking under the cloak and looking for the wound on his chest. A massive burn and scorch mark left the skin cracked and broken where it should have been bloody but of the stab wound, there was no sign.

"Are you both done?" Cerberus gasped and coughed. A watery trickle of blood slipped down his chin.

Cerberex's eyes went wide a the voice. Quickly, she rolled Cerberus onto his side. "Brother!"

Cerberus's face twitched painfully but he forced a grin. "I hope I didn't cause a spectacle."

Cerberex could feel wet tears of relief fall down her face. She sniffed, and shook her head. "You should be dead."

Cerberus coughed a laugh. "Well it didn't stick." He winced, coiling in on himself with a shiver. "I saw her leave."

Cerberex leaned in. "Tell me where Cerberus and I swear I shall..." She gasped as coils of heat began to pass up her arm, arcing from Cerberus like some pulsating current.

"No." Cerberus said firmly and clamped a hand down on her arm. The tendrils evaporated into mist. "She's too dangerous right now. She has allies and we are in her battleground."

"We have a route of assassins." Cerberex replied coldly, the rage making her voice shudder.

"We?" Cerberus squinted, forcing his eyes to focus on his sister and he beckoned her closer. "Why sister?" He whispered. "Why did you do it? Why with him in the name of all that is holy?! Why?"

Cerberex's mouth went dry. "I'm sorry." She whispered.

Cerberus gritted his teeth. "You let him do that to you?"

"I couldn't tell you. I didn't know what you would think." Cerberex choked on her own breath.

"Think? He beat you!" Cerberus's eyes looked more terrified than angry. "Do you have any idea what I would have done if you had never come back?"

"I killed him Cerberus." Cerberex tried to explain her voice small and timid.

"I know." Cerberus replied.

Cerberex looked up and sniffed in surprise.

"What? You don't think I've seen that look before?" He wheezed a sigh. "I just... I just wish I'd realised what it was sooner. It leaves a mark upon us sister. Each one. I never wanted you to be part of that."

Cerberex hiccoughed a strangled laugh and glanced at Kane. "I'm a Dhal-Marrah. It's in the blood."

Cerberus groaned as he tried to push himself up with barely enough strength to keep his arms from shaking. "There was another Drau - male. He was waiting for her. He knew she was coming."

"Sylas is in our custody." Kane interjected.

Cerberus turned to him as Cerberex pulled the cloak firmly around his body, taking off her own belt so that he wore it like a tunic. "Is he now?" He tried to walk and almost fell. "Well Meera's new friend doesn't wear our colours."

Kane looked at him in surprise. "What?"

"Gal-Serrek." Cerberus replied in two slow breaths. "A mage, or arcanist - I don't know. They disappeared as soon as she was in his arms."

"A lover?" Cerberex blurted out before she could stop herself.

"Perhaps." Cerberus leaned heavily against Kane. "We'll need to ask our mutual acquaintance back at the house."

Together they took a few cautionary steps. Cerberus hobbled and then stopped after a few feet rolling his eyes. "We have company."

Heavy footfalls of armoured feet hammered closer from all angles. Cerberex and Kane stopped. Kane pulled back up his scarf obscuring what he could of his face without the cloak just before a ring of armed soldiers hemmed them in from all sides. Long spears angled down in unison, pinning them to a single spot. Kane's eyes darted around taking in the ivory and electric blue of their armour.

"Lotheri soldiers." Cerberex hissed to Cerberus.

"Palace guard of the Queens." Kane muttered trying to turn away.

"I'm wounded. Not blind." Cerberus hissed back.

"Get on the ground!" An anonymous voice shouted from the circle of armour.

Cerberus opened his mouth to speak some retort as a flash of blinding white so bright it brought stars to their vision, burst into existence in the small intervening space between them.

"Put up your weapons." The voice was tinny as it exuded from the light. "This is Lord Dhal-Marrah and Lady Cerberex." The light began to fade but the voice brooked no argument. "And they are with me."

Cerberex shielded her eyes as the last of the light dispersed. Aunt Maleficent and her mother both held an arm of Queen Lida. Flickers of lightening crackled between them. It was the first time in over a hundred years that Cerberex had seen her aunt and mother working in unison and it was impressive. Cerberex heard the simultaneous clunk of armoured plating as each soldier bent to one knee. Her eyes glanced at Lida. An ugly red welt circled her throat. Her eyes flew to Cerberus then to Kane.

Kane's eyes looked back at her and his eyebrows raised just a little as with as much delicacy as he could manage he went down to one knee, pulling Cerberus along with him.

Cerberex followed a moment behind catching her brother whisper painfully "Shame. So much fun to be had, so little time."

Epilogue:
Turn Coat

Meera sat at ease among soft silk cushions. The hour was late or possibly even early - it was hard to say. The flicker of candle light barely illuminated the room. Small though it was, it had been sumptuously decorated to the point of absurdity. The walls had been coated in brushed velvet of deep maroon. The cherry wood parquet floor had been laid with tiny intervening squares of gold and black. Each piece of furniture was a masterpiece. Meera sat arms sprawled along the length of the couch, her legs crossed, her face passively emotionless despite the richness of her surroundings. Her eyes focused on the single small mahogany wood door recessed into the wall ahead.

Another figure in half-length coat of brushed silk the colour of nightshade, paced the nine feet from one side of the room to the other. The shadows in the room made him appear like a spectre.

"Mistress Korith..." The voice of the spectre was low and warm.

Meera twitched with irritation.

"Meera." It whispered. "This is a terrible idea!"

Meera huffed but said nothing.

"You don't know what you're getting yourself into." The spectre paced faster.

"Sit down." Meera murmured. "You're making me feel sea-sick."

The male Drau paused and slid to one knee in front of her. "Leave. I know these people." He implored. "I don't usually beg Meera but I will."

"Get up you idiot!" Meera growled issuing a slight kick. "If I leave now, I'll have two houses after me not just the one." She glanced back at the door. "I am expected after all."

"I will hide you then." He insisted. He had a boyish face that was contorted with worry.

Meera snorted and resumed watching the door, unblinking.

The Drau stood and began to pace once more. "I have money." He added after a while. "We could both leave."

Meera looked over at him with beatific smile. "Understand me well darling. There is nowhere in the world I would go with you. You love me - I can't love you. I don't run because I am not a coward."

The door clicked open letting a small stream of light through the gap. A bald half-human male entered the room, bowing low. "Lord Vor'ran will see you now." His voice was tinged with an accent unfamiliar to Meera who stood smoothly to her feet.

The Drau moved but the servant held up a hand sternly. "My apologies. Lord

Vor'ran called only for the lady."

He looked at Meera. "Please." He mouthed.

Meera ignored him and pushed past the servant into the adjoining room.

There was a slight whiff of cinnamon and umber as she entered. A small incense lamp rested on a desk, a curl of slightly blue smoke ran ribbons around the room. Unlike the former, this room was restrained. Discoloured patches on the wall indicated that pictures or mirrors had been removed and recesses in the heavy pile of the carpet ghosted the places where other furniture had once been. The newest owner of this study sat amidst the void with fingers steepled upon the desk. In the corner a heavily armoured house guard in black steel, stood so motionless that for a second she mistook him for a suit of armour.

Meera stood a few feet from the desk. The silence seemed thick. A moment passed. Meera glanced around the room impatiently.

"This is an unexpected surprise." Vor'ran's voice was quiet. His eyes were closed but Meera was confident that he knew exactly where she was.

"Surprise darling? We had an arrangement I believe." Meera smiled at him.

Vor'ran took a deep breath. "I have lost a cousin and a King, Mistress Korith. That was not part of the plan I think."

"Casualty of war darling. I can't be held responsible for stupidity or ego. He clearly intended to flaunt that personal victory. I warned you. You said he'd be well warded against such things." Meera folded her arms.

Vor'ran's eyes narrowed. "You blame me?"

"Of course not darling, a deal is a deal though." Meera did not blink as Vor'ran moved from behind the desk.

"I thought I was very clear..." Vor'ran began quietly. "About the need..." He picked up an inkwell and studied it. "For discretion!" He shouted throwing it at her before it smashed against the door behind as she dodged out of the way. "My directions were exact. Clear. Simple." He continued. "The Dhal-Marrah Dog was to be dead, the family incarcerated, the bitch Queen in exile." He slammed a hand against the desk causing the papers upon it to jump. "What do you bring me? Nothing! I already hear that Lord Dhal-Marrah lives. That the Queen now flies a silver dragon in the great hall again. Everything that we... that I have worked so hard to maintain has been unravelled at the seams. So Mistress, tell me what good news do you bring that you come to House Gal-Serrek in the dead of night, sweating like a mated hound?"

"I have cut my ties with Dhal-Marrah." Meera replied and calmly knelt. "I humbly ask to join the esteemed and rightful ruling house of Gal-Serrek."

Vor'ran turned. At first Meera thought he was choking until she realised that he was laughing so hard that his arms shook.

"Look at you." Vor'ran hissed. "Mistress Korith. Come to beg at the door of her betters." He sneered.

Meera's face shifted angrily as she tried to remain impassive.

Vor'ran stepped towards her. "My spies tell me you helped Cerberus Dhal-Marrah escape in the vaults." He circled her like a vulture. "I wonder what would have happened if the Queen had died? Would you have run into his arms and disappeared into the sunset together?"

"You doubt my loyalty?" Meera sneered. Her patience reaching its limits.

"You are a turn coat, a traitor, and a once Dhal-Marrah. I have doubted your loyalty ever since you came to me." Vor'ran smiled. The reply stung her but he ignored her discomfort. "You swear fealty when it suits you Mistress Korith." He whispered in her ear. "No. I'll tell you why you've come. You've come to beg for my forgiveness, for my salvation. Oh, you act well but I can smell the fear coming off you." He grabbed her wrist, squeezing it in a vice-like grip. "You're afraid of what's coming and you need my help. You're a fool Mistress Korith, and I have no need for fools." He let go and stepped away, nodding at the guard in the corner. "Throw this whore into the streets where she belongs."

Meera felt her arms forced behind her back. "We had a deal!" She shrieked.

Vor'ran held up a hand and smiled coldly. "And when you have upheld your part; when you bring me the blackened heart of Cerberus Dhal-Marrah, then I will be only too happy to fulfil my part." He nodded once more and the guard began to drag. "Till then, House Gal-Serrek has nothing to do with you."

Meera screeched with anger and twisted herself out of the guard's grip. "I will remember this Vor'ran." He pointed her finger at him.

Vor'ran didn't flinch. "See that you do. The Gal-Serreks don't brook failure as much as your former master. This time you keep your head."

Meera's breathing came in short gasps. Her face flushed with anger. "We will meet again Vor'ran, and next time you will ensure my reward is waiting."

"Lord Vor'ran." Vor'ran corrected. "Next time you Mistress Korith, will remember your manners."

Meera headed into the rain slick streets as the gates of House Gal-Serrek clanged closed noisily behind her. Three shadows moved from the rooftops. Dichta, Negari, and Seska were all soaked to the skin.

"Well?" Dichta urged hopefully. Her teeth were beginning to chatter.

Meera looked at them. Her face black with rage.

Seska sighed. "The bastard's gone out on us hasn't he." She rolled her eyes. "Bloody Gal-Serreks!" She muttered.

"The deal still stands." Meera snapped feeling the cold rain seep into her clothes. "We'll get our due ladies, don't you worry." She laid a hand on Seska's shoulder. "When the task is done."

"How are we supposed to complete it?" Dichta shrieked a little too loudly. "We've truly kicked the hornets nest. They - He won't rest until every last one of us is in the ground!"

Meera looked into the sky, blinking as the rain hit her face and smiled crookedly. "Let him come. I too can bring hell's fury and I will make him beg for death by the time I have finished with him." She laughed as a fork of lightening tore the sky asunder.

Cerberus and Cerberex return in Book II
Drau: Scion
Coming Soon

About the Author

Elizabeth Stephens lives in the riverside town of Kings Lynn on the Norfolk coast of the UK. Her first 'book' was written at the tender age of seven on precisely folded sheets of old dot-matrix print stock!
Despite initial set backs, she pursued her ambitions taking a degree in English and Creative Writing at the University of Winchester. A varied reader and procrastinator, she found herself drawn to studying a strange combination of graphic novels and Shakespearean drama. Her love for theater and the sheer empowerment of the fantastical, has never diminished.

Lightning Source UK Ltd.
Milton Keynes UK
UKHW011111080120
356576UK00001B/1/P